Awakening to the Immensity of the Mystery

Theory and Practice in Inter-Religious Relations

Awakening to the Immensity of the Mystery

Theory and Practice in Inter-Religious Relations

EDITOR

PACKIAM T. SAMUEL

HENRY MARTYN INSTITUTE (HMI)
2019

Awakening to the Immensity of the Mystery: *Theory and Practice in Inter-Religious Relations* —jointly published by the Rev. Dr. Ashish Amos of the Indian Society for Promoting Christian Knowledge (ISPCK), Post Box 1585, Kashmere Gate, Delhi-110006 and Henry Martyn Institute (HMI), Shivarampally, Hyderabad 500052.

ISBN: 978-93-88945-02-8

Cover Photo Credit: http://7-themes.Com/6862523-cosmos-wallpaper.Html

Laser typeset by
ISPCK, Post Box 1585, 1654, Madarsa Road, Kashmere Gate, Delhi-110006 • *Tel:* 23866323

e-mail: ashish@ispck.org.in • ella@ispck.org.in
website: www.ispck.org.in

Contents

Preface

*A*wakening to the Immensity of the Mystery: Theory and Practice in *Inter-Religious Relations* is an outcome of Henry Martyn Institute's sustain effort in building interfaith relations. This collection of 25 articles from renowned scholars on interfaith relations was sourced from *The Bulletin of the Henry Martyn Institute of Islamic Studies*, and *Journal of the Henry Martyn Institute*. This edition serves as a third of its kind—the other two being the work of Andreas D' Souza's *From Converting the Pagan to Dialogue with Our Partners: HMI's Fifty Years Work of Evangelism and Interfaith Relations*; and David Emmanuel Singh and Robert Edwin Schick's *Approaches, Foundations, Issues and Models of Interfaith Relations*. The former has a collection of selected articles from 1941 to 1986, and the latter from 1991 to 2001. The present book has selected articles on interfaith relation from 2001 to the present.

I acknowledge the contributors for their articles; the ISPCK as a joint publisher; Pamhor Thumra for helping in editorial work and other staff members in HMI for making this work a success.

Contributors

Marykutty Thomas
Marykutty Thomas was the head of the Department of Methods, Neelam Sanjeeva Reddy College of Education, V.V. Chambers, Hyderabad.

Samuel Rayan S.J.
Samuel Rayan has been a professor of systematic theology at Vidyajyoti Institute of Religions in New Delhi for over two decades. He was also the Principal of Indian School of Ecumenical Theology in Bangalore. He was a member of the Commission on Faith and Order of the World Council of Churches. Some of his books are *The Holy Spirit, Heart of the Gospel and Christian Hope*, and *In Christ: Power of Women*.

Vardit Rispler-Chaim
Vardit Rispler-Chaim is a lecturer in the Department of Arabic, University of Haifa. He received his Ph.D. from the University of California, Berkeley, U.S.A. He has published several articles on topics like Islamic law, medical ethics, human rights, and Islamic economics.

David Emmanuel Singh
David Emmanuel Singh was an Associate Director (Academics) in the Henry Martyn Institute. He co-edited the book *Approaches, Foundations, Issues and Models of Interfaith Relations*.

Anantanand Rambachan
Anantanand Rambachan is Professor of Religion at St. Olaf College, Minnesota. His major books include *Accomplishing the Accomplished: The Vedas as a Source of Valid Knowledge in Shankara, The Limits of Scripture:*

Vivekananda's Reinterpretation of the Authority of the Vedas, The Advaita Worldview: God, World and Humanity, and *A Hindu Theology of Liberation: Not-Two is Not One.*

S. L. Gandhi

S. L. Gandhi was the Secretary-General of Anuvrat Global Organization, Jaipur, Rajasthan.

Annette Meuthrath

Annette Meuthrath worked with the Foreign Department, Asia Desk. She is a lecturer in Religious Studies at the RWTH Achen University with a focus on far Eastern Religious studies. She studied Indology, Philosophy, Theology, and Religious Studies.

Clemens Mendonca

Clemens Mendonca is the Executive Director of the Institute for the Study of Religion, De Nobili College, Pune. She specializes in Asian cultural education and religious studies. She also works as the counselor of the Catholic and Inter-religious Issues Department.

Ch. Vasantha Rao

Ch. Vasantha Rao is the Principal of the United Theological College, Bengaluru, India. He holds a Doctorate from Hamburg University, Germany. He was a visiting Professor at the Harvard University, Boston, and Lutheran School of Theology at Chicago, USA and guest Professor at the EST, Porto Alegre, Brazil. He was also a Senior Visiting Scholar at the Princeton Theological Seminary, New Jersey, USA. He has authored several books and published several articles including one in *The Oxford Encyclopaedia of South Asian Christianity.*

T. Swami Raju

T. Swami Raju is a Professor in Religion, Culture & Philosophy in Andhra Christian Theological College and Advanced Institute for Research on Religion and Culture. He holds degrees in B.Sc., M.A (Eng)., B.D., M.Th. (Rel), M.A (Phil)., and D.Th (Rel). He is the author of 16 books and many articles.

Reeta Bagchi

Reeta Bagchi is an Associate Professor, Dept. of Islamic Studies, Hamdard University, New Delhi.

M.M. Abraham

M.M. Abraham is an Associate Director (Academics), Henry Martyn Institute.

Raimon Panikkar

Raimon Panikkar was a philosopher-theologian, a proponent of inter-religious dialogue, and a scholar of comparative religion. A well-known religious scholar, he authored nearly 50 books and many articles. Some of his books are *The Unknown Christ of Hinduism*, *The Vedic Experience: Mantramanjari: An Anthology of the Vedas for Modern Man*, *Pluralism and Oppression: Theology in World Perspective* (co-authored with Paul F. Knitter), *Interreligious Dialogue*, among others. For his initiation on inter-faith relations, he was known as the Apostle of Inter-religious dialogue.

Martin Repp

Marin Repp is a theologian from Germany. He worked at the National Christian Council in Japan (NCCJ) Centre for Study of Japanese Religion, Kyoto as Associate Director and Coordinator of Interreligious Studies from 2002-2004. In 2004, he became the Professor of Theology and Comparative Religion at the Graduate School for Pure Land Buddhist Studies of Ryukoku University in Kyoto.

Safia Amir

Safia Amir is an Asst. Professor, Department of Islamic Studies, Jamia Hamdard, New Delhi.

K. P. Aleaz

K.P. Aleaz was a Professor of Religion at Bishop's College, as well as Professor and Dean of the Doctoral Programme at North India Institute of Post Graduate Theological Studies, Kolkata (NIPGTS), and research committee member in South Asia Theological Research Institutes (SATHRI). As a renowned scholar of religion, he has authored many books and articles. Some of his contributions are *An Indian Jesus from Sankara's Thought*, *Christian Responses to Indian Philosophy*, *Indian Biblical Reflections and Other Essays*, *Theology of Religions: Birmingham Papers and Other Essays*, among others.

Victor Edwin

Victor Edwin is a doctoral degree holder in Islamic Studies from Jamia Millia Islamia, New Delhi. He is also the managing editor of *Salaam*—the journal of the Islamic Studies Association.

G.N. Khaki

G.N. Khaki is a Senior Professor in Islamic Studies at the Center for Central Asian Studies (CCSA), an international research institute, University of Kashmir.

Shabir Ahmad Mugloo

Shabir Ahmad Mughloo works with the Centre for Central Asian Studies, Kashmir University of Kashmir.

Adis Duderija

Adis Duderija served as a Visiting Senior Lecturer at the University of Malaya, Malaysia. He is a Lecturer, Study of Islam and Society, Griffith University. His main works focus on progressive Islam, Islam and gender, western Muslims' identity construction and inter-faith dialogue. Some of his books are *Islam and Muslims in the West: Major issues and Debate* (co-author with H. Rane), *Progressive Islam: Re-awakening Authenticity, The Imperatives of Progressive Islam*, among others.

Leo D. Lefebure

Leo D. Lefebure is the Matteo Ricci, S.J., Professor of Theology at Georgetown University and a priest of the Roman Catholic Archdiocese of Chicago. He is the author of *True and Holy: Christian Scripture and Others religions, The Path of Wisdom: A Christian Commentary on the Dhammapada* (co-author with Peter Feldmeier), *The Buddha and the Christ*, among others.

Teresa Joseph FMA

Teresa Joseph is the Secretary, Dialogue and Ecumenism, Catholic Bishop's Conference of India. She is an ardent advocate of inter-religious dialogue.

ʿĀshaq Ḥussain

ʿĀshaq Ḥussain is a Post-Doc Fellow at Centre of Central Asian Studies, University of Kashmir. He holds masters, as well as Ph.D. in Islamic Studies respectively from the University of Kashmir. He has contributed many articles in many journals. His major areas of expertise and interest are Islamic Civilization, Religious and Qur'ānic Studies.

Rudolf C. Heredia

Rudolf C. Heredia holds a doctorate in sociology from the University of Chicago. He was the rector of St. Xavier's College, Mumbai. He served as the Director of the department of research at the Indian Social Institute. His interest includes issues related to religion, education, and globalization. He has contributed articles on many journals, periodicals of repute.

Francis Gonsalves S.J.

Francis Gonsalves has been working with Jnana-Deepa Vidyapeeth for many years. He currently teaches systematic theology at Jnana-Deepa Vidyapeeth, Pune. He has lectured at Sagong University, South Korea, the Jesuit School of Theology, Berkeley, and other faculties. He has authored 5 books, edited 6 books, besides publishing many articles regularly in India and abroad.

Introduction

Marykutty Thomas "Making Religion A Force for Reconciliation: A Pragmatic Approach to Combating Communalism in the Indian Context," *The Bulletin of Henry Martyn Institute of Islamic Studies* IX/3 (July-September, 1986)

Marykutty Thomas' "Making Religion a Force for Reconciliation: A Pragmatic Approach to Combating Communalism in the Indian Context" emphasizes the values of common humanity in various religious tradition regardless of religious diversity. She viewed the 'frog in the well' attitude, the abuse of religion by various fundamental groups as the main reasons for sectarian violence. In this context of communalism, the author called on religion to promote reconciliation. In her approach for reconciliation, she suggests finding common similarities – the emphasis for oneness of God and humanity and morality in Hindu religious tradition, the Bible and Qur'ān. The author also suggests ways and means to combat communalism through various stages. This practical initiative, she opined, will translate religion as a catalyst for reconciliation.

Samuel Rayan "The Kingdom of God, Religious Pluralism and Communalism: The Kingdom Of Justice and Peace," *The Bulletin of Henry Martyn Institute of Islamic Studies* 10/4 (October-December, 1991)

Samuel Rayan, in his article, "The Kingdom of God, Religious Pluralism and Communalism: The Kingdom of Justice and Peace" writes on the issue of religious and communal conflict and the role of Christians as peace-makers. Rayan underlines India's religious diversity and the causes of communal violence post India's independence rooted *per se* not in Muslim-Hindu rivalry, but on economic standpoints citing Asghar Ali Engineer's assessment. Nonetheless, he asserted that 'primordial identities' such as religion, caste and race have often been manipulated to polarize community on religious lines. In this context, the author called for a Christian response for 'the kingdom of justice and peace' from the Lukan perspective.

Vardit Rispler-Chaim "There is No Compulsion in Religion (Qur'ān 2:256): Freedom of Religious Belief in the Qur'ān," The Bulletin of Henry Martyn Institute of Islamic Studies 11/3&4 (July-December, 1992)
Vardit Rispler-Chaim, in his article, "There is No Compulsion in Religion (Qur'ān 2:256): Freedom of Religious Belief in the Qur'ān" critically explores freedom of religious belief in the Qur'ān. The author is aware that while Qur'ānic injunctions calling for freedom of religious practice abounds, verses that express superiority of Islam over other religion cannot be ruled out as well. For instance, he examined Qur'ān 2:256 that calls for non-compulsion in religion, while also studying Qur'ān 3:19; 9:123 etc. which present an intolerant side of Islam. The author indulges in careful study of these texts and their varied interpretations that expounds the multifaceted nature of Qur'ānic injunctions.

David Emmanuel Singh, "The Main Line Christian Attitudes to World Religions and a Voice of Dissent," Journal of the Henry Martyn Institute 20/2 (July-December, 2001)
David Emmanuel Singh, in his article, "The Main Line Christian Attitudes to World Religions and a Voice of Dissent" studies the various stages of pluralism and inter-religious encounter of both the Roman Catholic Church and the Protestant Churches of the World Council of Churches. The author underlines the Catholic Church's long history of openness towards other religions as seen in the declaration of Vatican II and the work of Karl Rahner. The paper also discusses the contribution of Indian Christian theologians on the question of pluralism and inter-religious relations by P.D. Devanandan, S.J. Samartha and others, with a special focus on the work of Samartha. Singh assessed the position of W.C.C. on multi religions as ambiguous, needing a lot of soul searching insofar as the possibility of God's salvation for all religions is concern. This, he concluded by pointing out the Christo-centric approach of W.C.C. and remarked that W.C.C. has a lot of catching

up to do compared with the Roman Catholic Church's position on multi religious experience.

Anantanand Rambachan, "The Axe and the Sandal Tree: The Grounds and Necessity for Reconciliation in Hinduism," _Journal of the Henry Martyn Institute_ 21/2 (July-December, 2002)

Rambachan, in his article, "The Axe and the Sandal Tree: The Grounds and Necessity for Reconciliation in Hinduism" reflects on the need for reconciliation among all religions in the midst of religious conflict. In his proposition of reconciliation, he drew examples from Hindu religious resources like: Lord Krishna's teaching on God as the common and unifying reality through the analogy of the string in the necklace of jewels (Bhagavad-Gītā 7:7); the Advaita philosophy of unity in existence and non-duality; the philosophy of _vasudhāiva kutumbakam_; the compassion espoused in the Ramayana of Valmiki. The author identified _avidyā_ as the root of misunderstanding; he therefore invoked Mahatma Gandhi's satyagraha. The challenge today, according to the author, is to relive these core teachings of Hinduism.

S. L. Gandhi, "Anekānt: The Jaina Path of Peace and Reconciliation"; _Journal of the Henry Martyn Institute_ 21/2 (July-December, 2002)

Gandhi, in his paper, "Anekānt: The Jaina Path of Peace and Reconciliation" presents the Jaina concept of _anekānt_ – a philosophy of peace and reconciliation in the context of absolutism and violence. The author remarked that wars and conflicts have been either fought in the name of holding on to one's religious belief at the expense of the others, or on account of superiority complex. It was in this context Gandhi illustrated Mahāvīra's idea of non-absolutism, non-exclusivism and non-dogmatism. This philosophy of _anekānt_ accepts co-existence of gnosis and nescience, which is to imply that truth cannot be known in its completeness; that diversity is innate. The doctrine of non-absolutism, as the author implies, has potential to usher peace and harmony because, to cite his example, the forms and modes of clay undergoes changes, but clay remains as clay. The author rightly put forth that all were right and all were wrong when he referred to the story of the blind men and their description of the elephant.

Annette Meuthrath, "For Poverty is a Great Luminosity from within…"
The Notion of Poverty in Buddhism and Christianity and its Significance
for an Inter-religious Dialogue on Poverty, *Journal of Henry Martyn*
Institute, **25/1&2 (January-December, 2006)**

Annette Meuthrath, in her article, "For Poverty is a Great Luminosity from within…" The Notion of Poverty in Buddhism and Christianity and its Significance for an Inter-religious Dialogue on Poverty, proposes common inter-religious initiative on the issue of poverty – especially from Buddhist and Christian perspectives. The author explores the issue of poverty both in Buddhism as interpreted by David L. Loy and P.D. Premasiri and Christianity as interpreted by Aloysius Pieris. She underlines two types of poverty: self-chosen poverty and poverty by circumstances. While the former is a way to freedom, happiness and spiritual richness, the latter is a product of injustice, oppression and exploitation. Taking poverty as the issue, the author called for a common interfaith dialogue with the poor – how both religions can initiate towards realising a world of peace and harmony according to what Pieris eulogised as 'home-temple-garden' world. This paper is thus a call for collaborative actions, common projects, common understanding of poverty and struggle for liberation from Buddhist and Christian perspectives.

Clemens Mendonca, "Inter-religious Collaboration: The Response of
Religions to the Signs of Our Times," *Journal of the Henry Martyn*
Institute **25/1&2 (January-December, 2006)**

Clemens Mendonca, in her article, "Inter-religious Collaboration: The Response of Religions to the Signs of Our Times" reiterates the role of religions as the answer to the common struggle for a better society. The author affirms the statement of the Pontifical Council for Interreligious Dialogue that the meeting point of religions to address the signs of our times is not an option but a necessity. This calls for a cross-cultural approach of not just knowing but understanding others – it is to enter into the mythos of culture and traditions of the neighbors. But to do this, the author says, dialogue is indispensable. She went on to highlight the Catholic Church's statement of *Nostra Aetate* that calls for open dialogue with other religions; PCID principles of dialogue that emphasize speaking and listening, giving and receiving for mutual growth and enrichment. Dialogue, as the author cites the idea of Raymon Panikkar, is not about arriving at a total agreement – it is discovery of the deeper inner self. The main focus for inter-religious collaboration in response to the signs of our times is therefore to realise the world as eulogised in Nazareth's manifesto.

Ch.Vasantha Rao and T. Swami Raju, "Interfaith Cooperation and Political Context," *Journal of the Henry Martyn Institute* 29/1 (January-June, 2010)

Ch.Vasantha Rao and T. Swami Raju, in their article, "Interfaith Cooperation and Political Context," suggest means and ways to explore and execute interfaith cooperation and peace in the midst of divisions based on religious sects, castes, classes, political parties and others. For instance, the concern for the poor was highlighted as an important theme for various religious communities and cultures such as the Sumerian and Hammurabi Codes, the Bible, Hindu spirituality and Islam. In the context of the misuse of religion and communalization of politics, the authors called upon religious groups to draw meaning from the root study of the term '*religio*', meaning 'drawing people together' or 'bind together.' They called upon the people to address the issue of justice and equality on the basis of: equality of humans before God; concern for the poor; equal distribution of state's resources, co-operation in building healthy community etc.

Reeta Bagchi, "Muslim Understanding of Hindu Civilization," *Journal of the Henry Martyn Institute* 29/1 (January-June, 2010)

Reeta Bagchi, in her article, "Muslim Understanding of Hindu Civilization," underlines the fundamental concern for peace among religions by emphasizing on dialogue in the context of religious communalism, especially between Hindus and Muslims. With this focus, the author studies the contribution of al-Bīrūnī on Hindu philosophy, theology and jurisprudence in his famous book *Al-Bīrūnī's India* and cross-cultural and comparative study of Hindu and Muslim religious texts. Secondly, the author highlights the non-conformist attitude of Saint Kabīr, his teachings on unity of God and humankind, co-existence and cultural assimilation etc. The author also highlights Akbar's universal religion, the idea of common humanity, equality and emphasis on interfaith dialogue etc. Furthermore, the author discusses at length Dara Shikoh's attempt for religious and cultural synthesis by underlining Shikoh's study of both Hindu and Qur'ānic texts calling for 'mingling of the two oceans' and his study of Sufism and Hindu philosophy etc. The author's call for interfaith relations is echoed in Dara Shikoh's statement, "Thou art in the Ka'ba at Mecca, as well as in the Hindu temple of Somnath."

M.M. Abraham, "Pluralism, Dialogue and Mission," *Journal of the Henry Martyn Institute* 29/1 (Janaury-June, 2010)

The author, in his article, "Pluralism, Dialogue and Mission," reiterates Arnold Toynbee's assessment of the unsuccessful attempt for religious syncretism in the history of humankind. It is thus a call for inter-religious dialogue. The author mentions the standpoint of the exclusivist, inclusivist and the reality of pluralistic society. He cites, as an example A.J. Appasmy's call for indigenous Christian theology which will be enriched by Bhakti tradition, Hindu philosophy etc. The author underlines the indispensability of understanding the 'otherness' of the others. The paradigm of the Kingdom of God is illustrated as a motif through which Christians are called to engage with people of all faith; that God is in work with all humankind. The author however warns that mission as dialogue should not be construed as an attempt for conversion but towards openness, respect and love of all.

Raimon Panikkar, "The Ultimate Experience: The Ways of the West and the East," *Journal of the Henry Martyn Institute* 29/2 (July-December, 2010)

This is one of the articles of the late Prof. Raimon Panikkar republished by *Journal of the Henry Martyn Institute*. In his article "The Ultimate Experience: The Ways of the West and the East," the author studies the experience of the ultimate and its understanding in the East and the West. He underlines this experience based on sense, intellect and mystical dimensions. In the quest for the supreme experience, the author engages that one cannot see the seer of the seeing, think` the thinker of the thinking or know the knower of the knowing. It is possible only by being oneself – the knower and the understander. The quest for supreme experience, according to the author is not identification with the experience but becoming the experience itself. This experience is supreme experience which is pure consciousness. In the second part, the author discussed the nature of transcendence associated with Semitic religions and immanence with Hindu religious traditions. He called for a meeting point between the East and the West by being open to the freedom of the Spirit and through transcendent immanence. The mark of transcendent immanence is to doubt if one has experienced the supreme, doubts whether one has attained. This was a call to be open to real liberation.

Martin Repp, "An Inquiry into the Communicational Structures of the Early Sangha and King Ashoka's Edicts: A Model to Tackle Religious Diversity," *Journal of the Henry Martyn Institute* 30/1&2 (January-December, 2011)

Martin Repp's "An Inquiry into the Communicational Structures of the Early Sangha and King Ashoka's Edicts: A Model to Tackle Religious Diversity," responds to the nature of religious diversity towards intra and inter-religious communication and understanding through Lord Buddha's and Ashoka's call for self-control. The author elaborates Buddha's call for self-control through his advice to the early sangha to abstain from hostile communication, malice, ill will, anger etc. among different schools of thoughts. For instance, Ashoka taught that one cannot value one's own sect at the expense of injuring the others; that in doing so, it is like digging the grave of one's own sect and also doing harm to the other sect. It is to call for a live and let live attitude. The author illustrates the example of the Lotus Sutra in which Buddha said that there is no such thing as smaller or bigger vehicle or three vehicles when the goal is the same – *Nirvāna*.

Safia Amir, "Towards an Interfaith Encounter: Islamic Perspective," *Journal of the Henry Martyn Institute* 30/1&2 (January-December, 2011)

Safia Amir, in her article, "Towards an Interfaith Encounter: Islamic Perspective," underlines the resources for interfaith relations from the Qur'ān and the Ḥadīth by highlighting the qualities of kindness purity, chastity, love, affection, truth, neighbourliness, tolerance, forbearance, forgiveness etc. as ethical principle for interfaith relations. The Qur'ānic injunctions for non-compulsion in religion, acknowledgement of the multiplicity of religions constitute the base of this assertion. The author dwells on Muslims' contact with other cultures and religions that were conscious of other faiths and the shared primordial and monotheistic religion. For instance, al-Bīrūnī in his *Kitāb Tarikh al-Hind*, made a comparative study of religion; so also Abū al-Maali's *Kitāb Bayan al-Adyan* on comparative study of both Hinduism and Islam based on belief in one God. The author further mentioned India's 'Ulamā call for freedom struggle as a religious duty to further substantiate interfaith encounter from Islamic perspective.

K. P. Aleaz, "The Challenge of Religious Pluralism and the Indian Context," *Journal of the Henry Martyn Institute* **32/1 (January-June, 2013).**
K. P. Aleaz, in his article, "The Challenge of Religious Pluralism and the Indian Context," calls for Christian conversion from within towards relational convergence in Indian context. Aleaz was critical of Christian's violence against the gospel, i.e. the issue of proselytising and foreign tag labelled on Indian Christians. He points out that the freedom to propagate religions does not warranty proselytising as pointed out in various bills on freedom of religion. The author underlined the critique of Raja Ram Mohan Roy, Swami Vivekananda and Mahatma Gandhi on Christians' negative attitude to Indian religions. Another important issue the author dwelled on was the issue of de-nationalisation which Ambedkar and other Hindu right wing group have often expressed. In the light of these issues, the author calls for gospel from within India and conversion not proselytising. By conversion, the author meant, a total inward experience, conversion to Jesus in Indian context – this, he called it a relational convergence.

Reeta Bagchi, "Spirituality for Interfaith Thinking: A Hindu Perspective" *Journal of the Henry Martyn Institute* **32/1 (January-June, 2013)**
Reeta Bagchi's article "Spirituality for Interfaith Thinking: A Hindu Perspective," reflects on Hindu spiritual tradition as a resource for interfaith spirituality. She advocates the Hindu philosophy of *Vasudhāiva Kutumbakam*, commonality – that Truth is one with different names. The author elaborates the multi-sided Hindu spirituality: accommodation of various sects and traditions, emphasizing on realisation of spiritual consciousness and the divinity of all souls, unity of beings etc. She also called upon the importance of East-West dialogue by reiterating Swami Vivekananda's universal principle which he delivered in World Parliament of Religions on how the West can learnt from Hindu spirituality. The author opined that religion has brought many blessings than bigotry and fanaticism which breeds violence. Religion as the author asserts, is self-realisation, discovering the universal values inherent in every religions – love, peace and harmony.

Victor Edwin, "Christian Spiritual Resources for Christian-Muslim Relations," *Journal of the Henry Martyn Institute* **32/1 (January-June, 2013)**
Victor Edwin in "Christian Spiritual Resources for Christian-Muslim Relations" explores Christian spiritual resource for Christian-Muslim relations

in and through the lives and witnesses of five Christian personalities. Firstly, the author drew examples of interfaith relations from St Francis Assisi's message of peace and St. Thomas Aquinas' emphasis on God as the common meeting points between Christianity and Islam. Secondly, the author pointed out the interfaith praxis of Charles de Foucauld, Henri Marechal and Lious Massignon. Foucauld emphasised on a mutually enriching traditions, focussing on common concern such as poverty. Marchal was presented as the propagator of the message of God's spirit working in different ways therefore calling for conversion to God. The author also echoed Massignon's message on understanding the Muslims towards mutual relationship and hospitality. Thus, underlining the contribution of these Christian personalities, the author calls for interfaith relation based on solidarity with the poor as a common ground for both religions.

G.N. Khaki and Shabir Ahmad Mugloo, "Buddhism and Islam: Inter-Religious Dialogue on Ethics," *Journal of the Henry Martyn Institute* 33/1 (January-June, 2014)

Khaki and Mugloo, in their article, "Buddhism and Islam: Inter-Religious Dialogue on Ethics," emphasize on the common ethical principles of Muslims and Buddhist as an example for building inter-faith relations. The authors study both Buddhists' ethical principle such as generosity, following the eightfold path, kindness, compassion and Muslims' ethical principle of righteousness, love for God and the poor, humility, righteousness and welfare for the individual and the society. The authors call for a common meeting point for dialogue of life based on compassion, mercy, love, kindness towards living beings, patience, forgiveness, sincerity, patience, self-criticism, sympathy, open mindedness, tolerance and generosity, especially emphasizing on compassion as a common ground for understanding between Buddhism and Islam.

Adis Duderija, "Muslims Approaches to Interfaith Dialogue: The Authentic and the Apologetic," *Journal of the Henry Martyn Institute* 33/2 (July-December 2014)

Adis Duderija, in his article, "Muslims Approaches to Interfaith Dialogue: The Authentic and the Apologetic," studies both the authentic and apologetic approach of the Muslims towards people of other faith. While the former is sensitive to holistic, contextual and historicity of religious tradition, the latter attempts to score ideological points. The author points out Qur'ānic texts and Traditions interpreted by Neo-Traditional Salafism of exclusive and antagonistic nature. He calls for understanding the text within the context. He further pointed out that the early foundation of Islam was based on pluralism. But in the later part, religious consciousness, independent confessional identity, religious self-consciousness and exclusivism replaced tolerance and pluralistic Islam. The author remarked that genuine interfaith dialogue from the Muslims must accept all the good, bad and ugly nature of this fact to initiate a meaningful dialogue.

Leo D. Lefebure, "Spirituality and Interreligious Relations: Pope Francis and M. Fethullah Gülen," *Journal of the Henry Martyn Institute* 34/1 (January-December, 2015)

Leo D. Lefebure in his article, "Spirituality and Interreligious Relations: Pope Francis and M. Fethullah Gülen," studies the contribution of Pope Francis and Fethullah Gülen towards interreligious relations. The author presents Pope Francis' respectful attitude towards other religions, humility, openness, listening attitude, love, dialogue and his relations with the Muslims. He further reiterates Pope Francis' assertion of the plurality of God consciousness, cultures while denouncing Church's exclusive locus of salvation and Gülen's interreligious spirituality as search for truth in all religions ignoring polemics – that it is not a drive to dominate and satiate one's ego. He emphasized on respect of diverse cultures, its distinctiveness and uniqueness, asserting that the true knowledge of God is to recognise its limit; that the total truth is beyond comprehension. Thus, the inability to perceive the truth is stated as true perception.

Teresa Joseph, "*Nostra Aetate* – 50 Golden Years: A New Style of Relationship with Believers of Different Religions," *Journal of the Henry Martyn Institute* 34/1 (January-December, 2015)

Teresa Joseph in her article "*Nostra Aetate* – 50 Golden Years: A New Style of Relationship with Believers of Different Religions," commemorates and re-asserts the landmark change of the Catholic Church's approach to people of other faith. The *Nostra Aetate*'s declaration in the Second Vatican proclaimed God as the creator of all with common origin and one final goal. The declaration is based on the notion that throughout history there was a certain perception of the Supreme Being in every culture. The author highlights, further, the main thrust of *Nostra Aetate* in relation to the Church's renewed stand on Christian-Muslim relation, Jewish-Christian relation,

Buddhist and Hindus. This statement was a call for common humanity based on the creation of humankind in the image of God. The article reflects the spirit of *Nostra Aetate* by stating interreligious dialogue as mission of the Church in four forms: dialogue of life, action, theological exchange and religious experience.

'Āshaq Ḥussain, "The Qur'ānic and Prophetic Model of Inter-Religious Dialogue," *Journal of the Henry Martyn Institute* 35/1 (January-June, 2016)

'Āshaq Ḥussain, in his article, "The Qur'ānic and Prophetic Model of Inter-Religious Dialogue," expounds a model of inter-religious dialogue from the Qur'ān and the conduct of Prophet Mohammed. In his discussion, he relied mainly on Qur'ānic text that traces the root of humankind to one singe man and woman. The author elaborated on the Prophet's initiation for inter-religious dialogue with the 'People of the Book' based on commonness such as the worship of One God. The Prophet's Madīna Charter was discussed at length in the article. The charter called for understanding, tolerance, and protection of rights, freedom, peace, equality and relationship with the 'People of the Book', polytheist, and idolaters. Thus, the article incorporates both the Qur'ānic and prophetic tradition for peaceful co-existence of common humanity.

Rudolf C. Heredia, "Dialogue as Pedagogy: Learning Together with the Other," *Journal of the Henry Martyn Institute* 35/2 (July-December, 2016)

Heredia, in his article, "Dialogue as Pedagogy: Learning Together with the Other," calls for a pedagogic dialogue with the poor, cultures and religious traditions. The author reiterates Raymondo Panikkar idea of dialogue which is to open up oneself to others, to dare beyond the constraint of dialectics. In dialogue with the poor, the author calls for solidarity with the alienated. He calls for acceptance and tolerance, celebrating diversity – not just unity in diversity but diversity in unity which appreciates difference. Dialogue with cultures further leads to dialogue with religions. The author emphasises on faith that is humanising, dialogue beyond verbal exchange, reciprocity between the self and the other. He stresses for dialogue of life, action, religious experience and theological exchange which is, "to be person is to be inter-personal; to be cultured is to be inter-cultural; to develop is to participate and exchange; to be religious is to be inter-religious."

Francis Gonsalves, "Mercy and Compassion: The Womb of Interfaith Dialogue," *Journal of the Henry Martyn Institute* 35/2 (July-December, 2016)

Francis Gonsalves, in his article, "Mercy and Compassion: The Womb of Interfaith Dialogue," emphasizes on mercy and compassion as the heritage and common meeting point of all religions for interfaith dialogue. Based on Pope Francis declaration of the 'Year of Mercy,' the author incorporates the teachings of Abrahamic religions on God as the source of love, mercy and compassion and the Indic religions' emphasis on *karunā* and *dayā* (compassion and mercy). For example, he mentions Mata Amritanandamayi's praxis of love and compassion, Buddhist's call for compassion on all living beings, the Jains compassion of all jīva, the concept of *ren* which focus on compassion and loving kindness in the Far East tradition to illustrate his point. Moreover, concepts such as *ahimsā, satyagraha, kenosis, shūnyatā, tyaga, vairagya* and *karunā* from different religious perspectives are incorporated as common meeting point for interfaith relations.

Victor Edwin, "Christian W. Troll's Engagement with Sir Sayyid Ahmed Khan," *Journal of the Henry Martyn Institute* 36/1 (January-July, 2017)

Victor Edwin, in his article, "Christian W. Troll's Engagement with Sir Sayyid Ahmed Khan," studies Christian W. Troll's engagement with Sayyid Ahmad Khan's approach to the study of Bible and its influence on Troll's Christian-Muslim dialogue. The author highlights Sayyid Ahmed Khan's knowledge of the Bible that subscribe to the Oneness of God as a basis for building Christian-Muslim relations. He further mentioned Troll's assessment of Khan's *Tabyīn al-Kalām* which focused on the reverence of the gospel of Jesus Christ; witness to *tawḥīd* and Christians' monotheistic tradition; the idea of Christian discipleship and the kingdom of God and Jesus as the inner Truth as helpful resources for Muslim spiritual development. The author further reiterates the need on the part of the Christians to understand the Qur'ān as God's revelation and Jesus Christ as the incarnate of the Word of God, on the part of the Muslims. It therefore calls for openness, inter-scriptural reasoning from both the Muslim and Christian communities.

Making Religion A Force for Reconciliation: A Pragmatic Approach to Combating Communalism in the Indian Context

Marykutty Thomas

Unity in Diversity

Despite the numerous dissimilarities and diversities present prima facie of the various religions in India, one can certainly perceive the essential unity that goes far beyond and surpasses all their apparent difference. This common basis of all the religions is the source of tremendous energy which rightly utilized, can be the obvious force to bring about reconciliation, harmony and peace among the people. To quote from a popular hymn: "As the different streams having their sources in different place all minge their water in the sea, so, O Lord, the different paths which men take through different tendencies, various through they appear, crooked or straight, all lead to Thee." This simple hymn is a proud declaration of the wonderful doctrine preached in the Gita: "Whosoever comes to Me, through whatsoever form. I reach him; all men are struggling through paths which in the end lead to Me." In this regard, the Qur'ān says: "Say, we believe in God and in what has been revealed to us, as well as to Abraham, Ismail, Isaac, Jacob and their descendants: We also believe in what was given to Moses, Jesus and to all the prophets raised by the Creator of the Universe; we accept all of them" (Qur'ān 3:84). Elsewhere the Qur'ān says: "Every nation

had its guide" and "a divine messenger was sent to every class of men."
(Qur'ān 35:24).

History has proved to world that holiness, purity, and charity are
not the exclusive possessions of any religion in the world, and that every
system has produced men and women of the most exalted character. In
the face of this evidence alone one can proclaim that none can dream
of the exclusive survival of his own religion and the destruction of the
others, Unity among the people will not come by "the triumph of any
one of religions and the destruction of the others" pronounced Swami
Vivekananda, the luminous young monk illuminated by Light of lights,
who shook the world's Parliament of Religions 1993. "The seed is put
in the ground", he further said "and earth and air and water are placed
around it. Does the seed become the earth or the air, or the water? No.
It becomes plant, it develops after the law of its own growth, assimilates
the air, the earth and the water, converts them into plant substance, and
grows into a plant. Similar is the case with religion. The Christian is
not to become a Hindu or a Buddhist or a Muslim; nor a Hindu or a
Buddhist or a Muslim to become a Christian. But each must assimilate
the spirit of others and yet preserve his individuality and grow according
to his own law of growth". Hence the slogan of every religion interested
in progress, development, and peaceful and joyful co-existence should
be "Help and not Fight," "Assimilation and not Destruction," "Harmony
and Peace and not Dissension."

Why Do We Disagree?
Sectarianism, bigotry and its horrible descendent fanaticism have long
possessed our beautiful country. They have filled our country with
violence, drenched it often with human blood and sent the whole country
to despair. Had it not been for these horrible demons, India would have
been farther advanced than it is now. Currently India is at a cross road
of diversified communalistic tendencies threatening its very existence.
Unless death knell is tolled to all fanaticism, to all persecutions with
sword or pen, and to all uncharitable feelings between persons wending
their ways to the same goal, the future is frighteningly uncertain, but
why is there so much variance? A short story, familiar to many of you,

would illustrate the cause of this variance. A frog lived in a well for a long time. It was born there, brought up there: yet remained a little. Certainly, the evolutionists were not there to tell us the frog had lost its eyes or not. Anyway, our frog had its eyes, and every day it cleansed the water of all the worms and bacilli that lived in it with an energy that would do credit to the modern bacteriologists. In this way, it went on and became a little sleek and fat. One day another frog that lived in the sea came and fell into the well. Traditional pleasantries were exchanged between the frogs about the weather, the adverse effect of unseasonal monsoons: the severe drought etc. Then followed a sweet little conversation thus:

"Where are you from?"
"I am from the sea"

"The sea! How big is that? Is it as big as my well?" and he took a leap from one side of the well to the other as if to show the vastness of his empire. "My friend" said the frog of the sea, "how do you compare the sea with your little well?"

"Is your sea so big?" The frog of the well asked taking another leap, "What nonsense you speak, comparing the sea with your well!"

"Well, then", said the frog of the well to himself "Nothing can be bigger than my well; certainly there is nothing bigger than this. This fellow must be a liar. I'll turn him out."

And therein lays the difficulty. If only the frog of the well had tried to visit the sea utilizing his friendship with the frog of the sea, then he would certainly have had a taste of the vastness and the depth of the unfathomable sea. Instead, he turned his friend out and culled him a liar. I am a Christian. I am living in my own well, and believe fully that my little well is the whole world. The Hindu lives in his little well and thinks that is the whole world, and so also the Muslim. Unless we break down the barriers of our own little world we cannot have the vision of the wonderful universe which exists outside of it. To this one must, as J. Krishnamurti wrote, "feel perfect tolerance for all and a hearty interest in the beliefs of those of another religion, just as much as in your own. For, their religion is a path to the highest, just as yours is. And to help all, you must understand all."

The Abuse of Religion

According to the Old Testament of the Bible, God confronts Cain by saying: "Where is your brother?" The murderer answered: "Am I my brother's keeper?" In cutting down his brother, Cain showed his defiance, while in not owing up to his responsibility before God, he revealed his arrogance. God's judgment upon sin and the rejection of his method reveal that one cannot escape being the keeper of one's brother without having to meet the eternal consequences. But who is one's brother? And what does it mean to be his keeper? No one can read the Bible without the solemn discovery that brotherhood and sisterhood of humanity is one of the foremost concerns of the Scriptures. The prophet Malachi argues for human brother-hood from the point of the father-hood of God. This is what Jesus also had in mind when he taught his model prayer which begins with confession of the father-hood of God. "Our Father which art in heaven" immediately implies "Our brother which is on Earth." The Biblical concept of humankind affirms that he is a child of God, and that in Christ Jesus all barriers between human and human have been broken down. Says the apostle Paul: "For ye are all the children of God by faith in Christ Jesus ... There is neither Jew nor Greek, there is no bond or free – for ye are all one in Christ Jesus."

The religion of Islam went a step further and established means for practical community. In his *Islam, Aims and Scope*: Mirza Abul Fazl points out that "Muhammad preached the brother-hood of man [*sic*] by totally destroying all the barriers raised against it by the selfish interest of man [*sic*]. Humanity was one vast brotherhood with God as their Creator and master who looked upon them as all equal." To a Muslim therefore, this World presents a vast field for co-operation in the struggle of life towards its ultimate goal. A Muslim may with a quiet conscience even eat and marry with the people of other religions. Muhammad himself, strictly opposed as he was to the religion of the idolaters, married three of his own daughters to them. The opening verse of the Quran teaches a Muslim to believe that if the creator and provider of the whole Universe has given means of physical growth equally to all human on earth, God has also provided them with means of spiritual culture as well. This noble doctrine advocated by the Quran infuses the spirit of equality and fraternity among humankind.

The Vedas too proclaim the common humanity. The Atharvā Veda is full of such endearing pronouncements. "Let a brother hate not his brother. Let a sister be not unkind to her sister. With good intentions speak to one another." It is further added "Love one another with that intensity with which a cow loves its calf." Rig Veda also follows the same trends of thinking thus: "Let your hearts beat in unison with all human hearts." An inspired Vedic sage addressed the people as "the children of immortal bliss": and Swami Vivekananda proudly proclaimed that the people are "the children of God, the sharers of immortal bliss, holy and perfect beings."

I have just shown you some of the sentiments expressed on the doctrine common humanity by the religious scriptures of three main religious groups represented in India – Hindus, Muslims and Christians. Yet, religion remains the strongest force of cleavage in India today. It played a significant role in the past political history of India, culminating in the partition of the sub-continent. The forces of reconciliation were again threatened by religion when it mercilessly took away many innocent lives in the great Punjab tragedy. Not only India but the whole world was shocked at the brutal assassination of Indira Gandhi by a group of fanatic Sikhs. Religion is a growing force causing situations of difference and conflict in India today. I will now explain some of the reasons go this.

The most basic reason is the traditional outlook and the pattern of social thinking that the people of India have inherited. Extended kinship and in-group loyalties are characteristic of all pre-industrial societies. Such loyalties easily take the form of communalism where religion is played up as a dominant theme of social values. There are several voluntary organizations in the country with definite aims for safeguarding the interests of the members of a specific religious coup. Conventions are constantly being held in which prominent members of major religious groups give voice to such objectives and try to effect collective bargaining for social, economic and political benefits in the country.

Articles 15 and 16 of the Indian Constitution prohibit discrimination on the grounds of religion and assure equality of opportunity in matters of public employment to all the citizens of India. Safeguarding this Constitutional guarantee often takes the form of collective action by the major religious groups. The Hindū Mahāsabhā, the Muslim League, the Akali Dal of Sikhs, these and other similar organizations have the avowed objective of safeguarding and bargaining for the interests of specific religious denominations. Often these communal bodies do little in terms of religious and cultural activities and tend to become agencies of political and agitational activities. Such communal activities set out a chain of rival actions which tend to increase tensions among the groups and widen and crystalize the situations of difference in the country.

Probably all the factors that cause tensions among religious groups in India are present in the confrontations which arise between Hindus and Muslims. Moreover, since these two groups happen to be the largest communal groups in the country, a study of Hindu-Muslim relations is highly significant.

The chief method by which Islam influenced Indian political life was through a series of invasions over the sub-continent, culminating in the establishment of the Moghul Empire in India. In contrast to the violence and hostility which marked the beginnings of this influence, the trade links between the west coast of India and Muslim countries such as Arabia and Persia, were characterized by long-standing communication and, to some extent, intermigration.

By about the middle of the 16th Century with the stabilization of Muslim rule, Islam and its followers had become a force to reckon with in the social and political life of India. Although the settlement of Muslim conquerors in India introduced a new religion and a new culture in the sub-continent, it was not marked by animosity between the followers of Islam and the native Hindus until the 17th Century. During that period, the bigotry of Aurangzeb and his persistent attempt to proselytize the natives aroused the opposition of the Marathas, the Sikhs and the Rajputs. History also records a few instances of outrages perpetrated by Muslim rulers on Hindu places of worship and learning. We may also read of the actions of individuals like Sikander Lodi of Delhi and Jalaluddin of Bengal who raged against Hinduism in a violent way and made converts by force. But, by and large, such acts are few and far between; they are not generally characteristic of Islam in India.

In the courts and in the cities, patterns of common behavior grew out. In the moral areas common beliefs and customs developed. The Mughal rulers and the preceding Sultans were not always strictly orthodox in their following of Islam, Two of them Ala-ud-Din and Akbar contemplated founding new religions of their own. Moreover, many of these rulers were connected with Hindu sovereigns by marriage or political alliances. Such attempts at social integration were but natural. It is a universal phenomenon that when two peoples come to live together and have identical practical problems to deal with they evolve out a synthetic pattern of culture. Thus, while this process of integration was slowly taking place on the Indian soil, the emergence of the British power in the country adversely affected this process of synthesis and resulted in the playing up of the situation of differences between these two communal groups. In their masterly analysis of this problem Ashok Mehta and Achyut Patwardhan have given a fuller account of this "Communal Triangle" and have indicated how the British arm of the triangle kept apart the two sides in the 18th, 19th and 20th centuries.

However, to attribute the Hindu-Muslim tensions solely to policies of the British Government to what is popularly known as *'divide et impera'* would be an over simplification of the problem. There are other sociological forces which undoubtedly also had an influence: the conflict of Hindu commercial interests with the Muslim aristocracy in the latter part of the 18th century; the systematic shutting out of Muslim community from the Indian army – the Muslims ideal of profession in the 19th century; the State patronage of British Government of India weighing alternately between the two communities during the 19th and early 20th centuries, the non-cohesion of Hindu and Muslim cultures due to the total neglect of the regional and classical traditions facilitated by the spread of English education and so on. All of these factors have contributed to the stabilization of the Hindu-Muslim tension.

For nearly a quarter of a century preceding Indian Independence, there were also systematic efforts on the parts of both Hindu and Muslim leaders to widen the gulf between the two communities. These moves were based, at least in part, on mutual distrust of each other's secret political motives. Such antagonizing propaganda could not but reflect on the social and cultural aspects of the two communities. Thus, what was merely an intellectual difference between two theological concepts became a hard cultural cleavage between two communities.

The partition and post partition tensions and the anti-social activities indulged in by the members of the two communities have only contributed to making the two communities more bitter against each other: In addition to the situations of differences between the Hindus and Muslims, the tensions between other religious groups in the country – Hindu-Christian, Hindu-Sikh, etc. – have assumed fearful dimensions.

"Operation Blue Star" and the fanatic terrorist activities which occurred thereafter have become a nightmare to all peace loving citizens of the country. Religious fundamentalism is raising its head in parts of the country such as Ayodhya, Haridwar etc. Such abuse of religion socially and politically can be overcome only by a pragmatic attitude which includes (a) the belief that there is an essential unity of all and (b) the confidence that even the conflicting views should not prevent peaceful co-existence and common work for the common good.

Making Religion a Force for Reconciliation
This section of the paper includes three sub-sections

a) Terminological Clarifications
b) Similarity of Religions, and
c) Combating Communalism – Ways and Means

a) Terminological Clarifications

The term 'reconciliation' pre-supposes a state of enmity, estrangement, or disharmony, and connotes a variety of meanings such as 'to make friendly again', 'to settle a quarrel', 'to bring into harmony', 'to make content', etc. The most common type of reconciliation is 'a compromise that covers up differences, where enmity is subdued by glossing over difficulties' or 'a compromise that accepts a plurality of differing and even contradictory views, life-styles, and ideologies.' But true reconciliation is more than the acceptance of pluralism. To quote Notto R. Thelle, "It involves concilium"; meeting of two or more parts that initiates a process through which both parts integrate some of the others in themselves, mutual transformation". He further added "this can only happen in an atmosphere of trust, where the parts are not threatened by each other." This process involves sacrifice, suffering, forgiveness and repentance on both sides. It is bringing about a 'rapport', a 'relationship' between the two parties involved.

Etymologically speaking, the term 'communalism' is derived from the root word 'commune' which means an organized group of people promoting local interests. But in a pluralistic discord-ridden country like India, the word 'communalism' has obviously come to symbolize a negative tendency. It is a complex term denoting all those factors past, present, and which lend solidarity to a group of people living on a compact territory. It implies "community of ideas, ideals, beliefs which are consummated by two conditions – location and common loyalties to a political ideal or organization." The concept of communalism, in other words, indicates psychological feeling which stresses the loyalty of the individual to the group. It is fundamentally a way of looking at the group life of a people bound by the virtue of their common historical background and future aspirations.

The root causes of the communal riots which have occurred in our country have been associated with the mistrust between the communities. Misunderstanding of the others' religions leads to distrust, and this distrust combined with blind faith of the fanatics in their own religion often breeds communal tensions.

The apparent differences among the various religions are due to a number of reasons such as the regional, national and racial characteristics; the varying stages of the intellectual growth of the people concerned; the rites and ceremonies which are practiced; and the exaggerated misrepresentations and wrong interpretations of the basic truths taught by the founders of these religions. Truth may be expressed in different ways, but the whole truth can never be fully, perfectly expressed. The world's different religions represent the varied colors which in their union form the one white ray of truth. The essential unity of all religions, the common meaning behind the various words', can easily be established by a close examination of the similarities behind the dis-similarities of all the religions. If we want peace and unity among religions' followers, we must first seek to find the essential unity among religions. Unity is not uniformity. If we continue to say that religions differ but the followers should unite, we will never succeed in uniting them.

b.   Similarities of Religions

In this area too, the scope of the paper delimits itself to the study of Islam, Hinduism and Christianity. The cardinal principles in all three of these religions are essentially similar. For instance, on the doctrine of God, Hinduism says: "The One Being the sages call by various names" (Rig Veda); Christianity acknowledges the one God: "And this is life eternal that they might know thee the only true God, and Jesus Christ whom thou hast sent" (Gospel of St. John); and Islam is clearly monotheistic: "Your God is one God: there is no God but He, the Merciful, the Compassionate" (Qur'ān). Thus all the three religions acknowledge the unity of God.

Faith without morality is of little value. Righteousness is enjoined by all three religions. Hinduism strongly stands for righteousness: "single is each being born, single he dies, single he receive the rewards of his virtues, single also his bad deed" (Manu). Christianity enjoins righteousness emphatically "But in every nation he that feareth Him, and worketh righteousness, is accepted of Him" (Acts of the Apostles). Islam urges righteousness very forcibly: "... and do good – they have their reward with their Lord there is no fear for them. neither shall they grieve" (Qur'ān).

It is not difficult to multiply instances to show that essential features of all religions are fundamentally the same. One can only conclude that religion is that feeling of reverence which men entertain towards the Supreme Being.

c.   Combating Communalism – Ways and Means

"Since wars began in the midst of men, it is in the minds of humans that foundation of peace is to be built" (UNESCO), The same idea is also applicable in the war against communalism.   This is what I meant earlier when I noted that reconciliation involves 'concilium.'

To bring about this sort of reconciliation, there must be 'inter-religious dialogue.' The World Council of Churces (1977) defined 'dialogue' as "a fundamental part of Christian service within the community ... It is a joyful affirmation of life against chaos, and a participation with all who are allies of life in seeking the provisional goals of better humanity."

Reconciliation involves understanding rational process which combines within itself a sympathetic attitude towards other people. It suggests three stages of inter-religious understanding and these should be practiced either in sequence or simultaneously depending upon the given conditions.

i.   Awareness Stage

This stage is marked by the awareness of other religions. The gaining of information about the different religions in India has to proceed with knowledge of one's own religion, which should act as the basis of comparison in the individual mind.

ii.   Penetration Stage

Tolerance and respect for the dignity of the individuals of other religions are the characteristics of this stage. It is also marked by an open mindedness leading to recognition of the common humanness which binds all religions in the country. This implies a development of the ability to think critically with regard to inter-religious problems.

iii.   Involvement Stage

This stage is marked by an empathy with the persons of other religions leading to a sense of emotional involvement and co-operation.

With these stages in mind, we may map out a programme to make religion a force for reconciliation,

a.   To achieve inter-religious understanding, we need 'bridge builders.' Each religion or people or voluntary organization or committee of two or more religions must try to build bridges between two hostile communities or two religious groups.

b.   These bridge builders should function in two ways:

   –   As a stimulating agency i.e. to stimulate and initiate seminars, workshops, conferences and other activities through-out the country on important aspects of religion, communalism, communal harmony etc., in order to dis-seminate knowledge and encourage operative living;

   –   as a service agency i. e. to provide people or institutions with needed information on the subject

c.   Research studies should be undertaken and also encouraged on the various aspects of communal harmony. These researches should give priority to identifying positive stimuli in bringing about communal harmony so that they could be exploited while preparing text books and other books for children. Research on every religion should be encouraged by the Government and by each religion. Co-operative efforts in this area should also be welcomed.

d.   Every religion has to invite distinguished men and women of letters from different communities to deliver speeches on the various aspects of their religion.

e.   It has been rightly said that the battle of Waterloo was won on the playgrounds of Eton. The battle against communalism can be fought effectively in the class-rooms of our schools. The famous Kothari Commission Report thus begins with a bang: "the destiny of India is being shaped in her class-rooms." Education is the only instrument of affecting a bloodless revolution. This is all the more true in a country like ours where ignorance, poverty, superstitions and blind faith are the order of the day. Schools can organize different types of curricular and co-curricular activities in order to inculcate in students the right interests and attitudes towards religion and communal harmony. These may include exchange programme of the students from different religions, inter-religious camps; field trips to places of importance to different religious groups, celebrating the festival of every religion and so on.

The problem of communalism needs to be dealt with on many fronts. Making religion a force of reconciliation can be very fruitful in fighting against the narrow minded communal forces. The task is certainly herculean but a determined effort will never fail.

The Kingdom of God, Religious Pluralism and Communalism: The Kingdom of Justice and Peace[1]

Samuel Rayan

Through the organizers of this course you have asked me to reflect theologically "...on our multi-religious situation with direct reference to the communal violence that has occurred and continues to occur in various parts of our country." More specifically, you have asked me to

> ...give a Christian theological perspective on the concept of the Kingdom of God as alluded to in Saint Luke's Gospel, with particular reference to justice, peace and reconciliation, stressing the Christian role as peace-makers in times of conflict.

May I begin by observing that we, adherents of Hindu, Muslim, Christians, and other spiritual traditions should not and indeed cannot, wait for times of conflict to burst upon us in order to exercise our role as peace-makers. Peace-making and the ministry of reconciliation have to be an abiding concern and way of life for communities of faith. Our efforts must aim not so much at the healing of wounds as at the prevention of wounding; we must be prepared not only to smother the flames but to extinguish the sources of the flare-up. The demand of our faiths is that we set ourselves to identify and eliminate the causes of communal tensions rather than merely deal with their symptoms.

You may already have surveyed the situation in our country, and analyzed it historically, structurally and culturally. I understand that Dr. Andreas D'Souza has provided "concrete practical information on the communal situation in India as reflection on efforts at reconciliation." The matter need not be gone over again. All we need at this point is perhaps to refresh our memory by recalling the main outline and stressing certain salient points.

Diversity

India has many religions and spiritual traditions. Adivasi religions represented in the Indus Valley discoveries, yet un-deciphered, and by some present day Adivasi observances; the Dravidian traditions, be they aboriginal, be they immigrant; the Aryan concepts and symbols that came in later; the protest and dissent movements like Jainism and Buddhism; Christianity and Islam which also outside; the emergence meanwhile of yoga, bhakti advaita spiritualties. All these interacted and influenced each other in various degrees. A real osmosis has happened at the level of spiritualties and world outlook. The nation comprises numerous castes, sub castes, outcasts; and many races and ethnic groups; several language families and cultures; diverse historical experiences of war and peace, of poverty and plenty; of different socio-political ideologies and a hierarchy of economic classes. A close look at our recent history would reveal a mounting concentration of wealth and power in a few hands, resulting in a deep distortion of democracy, in spiraling political violence and corruption, and in disillusionment and frustration for the masses. The majority of the people of India have become marginal and dispensable while the rich, the clever and the crafty are provided with ever-widening opportunities for self-aggrandizement and national plunder. Our land has become the private fief of an unscrupulous clique.

The growing gap between the poor and the non-poor has effectively divided the nation. There are two Indias: the India of the wealthy and the powerful and the India of the destitute, the wretched and the hungry. It is perhaps truer to speak of many Indias than of two: truer perhaps to speak of India's fragmentation than of its division. Ours is a nation torn to shreds by the caste myth, and by the sharp practices of an individualist, competitive economy. Caste and class divisions and fragmentations are assisted, reproduced and perpetuated by disruptive educational systems with differential socio-economic possibilities and promises attached to each. There are vested interests keen on keeping the poor poor and the masses illiterate. Our development has, as a result, been lopsided and unbalanced region-wise, population-wise and class-wise. Our priorities have gone wrong: we have been caring first and most for the well-to-do and for consumerist cravings, with little time or resources left for the basic needs of the masses. The result as stated by the international Hunger Project is that: "In India nearly 11,000 people die each day of hunger. India is the country with the largest number of people who go hungry. One third of the world's hungry people live here."[2]

That means our economic and cultural life has become twisted out of shape. And we know that our life and thought, at leadership levels, are oriented towards and controlled by the ideas, interests and manipulative tactics of our former colonial overlords, the oligarchies and banks of Western Europe and the U.S.A.

Communalism: A National Malaise

It is in this context that we center our attention on communalism. Studies done by social scientists and published over the years in books and in periodicals such as the *Economic and Political Weekly*, show that communal conflicts and violence have been on the increase. They appear to have acquired the features of semi-permanent group warfare. Communal disturbances, frequent enough up to independence, declined in number after 1947. But their frequency suddenly rocketed in 1964: between 1947 and 1963 the average number of incidents per year was 81.5. In 1964 alone the total number of events was 2115. And the average per year between 1964 and 1970 came to 1025. After 1970 the situation has continued to cause to the nation. Social analysts ask if communal violence has not become for us a way life. They point out that communalism is a complex reality with many faces it passes economic, political, social, cultural and intellectual factors. They define it as: a sharp divide between communities, each pulling itself apart from the rest, and feeling superior, inferior, aggrieved, and hostile. Hostility can go to the extent of calling for a blanket denial of historical facts and for the de-recognition as religion of traditions other than one's own.[3]

Causes

Communal riots may be caused or occasioned by a variety of factors including 1) religious disputes; 2) revivalist movements; 3) hegemonistic ideologies presuming to prescribe to others standards of patriotism; 4) manipulation of minorities of religion by the ruling class to save their vested or naked interests; 5) the emergence (for various reasons) of smaller identities based on region, caste, language or regional group; 6) the political use of communal sentiments and tensions in order to build up personal or party power; 7) economic competition breaking into divisive struggles fed by perceptions of unequal growth and discriminatory development; 8) the ascendancy of capitalism with its ethos of greed and individualism seeking domination and of balkanization; and finally, 9) ignorance of each other's culture and religion causing a litter of prejudices and negative stereotypes about each other.

One conclusion drawn from such cause analysis is that communalism in India, "does not originate totally, or even primarily, in the religious concerns of the Hindus or the Muslims."[4] Where then lies the primary cause? In the sphere of economic and class, answers Asghar Ali Engineer:

> A modern democratic society with inbuilt unjust structures becomes highly explosive. Primordial identities on the basis of religion, caste, race, ethnicity or region acquire new potency and violence erupts frequently if politicians decide to appeal to these primordial identities without changing unjust social structures. Communal and ethnic polarization is a natural consequence to a class polarization and increasing gaps between the riches and poverty, and monopolization of economic and power resources by a few castes or communities, religious or ethnic.[5]

Solutions

The remedies and solutions suggested are: 1) education which should remove ignorance, prejudices and active images of other; 2) each group's conversion and fidelity to its own religious/spiritual ideals; 3) practice of sustained self-criticism by every religious community, political and social groups; 4) struggle by all religious movements, singly and together, against every sort of injustice, against all oppression, exploitation, discrimination and corruption without distinction of creed or color, as well as against unbalanced development and concentration of wealth; and, more positively; 5) work together for proper, democratic, distribution or redistribution of power and hence of productive wealth.

A search for solutions has arrived at the conclusion spelt out by Bipin Chandra that social transformation leading to a more egalitarian, collaborative and participatory social system is alone the comprehensive way of fighting communalism effectively.[6]

Challenge

The challenge to Christian faith and theology is clear. Our life and thought stand challenged to self-criticism, to reconciliation of memories, to fidelity to the finest visions of the faith, to commitment to justice and to a communitarian and participatory restructuring of economic and political realities. We stand summoned to solidarity with all the victims of oppression. We are called to clarify meanings and unmask pseudo-religions and undermine the religious props used by communalist politicians and manipulators. We are to reassert the radical opposition which Jesus closed as existing between God and mammon. Our task is to reaffirm the primacy of the human and of love as the concrete image and temple and worship of the Ultimate Mystery we point to when we speak of God.

Faith and theology must provide the spiritual and mental grid which can hold the many human and religious experiences together in critical tension and in conscious mutual complementarity. Faith and theology have to furnish a horizon vast enough to include in one reconciling embrace the whole sweep of creation and the spiritual dimensions or movements of the entirety of history.

The King and His Reign

Even before his conception, Jesus is introduced in Luke as a king who would inherit the throne of David and whose reign would be never-ending (1:32-33).[7] As he dies on the cross he is acknowledged as king by a co-sufferer, crucified for flouting the laws of the imperial colonial rule which had also passed the sentence on Jesus (23:42).

The content and purpose of Jesus' kingship is presented by Jesus himself as the manifestation and proclamation of God's kingly rule which differed from and called into question Roman imperial domination (4:43; see 4:16-41; 8:1; 9:11). Of the excellence and wonder of this realm and reign of God, we have a hint in the observation that the least in that divine realm is greater than the Baptizer who is the greatest of all these born of women (7:28). It is incomparable privilege for Jesus' disciples to be confided with the secret of God's reign to others who are reluctant to follow Jesus, the secrets are served in parables (8:10; 10:23-24). For it is the Father's good pleasure to give the Kingdom to Jesus' disciples (12:32); and this Jesus conferred on them a little before his arrest and execution (22:29).

But gifts and privileges entail responsibilities and tasks. The disciples, recipients of the Kingdom with its secrets, are to go out to proclaim it and make its blessings available to everyone (9:2, 60). The mission has such priority and urgency that not even the duty of burying one's father may be allowed to retard or postpone it (9:59-62). The urgency springs from the fact that the Kingdom is near, very near; it has caught us unawares (11:20). This proximity is the pressing point of the proclamation (10: 9, 11), and of the prayer for the kingdom instead of worrying over food and drink which God knows we need (12:29-31). And yet the coming of the kingdom does not admit of observation; it is in our midst and within our grasp (17:20-21).

Jesus is the voice and sacrament of the Reign of God which has always been I the midst of people and within their grasp, and which has always been active in history, enlightening, gracing, guiding and saving people. The coming of Jesus enables us to name the kingdom, see its face and touch its blessings in Jesus' person, work and word.

Peace
Luke portrays Jesus not only as king, but as a peaceful king, peace-making and reconciling, He surrounds the story of Jesus' birth with thoughts of peace. In Zechariah's song Jesus is referred to as the Rising Sun come to visit us, to give us lights, and to "guide our feet into the

way of peace" (1:78-79). The birth of Jesus is then directly associated with glory to god in heaven and "peace on earth to those he favors" (2:13-14). At his presentation in the temple, old Simeon is shown as experiencing the peace that was to crown his life (2:28-32). "Go in peace" is Jesus' life giving word to the woman from the city who had "shown such great love" (6:50), and to the woman with a hemorrhage who touched Jesus' cloak and got healed (8:48). Both women had been social outcasts, shunned for moral or ritual pollution. Restoring them to health and dignity and rebuilding their pride and self-respect, Jesus is bidding society be converted and be reconciled. His peace was non-conformist, counter-cultural and socially transformative.

The first word his disciples sent out like lambs among wolves – are to speak on entering a house is, 'Peace.' Salvation is offered as peace. This wish bears all the spiritual and temporal blessings of the Reign of God. If a person open to these blessings lived in the house, "your peace will go and rest on him; if not, it will come back to you" (10:5-6). Jerusalem is an example of the refusal of the King's peace. In the last week of his life Jesus rode a colt and entered Jerusalem. On the way his disciples praised God with words that rejoined the song the angels sang at his birth: they named Jesus king and proclaimed peace and glory in heaven. But Jerusalem would not, even on that day, recognize "the way of peace" or "the moment of her visitation" (19:37-44; cf. 13:34-35).

Refusal of peace and rejection of reconciliation amount to choosing the path to ruin. On seeing the city, therefore, Jesus shed tears over it (19:41). That is how he could see his mission not only in terms of peace and reconciliation but of division as well, and of dissension (12:51-53).

Peace is born of Justice

The word about division and dissention (about the sword according to Matthew 10:34) means that the peace-salvation which the Messiah King brings overturns the peace of the world, and denounces all false securities (17:26-36). Luke points to two main factors on which false peace bases itself. One is hoarded wealth which engenders snobbishness and arrogance. The other is religious observances with their brood of self-righteousness, conceit and contempt for others. These are denounced and a summons is sustained throughout Luke to renunciation of riches, sharing of wealth and sobriety of living, to solidarity with the oppressed and action for justice and liberation. There is strong warning against religious chauvinism and religious pride along with a consistent call to littleness and lowliness.

Mary's visitation hymn confesses God as friend of the lowly and router of the arrogant. God fills the starving with many good things including the courage to stand for their rights, but he sends the rich away empty (1:46-55). The song is governed by an egalitarian vision of God's people/family on this earth; it constitutes a call for justice. This perspective is maintained in the infancy stories through reference to the manger, to the child as one destined to be oppressed and to its mother as destined to be pierced with a sword (2:6-38). Jesus' Nazareth manifesto is a clear option for the oppressed and the deprived, a firm commitment to justice and liberation; that is, to the construction of a community without prisons and chains, one that will be equal and free, reconciled and humane (4:18-19). The option was already contained in Jesus' rejection of temptations to walk the ways of the wealthy (4:1-13). It continues to express itself in Jesus' concern for the possesses and the sick (4:22-41; 5:12-14; 17-26; 7:1-17; 8:26-56; 13:10-17; 17:11-16); in his association with outcasts (4:23-27; 5:27-32; 7:36-50; 8:26-45; 10:30-37; 14:12-24; 15:11-32; 16:19-31; 19:1-10); in his inclusion of women among his travel companions (8:1-3); in his invariable positive and affirmative attitude to women of all occasions (7:36-50; 11-16; 8:40-56; 10:38-42; 13:8-10; 21:33; 23:27-31); in his offer of the Kingdom and its blessings to the poor, the hungry and those persecuted on account of the Son of Man (6:20-23); and inn the way he identified himself to the Baptizer's disciples in terms of socially transformative services to the poor and the afflicted (7:18-23).

The same option and approach is reflected in Jesus' self-identification with little ones and his word about the greatness of the least (9:46-48), and about revelation hidden from the earned and the cleaver but given to little ones (10:21-22; cf. 18:15-17). A high point is reached and extra emphasis laid on options for the poor and for justice where Jesus lays down clear norms for choosing guests to be invites "when you give a lunch or dinner." "Do not invite your friends or brothers or relatives or wealthy neighbors ... No ...invite the beggars and the crippled, the lame and the bind" (14:12-14). Or ways and views, our value sets and social relations are being radically questioned, remodeled and re-oriented.

Hence, Luke's and Jesus' relentless attack on greed and hoarded wealth and selfish pleasure. We may recall how Mary's song portrays God as one who topples throned princes and dismisses the rich with empty hands (1:52-53). "Alas for you who are rich" is as much part of Jesus' message as "blesses are you who are poor" (6:20-26). The contrast is stunning. The demand is for reconciliation through elimination of class-based imbalances which are always big with oppression and conflict. The rich man who feels secure in the plenteous good things he has amassed and stored away is unmasked as a fool (12:16-20). "Be therefore on your guard against every avarice." Life does not consist in possessions; and worry is no provider of life's necessities. Set your hearts after on the Kingdom (of Justice and mercy); seek out God's kingship over you, and rest will follow in turn (12:13-15, 22-32).

Jesus exposes the craftiness which becomes practical necessity in the exalted spheres of hoarded wealth (16:1-8). He denounces the 'holy' Pharisees' love of money (16:14-15). No one can be slave both of God and money (16:13). The real purpose and meaning of wealth is fellowship and friendship and community existence which are the really genuine human values (16:8-12). That is why the great Eater, insensitive to the wretched at his gate and around his palace, belongs with death and with the subhuman; and the chasm between the like of him and the destiny of the oppressed is unbridgeable (16:19-31). For it is incredibly hard "for those who have riches to make their way into Kingdom of God" – harder than it is for camel to pass through the eye of a needle (18:24-27).

Jesus therefore insists on renunciation which liberates the heart from slavery to wealth and liberates wealth for the life of the whole human family, and for the up building of a world of friendship and a culture of tenderness. A rich aristocrat and who has kept all God's commandments, is told there is something he lack. He had everything he owns, distribute the money to the poor and come, follow Jesus (18:18-23). The man cannot respond; he is very rich. The story is followed soon after by a different story in which a rich man, in growing friendship with Jesus, does part with his ill-gotten wealth, makes ample restitution and shares property with the poor. This practice of justice and solidarity with the dispossessed meant salvation to Zachaeus' house (19:1-10). One has to renounce all that one holds dear, no one can be Jesus disciple "without giving up all that he owns (14:25-33). "Sell your possessions and give to those in need" – is almost a refrain (12:33-34).

Self-Righteousness

The other ground of false peace, the other obstacle to reconciliation and fellowship is self-righteousness. This is illustrated by a Pharisee's boastful 'prayer', contemptuous of those who confessed themselves sinners (18:9-14). Self-righteousness, in league with legalism and fundamentalism, took its stand on strict observance of traditions of purity and pollution, and of laws concerning fasting, foods and Sabbaths. These were erected into divisive walls separating the holy few (of the well-to-do) from the many sinners (the common people). Jesus showed that God's reign of peace went beyond all human restrictions and offered people abundant life and freedom. Rules of food and fast and Sabbath must yield to the possibilities of the Kingdom of life and mercy and fellowship (5:33-39; 6:1-11). Jesus insists that traditional socio religious attitudes to sinners, prostitutes, and women in general, Samaritans and other non-Jews must change; prejudices must go; discrimination must end; and gulfs that separate people from people must be bridged (7:36-50, 10:24-37, 13:10-17, 37-41). Jesus reshapes and re-centers religion on justice and love, thus laying the foundations of a world of fellowship (13:42).

Openness

A basic feature and an essential requirement of the Kingdom is love for enemies, love for the unloving and the unlovable together with glad sharing of property. God is kind even to the ungrateful and the wicked (6:27-38). Such large-heartedness persuades us to shed all monopolistic claims, especially in religion, and enables us to live the openness and universalism of the Reign. Jesus' disciples are not to stop anyone, "because he is not one of us", from using Jesus' name to liberate people. That he who is not against you is for you is a principle or perspective particularly relevant in inter-religious relationships (9:49-50). The Kingdom is neither parochial nor ethnic.

"People from east and west, north and south, and one might add: from ancient times as well as modern), will come and sit down at the feast in the Kingdom" (13:29). For it is not saying Lord, Lord, or the possession of creeds and rites matters, but doing the Father's will. Hence calling down fire from heaven is not kingdom-response to prejudice and hostility (9:51-56). A different, positive, approach is called for. Jesus' own approach is represented by that astonishing prayer from the Cross, pleading for forgiveness for his killers (23:34). Such memories are for us more than models. They are invitations and imperatives. They are religion and life.

The Feast of the Kingdom
The experience of the Kingdom with its offer of peace and its demand for renunciation and community is summed up and socially expressed in table fellowship. A picture of feasting is the Bible's favorite symbol for the (final) Kingdom.[8] The time of the Kingdom as history's fulfillment (in process) is a time of life and life's celebration. It is distinct from the day of the Baptizer which was period of expectation and asceticism (5:33-39; 7:33-34). Among the Jews a banquet was an acted parable, in prophetic style, of final fulfillment – a metaphor for messianic salvation.[9] The messianic banquet was a prophecy of universal reconciliation. It represented the messianic community.[10]

Nearly all the meal passages in Luke occur in the context of the Kingdom, and allude to God's kingly activity or to the blessings of God's Reign. In Mary's song, God's saving action includes the provision of food for the poor, the filling of the hungry with many good things

(1:46-53). The theme of the hungry having their fill is soon repeated in connection with Jesus' offer of the kingdom to the poor (6:20-21). In the prayer Jesus taught his disciples the petition for the coming of the Kingdom becomes concrete in the immediate plea for daily bread each day (11:2-3).

There are three instances of Jesus accepting invitations from Pharisees to dine with them (7:36-50; 11:37-52; 14:1-24). On each occasion Jesus provokes a controversy by letting a woman of ill repute come in, touch and kiss him; by omitting the ablutions prescribed before eating; and by healing a man on a Sabbath day. Through such non-conformist behavior Jesus was inserting into crabbed and confined situations the liberating, life-giving, transforming realties of the Kingdom of God, like forgiveness and love (7:47), justice and inwardness (11:41-42), and solidarity with the poor and the lowly (14:11, 13, 21-29). Jesus was thus transmitting the Pharisee's table into a Banquet of the Kingdom by opening it up for the prostitute, the sinner, the cripple, the poor, the unwashed and despised nobodies. "Thus there are two banquets simultaneously in progress."[11]

The practice of table fellowship comes to a high point in Jesus' farewell supper with his working class friends, women and men. In the course of the supper, the banquet of the Kingdom receives repeated mention (22:16, 18, and 30). In the concluding chapter of Luke, a shared meal is the place of the definitive revelation of and meeting with the risen Jesus, the place and the seal of saving faith.

The meal scenes often imply a criticism of existing social relations, and the initiation of an alternative social order structured with equality and freedom and joyful creativity. They issue a call to reconciliation in truth of groups in conflict. From the Magnificat onward, Luke's work envisions the leveling of social and economic classes to create the family of God on this earth (1:50-53). The meal with publicans and sinners in Levi's house rejects the social system and the religious traditions which ostracize some people.

A banquet is a community reality. Jesus' table, symbol and foretaste of the feast of the Kingdom, is open table: it welcomes all sorts of people, for at the feast in the Kingdom people from all corners of the world will sit with the patriarchs and prophets (13:28-29). His table invites, and indeed presses to come in those who are normally excluded from decent society. Outcasts, prostitutes and prodigals are made welcome together with the crippled and the poor and the women as well as the dispirited who tend to withdraw into themselves (5.29-32; 7:36-50; 14:12-14, 21-23; 15:22-32; 24:13-35).

Conclusion

Luke introduces Jesus as king who proclaims and realizes in history the kingdom of God. The Kingdom is God's action transforming the world into reality of love and justice, equality and community. It is therefore primarily concerned with and involves the oppressed and the afflicted, those whom the world despises, tortures and rejects, the victims of subhuman non-history. On that account the Kingdom constitutes a challenge to the wealthy and the powerful, the managers of wars and misery; it implies a criticism of existing socio-economic structures, and call to remake them so that all women and men may live in glad and creative fellowship around the Father's table in the New Age. Jesus expressed and celebrated the presence of the New Age in fellowship meals with the lowly. His table was as open as the Kingdom and its feast.

This portrait of the Kingdom has consequences for all of us, living as we are in fragmented and conflictual society marked by deep oppression, the sin of untouchability, dehumanizing poverty inflicted on the vast majority of the population, and communal conflicts engineered for the economic and political benefit of a few using religion as tool and cover. In this context our task is:

1. To become a kingdom community: not one of greed and competition, or individualism and unconcern, but of justice and equality, and of great tenderness; a fellowship of people who share, nurture each other and grow up together.

2. To remold and transform parish life, on the basis of the social indications of the Our Father and after the social patterns suggested by authentic Eucharistic assemblies and by the understanding of God as Trinity. It would mean retrieving the lost vision and innovative boldness of our beginnings as enshrined in the accounts in Acts 2:42-46 and 4:32-37.

3. To give up silence and rick speech – personally and corporately – in the face of injustices and atrocities against the powerless and the poor.

4. To keep studying the evolving social and institutional situation, and relate the analysis constantly to our faiths and tis demands.

5. To promote egalitarian thought and practice, a culture of sharing and fellowship.

6. To stress the human as the center of religion.

7. And finally, to strive to live out the openness and universality of the Kingdom and its banquets, and to remember that God is greater than our hearts and our churches, and that God is with the other too, and may be speaking to me from there. To this last point we shall return in the talks that follow.

Endnotes

[1] This is one of three papers presented by Dr. Ryan on the topic "The Kingdom of God, Religious Pluralism and Communalism" at H.M.I.'s October 1991 residential course, the first in the series "Foundations for Reconciliation."

[2] *Hindustan Times*, October 9, 1991.

[3] Cf. S. Rayan, "The Other and the Theologian," in *Responding to Communalism*, edited by S. Arockiasamy (Anand: Gujarat Sahitya Prakash, 1991), 107-110.

[4] Gopal Krishna, "Communal Violence in India. A Study of Communal Disturbances in Delhi," in *Economic and Political Weekly*, xx/3 (Jan 1985), 124ff; also see, Rayan, "The Other and the Theologian," in *Responding to Communalism*, 112-120.

[5] Asghar Ali Engineer, "Communal Riots Before, during and After Lok Sabha Elections," *Economic and Political Weekly*, 14 September 1991, vol. 26, issue no. 37, 2138.

[6] A.A. Engineer, "Report on Seminar of Communalism," in *Economic and Political Weekly*, XIX/19 May 5, 1984), 755; Rayan, "The Other and the Theologian," in *Responding to Communalism*, 121-123.

[7] All biblical verses henceforth cited are from Luke's gospel, unless otherwise indicated.

[8] G. Wainwright, *Eucharist and Eschatology* (London: Epworth, 1971), 147.

[9] G.F. Moore, *Judaism II* (Cambridge: Harvard University Press, 1927), 262; also see Isaiah 25:6-9; 55:1-3; 65:11-14; Proverbs 9:1-6.

[10] J. Navone, *Themes of St. Luke* (Rome: Gregorian and Biblical Press, 1970), 11-14.

[11] Navone, *Themes of St. Luke*, 14, 27.

There is No Compulsion in Religion (Qur'ān 2:256): Freedom of Religious Belief in the Qur'ān

Vardit Rispler-Chaim

Muslims have recently begun to share a universal interest in the study of human rights. This study has been going on in the West for about thirty years.

Modern Muslims especially lawyers and religious scholars have taken upon to prove that Islamic law since its early stages of development has demonstrated understanding towards the needs of man in the basic freedoms. Islamic law, claim has taken precautions as well against the violation of these freedoms.

Freedom of religious belief, for example, is claimed to have been preached in Qur'ān 2:256.[1] This verse will therefore be the focus of our study. The recurring call for *jihād* had today, and the resurgence of Islamic powers all over the world make the question of whether the Qur'ān indeed advocates freedom of religious belief even more relevant and worthy.

Qur'ān 2:256 reads, "There is no compulsion in religion."[2] If this was the only verse in the Qur'ān relating to the problem of freedom of religion, and if religion is understood to refer solely to Islam, then Islam would appear to be an extremely tolerant religion. This view could be of great service in defending Islam against the claim that Islam allows no freedom of religious belief and is, therefore, unsuitable for our times.[3]

There are, however, other verses in the Qur'ān relating to freedom of religion. Some like Qur'ān 2:256 supporting it and others denying it; emphasizing, rather, the unique ness and the superiority of Islam.

For example, Qur'ān 73:10 reads, "And bear with patience what they utter, and part from them with fair leave taking."[4] Similarly, Qur'ān 2:282 reads "… and let no harm be done to scribe or witness. If we do (harm to them) lo! It is a sin in you." This verse appears to advocate not only freedom of religious belief, but also freedom of speech and of belief in general. It also denounces violators of these freedoms.

Against the above verses, we have Qur'ān 3:19 which read "Lo! Religion with Allah (is the Surrender", meaning that Islam translated literally as "The Surrender", is the only religion acceptable to God. And Qur'ān 3:85 reads: "Whoso seeketh as religion other than The Surrender (to Allah), it will be accepted from him, and he will be a loser in the Hereafter."

Many verses encourage fighting "in the path of Allah", the common definition of *jihād* (holy war), and declare it to be the highest virtue of Muslim believers.[5] Qur'ān 9:123 contains an even more cogent call to fight disbelievers mercilessly: "O ye who believe! Fight those of the disbelievers who are near to you, and let them find harshness in you, and know that Allah is with those who keep their duty (unto Him)."

Qur'ān 9:29 contains a similar call to fight the People of the Book until they agree to pay a special tax (*jizya*): Fight against such of those who have been given the Scripture as believe not in Allah nor the Last Day and forbid not that which Allah hath forbidden by His messenger, and follow not the religion of truth, they pay the tribute readily, being brought low.

Muslim commentators were already aware in the early Middle Ages of the equivocality of the Qur'ān verses regarding freedom of religious belief. The number of different interpretations each commentator sometimes offers for a single verse is evidence of the difficulty they experienced in their attempt to resolve the ambiguity. At the same time we cannot fail to discern a strong motivation among the commentators to demonstrate that the Qur'ān's verses, though apparently contradictory in fact consistent and speak with one voice.

Our main concern in this article will be to describe the means by which these commentators attempted to reconcile the Qur'ān's apparently contradictory attitudes, and the outcome of their efforts. For this purpose we propose to focus on the verses cited above, both those advocating as well as those condemning freedom of religious belief. Additional verses could be cited on either side, but this would take beyond the scope of this article and is, I believe, not essential for its purpose.

Islamic legal literatures dealing with the treatment of non-Muslims, often has recourse to the commentaries on the verses we have cited, since the verses are laconic and call for elucidation. The commentaries thus provide a major contribute to Islamic law. This adds to our scholarly purpose a valuable practical reason for studying them.

Verses Advocating Tolerance

"There is No Compulsion in Religion" (Qur'ān 2:256)
The commentaries on this verse, which are of the most general kind, tend to be utopian. They draw from popular psychology the assumption that belief belongs to one's innermost and can therefore never be subject to compulsion. Since religion is a form of belief, there can never be any truly effective imposition of religion. Compulsion can affect a person's external behavior, but can never affect a change of heart or alter an inner conviction.[6]

A more specific interpretation suggests that this verse should be read as a negative imperative, "Do not compel!" rather than as a statement of fact.[7] The verse thus clearly prohibits the imposition of Islam since Islam should be freely chosen and not imposed. This interpretation, too, is utopian. It may, however, be seen as having a realistic purpose if we assume that the command "do not compel!" was intended to correct a situation in which compulsion actually existed.

The most 'Islamic' interpretation argues that since Islam is such a true and persuasive religion, once a person becomes acquainted with tis principles which 'obvious sings of truth' (āyāt *bayyinat*) conversion must follow. Islamic inner meanings speak for themselves, and there is no need for violence to convince a person that it is a religion worth adopting.[8]

Most commentators were not satisfied with such utopian explanations of the verse, mainly or reasons deriving from Islamic history itself, and offered other explanations. These narrow the scope of the verses either by: i) time, meaning that 'no compulsion' was true only for certain periods in Islamic history, or that it was once a legal practice that had later been abolished; or ii) scope, meaning that is applied to certain groups of people and not to humanity in general; or iii) terminology, meaning that an act which may rightly be defined as compulsive under certain circumstances may not be compulsive under different circumstances.

Many commentators cite traditions according to which compulsion prohibited by the Prophet and his immediate successors on certain historic occasions some of which are given below:

a. When the two Jewish tribes of Qaynuqā and Nadīr were expelled from Medina, they had in their charge children of the *Anṣār* who had been placed with Jewish families to protect them from the evil eye and to ensure them long life. The biological parents asked the Prophet's permission to take their children back and raise them as Muslims, but the Prophet said "there is no compulsion in religion". The Prophet gave the same answer to the woman whose babies used to die at birth and who therefore placed those that survived with Jews for nursing upon the expulsion of the Jews from Medina. The Prophet's words meant 'Let them go with their foster parents and grow up in their religion too' (Judaism).[9]

b. A Muslim named Al-Ḥusayn had two sons, who having been influenced by Christian merchants, converted to Christianity and left Medina to go to Syria with these missionary merchants. Al-Ḥusayn pleaded with the prophet to pursue the convoy and bring his sons back to Islam. But the Prophet once again said "there is no compulsion in religion", that is, let them follow the religion of their choice, even though it is not Islam.

c. The Caliph Umar proposed to his Christian servant, Asbaq, that he adopts Islam. When the latter refused, Umar simply explained to him that as a Muslim he could bring more benefit to other Muslims, through marriage and participation in *jihād* etc. than as a Christian. Umar did not impose Islam even on a servant[10] despite the fact that in those days servants being part of the property[11] could be compelled to adopt master's religion.[12]

Earlier, I mentioned ways in which commentators narrow the scope of the 'no compulsion' verse in the sense of time. Yet another way of narrowing it was by the application of the legal doctrine of abrogation (*naskh*). According to this doctrine which is based on the tradition that the Qur'ānic verse were gradually revealed to Prophet Muhammad, some verses were legally valid until superseded by later verses. Verse 2:256 was therefore valid until verses ordering the waging of *jihād* were revealed to Muhammad by God and the "no compulsion" rule consequently ceases to apply.[13] Accordingly to Al-Sūytī this happened in the year 628 C.E.[14]

The scope of the 'no compulsion' verse is narrowed by regarding it as a legal prescription applicable exclusively to the People of the Book and enjoining Muslims to treat them with tolerance.[15] The People of the Book were accordingly granted the option of paying *jizya* (poll tax) in exchange for freedom of worship and safety of life and property. The legal definition of 'People of Book' varies according to the legal doctrine adopted. However, Jews and Christians are always included.

According to several commentaries the definitions of 'compulsion' and of 'those considered compelled', which determine the presence or absence of compulsion vary by narrowing the scope of the verse in different ways. The following are some examples:

> Compulsion is permitted only in respect of those who have no religion, such as pagans. The reason being that compulsion in their case is for their benefit, since they are mentally incapable of arriving at the true faith out of choice.[16] Compulsion in this case is like education which has to be imposed

on a child since he is too young to know its value. Compulsion of pagans is therefore not really compulsion. In fact some commentators claim that with the pagans no compulsion occurred since they had no religion which they were compelled to abandon.[17]

For the same reason, the conversion to Islam of children taken as captives in war is not considered compulsion. Since they have no religion of their own, children must adopt the religion of their captors.[18]

Forced conversion to Islam ceases to be "compulsion" if the convert later becomes convinced of the merits of Islam and embraces Islam sincerely out of conviction. Conversion following a war is not considered a compulsion since the conduct of war is guided by laws and rules which differ from those of peace time.[19]

There is a tradition that Allah likes those who are dragged into paradise in chains.[20] This means that force conversion ceases to be a "Compulsion", if and when the ultimate goal of attaining Paradise is achieved.[21]

In other words, the circumstances and result in each case, retrospectively determine whether or not there has been 'compulsion.' 'Compulsion' in the commentaries thus becomes a relative and not an absolute term.

"And Bear with Patience what they Utter" (Qur'ān 73:10)

According to commentaries, 'patience' should be practiced toward the heretics of Mecca,[22] heretics in general,[23] polytheists,[24] and the "fools from among the tribe".[25] Patience was required in order to endure the hurt, the curse and the contempt which the Prophet suffered from the above mentioned categories,[26] which accused the Prophet of lying,[27] and made other false accusations against him.[28] Patience was required for the Prophet to withdraw from those who had hurt him, without expressing anger or reproaching them.[29] Patience is the missionary's only weapon. During the Prophet's early years in Mecca, Islamic propaganda concentrated on appealing to human's hearts and conscience through 'quiet' preaching.[30]

However, several commentaries claim that this kind of patience toward the heretics did not last long. Quran 73:10, they say, was abrogated by the order to fight the heretics until they embrace Islam or die by the Sword.[31] This interpretation of 73:10 tallies with the interpretation of

2:256 which claims that the advocacy of tolerance was preceded by the encouragement to us e the sword for the spread of Islam.

"And let no Harm be done to Scribes or Witness" (Qur'ān 2: 282)

This verse has been variously interpreted by the commentators as: a) do not punish the secretary for refusing to write down what was not dedicated to him or the witness to testify what he has not sworn to testify;[32] b) do not prevent the secretary from writing and the witness from giving evidence;[33] c) do not punish a secretary or a witness who refuses to show up to perform their duty when called to, because they are busy;[34] d) an indirect warning to the secretary and witness not to neglect their duty or commit forgery, or add to or delete from the text, even if pressured to do so.

According to the verse, no one can harm them and escape punishment. The scribe and witness are likely to displease one of the parties who, as a result wish to harm them.[35] Some commentators explain 'harm' as denying the scribe or witness the wages they are entitled to, if what they have recorded or the evidence they have given does not satisfy the party that engaged them.[36]

Each of the interpretations of 2:282 emphasizes that even those paid for their jobs must not be forced to act against their conscience to say or write things they do not believe to be true. It is not merely freedom of religious belief which protected here, but freedom of belief in general.

Verses Declaring the Superiority and Exclusiveness of Islam

"lo! Religion with Allah in the Surrender" (Qur'ān 3:19)

The most bigoted commentary on this verse bases itself on the explicit wording of the verse and concludes that for Allah there is only one true religion – Islam;[37] and that reward in the hereafter will be granted only to those who practice Islam.

The most tolerant interpretation of the verse is based on the interpretation of "Islam" as *istislam* (submission) or *taa* (obedience), thus equating Islam with 'imān (religious belief in general).[38] Sheikh Al-Marāghī extends this idea, claiming that a true "Muslim" is anyone who is free from all traces of paganism and is devoted in his deeds, regardless of the religious community to which he belongs or the period in which he lives.[39]

A somewhat similar opinion is expressed also by the Shī'ī Al-Tabātabā'ī who claims that all nations have the same basic religious faith differing only in the degree of "preparedness" or "qualification", but he does not specify if this means "preparedness" to accept, to practice or to comprehend.[40]

Most commentators, however, point out the ambiguity of the verse. Though they agree that 'Islam' literally means submission to God's will, they nevertheless link submission to God with acceptance of the Prophet Muhammad, God's mouthpiece and spokesman.[41] This extension of the meaning of 'Islam' to include Muhammad makes the word 'Islam' in the verse indicates the religion of Islam and not simply submission to one God, which would apply to all monotheist religions. The exclusiveness Of Islam presented thus, not dogmatically, as in the first commentary on this verse, given above, but reasonably, becomes both evident and acceptable.

Judaism and Christianity, which also taught submission to one God, are dismissed as unacceptable to God, since they fail to recognize the Prophet Mohammed as a source of authority. Sayyid Qutb even suggests that the verse ridicules the People of Book who claim to accept the religion of God, but refuse to be judged by his book (Torah or New Testament). Qutb declares that "Islam" obedience to both God and His messenger. Therefore the conviction of the heart or the utterance of the tongue that is mere belief is not enough.[42] In other words, Islam involves spiritual activity, but also the observance of a code of behavior and ritual.

"Whoso Seeketh as Religion other than the Surrender; It will not be Accepted from him" (Qur'ān 3:85)

Like the interpretations for 3:19, 'The Surrender' is here again interpreted in its widest sense as monotheism.[43] It is the Shī'ī Al-Tūsī this time who claims that 'Islam' means *istislam* (submission), that is 'religious belief.' Consequently, it does not matter by which legal system or theological approach submission is achieved.[44]

Several commentators connect the verse with the historic case of the withdrawal from Islam (irtidad) of a group who had previously adopted it. Al-Ourtūbī and Al-Alūsī more specifically connect the verse with the irtidad of the Ansārī Hārith b.Suwayd and twelve others from among the Ansār.[45]

Al-Zamakhsharī, besides expressing the above view, also interpreted the verse as a rebuke to the Jews who had first believed in the Prophet and then later rejected him. This may be an allusion to an actual historic fact, namely, that some Jews had been inclined to accept the Prophet Muhammad at the beginning of the Islamic era as the promised Messiah, but changed their minds or failed to convince their brothers to follow them.

In this interpretation, as in the interpretation of 3:19, we are told once again that Muhammad was God's last Prophet and that Islam is therefore the last legal religious option.[46] Therefore we are to understand "Islam" once again as the name of the religion associated with the messenger, Muhammad.

Ibn Kathīr adds to the ambiguity of the verse by saying that "other than The Surrender" means "other than what God decreed as Law" (shara'a).[47] This leaves it to us to decide whether his paraphrase "what God decreed as law" incudes all heavenly ordained religions, or only the one revealed through Muhammad.

Verses Encouraging the Spread of Islam by Warfare

"O ye who Believe! Flight those of the disbelievers, who are near to you and let them find harshness in you" (Qur'ān 9,123)

The commentators agree in understanding the verse as a general call to fight disbelievers (jihād) in order to spread Islam. This jihād is to be conducted by stages starting with the disbelievers who are geographically nearest to the Muslims, and gradually proceeding to those further away.[48]

Islamic history shows that these guidelines were in fact followed. Muhammad started by fighting first against his own tribesmen and the other Arab tribes in Hijāz, then against the Jewish tribes of Qurayza and Nadīr, the Jews of Khaybar and finally against the Byzantines.[49]

'Disbelievers' in the verse includes pagans and monotheists alike, i.e. all those who do not believe in the message of Islam. Tolerance seems to be quite absent in this verse. Yet Sayyid Qutb asserts that the jihād was not intended to compel one to adopt Islam by force, but rather, it was meant to guarantee freedom of faith. The completion of jihād provided the conquered people with the option of conversion to Islam or of maintaining their faith by paying jizya.[50] In the same line, "harshness", on the part of Muslims is not explained as ill-treatment and torture, but rather of protecting the call to Islam and Muslims.[51]

The call to jihād in 9:123 requires those who believe to fight those who dis-believe, i.e. all the rest of humanity. The purpose of this fight is not specified in the verse. It will be explained in 9:29. Only the modernists, Al-Marāghī and Qutb probably influenced by the modern sensitivity to human rights attempt to justify jihād by explaining it as a defensive measure – to protect the faith and to protect Muslims.[52] It is this latter mistaken view of jihād that gives Muslims a bad name and provides their enemies with evidence to support the old, traditional charge against Islam, namely, that it is an intolerant and brutal religion.

"Fight against such of those who have been given the Scripture as believe not in Allah nor the Last Day, and forbid not that which Allah hath forbidden by His messenger, and follow not the religion of truth until they pay the tribute readily, being brought low" (Qur'ān 9:29)

The verse is an injunction to fight the People of the Book on account of the three offences which they have committed in violation of the true message of God.

The purposes of the fight against the People of the Book may be:

(i) To defend Islam and the Muslims;[53]

(ii) To force the People of the Book to pay the *jizya*,[54] not in order to satisfy a Muslim ruler's greed, but to strengthened the true faith and enable it to dominate.[55]

The commentators indulge in legal debates concerning who are the People of the Book. However, I do not propose to go into the details of this debate. According to Al-Tabātabā'ī, any partial belief is perceived as *kufr* (heresy). So that not only those faiths which do not accept monotheism, but even those which accept monotheism, but not as preached by the Prophet Mohammad fall within the definition of *kufr*.[56] However, the degree of *kufr* may differ in a westerner's judgment.

We shall also not dwell on the debate concerning who among the People of the Book are to be taxed and who are exempt, or the question of the amount of the tax to be levied.

Jizya is justified as payment for the right to live in the Islamic state and be protected by it, [57] as a compensatory payment for not fighting with the Muslims;[58] as an opportunity for the People of the Book to consider the merits of Islam and to adopt it;[59] or as a punishment for their *kufr*.[60] Thus, except for the last point, the imposition of *jizya* emerges as a payment for benefits granted by the Islamic state to the non-believer. The last reason is in the nature of revenge, which accords with the last phrase of the verse, "being brought low" (*saghirun*). This is often explained as the humiliation of the People of the Book and their subjection to the Muslim.[61]

If the verse is correctly dated by Ibn Kathīr as being revealed in the year 9 H after the conquest of Mecca, then 9:29 serves to emphasize that the duty of *jihād* is not abrogated by the conquest of the Arab polytheists (*mushrikun*). The Muslims must then proceed against the next enemy, as instructed in 9:123.

Summary

The Qur'ān clearly contains a double message regarding freedom of religious belief. On the one hand it advocates tolerating of other faiths. This is toleration is based on the confidence of Muslims in the superiority of their own faith as evidenced by statements in the Qur'ān that the religion most acceptable to God is Islam as taught to Muhammad. On the other hand, there are verses commanding Muslims to fight against non-Muslims, polytheists and monotheists alike, until they submit to Islamic domination, either by conversion or by paying the *jizya*.

If we accept the Muslim doctrine of the chronology of the Qur'ānic revelations, we can trace a trend from tolerance at the beginning of the Prophet Mohammed's mission (73:10; 2:256; 2:282) to intolerance in his last years in Medina, culminating in the clear command to fight the disbelievers (9:29; 9:123).

Sūrat Al-Tawba (9) of the Qur'ān is supposed to have been revealed in the year 9H/631,[62] a year after the conquest of Mecca; or, if it was the last to be revealed in 632.[63] This confirms the assumption regarding the Prophet's increasing inclination toward intolerance in the last years of his life.

This regress from tolerance to intolerance can be explained on at least two levels: i) on the personal level: the Prophet had come to realize over the years, how utopian and unrealistic had been his expectations that Jews and others would join the growing Islamic community if approached gently and shown the essential similarity between Islam and their own faith; ii) on the national level, the Muslims themselves came to realize over the years that they could survive as a community without the approval of other religious communities. What is more, they were strong enough to fight these other communities and to prosper at their expense.

Muhammad's period of tolerance may be explained as a sort of *taqiyya* (the tactic of concealing your true belief in time of danger, especially when you are minority in a hostile environment). When the Islamic community was more firmly established and had already won several military victories over its enemies, *taqiyya* was no longer necessary. The promotion of Islamic interests took precedence over all the other considerations.

In the light of the long list of Islamic military campaigns, some of which became symbol of heroism, of justice and of God's guidance, the commentators could not accept, "there is no compulsion in religion", as the true and sole guiding principle in Islamic history. They explained the contradictory attitudes in the Qur'ān either on a 'time line', using the abrogation theory (*naskh*), according to which the chronologically later verse supersedes an earlier verse. Or else they relied on the relative import of several key terms in the Qur'ān, such as *ikrah* (compulsion), *din* (religion), *kuffar* (disbelievers), *jihād* (holy war), and even 'Islam' itself. Sometimes they used both methods to explain the apparent contradiction.

All in all, the question whether or not the Qur'ān preached freedom of religious belief is more complex than modern human rights proponents who proclaim "there is no compulsion in religion" as Islam's unequivocal message of tolerance are ready admit. Their over simplified conclusions may serve some polemic purpose, but clearly ignore about 1200 years of Qur'ān commentaries and other relevant scholarly writings, as well as the evidence of Islamic history.

Endnotes

[1] Among those who share this view, most typical are: Abdul Ali, "Tolerance is Islam," in *Islamic Culture*, 56 (1982), 105-120; Fawzi Muhammad Tāyi, "Damānāt Al-Hūqūq Al Islāmiyya," in *Majallat al-Azhar* (June-July 1988), 1462-1466; Hassan Riffat, "On Human Rights and the Qur'ānic Perspective," in *Journal of Ecumenical Studies* 19 (1982), 51-65; Fazlur Rahman, " "Non-Muslim Minorities in an Islamic State," in *Journal Institute of Muslim Minority Affairs* 71 (1986), 13-24; Ali Abdel Wahid Wafi, "Human Rights in Islam," in *Islamic Quarterly* 11 (1967), 64-75; Tufail Ahmad Qureshi, "Justice in Islam," in *Islamic Studies* 21 II (1982), 35-51; Ihsan Hawid Al-Mafregy, "Islam and Human Tights," in *Human Rights Teachings* 2 (1981), 11-14; Mahmud Abdulmalik Boppa, "The Fundamental Human Rights in Islam," in *Nigerian Current Law Review* (1982), 351-362.

[2] The English translation of the Qur'ānic verses quoted in this paper is from M.M. Pickthall, *The Meaning of The Glorious Koran* (New York: n.d.).

[3] See for example, Yūsuf Al- Qirdāwī, *Fatāwā Mu'āsira*, 3rd ed. (Kuwait: 1987), 701-703.

[4] This injunction is repeated in 38:18; 20:130; 50:39.

[5] 2:190; 2:128; 2:244; 2:246; 3:13; 3:157; 3:167; 4:74; 4:76; 4:95; 5:54; 8:72; 8:74; 9:20.

[6] Al-Tūsi, *Al-Tibyān fī Tafsīr Al- Qur'ān*, Vol. 2 (Najf:1957), 311-312; Al-Zamaksharī, *Al-Kashshāf*, Vol. 1 (Beirut: 1947), 303-304; Al-Ālūsī, *Rūh Al Ma'ānī*

fī Tafsīr Al-Qurān Al-Azīm, Vol. 1 (Cairo 1301-1310 H), 478; Al-Marāghi, *Tafsīr Al- Marāghi*, 3ʳᵈ ed., Vol. 3 (Cairo: 1962), 15-17; Al-Tabātabā'ī, *Al-Mizā fī Tafsīr Al-Qurān*, Vol. 2 (Tehran: 1956), 360-362; Sayyid Qutb, *fī Zillāl Al-Qurān*, 3ʳᵈ ed., Vol. 1/3 (Beirut: 1961), 29-30; Hasanayn Muhammad Makhiūf, *Al-Qurān Al-Karīm*, 1ˢᵗ ed., Vol. 1 (Cairo: 1955), 83-84; Abd Al- Karīm Al-Khatib, *Al-Tafsīr Al-Qurānī*, Vol. 3 (Cairo: 1967-1970), 317-320; Al-Tabātabā'ī and Al-Khatīb died in the seconf half of the century.

⁷ Al-Nasafī, *Madārik Al-Tanzī was Haqā'iq Al-Ta'wīl*, 1ˢᵗ ed., Vol. 1 (Cairo: n.d.), 97.

⁸ Al-Baydāwī, *Anwār Al-Tanzīl wa Asrār Al-Ta'wīl*, Vol. 1 (Osnabruck: 1968), 132; Ibn Kathir, *Tafsīr Al-Qurān, Al-Azīm*, Vol. 1 (Cairo: n.d.), 310-311; Al-Shawkāni, *Fath Al-Qadīr*, 2ⁿᵈ ed., Vol. 1 (Cairo: 1964), 275-277; Al-Qāsimī, *Mahāsin Al-Ta'wīl*, 1ˢᵗ ed., Vol. 3 (Cairo: 1957), 644-665; Makhlūf, see note 5; Sayyid Qutb, see note 5.

⁹ At Tabari, *Jāmi Al-Bayān*, Vol. 5 (Cairo: 1954), 407-416; Al-Tūsī, Vol. 2, 311-312; Ibn Al-Arabi, *Ahkām Al-Qurān*, 2ⁿᵈ ed., Vol. 1 (Cairo: 1967), 233-234; Al-Qurtubi, *Al-Jāmī li Ahkām Al-Qurān*, Vol. 3 (Cairo: 1957), 279-281; Ibn Kathir, Vol. 1, 310-311; Al-Shawkānī, Vol. 1, 275-277; Makhlūf, Vol. 1, 275-277.

¹⁰ Al-Tabarī Vol., 5, 407-416; Al-Zamaksharī, Vol. 1, 303-304; Al-Qurtubī, Vol. 3, 279-281; Al-Baydāwī, Vol. 1, 132; Al-Nasafī, Vol.1, 97; Al- Al-Shawkānī, Vol. 1, 275-277.

¹¹ Ibn Kathīr, vol. 1, 310-311.

¹² R. Roberts, *The Social Laws of the Qur'ān* (London: 1925), 59.

¹³ Al-Tūsī, Vol. 2, 311-312; Al-Zamaksharī, Vol. 1, 303-304; Ibn Al-Arabii, Vol. 1, 233-234; Al-Qurtubī, Vol. 3, 279-281; Al-Baydāwī, Vol. 1, 132; Al-Nasafī, Vol.1, 97; Ibn Kathīr, Vol. 1, 310-311; Al-Shawkānī, Vol. 1, 275-277; Makhlūf, Vol. 1, 83-84.

¹⁴ It is mentioned in his *asbāb al-nuzūl* to verse 2, 190 which appears in *Tafsīr Al-Jalālayn* (Beirut: n.d.), 90-91.

¹⁵ Al-Tabarī, Vol., 5, 407-416; Al-Tūsī, Vol. 2, 311-312; Ibn Al-Arabī, Vol. 1, 233-234; Ibn Kathir, Vol. 1, 310-311; Al-Shawkānī, Vol. 1, 275-277; Makhlūf, Vol. 1, 83-84.

¹⁶ Al-Tabarī, Vol., 5, 407-416; Al-Qurtubī, Vol. 3, 279-281; Al-Shawkānī, Vol. 1, 275-277; Al-Tabātabā'ī, Vol. 2, 360-362.

¹⁷ Al-Tabarī, Vol., 5, 407-416; Al-Qurtubī, Vol. 3, 279-281; Al-Shawkānī, Vol. 1, 275-277;

¹⁸ Al-Qurtubī, Vol. 3, 279-281.

¹⁹ Al-Tūsī, Vol. 2, 311-312; Al-Shawkānī, Vol. 1, 275-277.

²⁰ Ibn Kathir, Vol. 1, 310-311; See the tradition in Ahmad Abd Al-Rahmān Al-Banā, *Al Fath Al-Rabbānī*, 1ˢᵗ ed., Vol. 14 (n.p. 1358 H), 108.

21 Al-Banā, *Al Fath Al-Rabbāni*, 1st ed., Vol. 14 (n.p. 1358 H), 108.

22 *Tafsīr Al-Jalālayn*, 773.

23 Al-Tūsī, *Al-Tabiyān*, Vol. 10, (Najf: 1963), 164.

24 Al-Tabarī, *Tafsīr Al-Qurān*, Vol. 29 (Cairo: 1912), 73.

25 Ibn Kathir, Vol. 4, 437.

26 Al-Shawkānī, Vol. 5, 318; Al-Marāghī, *Tafsīr Al-Marāghī*, 3rd ed., Vol. 29 (Cairo: 1966), 115.

27 Ibn Kathir, Vol. 4, 437.

28 Al-Baydāwī, *Anwār Al-Tanzīl*, Vol. 2 (West Germany: 1968), 365; Al-Qurtubī, *Tafsīr Al-Qurtubī*, 2nd ed., Vol. 18 (Cairo: 1967), 45; Al-Ālūsī, Vol. 9, 205; Al-Marāghī, Vol. 29, 115.

29 Sayyid Qutb, Vol. 8/29, 175.

30 Sayyid Qutb, Vol. 8/29, 175.

31 Al-Tabarī, Vol. 29, 73; Al-Zamaksharī, *Al-Kashshāf*, Vol. 4 (Cairo: 1966), 177; Al-Qurtubī, Vol. 19, 45; Al-Jalalyn, 773; Al- Shawkānī, Vol. 5, 318.

32 Al-Tabarī, *Tafsīr Al-Qurān*, Vol. 6 (Cairo: 1954), 85; Ibn Al-Arabī, Vol. 1, 259-260; Ibn Kathir, Vol. 1, 336.

33 Ibn Al-Arabī, see Note 31; Al-Qurtubī, Vol. 3, 405-406.

34 Ibn Al-Arabī, Vol. 1, 259-260; Al-Qurtubī, Vol. 3, 405-406; Al-Shawkānī, Vol. 1, 303.

35 Al-Baydāwī, Vol. 1, 142; Al-Nasafī, Vol.1, 106; Al-Shawkānī, Vol. 1, 303; Al-Marāghī, *Tafsīr Al-Marāghī*, 3rd ed., Vol. 3 (Cairo: 1963), 77.

36 Al-Zamaksharī, Vol. 1, 404.

37 Al-Zamaksharī, Vol. 1, 418; Al-Allūsī, Vol. 1, 540; Sayyid Qutb, Vol. 1/3, 138-139.

38 Al-Tabarī, Vol. 6, 273; Al-Qurtubī, *Tafsīr Al-Qurtubī*, Vol. 4 (Cairo: 1957), 43; Al-Shawkānī, Vol. 1, 326.

39 *Tafsīr Al-Marāghī*, 3rd ed., Vol. 3 (Cairo: 1962), 119.

40 Al-Tabātabā'ī, Vol. 3, 126-127.

41 Al-Tabarī, Vol. 6, 275; Al-Tūsī, *Al-Tabiyān*, Vol. 2, (Najf: 1957), 418-419; Al-Qurtubī, vol. 4, 44; Al-Allūsī, Vol. 1, 540; Al-Tabātabā'ī, Vol. 3, 126-127; Sayyid Qutb, Vol. 1/3, 138-139.

42 Sayyid Qutb, Vol. 1/3, 159.

43 Al-Zamaksharī, Vol. 1, 442; Al-Alūsī, Vol. 1, 622-623; Al-Marāghī, Vol. 3, 204.

44 Al-Tūsī, Vol. 2, 520-521.

45 Al-Zamaksharī, Vol. 1, 442; Al-Qurtubī, Vol. 4, 128; Al-Alūsī, Vol. 1, 622-623.

46 Al-Tabarī, Vol. 6, 570; Al-Alūsī, Vol. 1, 622-623; Sayyid Qutb, Vol. 1/3, 230-231.

47 Ibn Kathir, Vol. 1, 379.

[48] Al-Tūsī, Vol. 5 (Najf: 1965), 323-324; Al-Qurtubī, Vol. 8; (Cairo: 1967), 297-298; Al-Shawkānī, Vol. 2, 417; Al-Tabātabā'ī, Vol. 9, 428-429.

[49] Al-Tabarī, Vol. 14, 574-576; Al-Zamaksharī, Vol. 2 (Beirut: 1947), 323-324; Al-Alūsī, Vol. 3, 391.

[50] Qutb, Vol. 4/11, 77-84.

[51] Qutb, Vol. 4/11, 77-84.

[52] Al-Marāghī, Vol. 11 (Cairo: 1963), 48-50); Qutb Vol. 1, 77-84.

[53] Al-Marāghī, Vol. 10, 91-96.

[54] Al-Qurtubī, Vol. 8: 109-116.

[55] Al-Tabātabā'ī, Vol. 9, 246-253.

[56] Al-Tabātabā'ī, Vol. 9, 246-253.

[57] Al-Tabarī, Vol. 14, 198-201; Al-Qurtubī, Vol. 8, 109-116.

[58] Al-Qurtubī, Vol. 8, 109-116; Al-Alūsī, Vol. 3, 292-295.

[59] Al-Alūsī, Vol. 3, 292-295.

[60] Al-Alūsī, Vol. 5, 201-204.

[61] Al-Tabarī, Vol. 14, 198-201; Al-Alūsī, Vol. 5, 201-204; Al-Zamaksharī, Vol. 2, 262-263; Ibn Kathīr, Vol. 2, 347-348; Al-Shawkānī, Vol. 2, 349-352; ; Al-Alūsī, Vol. 3, 293-295; Al-Tabātabā'ī, Vol. 9, 246-253; or the debate between M.J. Kister and Meir M. Bravman over the interpretation of "an yadin" ("readily"), in 9: 29, See, Arabica 10 (1963), 94-96; 11 (1964), 272-278; 13 (1966), 307-314; 14 (1967), 90-91.

[62] Ibn Kathīr, Vol. 2, 347-348.

[63] Tafsīr Al-Jalāyan, 239.

The Main Line Christian Attitudes to World Religions and a Voice of Dissent

David Emmanuel Singh

Introduction

Gérard Vallée mentions three stages of development in the area of inter-religious encounter of the Protestant ecumenical debate.[1] The period from 1955 to 1961 marks the first stage, when among other things the issue of Christianity and non-Christian religions was in vogue.[2] In the second stage from 1962 to 1968 the emphasis shifted in favor of the issue of the finality of Jesus Christ, while the debate continued on the word of God and the living faiths.[3] Stage Three, since 1968, marked a new beginning, when the endorsement of the need for dialogue with those of other faiths and ideologies crystallized and thus opened the way for further debate.[4] The official position of the World Council of Churches came to lay ample accent on dialogue and especially listening in situations of dialogue, but there still remained a reluctance to accept the possibility of God's work in other faiths. It therefore remained unclear what the goals of dialogue were.

The Catholic position on the other hand, has a slightly different story. It has pointed out that all religions/faiths other than Christianity were not on the agenda of the Church to begin with.[5] The Church's concern was to issue a more open and affirmative declaration of how Christianity/the Church relates to the Jews. This proposal is said to have encountered some opposition from Arab Clergy. Consequently, the resultant document saw the addition of the term 'non-Christians' alongside the Jews. The controversy did not end with this because it is known that the Eastern Christians opposed the special mention of the Jews, which resulted in the deletion of the word 'Jews.' The document was finally approved in October 1965.[6]

The beginnings of the Roman Catholic interest in the people of other faiths did not therefore, issue from any serious theological questions concerning how God was operating in other religions, which would then be the basis for the Churches' relations with other faiths. It was rather occasioned by the Churches in-house diplomacy. The document containing a positive statement on religions vis-à-vis the Church may also be seen as the outcome of a democratic process whereby the Church is saved from taking a powerful minority position respecting the Jews only and is forced to widen its focus on 'faiths' as a result of the disapproval of the Arab clergy on the one hand and the Eastern Christians on the other hand.

But that is not all. The Catholic Church has had a long history of theological openness, which one must agree crystallized in the official statement of their position in Vatican II. The scholar who can be singled out as a prime mover of the Catholic position reflected in Vatican II is Karl Rahner. He has been credited with being the one who prepared the way for the Council's declaration, leading to an attempt at reconciling two official doctrines of the Catholic Church: (1) the universality of God's grace and salvation and (2) the necessity of the Church and Christ.[7] Paul Knitter has aptly phrased this position as "Many ways-one norm."[8]

The position holding on to the notion of the universality of God's grace and salvation and the necessity of the Church and Christ reflects the predicament of the Church. In the emerging environment of openness to other faiths the Church found if necessary to reflect on the soteriological value of "non-Christian faith" but also could not abandon the traditional belief in the centrality of the Church and Christ in the economy of divine salvation.

The great shift of emphasis on the inter-religious ethical issues, praxis of liberation, dialogue and inculturization, where one meets the other religions in the context of relatedness and not theological conflicts, reflects the Church's awareness of the ludicrousness inherent in this tension between "the Church/Christ alone and soteriological value of other religions" syndrome. In this context, one also encounters position papers such as the statement of the Indian Theological Association, which clearly deals with the theological issues in the face of pluralism.[9] There are individual theologians in this country who belonged to the Church but had the courage to step out and state individual theological opinions. I am of the opinion that the roots of such theological creativity go back to P.D. Devananda's bringing together a consensus position between those sympathetic toward other religions (Chenchiah, S.K. George, and C.F. Andrews), and those who pressed for the universal aspect of Christianity (Marcus Ward).[10] These two streams were brought together by P.D. Devanandan, who wanted to strike a balance between the proclamation of the central path of Christianity and sharing in the religious experience of the other faiths. Over the years though the emphasis has shifted to 'sharing in the religious experience', with the absolute neglect of proclamation,[11] there is one courageous theologian who has taken pains to keep the balance suggested by Devanandan intact, while also 'creatively reinterpreting' the two poles. He is S.J. Samartha. His 'theological creativity' tries to maintain, *from his own point of view*, the core Christian faith an also makes a large space to accommodate the living faiths of the entire world.

While one recognizes the need for theological creativity, bot least in the realm of interfaith, no creative theology or labels can be coercively dumped on the body of believers – that would be nothing short of an abject ignorance of the vitality of the body. My purpose is to outline changes that have already occurred in the direction of pluralism initiated and affirmed and within the body and to sound a caution against indiscriminate individual 'theological creativity.'

Individual creativity must and should be expresses in the context of the representative body as in the case of Rahner and Samartha, who operated within the confines of their respective representative bodies. Samartha in particular represents the potentially expansive and liberal extent of the Christian position *vis-à-vis* the other faiths because he breaks away from the ambiguities if the traditional theology of religions and incorporates extra-Christian insights. His system attempts to make space for Christ – thus safeguarding the issue of Christina identity and as fir the other faiths – thus moving beyond the confines of narrow triumphalism. While the body allows such adventures of the individuals as Samartha, they remain marginal to the official dogmas of the body. Such marginal attempts at understanding Christianity in relation to the other faiths are still important because they provide firm contextual foundations and also to some extent represent the developmental aspects of the Christian faith.

The Position of the Mainline World Council of Churches on Pluralism

Background

Beginning from Gérard Vallée's stage two,[12] the ground breaking decision was taken in the second assembly of the East-Asia Christian Conference (February 25-March 4, 1964) in Bangkok.[13] That decision was to enter into "true conversation with men of other faiths."[14] The Church was quick to affirm the scriptural basis for mission, the Lordship of Christ, the universality of the gospel message and the finality of Christ.[15] In a move to radically bring all religions, including Christianity on the same plane, it was recognized that religions are not necessarily good. It was also recognized that often religions of the people are instrumental in leading people away from God. However, once again, it was found necessary to hold the Gospel as the judge of all religions alike, and Jesus as one who confronts all religions of humankind equally, including Christianity. Once again, the awkwardness of holding on to the belief in the universal grace and the absoluteness of the Gospel and Jesus reflect in the special emphases on praxis as follows: (1) a need to understand faiths with whom the Christians converse, and (2) a need to share in the common secular life – a life of mutuality and cooperation. The dominant tone however, appears to have remained evangelistic in import.

The other consultation, though following the same line as the above, had a thoughtfully bold and a fresh theo-centric language.[16] It emphasized God's concern for everyone on the one hand, and indispensable status of the Church on the other, reflecting the Catholic debate on the same issue. Yet it differed noticeably from the others in its rider for "those who do not know the gospel of for it was stated that God has no favorites."[17]

The Position of the World Council of Churches on Religions

The negative exclusive position reigned under the influence of Barth and Kraemer (1928) until the third assembly of the WCC at New Delhi (1961).[18] But by now the attitudes had already become more open, and less aggressive. This led to the WCC's support of Christians associating with other faiths. The specific document that was the result of such transformation is "The WCC and dialogue with men of other faiths and ideologies", adopted at the Central Committee meeting at Addis Ababa, Ethiopia (January 10-21, 1971).[19]

Samartha summarizes briefly steps leading to the formation of 'Guidelines' on dialogue.[20] But first let us briefly look at the theological basis of the statement on dialogue with people of other faiths. It seems that the specific statement adopted was based on the doctrine of cosmic Christology.' That is to say that it was believed that somehow the benefits of what Christ did are not just for Christians. In some inexplicable manner 'Christ present cosmically illumines every heart.' Interestingly the notion of 'anonymous Christianity' of the Catholic Church is also based on the same foundation.[21] In fact Vatican II came before the WCC in issuing a clear statement on the Church's position with regard to the other faiths, in a specific document called 'Non-Christian religions: Nostra Actate',[22] and the WCC picked up the debate properly only after Vatican II.

Coming back to Samartha's article referred to above, it may be necessary to mention the issues raised in the Committee just preceding the publication of the 'Guidelines': (1) What is the purpose and the theological basis of dialogue? (2) Does not dialogue lead to syncretism? and (3) Would not dialogue blunt the cutting edge of the mission?

It is clear that the fear of syncretism, concern for proclamation, and confusion concerning the meaning and relationship of dialogue with mission touched off a controversy that resulted in what is termed as an 'unsatisfactory – inconclusive' position.[23] The document is against the use of dialogue as a weapon in Christian mission or to assert a position of superiority but leaves out the question of 'uniqueness and normativity of Jesus.' What While affirming that the 'universal creative and redemptive acts of God' are for all it, it does not clearly state if God unveils himself completely to all. Samartha was closely involved in the WCC Central Committee looking into this area ever since 1969, but this silence annoyed him. Samartha was personally disappointed with the Church diplomacy aiming at stability elected through compromise rather than dynamism effected through exploring fresh thresholds of the awareness of God in relation with all people. It was perhaps clear to him in this context of the politics of compromise that a theology of religions was not immediately imminent. He knew that the process of change in the thinking of the Churches respecting other faiths was staggering on account of the fear of syncretism and a concern for proclamation in certain quarters of the participant Churches.[24]

The WCC's position on the issue of religious pluralism remained understandably vague, because it held on to the belief in the "universal creative and redemptive act of God for all." and "particular creative and redemptive acts of God in Christ." One is left wondering whether one should interpret the above ambiguity to mean that God discloses himself positively to all or not? It bids fair to assume that the ambiguity was deliberate, a sort of a middle position to pacify the factious opinions.

As for the progress on the issue of the WCC position from Addis Ababa to Vancouver (1971-1983),[25] there was a suspicion about moving from Christo-centricism to theo-centricism. These two terms go a long way to explain the stalemate in the WCC consultations between the conservatives and the liberals, respectively. Generally speaking the WCC position may be plotted between the conservative Protestant Christo-centricism and the Roman Catholic Church's 'Christo-ecclesio-theocentricism', to which we presently turn our attention.

The Roman Catholic Position on Pluralism: Vatican II

Background

Paul Knitter examines the change in the Catholic attitude to the religions,[26] and goes on to examine the evolution of the Catholic position culminating in Vatican II and beyond. A cursory look at the table of contents reveals that he devotes much larger space for the survey of the Catholic position than for Protestants. That is understandable, though one obvious reason may be in the fact that the Catholic Church's position appears more positive than the WCC position. He therefore, calls it the "end point in Christian effort to a more positive approach". The Catholic position had become the plateau, as it were, of theological creativity of the organized Church, and a goal for the Protestant Church for many years to come. In the interim, it was the task of the individual dissenters to continue their theological creativity, hoping that at some point their thinking will become the architectural blocks of yet another milestone in the history of the Church, just as Carl Rahner's thinking proved to be for the Catholic Church in preparing the way for Vatican II.

The pre-Vatican II stage may best be précised as "the struggle of the Church to bring together the opposites, namely ecclesio-centricity and theo-centricity." This is not to suggest that the pre-Vatican stage was devoid of the concern for Christology, in fact the *Lumen gentium, Decree on missionary work*, and *the constitution on Church and world*, continued to underline the need for proclamation, based on Christology. The Christological content was understood to be innate in the ecclesiological spotlight.[27] The explicit concerns of the Catholic Church however, were (1) God's universal love for all, and (2) the necessity of the Church for salvation. The Church inherited these concerns from early Council of Arles (473).[28] Throughout the intervening period from 413 AD to the 20th century, the Church has struggled to reconcile those opposites.

In addition to the above concerns the Catholic Church also received a passive universalism in Origen's idea of *logos spermatikos*, and Tertulian's idea of *the naturally Christian*[29] *soul notion*[30] that underscore the principle of God's universal concern for all.

The period between the Council of Trent and the 20th century may briefly be recapitulated if we keep in focus the major shifts in the Church's emphasis. One feels convinced as a result of the study of the history of Christianity that it was primarily the theological controversies and the threat of Islam that led the Church to assume a defensive posture.[31] The zealous exclusivism of 'limited grace', 'double predestination', and the belief that some were prepared by God for sin etc. were perhaps a result of a negative response to the image of belligerent Islam.[32] The resultant extreme inwardness of the Church is reflected in her ecclesio-centricism, far outweighing the other principle of God's concern for all.

The Council of Trent[33] had much to do with letting the steam of insecurity out of the Church, and made it possible to incorporate a notion of "implicit desire" into its position on the people of other faiths. That is that if a 'pagan' lived according to his conscience it was tantamount to desiring to join the Church implicitly, and in as much as they join the Church implicitly, even if without being conscious of it, they were legitimate recipients of salvation. Thus a reconciliation of ecclesio-centricism and theo-centricism was effected. This position continued to be the mainline Catholic position until Vatican II.

Vatican II was a six-year-long period of deliberation from 1959 to 1965. The program of the declaration of Church's position on non-Christian religions was taken in 1964.

As pointed out earlier the Vatican II position crystallized both on account of long-standing theological debate on the concern of God for all, and its relationship with the Church, and the curious results of the dialogue on the position of the Jews in relation to the Church.[34]

> That God's supernatural saving designs extend to all men,[35] [sic] and the full extent of God's redemptive plan is for all individuals, societies and non-Christians.[36]

> That all persons are united in their sense of need, mysteries of human conditions... for which all religions offer some answers.[37]

> All kinds of discriminations based on race or religion were condemned.[38]

This was the first time in the history of the Church that it declared a positive statement about other religions officially.

The Bishops conference of Barundi-Ruanda (Africa),[39] in its preliminary marks, also brought out specific Biblical texts that dealt with the Church and the non-Christian world. The specific texts that clarified the 'divine plan for the non-Christians' were identified as Acts 10, Acts 17, and texts in Romans, Ephesians and Colossians. The document affirms the universal function of the incarnate word, but also adds 'the Church' in this affirmation, the fact of the universal religious aspiration toward the unknown God; the good in the non-Christian religions, etc. Interestingly enough the Church also maintained the earlier position by stating that the full light of revelation is in God and Christ, who then lead people to the Church.[40]

It is clear that the Vatican II position is also somewhat ambiguous in its statements. Though it recognizes the positive content in other faiths, it interpolates the necessity of Christ and the Church, effectively denying the possibility of salvation apart from this norm. Christ alone and the fellowship of the Church as a necessary outcome of knowing Christ mean, however, that though there are different ways, typified in the fact of a plurality of world religions, there is only one norm, namely Christ Church, and God behind it. There is therefore, a move in its seminal form towards a theo-centric theology of religion, which was developed further by a number of Catholic theologians, who go far beyond the Vatican II position. Scholars like Hans Kung and Carl Rahner, who move away from the 'Christo-ecclesio-theocentrism' of Vatican II to an explicitly theo-centric position that effectively wipes some of the ambiguity off the Vatican II declaration, still fall short of a precise theology of religion in the direction of pluralism.[41]

One feels convinced that a precise theology of pluralism was still forthcoming even as the scholars continued their search. It appears that the Protestant theologians would steal a march on their Catholic counterparts owing to their freedom from the centralizing authority of the official church.

But the question is how much can one depend on individual theological creativity in the face of historic Christianity's consensus on some form Christo-centricism, especially now that the organized body representing popular mass belief seems to have reached an impasse, with the body's unwillingness move beyond. Can world Christianity remain Christianity without Christ in the center of the Churches' faith and profession? S.J. Samartha's contribution in this direction is monumental.

S.J. Samartha's Contribution to the Theology of Religion

The hubs of Samartha's answer to the fact of pluralism are two basic ideas namely (1) rejection of normative exclusivism, and (2) acceptance of a sense of mystery. Those ideas are traceable to two backgrounds that Samartha straddles: the Indian-Hindu approaches to the other religions,[42] and the global trend toward some sort of relativity.[43] Samartha raised three basic points:[44]

Can Christian particularity be extended to have universal relevance? That is to say, is Christ as Lord, Lord of all or is there another way of understanding it without discarding it?

Could people of other faiths not make similar claims? If yes, what then is the meaning of the Christian mission?

Is not the manner in which we use the word Lord, developed in the west, where religious pluralism was not a significant factor?

In dealing with these questions Samartha reiterates a need to take a fresh look at the New Testament evidence and the tradition of the Church. In his treatment of the issue of the Lordship of Christ, Samartha connects the confession of the early church to a particular event called the resurrection through suffering and death. Jesus is Lord, therefore, in that he conquered sin and death. It has a particular context, beyond which one cannot extend, without doing violence to other confessions in their historical situation. One can detect here a tinge of the historical relativism of E. Troeltsch and the 'school he founded' after him represented by scholars such as B. Lonergan, L. Gilkey and D. Tracy.

Samartha though, deems it necessary to look at the New Testament to examine the meaning of the Lordship of Christ. His interpretation of the texts however, seems less than adequate, for a patent lack of thorough exegesis. For example he does not fully explain the perspicuous references (Phil. 2:1-11; Col. 1:15-20) to the absolute Lordship of Christ.[45] Further, although he does refer to the fact that in the resurrection, Christ was exalted above all Lords,[46] he does not identify who these Lords are. If Christ was indeed exalted above the others then it may be said that the Bible underscores the extension of grace of the events of the works and the person of Christ beyond his immediate context. Samartha recognizes this inadequacy in his explanation and a possibility of a faulty hermeneutics,[47] and thus adds his belief that after the entire Bible is not a 'blue print' to solve all the modern problems.[48] That is to say that the Bible is essentially relative, in that there are other resources to provide answer as well. If the Bible is not singularly authoritative, then what else may be applied to for help? Samartha's answer would be, "The experience of the Church, and Guidance of the Holy Spirit."

We have seen in our review of WCC and Vatican II that the mainline Churches have not felt free to revise their Christologies. They have given up much of what may be called 'Classicist Culture', but Christo-centricity has been very lynch pin of organized Christianity.

Although Samartha does not accept the absolute Biblical reference as normative, would he not accept the witness of the Church expressed in the official position as normatively guided by the Holy Spirit, which he himself states must be taken seriously? His point is well taken that the manner in which we used this word was developed in the West where pluralism was not a significant problem. It is however, a fact that (1) the experience of some kind of pluralism was always there, and (2) the WCC and the Vatican statements do in some sense reflect world Christian opinions in the face of pluralism. Would we not then recognize them under the guidance of the Holy Spirit, a criterion he himself has proposed? As it is, the word "guidance" is too ambiguous, that is to say that anyone could chain it for anything one states. One may adjudge the consensus of opinion sought by the representative bodies to be more authentic than an individual dissent.[49]

It may be necessary now to point out that Samartha gives tentative answer to the problem of the authority of the scriptures in his book, *One Christ – Many Religions*, where he prescribes an approach that recognizes a plurality of scriptures – the scriptures according to him in 'relation to' each other and not 'over against' each other.[50] The reason for this is that just as no one religion can make an exclusive claim to itself at the expense of the other, no one scripture can be set over above the others. All scriptures are then to be understood as valid in their own context. He therefore calls for change from 'monologue' to 'dialogue.'[51] However, since the relativity of the scriptures demands its particular authority for the believer, the Biblical witness to Christ's Lordship must be reviewed with this insight from Samartha – bracketing his suspicion of the scriptures.[52]

One problem in the way to establishing the particular authority of the scripture for the believer is that there are a variety of interpretations already in existence on the "difficult texts" or "exclusive texts" especially in the intra-denominational level, which Samantha himself recognizes.[53] But if his experience of seeking a debate on such texts in ecumenical debates drew a blank, one needs to ask if the direction suggested by Samartha is at all the one that the community of faith feels led to follow, or should we seek other ways mutually accepted, more open and non-coercive!

Elsewhere, Samartha deals more fully with the 'exclusive claims' of the Christian community, on behalf of Christ, in which he also tries to crystallize his new theology of religion.[54] He tries to answer why there is a need for a revised theology of religions, and gives four different answers:

> Theological claims have political consequences, in that cooperation and harmony with other communities is impeded by exclusive claims.

> Exclusivism raises some very basic questions about God's relationship with humanity.

> Christ has relativized himself in incarnation. The implication of which is that Christians must not absolutise what has been relativized. There is a ferment taking place within the Church for change in the direction of pluralism.

Samartha then goes on to survey the Church's official change in position is relation to other faiths, where he refers both to the WCC and the Vatican positions and observes that the Church's attitude is one of reluctance to move forward.[55] It is at this point that he moves on to give an alternative theology of religions with his reference to the "mystery of Truth".

One could not agree more with Samartha that a "radical change in the Christian stance" towards the other faiths is a theological necessity. The political and social factors are secondary in nature. That is because the politico-social factors must not in any way dictate the configuration of theology. It must rather be the other way around, if one hopes for true stability of society. Samartha recognizes the necessity of the primacy of theological concern behind pluralism and proposes the notion of 'normative plurality' as a newer paradigm in place of the Classical 'normative exclusivism.'

He attempts to go beyond the status quo of the representative Church's position in seeking a paradigm suited for the multicultural milieu. He finds a basis for 'normative plurality' in the notion of 'the Mystery' or 'the Ultimate Truth' clearly derived from his philosophical Hindu context. Samartha's doctoral work was on the great Hindu philosopher, Radhakrishnan.[56] The image of God as the Mystery always remains larger than any conception of God. No single apprehension of Him (It), can ever capture all of it. It is in other words always apprehended in part.

Since Samartha believes in the normative relativity of all religions and the scriptures, no religion, no single religion is absolute, yet all religions are necessary to help increase our knowledge of the Mystery. He brings therefore insights from the Hindu concept of *Satcidananda* and compares it with the concept of the Trinity of the Christian faith. He considers them as two different responses to the Mystery, arising out of two different cultural settings.[57] It then follows from this that the Mystery, being what it is, cannot be trapped or confined fully in any historical particularity. If such a possibility did exist the Mystery then would not remain a Mystery. This is why Samartha believes that the fact of Jesus is normative to the Christian alone; Christ is not to be made out to be an absolutely singular manifestation of the Mystery.

But since the particularity is normative for Christians, logically it is not impossible for Christ to be more relevant than He is, for Christianity as a community of faith is not a static entity. It has a history, and their history is the story of conversions and mission. Christ was not revealed to a community already isolated as one to receive a revelation of the Mystery in Christ. Samartha knows the logical possibility of a universal extension of the Christo-particularity and gives a very practical motive for desisting from making exclusive claims. That is, an exclusive claim "for our particular tradition is not the best way to love our neighbors as ourselves."[58]

Samartha's caution against 'Jesuology' and 'Christomonism' are extremely necessary correctives. He proposes a "theocentric or Mystery-centric Christology" that gives rightful priority to God, for he believes that Christ himself was theo-centric.[59] This insight is not novel. The ontological priority of the Mystery may be identified with the priority of God over Jesus in Biblical theology. Here Christ appears functionally subservient to God.[60] What one feels constrained to assert is that the ontological priority of God is the priority of the Father in the Trinity, not God if He was conceived of as an absolutely separate, independent and self- contained whole; for wholeness of God the Father is in His relatedness with the Son and the Holy Spirit, according to Biblical theology.

The theo-centric Christology of Samartha does provide a basis to "retain mystery of God, while also acknowledging the distinctiveness of Christ",[61] but it does so by relativizing the existence of Christians down through the ages until today. What the Church or the Scriptures have sought throughout history is not the distinctiveness of Christ's particularity, but rather the universality of Christ's particularity. One might wonder if by coercing the Church to accept this paradigm as the only one Samartha does not overstep his own principle of anti-exclusivism.

Samartha seems largely consistent in the internal reason of his system.[62] He does not easily resort to 'semantic mysticism.' He also is aware of the inalienable association between 'all religious life', and the notion of 'mission' and 'conversion.' He thus devotes fairly adequate attention to the logic of conversion and mission in the history and life of all the world religions. If this is so, why then does Samartha stridently advocate anti-exclusivism especially knowing that the logic of mission and conversion is in self-conscious universal particularity of each missionary religion?

His anti-exclusivism is:

An exaggerated reaction to the 'hobnobbing' of mission and conversion with military conquest, political domination, and racial arrogance.

A neutralizer to a ferment seeking to destroy other religions and cultures and replace them with a mono-religion and culture. That is just to replace and repudiate a religion but all that goes with it, for example, art, music, and so on. A mindset that is too militantly committed to the normativity of one's particular religious culture with a complete disregard and a negative evaluation of the other. Christianity as a social fact has been no more imperfect than any other world religion.

A valuable critique of the goal of conversion and mission. What is the direction of the missionary zeal on the part of the evangelizing religions? What is the direction of the respondent in deciding to convert to a particular religion? If it is a desire for numerical growth and a sense of religious and cultural superiority in the former case, and economic benefit, power, and a mere social uplift in the latter case, then that is neither a true mission nor a true conversion.

Samartha's critique is to be humbly accepted, and a renewed commitment made to the fact that the primary goal of conversion is God, that is conversion is primarily vertical. Conversion is not a movement of people from one community another that is, it is not primarily 'horizontal.'

What then is the meaning of mission in a pluralistic situation?[63] Samartha devotes an entire chapter on this question. He traces the historical context of mission as far back as the Tambaram conference

(1938), monopolized by Kraemer's 'Biblical realism' and his harsh opinions of other religions. He rightly points out that the Tambaram conference wholly ignored the Asian participants, though he finds Chenchiah's 'rethink group' especially significant, in that they mounted their criticism despite their minority status.[64]

Samartha then goes on to delineate some major issues in response to the question "what is Christian mission in a pluralistic world?" One finds him surprisingly orthodox in his treatment of Christian mission, and if the reader dwelt only on the sections elaborating his notions of 'Mystery' and 'anti-exclusivism' one would miss a very insightful facet of his arguments, without which his notion of 'Mystery' and 'anti-exclusivism' would amount to relativism, not as one of the contending philosophies explaining the phenomenon of pluralism, but *the only one*. That one feels would be disastrous for Samartha's own stance against triumphalistic arrogance of the classicist Christian culture.

He warns the Church that there is a plural way of doing mission.[65] Mission '*as the conquest*' for Christ is one of the ways. The other ways are, '*mission as Christian presence*', mission as '*being in Christ*', and mission as '*participating in God's mission*'.[66] He rightly rejects the first model and affirms the other three ways as the ways to do mission in the pluralistic context.[67] Participating in God's mission is essentially witnessing through presence by participating in Christ's suffering, in meekness and humility. Conversion may happen in the process of dialogue of this nature but not necessarily to Christianity.[68]

It is clear then that what Samartha really wishes to see happen is, conversion of the Church itself from arrogance and intolerance inherent in conquest pattern, and a positive acceptance or owning of Christ's own way of humble suffering and an enduring witness through it.

Samartha's 'anti-exclusive' point of view however does not make adequate space for a word like mission, for mission involves an idea of being sent for particular purpose; a purpose, unique and particular, necessarily active, horizontal, and vertical or both. Mission necessitates some sort of an experiential conviction of truth as wholly true, best or better truth; otherwise there is no rationale for mission. This however, does not mean that what others are saying is necessarily false.

Toynbee spoke of 'abandoning Christian intolerance' and W.C. Smith of 'theological surrender.'[69] That is a call to sacrifice the very hub of the Christian experience of Christ. Though intolerance must be decisively discarded, a call to surrender the core of one's faith, expressly in order to fabricate a space for others amounts to mere "swimming" on the surface. That concern may appear to be occasioned by diplomacy and socio-political acceptability rather than a passion for Truth. For it may be argued that if God is truly Mystery, one may never know if God really wishes to choose universalization of a particularity or requires surrendering of, and incorporation of all in the Christo-particularity. From the point of view of Samartha and the other relativists, there can be no absolute certainty when it comes to matters of ultimate concern. Why one may then argue demand a surrendering of theology and exclusivism in absolute terms, in favor of boundless mystery that one can never intelligibly comprehend even in part, unless one makes provision for some sort of possibility of 'absolute truth.'

Seyyid Hossein Nasr, an Islamic scholar, and W.C. Smith[70] have recognized this difficulty and therefore make a reluctant concession through terms such as 'relative absolute', and 'personal truth.' I am of the opinion that the future of credible theology of religion rests on humility on the part of the scholars to surrender fashionable concepts in favor of at least a possibility of a universal, stable, and solid reference point. It is this that will test the humility of any religious tradition as it seeks to re-conceive its contents, not giving in to the fluid relativism on account of the tremendous moral pressure applied by its votaries. The climate of debate on this has been turned into a battleground far from the notion of humility that they subscribed to. One feels that the crest of the mount has been scaled, where relativism is the king.

The future is going to witness a backward trend toward re-conceiving some sort of a 'stable reference point.' If the WCC, Vatican II, and popular Christian reluctance to adopt a strict theo-centrism are some indication, they point in that very direction.

Conclusion

We have seen that the Catholic Church has had a very long history re-conceiving its central emphasis on God's universal concern and the necessity of the Church and Christ. Vatican II accomplished a clear definition of what Church considers as the former doctrine's import. The Church thus moved from an exclusive plane by expanding the doctrine of the universality of God's concern over all the religions, but retained the implicit normativity of Christ of the Church, which the writer has tried to capture in the phrase, 'Christo-Ecclesio-Theocentricism.' It underlined the normativity of Christ of the Church, by placing Christ of the Church in the center of God's grace for all. The WCC seems however, to be lagging far behind the Vatican II position, in that its position on the possibility of God's grace for all is still ambiguous. Christo-centricism is therefore still the basis of the WCC position on other faiths. The Vatican II position will for some time to come remain the goal of WCC deliberations.

But for a minority in both the Churches' positions, an anxiety to seek 'unitive-pluralistic' model is quite patent, particularly among the individual voices within the Church. There is much that is conflicting between these scholars; the latest trend in this direction is to somehow preserve a 'normativity of Christ,' on the one hand, and to explain it away as the unique particularity of the Christian faith alone. It is particularly in the writings of Samartha. 'Uniqueness' is 'scotched' by his notions of 'Mystery' and 'anti-exclusivism.' We have also seen that if these are seen in the context of popular Christian attitude, they can serve as useful reminders of a need for 'suffering, weakness and even death', factors in the Christian mission.

I also think that the notion of 'surrender theology' is also not the only option for Christians today. Some scholars are beginning to realize the need for 'some sort of' absoluteness and universality, not just for preserving a particular identity, but for a possibility of universal validity of the particularity, without necessarily condemning others. The confession of the normativity of Christ in weakness and altruistic self-suffering, and confession of Christ in the christo-pneumatic ambience of the universal expansion of the particular Christic event is also a clear possibility. This, I wish to explore in the future, with insights from Islamic metaphysics.

Endnotes

[1] Gérard Vallée, "From Tambaram to Uppsala, 1938-1968 an Ecumenical Debate on the Interreligious Encounter," in *Study Encounter* 6.4 (1970): 207-214; Gérard Vallée, "The Word of God and the Living Faiths of Men: Chronology and Bibliography of a Study Process," in *Living Faith and the Ecumenical Movement*, edited by S.J. Samartha (Geneva: WCC, 1971), 165-182.

[2] Vallée, *Living Faith*, 165ff.

[3] Vallée, *Living Faith*, 165-173.

[4] Vallée, *Living Faith*, 182 (WCC meeting in Addis Ababa). See S.J. Samartha, "Dialogue as Continuing Christian Concern," in *Living Faith and the Ecumenical Movement*, edited by S.J. Samartha (Geneva: WCC, 1971), 143-157 and G. Khodr, "Christianity in Pluralistic World: the Economy of the Holy Spirit," *Ecumenical Review* 23 (April 1979): 118-142.

[5] Adrian Hastings, *A Concise Guide to the Documents of the Second Vatican Council*, vol. I (London: Darton Longman and Todd, 1968), 195-203.

[6] Hastings, *Concise Guide*, 197.

[7] Justo L. Gonsaler, *The Story of Christianity: The Early Church and the Dawn of Reform* (San Francisco: Harper and Row, 1984), 79

[8] Paul Knitter, *No Other Name? A Critical Survey of the Christian Attitudes to the World Religions* (London: SCM, 1985), 120.

[9] The Association's position on the Christian's relationship with the people of other faiths made in the 13th annual meeting December 28-31, 1989, at St. Paul's Seminary Tiruchirapally (Trichy in southern Tamil Nadu).

[10] Marcus Braybrook, *The Undiscovered Christ: A Review of the Recent Approaches to the Hindus* (Madras: CLS, 1973).

[11] Braybrook, *The Undiscovered Christ: A Review of the Recent Approaches to the Hindus.*

[12] Vallée, *Living Faith*, 175.

[13] The statement: "Christian Encounter with the Men of Other Faiths" was originally published in the *Ecumenical Review* 16 (July 1964), 451-455. This was given as a recommendation to the Churches after being adopted for the years 1964-1968, as the Churches' witness in relationship to religions and society, international affairs, and religious liberty.

[14] Vallée, *Living Faith*, 175

[15] "Christian Encounter with Men of Other Faiths," in *Ecumenical Review* 16 (1964), 455.

[16] "Christians in Dialogue with Men of Other Faiths," in *Study Encounter* 3/2 (1967), 52-72 and also *International Review of Mission* 56/223 (July 1967), 338-343. This consultation was held in Kandy, Ceylon February 27 to March 6, 1967 and was organized by Victor Hayward. An important feature of this consultation was the fact that it had Catholic participants for the first time along with the Orthodox and Protestant participants.

[17] See the statement by the Protestant, Orthodox and Catholics at the consultation in Kandy as above, *International Review of Missions* 56/223 (July 1967), 342.

[18] The materials related to this may be found in *Evanston to New Delhi* (Geneva: 1961), 3-26 and 63-66; W.A. Visser't Hooft, ed., *New Delhi Report* (London: SCM, 1962), 77-93; *The Work Book for the Assembly Committee* (Geneva, 1961), 68-73.

[19] The extracts of the document are found in S.J. Samartha, "Guidelines on Dialogue," in *The Ecumenical Review* 31/2 (April 1979), 155-162. See also S.J. Samartha, "Dialogue as Continuing Christian Concern," in *The Ecumenical Review* 23 (April 1971), 118-142 and Carl Hallen Hallencreutz, ed., *New Approaches to Men of Other Faith: A Theological Discussion* (WCC 1970). This book traces the history of the theological discussions since Kraemer's book The Christian Message in the non-Christian World. It traces Christian approaches within ecumenical movement to other faiths.

[20] Karl Rahner, "Anonymous Christianity and the Missionary Task of the Church," in *Theological Investigations* 14 (1974), 161-178.

[21] Hastings, *Concise Guide*, 195ff.

[22] Samartha, *Dialogue*, 156.

[23] S.J. Samartha, "Reflections on an Asian Visit" (WCC, 1969); Samartha also read a paper on "more than an encounter of commitment" in the Zurich consultation on "Christian dialogue with men of other faiths", on May 20-23, 1970.

[24] Knitter, *No Other Name?* 91.

[25] Sudharhan Devadhar, "Stanley Samantha's Contribution to the Interfaith Dialogue" (Ph.D. Dissertation, Drew University, 1987), 120-125.

[26] Knitter, *No Other Name?* 91.

[27] S. Mason, "The Roman Catholic Church and the Time of the Second Vatican Council," in *World Christian Handbook*, edited by H, Wakelin Coxill, et al., eds. (London: Lutterworth, 1967), 5-10 The article gives brief information on Catholic relations with the WCC, and Orthodox Churches, etc.

[28] Knitter, *No Other Name?* 91.

[29] Gonzalez, *Story of Christianity*, vol. 1, 79.

[30] Gonzalez, *Story of Christianity*, vol. 1, 79.

[31] Some official statements of the Church are as follows. In 1215 C.E., at the time of the fourth Lateran Council, the Council adopted the age-old doctrine of 'outside the Church no salvation' and added 'at all' for emphasis in 1305 C.E. Pope Boniface VIII also added 'Pope' to the above sentence. See also Palagianism and Augustine's

response in Williston Walker, *A History of the Christian Church* (New York: Charles Scribner's Sons, 1959), 160-168.

[32] *The History of Christianity in the Light of Modern Knowledge: A Collective Work* (London: Blackie and Son, 1929), 631-32, and 634-651.

[33] Hastings, *Concise Guide*, 198.

[34] Hastings, *Concise Guide*, 199.

[35] Hans Kung, Yves Congar and Daniel O' Hanlon, eds., *Council Speeches of Vatican II* (London and New York: Sheed and Ward, 1964), 181.

[36] Hastings, *Concise Guide*, 199.

[37] Hastings, *Concise Guide*, 202.

[38] Kung, Congar and Hanlon, eds., *Council Speeches Council Speeches of Vatican II*, 181.

[39] Kung, Congar and Hanlon, eds., *Council Speeches Council Speeches of Vatican II*, 182-183.

[40] Kung, Congar and Hanlon, eds., *Council Speeches Council Speeches of Vatican II*, 182-183.

[41] Scholars like Lonergan, Scheltte and Kung all subscribe to pluralism, but though there is a large hearted response to other faiths, the limitations of their own Church association force them to keep hinting at the normativity of Christ and the Church as 'the focus of orientation of all.' For further details, see Knitter, *No Other Name?* 130-135. See also Austin Flannery, ed., *Vatican II: More Post Conciliar Documents; New Authoritative Translation of Post Conciliar Documents*, vol. 2 (Michigan: Wm. B. Eerdmans, 1982), 711-761 and Francis X. Clooney, "The Study of non-Christian religions in the post Vatican II Roman Catholic Church," in *Journal of Ecumenical Studies* 28/3 (1991), 483-494.

[42] S.J. Samartha, "The Lordship of Christ and Religious Pluralism," in *Christ's Lordship and Religious Pluralism* (New York: Orbis, 1980), 19-36. See his "Commitment and Tolerance in Pluralistic Society," in *NCCR* 105/2 (February 1986), 71-77, originally convocation address delivered at the convocation celebration of Serampore College at Union Biblical Seminary, Pune, 1 February 1986. For Samartha's earlier position on pluralism, see "Unbound Christ: Toward a Christology in India Today," in *Asian Christian Theology: Emerging Themes*, edited by Douglas J. Elwood (Philadelphia: Westminster, 1980), 145-160 an extract of Dr. Samartha's first book *The Hindu Response to the Unbound Christ* (Bangalore/Madras: CISRS, 1974) originally published in German as *Hindus vor dem Universalen Christus* (Stuttgart: Evangelisches Verlagswerk, 1970).

[43] Samartha, *Christ's Lordship and Religious Pluralism*, 23.

[44] S.J. Samartha in his opening address at the consultation on "Christ's Lordship and Religious Pluralism," (Richmond, Virginia, USA, 24-27 October, 1979).

[45] Samartha, "Christ's Lordship and Religious Pluralism," 24.

[46] Samartha, "Christ's Lordship and Religious Pluralism," 24.

[47] Samartha, "Christ's Lordship and Religious Pluralism," 24.

[48] Samartha warns that WCC's aim is consensus and not to provide a theology of religion. One however, feels that the position presently held by the WCC is in fact a theology of religion arrived at after a serious deliberation.

[49] S.J. Samartha, *One Christ – Many Religions* (New York: Orbis, Maryknoll, 1991), 61-84. He emphasizes the normativeness of a plurality of scriptures, 'Spokenness' over against 'Writtenness', and seeks to deliver a new hermeneutics in the context of Asia.

[50] Samartha, *Christ's Lordship and Religious Pluralism*, 24. See also the response of Glasser to the article in the same book page 37ff, where he seeks to prove that the scriptures are the 'written' word of God, having the force of law. Also see Samartha's response to Glasser's critique, where he confesses that the idea that the scriptures have the force of law bothers him (page 54ff).

[51] S.J. Samartha, Dialogue in a Religiously Plural Society. Pp. 1-16 in *The Multifaith Context of India: Resources and Challenges for Christians*, ed. Israel Selvanayagam (Bangalore: Board of Theological Textbook Programme of South Asia, 1992).

[52] S.J. Samartha, "In Search of a Revised Christology: A Response to Paul Knitter," in *Sathri Journal* 1 (1993). See also Paul Knitter's critique, "Stanley Samarth's One Christ – Many Religions: Paludits and Problems," in *Sathri Journal* 1 (1993), 1-9.

[53] S.J. Samartha, "The Cross and the Rainbow: Christ in a Multi-religious Culture," in *Christian Response to the Multiform Faith in India* (Bangalore: UTC), 15-47; see also Samartha, *One Christ – Many Religions*, 87-104.

[54] Samartha, "The Cross and the Rainbow: Christ in a Multi-religious Culture," 16-17.

[55] Samartha, "The Cross and the Rainbow: Christ in a Multi-religious Culture," 17-20.

[56] Samartha, "The Cross and the Rainbow: Christ in a Multi-religious Culture," 30.

[57] Samartha, "The Cross and the Rainbow: Christ in a Multi-religious Culture," 30.

[58] Samartha, "The Cross and the Rainbow: Christ in a Multi-religious Culture," 32.

[59] Samartha, "The Cross and the Rainbow: Christ in a Multi-religious Culture," 37.

[60] John 3:16; 2 Cor. 5:19.

[61] Samartha, "The Cross and the Rainbow: Christ in a Multi-religious Culture," 40.

[62] Samartha, *One Christ – Many Religions*, 162-174.

[63] Samartha, *One Christ – Many Religions*, 163.

[64] Samartha, *Dialogue in Pluralistic Society*, 14.

[65] This approach was first defined by Kenneth Cragg in relation to Islam. Its focus is reverence for other traditions and an emphasis on common heritage. See Paul Loffler, "Representative Christian Approaches to People of Other Faiths: A Survey of Issues and Evaluation," in *Faith in the Midst of Faiths*, edited by S.J. Samartha (Geneva: WCC, 1977), 16-27.

[66] Samartha, *Dialogue in Pluralistic Society*, 169.

[67] Samartha, *One Christ – Many Religions*, 149-150.

[68] Samartha, *One Christ – Many Religions*, 147-150.

[69] Knitter, *No Other Name?* 44-54.

[70] Seyyid Hossein Nasr, "Philosophia Perennis and the Study of Religions," in *World Religious Tradition*, edited by Frank Whaling (New York: Cross, 1981), 181-200.

The Axe and the Sandal Tree: The Grounds and Necessity for Reconciliation in Hinduism

Anantanand Rambachan

The poet Tulasidasa in his most famous work, *Sri Ramacharitamanas*, employs a striking example to highlight the contrast in conduct between a saintly and an unsaintly person. He likens a saint to a sandal tree and an unsaintly one to an axe. Even when the axe cuts or fells the tree, the axe is saturated with the fragrance of the tree. It is the nature of the sandal tree to exude and share its soothing fragrance, and this defining quality is not altered by the behavior of the other. The cruelty and injustice of the axe cannot provoke a change in its nature. Like the sandal tree, a virtuous person does not become unjust because others are unjust and does not respond with hate towards those who are hate-filled. Goodness is not transformed by the destructive behavior of others.

The urge for reconciliation, nurtured by religious impulses, shares a fundamental similarity with the sandal tree. It is not extinguished by its encounter with hostility and cynicism. It never ceases to share the fragrance of its hope for an inclusive human community where relationships are compassionate and just. Even under the most oppressive conditions, it remains faithful to its vision of united humanity and gives of itself unselfishly to this end.

The necessity for reconciliation presupposes a condition under which relationships, such as those obtaining between individual human beings or human communities of various kinds are broken and characterized by suffering and hostility or indifference and isolation. Unfortunately, examples of such painful and fractured relationships abound in our contemporary world, and in every nation and continent there are relationships requiring healing and wholeness.

Why should the attainment of reconciliation be a central concern of religious traditions? What resources do our religious traditions offer that may inspire and energize us to work for reconciliation? These questions become especially significant in the light of the fact that religion is a factor and a contributory cause in many of the situations of conflict and discord, past and present, active and dormant. Among these are the struggles between Muslim Palestinians and Jewish Israelis, Christian East Timorese and Muslim Indonesians, Protestants and Catholics in Northern Ireland, and the Muslim North and Christian South in the Sudan. The list can be quite easily extended to include conflicts in Sri Lanka, India, Bosnia and Pakistan where religion is an important part of the identities of the communities in conflict.

Religion, admittedly, is not the sole explanation for any of these conflicts and the religious factor is intermeshed with historical, political, economic, ethnic, racial and cultural dimensions. Yet we cannot overlook the role of religion in intensifying narrow loyalties, providing a motivation for violence and entrenching divisiveness. We also cannot explain away the relationship between religion and violent conflict by the argument that in all these instances religion is being used or misused for the achievement of power in its various forms. It is too simplistic as well to attribute responsibility for conflict and violence to what we may regard as extremist and fundamentalist elements within religious traditions. The relationship between religion and violence is too ancient to be so easily explained. The boundaries of community are not determined only by geo-political factors but also by theological considerations, which are often more resistant to change and transformation. When we reflect on the role of religion as a force for reconciliation, we cannot ignore its continuing contribution to human discord and divisiveness.

In spite of the fact that the historical legacy of every world religion is tarnished one, religions continue to be a potent source of the visions, values and moral energies that are capable of renewing, transforming and healing human communities. While we must never underestimate and ignore the destructive side of religion, our challenge is also to discover and recover the spiritual and ethical insights, often ignored and forgotten, that are essential for the well-being of the world community. We may find encouragement and hope in the fact that the religions that have survived are those that are capable of self-correction, adaptation and change. One of the unprecedented opportunities in our present context is the possibility of growth and mutual transformation through inter religious dialogue and encounters.

We may begin our exploration of Hindu resource for reconciliation by noting that the will and desire for reconciliation as well as the possibility of its attainment is significantly enhanced when there is some form of shared identity with the estranged other. The significance of this truth may be appreciated, from another direction, by noting the extent to which parties in a conflict often go in alienating the other, emphasizing otherness and denying any common identity. "It is difficult," as Mark Juergensmeyer reminds us, "to belittle and kill a person whom one knows and for whom one has no personal antipathy."[1] The denial of the personhood of the other is a predictable and persistent feature of communities in conflict, past and present. The Irish Protestant leader, Rev. Ian Paisley, speaks of the Pope as "a black-coated bachelor" in his effort to caricature him and the religious community that he leads. The conservative Christian identity movement in the United States uses the term *mudpeople* to describe blacks and Hispanics and links the Jews with the origins of evil. Jewish and Arab activists in Israel engage in mutual dehumanization and demonization.[2]

One of the central insights of Hinduism, consistently proclaimed by its diverse traditions, is the unity of all existence in God. While this truth is affirmed philosophically in various dialogues of the Upanishads and in numerous other texts, it is also beautifully expressed in suggestive poetic metaphors and similes. One of the most striking occurs in the

Bhagavad-Gītā (7:7) where Krishna likens the divine to the string in a necklace of jewels. "Everything that exists," says Kṛṣṇa, "is strung on me like jewels on a string." While the gems constituting a necklace differ in form and properties, the string, which runs through each, is one and the same. The string links and unites each gem with the other, however separate they are spatially. In an analogous way, God is the common and unifying reality in all created beings, however different each one may appear to be. The Hindu tradition understands God to be the one truth in each one of us, uniting us with each other and with all things.

The non-dual tradition of Hinduism (*advaita*) articulates the most radical doctrine of the unity of existence in its denial of any ontological dualism and in its view that reality in not two. *Brahman*, the Brahman, the infinite, constitutes the essential nature of all that exists and is present in all beings as the self (*atman*). The wise person sees the sell in all and all in the self. As the Brhadaranyaka Upaniṣad (4.4.19) puts it, "there is here nothing diverse at all." This *advaita* teaching may be thought of as the spiritual parallel to the belief of science that life, in its totality descended from a single cell. The cells of all living things share a basic similarity, including the same DNA code and similar amino acids. Science suggests a common origin and nature for the countless expressions of life.

The significance that Hinduism grants to the truth of life's unity may be appreciated from the fact that its discernment is considered to the hallmark of wisdom and liberation. We are invited to recognize the sameness of the divine in ourselves and in all beings. The Bhagavad-Gītā (18:20) commends the knowledge that enables a person to see, "one imperishable Being in all beings, undivided in separate beings." A false and inferior way of seeing reality is to regard existing things as isolated, separate and independent of each other and to see in all beings "separate entities of various kinds" (18:21). This Hindu understanding of life's unity is the justification of its regard for the entire world as a single family (*vasudhaiva kutumbakam*). It is also the source of its core values such as non-injury (*ahiṃsā*), compassion (*dayā*) and generosity (*dana*). Compassion is an integral expression of the vision of life's unity and fundamental inter-relatedness.

The Hindu understanding of life's unity enables us to recognize and celebrate spiritual union with all beings. No one can be excluded, since the divine, which constitutes the unifying truth, does not exclude anyone and anything. 'God,' as the Bhagavad-Gītā (13:28) puts it, "abides equally in all beings." This is the antidote to our human tendency to deny the personhood, worth and dignity of the other. It is from the perspective of life's unity that we question exploitative and unjust human relationships that foster conflict and divisiveness, and it is the same perspective that urges us to seek and work for reconciliation and for the quality of human relationships that expresses this central truth of our existence. If our world is indeed a single family (*vasudhaiva kutumbakam*), both spiritually and biologically, the quality of our relationships should reflect the moral and ethical implications of this truth. Isa Upaniṣad (6) reminds us that the wise person who beholds all beings in the self and the self in all beings does not hate anyone. From profundity of the Hindu understanding of the nature of life's unity, estrangement from another is estrangement from one's own self and the hate of the other is the hate of one's self. To be in conflict with another is also to be in conflict with one's self. To inflict suffering on another is to violate one's own self.

The Hindu tradition assumes that a person who is truly grasped by the truth of life's unity in God will find delight in unselfishly working for the well-being of others. Ignorance of life's unity, on the other hand, expresses itself in greed self-centeredness and the infliction of suffering on others through reckless exploitation. This is the reason why the traditions of Hinduism have almost uniformly described the fundamental human problem to be one of ignorance or in Sanskrit, *avidyā*. Human conflict and the suffering that it causes are rooted in a fundamental misunderstanding of the nature of reality. The consequence is optimism about human nature, which is not considered to be inherently flawed and defective. Ignorance can be overcome and when it is and when we are awakened to the truth of life's unity, there will be a corresponding transformation in the quality of our relationships with others and greater social harmony.

The view that the human problem at its most fundamental level is one of ignorance and that this ignorance expresses itself in our failure to discern the unity of all existence is central to the development of a Hindu approach to reconciliation. It enables us to see the other, the one with whom we disagree and with whom we may be locked in struggle, as a fellow human being. We cannot dehumanize the one in whom we see ourselves or long for their humiliation. This approach was at the heart of Gandhi's philosophy and practice of non-violent resistance (*satyagraha*). Even in the midst of the strongest disagreements. Gandhi never sought to win support for his case by demonizing his opponent. He understood clearly that when a conflict is constructed sharply in terms of *we* and *they*, victory and defeat, the doors to reconciliation and a transformed community are shut. One is left with an enemy, a defeated enemy perhaps, and the next round of the conflict is only postponed. Gandhi included the opponent in the circle of his identity.

In restraining a disciple from violence towards some thieves who had stolen a few items from his monastery, the saintly Hindu teacher, Ramana Maharishi asked a provocative question, "If your teeth suddenly bite your tongue, do you knock them out in consequence?" Ramana's question implies the truth of life's unity as well as the reality of ignorance. The teeth and tongue are part of the same body and the biting, however, painful, is more in the nature of an error. The consequence is a disposition to compassion and forgiveness, without which reconciliation is impossible. Belief in the goodness of human nature and in ignorance as the source of evil disposes one to an attitude of forgiveness since it orients one to look beyond the immediate action to its underlying causes. As human beings, we are more likely to respond with hate when we believe that those who hurt us have done so because of intentional malevolence. If we see the action rooted in ignorance and a flawed understanding of God, self and world, our attitude to the other will be compassionate. We are liberated from hate, bitterness and the desire to inflict pain on the other and we are open to reconciliation.

One of the finest examples of the practice of such compassion and forgiveness occurs in the Rāmāyana of Valmiki. After the defeat of Rāvana, Hanuman sought the permission of Sita to destroy the female servants of Rāvana who had guarded and taunted her during her imprisonment. Sita, however, saw them as victims like herself and offered the superior ideal of forgiveness and reconciliation. "Who would be angry," asks Sita, "with women who are dependent on a monarch who is their superior and who acts on other's advice as mere servants or slaves? I wish in compassion to protect the slaves of Rāvana .... A superior being does not render evil for evil, this is a maxim one should observe; the ornament of virtuous persons is their conduct." Forgiveness and compassion are attributes of the divine in Hinduism. The one quality of God most emphasized by Tulasidasa, for example, in his *Ramacaritamanas* is compassion. He uses the term 'abode of mercy' (*krpanidhana*) on at least five hundred occasions to describe Rama, and Rama, in the *Sundarakanda*, makes one of the most remarkable statements in the entire text – I would not abandon even the murderer of ten million brahmins if he sought refuge in me.

If one keeps in mind that brahminicide was one of the gravest of crimes, the significance of Rama's statement becomes obvious.

It is clear that the traditions of Hinduism, in both their distinctive as well as shared insights, provide resources that justify and inspire the work of reconciliation. The challenge for us today is to highlight these core teachings of Hinduism and, more importantly to simultaneously employ these teachings as the basis of a rigorous Hindu self-examination that identifies exploitative and oppressive structures. These are the structures that alienate and estrange beings from each other and from the natural world and that are fundamentally unjust. It is easy to succumb to the temptation to speak in enticing and platitudinous ways about the need and value for reconciliation while ignoring the challenges of addressing and overcoming those structures that sanction and enable some human beings to inflict suffering on others. Discourse about reconciliation must not become like a silken robe that conceals a diseased body. Reconciliation will always remain an intangible ideal as long as we are unwilling, from insincerity or fear, to unearth and confront the underlying causes of human conflict and divisiveness. The voices of those within and outside our tradition who feel despised, rejected and stripped of dignity must be heard, even in silence and absence.

Hinduism, like other world religions that developed in patriarchal cultures, reflects assumptions about male gender supremacy that have been oppressive to Hindu women. Gender reconciliation, therefore, is one of the important tasks for Hindus to undertake. The work of gender reconciliation, however, cannot be meaningfully pursued by simply pointing to Hindu teachings about the spiritual equality of men and women or to the presence of feminine images of God. We must ask why a disproportionate percentage of the illiterate in India are women. We must grapple with the reality that women are oppressed when they are forced because of social values to abort fetuses merely because the fetus is female. We must question the relationship between female abortion and the custom of dowry, which depletes the economic resources of families into which girls are born and which makes them feel guilty for being women. The practice of dowry demeans women by signifying that the value of a woman is so low that she becomes acceptable to another only when her family is able to satisfy his greed for the latest gadgets of materialistic fancy.[3] Reconciliation between men and women requires overcoming the gender-oppressive structures of Hindu society.

Similarly, the inequities of the caste system cannot be addressed only by offering concessions to those who have been disadvantaged and who have not traditionally enjoyed the privileges accorded to male members of the upper castes. While supporting such measures, religion must also get to the heart of the matter by questioning the very legitimacy of a hierarchical social system that assigns different privileges and value to human beings on the basis of exclusive notions of purity and impurity. The role of religious doctrine and ritual in providing legitimacy for the system of caste must be examined. Reconciliation from religious standpoint cannot be content with the mere amelioration of questionable system in the interest of social harmony. A self-critical sincerity is needed to acknowledge the ways in which many, especially those from the so called untouchable castes, experience the tradition as oppressive and as negating not be liberative must be admitted.

While an acknowledgment of the past and present indignities of the caste system by those who have enjoyed its benefits is a necessary step in the process of reconciliation, there must be the will for the reform and reconstruction of Hindu society on the basis of those central insights and values of Hinduism that promote the freedom, dignity and equal worth of human beings. The major traditions of Hinduism, as noted before, are unanimous in their view that the divine exists equally and identically in all beings. While the social implications of this truth are not always consistently and clearly drawn out in the classical texts, all of them articulate it in one way or the other. When the implications for human relationships are enunciated, they are done in terms of a vision of equality and this equality must be the norm by which we critique social structures and gender relationships. The doctrine of divine equality and the worth of all human beings must inspire and impel us to identify and heal the exploitative and oppressive structures of Hindu society. Such work is vital and inseparable to the quest for reconciliation.

Endnotes

[1] Mark Juergensmeyer, *Terror in the Mind of God* (Berkeley: University of California 2001), 174.

[2] Juergensmeyer, *Terror in the Mind of God*, 171-178.

[3] Anantanand Rambachan, "A Hindu Perspective," in *What Men Owe to Women*, edited by John C. Raines and Daniel C. Maquire (Albany: State University of New York, 2000), 17-40.

Anekānt: The Jaina Path of Peace and Reconciliation

S. L. Gandhi

Diversity of Beliefs and Conflicts

Human life is marked by contrary beliefs, ideas, thoughts and philosophies, and the wonder is that despite contradictions and the apparently heterogeneous character of social life, civilization has continued to march ahead and has achieved spectacular successes in all areas. However, the calmness of the stream of social life that seems to have flowed through zigzag paths and barren lands for thousands of years has been disturbed by wars, genocides, murders and bloody conflicts that raged through century after century, taking a heavy toll of innocent lives.

With the passage of time intolerance based on caste, color, geographical boundaries, race, different political systems, divergent approaches to problems and loyalties increased to such an extent that each opposing group of human beings sought the annihilation of the groups not agreeing with them. Wars were resorted to for settling disputes arising from different viewpoints. Some wars were also fought for the expansion of territories, wealth and women.

Most wars were caused by the dogmatic attitude of an individual or a social, political or religious group. They held that what they believed alone was the absolute or the whole truth and all other beliefs were heretical and false. A root cause of violent conflicts is the adherence of an individual or a group to a set of beliefs considering them to be absolutely true and regarding the opposite views as nothing but false.

Adolf Hitler's belief in racial superiority led him to kill Jews on a large scale and push mankind into the bloodiest Second World War. Racial segregation in South Africa for years was the result of inbuilt feelings of hatred against the blacks. Most conflicts and wars in the world are being fought either in the name of protecting a particular religious belief or on account of the belief in ethnic and racial superiority. The rising trends of intolerance in all parts of the world that stem from opposing beliefs pose a real threat to human survival. The human race now possesses weapons of mass destruction, which makes it vulnerable to complete destruction.

Lord Mahāvīra, the 24th Tīrthaṅkara of the Jain religious tradition, exhorted his disciples to avoid an absolutist attitude in their exposition of the object. He advised monks and nuns to have recourse to *vibhajyavad* or the doctrine of alternatives while expounding the nature of a thing. He was opposed to the dogmatic assertion of individual beliefs. On being asked by one of his disciples which was the better of the two states (i) the state of slumber and (ii) the state of awakening, Mahāvīra said:

> For some souls the slumber is commendable but for others awakening is wholesome.
> Why is it so O Lord!?
> The slumber is wholesome for those who are engaged in sinful activities while for the virtuous awakening is commendable.

Mahāvīra did not approve of the exclusive assertion of the wholeness of slumber or awakening. He avoided exclusiveness in answering all questions. The *Anekānt* approach to dealing with others adopted by Lord Mahāvīra is relevant even today.

It is the only way to promote religious harmony, reconciliation and unity in diversity. In the midst of the chaotic situation prevailing in all parts of the world what encourages us most is the emergence of a new trend on the international horizon, giving rise to initiatives that encourage dialogue, talks and mediation for the resolution of conflicts. The world is now familiar with such terms as relativity, reconciliation and co-existence. The philosophy inherent in the above words that radiates the hope of human survival is the Jain philosophy of *anekānt* and *syadvad*. As a matter of fact '*anekānt*' is an eye. A human eye can only see the physical appearance of an individual or an object but it can neither see nor perceive what he is thinking and why he is thinking so. Unless one is able to realize this subtle aspect, one cannot do justice to the viewpoint and thinking on others. One cannot understand even the modes of changes taking place in an object. *Syadvad* or conditional dialectics is a mode of expressing the philosophy of *anekānt* (non-absolutist viewpoint).

The *anekānt* eye is the best way to perceive the physical as well as the subtle modes or changes occurring in the world of objects. With its help we can develop flexibility and a non-dogmatic attitude towards the viewpoints of others, resolve disputes and vanquish the sparks of war. It is only through the non-absolutist approach (*Anekānt*) that harmonious social climate can be created.

The Jaina Philosophy of *Anekānt*

One of the most important achievements of the philosophical period consisted in a synthetic view of the divergent schools of philosophy and the development and extensive employment of the *anekānt* dialectic for such synthesis.

The two important questions of the philosophical debate since the times of the Upanishads were: Is it possible to know the absolute truth, the truth in its completeness? Is it possible to give it a verbal expression and exposition?

Different philosophies have offered different solutions to those perennial issues of philosophy. The Jaina thinkers have also presented their solutions. They answered the first question through their epistemological critique, while they tried to answer the second question through their doctrine of *anekānt*. The Jains believe that it is the omniscient Jaina alone who is capable of knowing the truth in its entirety. His knowledge is absolutely perfect, free from all layers of illusion. That explains why such knowledge has no obstruction or hindrance. The non-omniscient are incapable of knowing the truth in its fullness, because their knowledge is imperfect, being a mixture of gnosis and nescience. With the acknowledgement of the gnosis of the non-omniscient, we simultaneously acknowledge his nescience also. In the veiled state of consciousness we find truth and untruth entwined in one. It is only the omniscient whom we can designate as having perfect knowledge. The term 'kevalin' (omniscient) can also be explained as one who is possessed of knowledge alone and nothing else. His is pure knowledge, absolutely free from nescience. From the viewpoint of knowledge all persons other than the omniscient are possessed of gnosis as well as nescience. This acceptance of the co-existence of gnosis and nescience implies that the truth in its completeness can be known only by omniscient and not by any other person even though he may be an ascetic of great repute.

The real has two facets – the substance and the mode. The possessor of scriptural knowledge knows all the substances, material as well as immaterial, but it is impossible for him to know all their modes. The omniscient knows all the substances with all their modes, and therefore it is said that he knows the complete truth. The possessor of scriptural knowledge knows the substances through the scriptures. The omniscient knows them directly and so he knows the whole truth. In the words of *Āchārya* Samantabhadra, both *syadyad* and omniscience are revealers of all objects. The difference between them if any, consists in the latter being a direct cognition and the former being an indirect cognition. All other objects, which are not cognized by either of them are unreal.

In Jaina ontology two kinds of substances are accepted (1) sentient, and (2) non-sentient. Each substance is divided into infinitely infinite units, and each unit into infinitely infinite modes. All these substances with all their integral units together with their modes in their totality constitute the complete truth. The monist can postulate the Absolute Truth (independent of anything else), but the dualist cannot agree with him. This is the reason why the Jaina philosopher, as an upholder of dualism, explains truth on the basis of the doctrine of non-absolutism. Truth has infinite modes and the capacity of language is limited. A word can express a single mode at a single moment, and as such the speaker can, in his whole life, give expression to only a limited number of modes. It, therefore, follows that the complete truth can never be explained through words; it is only part of a truth that can be the subject matter of linguistic expression.

Syadvad: the Methodology of Reconciling the Opposites

The method of viewing or explaining a thing from different standpoints is *syadvad*. The doctrine that an object can be described from different points of view and that a person expresses it in different points of view and that a person expresses it in different ways is characteristically expressed in *syadvad* – the doctrine of conditional dialectics. In other words, we can say that *syadvad* is the language by means of which the Jaina doctrine *anekānt* is explained.

Syadvad is composed of two words viz. '*syat*' and '*vad*.' '*Syat*' is a Sanskrit word that means 'from a particular standpoint'. It stands for multiplicity. The word '*vad*' means a doctrine. Thus the combination of the two words '*syadvad*' means doctrine that expounds the nature of a thing from different standpoints. The nature of an object in this universe is so complex that making an assertive statement may either be incomplete or untrue. The Jains therefore emphasize utmost care in the exposition of the nature of an object and advise adherents of truth to avoid making exclusive statements. In order to determine the character of thing the Jains recommend sevenfold predication, which is as follows:

i.   The pot certainly (*eva*) exists from a certain point of view

ii. The pot certainly does not exist from a certain point of view

iii. The pot certainly exists from one point of view but it certainly does not from another point of view.

iv. The pot is certainly indescribable from a certain point of view

v.   The pot certainly exists from one point of view but it is certainly indescribable from another point of view.

vi. The pot certainly does not exist from one point of view and it is certainly indescribable from another point of view,

vii. The pot certainly exists from a certain point of view but it certainly does not exist and is certainly indescribable from another point of view.

The above proposition is philosophical in nature, but the truth is that all our statements in relation to our dealings in this world are made from one or the other standpoint. The seven-fold predication or judgment that the Jains call *saptabhangi* is formulated on the basis of the two modes, i.e. affirmation and negation. Technically *saptabhangi* can be defined as a statement in seven different ways. According to Jainas all religious or philosophical systems contain a grain of truth. The fragmentation of humanity into innumerable sects and schisms is the result of the dogmatic assertion made by adherents of a particular faith that what their religious tradition says alone is true and all else is heretical. Any proposition of this sort based on extreme sense of insistence will give rise to intolerance and conflicts. The Jains claim that their *anekānt* approach has in it the potential for ushering in an era of peace and harmony.

The method of honestly accepting and reconciling the apparently contradictory attributes in in a thing from different standpoints is called *syadvad*. In a man, we accept seemingly contradictory attributes – that is, we call him father and son, uncle and nephew, son-in-law and father-in-law, etc., because they are reconcilable from different standpoints of different relations that he holds with different persons. Similarly, one accepts apparently opposite attributes, viz., permanence and impermanence, etc., in a thing, say a pot, because one reconciles them with one another from different standpoints. The contradiction of opposite attributes in a thing is really apparent and can be removed by viewing the thing from different standpoints. Different standpoints yield contradictory attributes which are synthesized in a coherent whole by *syadvad*. Thus *syadvad* is a method of synthesis.

One and the same person is father with respect to his son and son with respect to his father, uncle with respect to his nephew and nephew with respect to his uncle, father-in-law with respect to his son-in-law and son-in-law with respect to his father-in-law, and so on and so forth. Accordingly, we accept all those opposite attributes – father and son, uncle and nephew, etc. – in one and the same individual from different standpoints of relations he has with different persons. In the same way, why should we not accept in one and the same thing the opposite attributes, if on reflection we find them reconcilable from different standpoints?

What is a pot? It is well known that earthen vessels like a pot, a bowl, etc. are produced from the same clay. After having broken a pot, a bowl is produced from the same clay; now, will anybody call the bowl a pot? No. Why? Is clay not the same? Yes, clay is the same but the form or mode has changed. As the form has changed, clay cannot be called a 'pot'. Well, then it is proved that a pot is particular form or mode of clay. But one should remember that the mode or form is not absolutely different from clay. Clay itself is called a 'pot', 'bowl', etc., when it assumes different forms or modes. So how can we consider clay and pot to be totally different? From this viewpoint it is proved that both the form-of-a-pot and clay constitute the nature of the thing called 'pot'. Now let us see which of the two natures is permanent and which is impermanent. We observe that the form-of-a-pot is impermanent. So one nature of the pot, viz., the form-of-a-pot is established as impermanent. And how is the other nature, viz., clay? It is not impermanent. It is so because the forms or modes that clay assumes go on changing but clay as such remains the same. This is established by experience. Thus, we see that a pot has both these natures – one permanent, and the other impermanent. From this we can naturally maintain that from the standpoint of its permanent nature, a pot is impermanent and from the standpoint of its permanent nature it is permanent. In this way to see and ascertain both the permanent and impermanent natures in one and the same thing from two different standpoints is a case of *anekānt* (synthetic or synoptic or many-sided) viewing.

Anekānt: A Path of Reconciliation and Co-existence

I bow before the principle of *anekānt*, which forbids quarrelling on account of divergently opposed views and lays emphasis on discovering common values in all systems of thought. I bow before it because without inculcating an attitude of *anekānt* in the masses there can be no interaction, no dialogue and the world will come to a grinding halt. Diversity is inbuilt and innate. It cannot be abolished. This reality has to be accepted. Nothing can be said to be absolutely true and nothing is wholly untrue. *Anekānt* synthesizes the opposite modes of thought. Without *anekānt* truth will remain elusive and will never be realized. Leave apart the question of knowing the whole truth, even the relationship between family and society can no longer be maintained. *Anekānt* is our real Guru who shows us the path to universal peace.

Human has been inquisitive to know the reality from time immemorial. 'What is reality?' This question has been asked thousands of time in human history. Whosoever became knowledgeable asked the above question. Once Gandhar Gautam asked Lord Mahāvīra *'kim kattam'* – what is reality? Lord Mahāvīra replied, *'upnnei'* – that one is born is a reality. But Gautam was not satisfied. If being born is a reality, the world would be over-populated. So he asked the Lord again. Lord Mahāvīra replied, "*vigmei va*" – to perish or to be destroyed is reality. Gautam's doubt remained unresolved. If destruction alone is a reality, nothing will be left behind. He repeated the question. Lord Mahāvīra replied, "dhuvei va" – to remain eternal or steadfast is a reality.

Now Gautam's inquisitiveness was satiated. He was fully satisfied with the answer provided by the Lord. The truth is threefold. It consists in birth, death and eternity. The reality has three ingredients: Creation, total destruction and survival. Both eternal and perishable are reality. Just as we see a pair of man and woman, we find the same in nature, i.e. eternal and non-eternal. We find the opposite modes everywhere. Mere oneness is unthinkable. If there is knowledge, there is ignorance. If there is winter, there is spring. If there is day, there is night. Life goes on the basis of opposite modes. We need the opposite as well as homogenous. Our entire system is regulated by contrary modes. We need both opponents as well as supporters.

The Jain philosophy of *anekānt* alone can extricate the world from the mire of violence and hatred. We should always accept the fact that everything we see around us has some or the other element of truth. We cannot dismiss anything as wholly untrue. This approach will minimize violence and hatred to a great extent. It is because of the philosophy of *anekānt* that the Jain *Shravaks* refrain from criticizing and censuring others' viewpoints.

The well-known parable of six blind persons seeking to know what elephant looks like illustrates it further. They were born blind and had no idea what a huge animal like an elephant looks like. They decided to know the truth by touching the elephant. One blind person touched the trunk of the elephant said, "Oh! It is like a serpent." The second blind person touched the body of the elephant and said, "Oh! It is like a wall." The third blind person touched the tail and said, "Oh! It is like a snake." Others found it like a pillar, a winnowing etc. All were right and all were wrong. Everyone was partially true. The *anekānt* approach is the basis of our survival since it supports coexistence and reconciliation. The world will be a better place to live by if we can realize the truth that the diversity of beliefs in a human society is a natural phenomenon. Any attempt by a fanatic to wipe out the groups who hold different views and enforce the rule of just one faith will be met with still resistance and will unleash violent conflicts in all parts of this planet. We must accept diversity as a natural trait of humanity and learn to live in it. Co-existence is possible only if dogmatic insistence on a viewpoint is given up. The Jain philosophy of *anekānt* has in it a potential for survival into the third millennium.

'For Poverty is a Great Luminosity from within…' The Notion of Poverty in Buddhism and Christianity and its Significance for an Inter-religious Dialogue on Poverty

Annette Meuthrath

"For poverty is a great luminosity from within."[1] This sentence of Rainer Maria Rilke, the famous Austrian poet, has often been harshly criticized. The reasons for this criticism seem to be obliviously given. Is not it scorn seeing emaciated bodies or shrunken bellies? Poverty all too often as the face of shortage or lack, of sorrow and distress and also of hate. "Why does rioting take place always in the old city of Hyderabad, where most of the poor live, and not in Banjara Hills, the habitat of the rich?" It was exactly this question in Andreas' call for the papers to the conference "Drop by Drop: Building a Community': A Conference on Interfaith Collaboration" that motivated me to reflect on poverty and its challenge to interfaith dialogue and praxis. And in defence to Rilke who is my favourite poet, I would like to distinguish between two kinds of poverty, optional or self-chosen poverty and poverty by circumstances that are forced or imposed. While the latter is a consequence of injustice, oppression and exploitation and goes along with the destruction and death, the first is a possible way to freedom and happiness that may lead to spiritual richness and liberation. I will demonstrate these two kinds of poverty with regard to Buddhism and Christianity that both make this distinction.

The notion of poverty in Buddhism and Christianity is a wide filed. Therefore I have to concentrate on a few aspects. In the following contribution I will elaborate on what is said about two kinds of poverty in Christina revelation, namely the New Testament, according to the interpretation of Aloysius Pieris, and in some parts of the Buddhist Pāli canon interpreted by David L. Loy and P.D. Premasiri. Moreover, I would like to reflect on the meaning of these authoritative passages for our lives within and as religious communities and for an interfaith praxis.

What is poverty?

For economists, "lack of income remains the basic criterion of ill-being."[2] In accordance with this view some definitions of poverty still referred to it solely with regard to material goods as:

"The state of having little or no money and few or no material possessions."[3]

Other definitions include non-material aspects. Here poverty means:

"to lack or be denied adequate resources to participate meaningfully in society."[4]

More adequate definitions with regard to a holistic understanding of human beings and poverty include factors such as education and social status. Wikipedia gives an overview about different starting points or approaches in defining what poverty is:

Poverty is the state of being without many or most of the necessities for daily living (e.g., food, clothing, shelter, education and health care), relative to some other reference group. Those who live in conditions of poverty lack a wide range of economic and other resources and may be described as 'poor' or 'impoverished.' Same see the term as subjective and comparative, others see it as moral and evaluative, while others consider that it is scientifically established.

There are varying degrees or levels of poverty. The Copenhagen Declaration absolute poverty as "a condition characterized by severe deprivation of basic needs, including food, safe drinking water, sanitation facilities, education and information." The World Bank defines extreme poverty as living on less than US$ (PPP) 1 per day, and poverty as less than $3 a day.

As of 2001, this meant that 21% of the world population (or about 1.1 billion people) was living in extreme poverty, and more than 50% were living in poverty. By comparison, in 1981, 1.5 billion people were living in extreme poverty (40%of world population); in 1987, 1.227 billion people (30%); and in 1993, 1.314 billion people (29%).

It is estimated that about 8 million people die each year because they are too poor to survive.[5]

What is missing in all these definitions is that kind of poverty that may go along with even extreme wealth and could be named by terms like "moral poverty" or "spiritual poverty". Morality or spirituality are no economic categories. They are within the field of philosophies or religions and their theologies. Religions have their own approach to and sense of what poverty is including (besides spiritual and moral aspects) the liberating approach. This holds true for Buddhism as well as for Christianity.

The Buddhist View on Poverty

The goal of the Buddhist path is to end *dukkha* ('suffering', 'ill-being'). Ill-being arises from *tanha* ('thirst', 'craving'). To reduce ill-being therefore means to reduce craving. Craving is closely attachment (*upādāna*). With regard to material goods non-attachment means: "to possess and use material things but not to be possessed or used of them."[6] This applies for lay persons (*upāsaka*) as well as for those people who have chosen a life in homelessness (*pabbajjā*), for example as monk (*bhikkhu*) or nun (*bhikkhunī*).

P.D. Premasini gives an appropriate summary of the Buddhist understanding of poverty (*dāliddiya*):

> According to Buddhism poverty involves suffering. As a philosophy of living which advocates the elimination of suffering, Buddhism does not value poverty. Buddhism values detachment towards material goods in commending having less wants as a virtue. Poverty, as ordinarily understood, consists in the non-possession of the basic material requirements for leading a decent

life free from hunger, malnutrition and disease. Buddhism recognizes the importance of the fulfillment of the minimum material needs for a decent living, even in the case of the aspirants of its higher spiritual goal. Poverty, from this point of view does not involve the absence of an abundance of goods that stimulates the insatiable of man [sic!]^{7}.^{8}

From this summary it becomes clear that it is equally right to say that the Buddha, according to the Pāli Canon, did on the one hand "not praise poverty at any stage"[9] and on the other hand "attached very little value to all the material riches that ordinary folk usually crave for."[10] This has to do with the difference between the moral rules (*sikkhāpada*) laypersons should follow and the additional rules for ordained persons (monks and nuns), i.e., for those who have chosen the homelessness as *pabbajati* ('religious wanderer').[11] *Bhikkhus* ('almsmen', 'monks') and *Bhikkhunis* ('almswomen', 'nuns') are supposed to live a material poor life, but this does not hold for laypersons.

While it applies for all human beings that those "who are intent on attaining the supreme goal of Buddhism were expected to break of all physical connections and psychological attachment to such riches [ordinary people crave for]"[12] It is also said that "poverty is an ordeal for a person living a household life."[13] Some Pāli texts even stress that householders should increase their fortune and try to keep it on condition that it is spent properly and that it is earned by right means "so that their lives are useful."[14] Wrong means would be, for example, the work as a butcher, pub owner or arms dealer, i.e., all such work that are not in harmony with Buddhist ethics (*sila*) that teaches, for example, the abstinence from taking lives (*pānātipātāveramanī*) and the abundance from any indolence arising from the use of intoxicants (*surāmerayamājjappamādathānā veramānī*). A.B. Ananda Maitreya writes: "There are some people who are satisfied with a little income and live simple life. But if a person expects to do great service, to help the people who are in need of this help, he [sic!] should try to earn wealth by right means."[15]

According to the Pāli Canon poverty as such is not a "recommendable soteriological basic condition."[16] This becomes clear by two facts:

a) Lay persons and ordained persons like monks and nuns are living
    in a complementary way in so far as the laypersons or householders
    need material goods to support the *Bhikkhus* and *Bhikkhunis*.
    Through the act of giving laypersons are earning merits. Giving
    (*dāna*) is the first of the meritorious actions (*punnakririyavatthu*).[17]

b) Poverty may lead to moral degeneration. Hence, it can have non-
    meritorious (*akusala*) effects on a person in leading to spiritual or
    moral poverty.

It is the laypersons for whom material poverty may have bad consequence
with regard to their spirituality or morality. Accordingly we find in
Buddhist teachings a double connotation of poverty, which can be
expressed by the terms "material poverty" and "spiritual poverty".

Premasiri states: "When any section of human beings are deprived
of the basic material needs due to an unjust economic order, there is
a natural tendency towards the moral degeneration of a society".[18] For
Premasiri this is "clearly illustrated" in the *Cakkavattisihananda Sutta* and
the *Kutadanta Sutta*. Criminal behavior is, according to the *Kutadanta
Sutta*, a consequence of oppression, exploitation, and marginalization
that is often accompanied by material poverty.

From what has been said so far it is clear that we have to make
another distinction with regard to material poverty. There is a voluntary
material poverty as well as a non-voluntary poverty. The latter one can
lead to that other kind of poverty that Premasiri calls the spiritual one.

Spiritual Richness and Optional Material Poverty

While compulsory poverty can lead to moral or spiritual poverty, self-
chosen poverty may lead to spiritual richness and to liberation. Buddhism
"sees a clause casual connection between poverty in the material sphere
of human living and man's [*sic*] ability to attain or preserve spiritual
riches."[19] Premasiri writes, "the seeker after the supreme goal of *Nibbāna*
in Buddhism is one who breaks of all ties with material riches and takes
up voluntarily a life of few wants (*appichata*)."[20] Those people who decide
to live with regard to material goods are considered by Buddhism as

belonging "to the community of the noble ones (*ariyapuggala*)." The minimum needs however should be met also for the voluntary poor. That means:

> Food sufficient to prevent the affliction of hunger and adequate to maintain the health of the body, clothing sufficient to appear socially decent and conducive to the protection of the body from any harm from the natural environment; housing which gives sufficient safety and security conducive to one's serious engagement in the culture of the mind; and medicine and health care which cures and prevents disease.[21]

Although the basic material needs to live a dignified life should be covered for all human beings, including those who have chosen to go the noble path as *Bhikkhu* or *Bhikkhuni*, and although Buddhism does not teach poverty as a value as such, attachment, referred to here as the wish to possess material goods is a cause of suffering (*dukkha*) and a hindrance on the way to deliverance from the entanglement in the circle of life and death (*samsāra*). To gain deliberation from suffering one has to recognize the four noble truths: life is *dukkha*, the cause of *dukkha* is craving (*tanha*, 'thirst'), there is an end to *dukkha* which is *nibāna* (Sanskrit: *nirvāna*), and there is a way to end *dukkha*, i.e. the Eightfold Path (*magga*). This path leads to richness or wealth that is beyond all material goods and that has final deliverance as its consequence. Optional material poverty makes it easier to follow this path.

Consequences of the Buddhist View of Poverty for the Daily life

Premasiri's words "While Buddhism recognizes the greater value of man's [*sic*] spiritual riches than material riches applied to poverty means that even worse than material poverty would be spiritual poverty."[22] According to this understanding it is not sufficient "when measuring poverty to measure merely the material conditions of living. For a more complete measurement of poverty it is necessary to measure the moral quality of people's lives."[23] And since Premasiri brings together non-voluntary poverty with a possible degeneration of moral behavior or attitude, the conclusion suggests itself that a society that wants to reduce unmoral behavior in its members has to see to it that the basic material needs of all are covered. Nevertheless Premasiri qualifies what has been said to a certain extent in so far as he also states that rich societies must not be happier as poorer ones:

> From the Buddhist point of view the elimination of poverty needs to be demonstrated by the establishment of a society free of crime, social tensions, wars and conflicts where people can live in harmony, friendship and peace. The quality of life of a community that possesses not even a fraction of the goods possessed by a so-called affluent community may be far superior to that of the latter. For the abundance of material goods does not necessarily correspond to an abundance of human happiness.[24]

Not only can great material poverty lead to the moral degeneration of a society but also great richness can increase attachment and selfishness.

Nevertheless, as a consequence of what has been said about the effects of material poverty on a society, Buddhists would have to work for a society where at least the basic material needs of all people would be satisfied. Moral integrity seems to be closely connected with a materially safe life. The guarantee of a dignified life in which the basic material needs are covered is an important condition for a moral and spiritually rich life. This is true not only with regard to laypersons or householders but also with regard to nuns and monks. Buddhism never favored an extremely ascetic way. It was the Middle Way that the Buddha taught. Even though the material possessions of nuns and monks were reduced to minimum, this minimum provided sufficient food, clothes and shelter.

The Christian Notion of Poverty

As reported above, Buddhism distinguishes between two kinds of poverty, material and spiritual, and between two kinds of lived poverty: self-chosen or imposed. Whereas optional poverty can aid spiritual or moral richness, imposed poverty may have moral or spiritual poverty as its effect. Similar distinctions between different kinds of poverty can be found in Christianity, although the connection between involuntary material poverty and moral or spiritual poverty is not apparent.

The Significance of Poverty and the Poor in the Gospels

It is the poor to whom Jesus addresses His good news (Lk. 7:22. Mt. 11:5). They are blessed whereas the rich are sorry or unhappy (Lk. 6:20,

24; Mt. 5:3). It is the poor who are our neighbors (Lk. 10:30-35) whom we should love. And it is they with whom Jesus identifies Himself (Mt. 25:351). The rich are ones who, in following Jesus, should spend all their riches for the poor and for whom it is more difficult to enter the Reign of God than for a camel to pass through the eye of a needle (Mt. 19:20-24, see also Mk. 10:21. Lk. 18:22) Therefore, according to Aloysius Pieris, "my resources or 'riches' (time, money, competence, influence) acquire their salvific value only when they are expended for my poor neighbor. Unless shared with the victims of exploitation, such resources become Mammon, a source of my enmity with God."[25] Because it is impossible to serve God and Mammon[26] (Mt. 6:24, Lk. 16:13), only if Mammon is used in a reasonable way and shared with the poor will it receive what is of real value (Lk. 16:11).

From the quotations above it is clear that there are also two categories of the poor in the Christian understanding: The poor by circumstances who are the "true vicars of Christ" (Mt. 25:31-46. Mk. 9:36f., 41) and in whom "one meets and serves Christ" and the poor by option who are the "true disciples of Jesus" (Mk 4:21, 28, Lk. 5: 28 etc.) the 'God-lovers' who "share their possessions with the dispossessed and accumulate no surplus."[27] It is not the material indigence as such that is seen as a salutary quality but the attitude of the poor, who seek their salvation and their rescue only in God. It is the bigger nearness of the poor to God that is salutary whereas the rich always tend to trust in themselves and believe in their property and own power.[28] Both categories of the poor are the "inheritors and the carriers of the Reign of God." But, as Aloysius Pieris states, "each group has its own specific mission in God's Reign."[29]

The Mission of the Poor in God's Reign
Aloysius Pieris in his book "God's Reign for God's Poor" gives six features of the poor by circumstances:[30]

a) They are "the victims of nations who act as eschatological judge of nations" (Mt. 25:36ff).

b) "Their poverty is forced upon them because of a wrong 'house-management' (*oiko-nomia*) of the world of Mammon-worshippers."

c) They are "far from being holy: they are sinners as much as the rich."

d) "Their victimhood is, therefore, the sole basis of their *election*" as "God's covenant partners."

e) "Their *holiness* consists in responding to their calling to be God's covenant partners, to be a liberative force in the world. Their election is *for* others, not above others."

f) "To bring them to this awareness they may need the help of the second category of the poor."

While the mission of the involuntary poor is to be a liberative force[31] in the world, the mission of the renouncers of Mammon, the poor by option, is solidarity with the socially poor. The mission of both groups is God's Reign.

But what is meant by "Reign of God"? According to Pieris it is "love of God" "which is simultaneously a radical option for the poor"[32] (love of neighbor):[33]

> The reign of God is, incipiently, just that kind of earth (a home-temple-garden) which, at the end-time will leap into another dimension of existence that has been promised to us a 'new heaven and a new earth, home of righteousness' (2 Pe. 3:13). It is what God and the poor dream about together in Jesus.[34]

The mission of the poor as well as the mission of the true disciples of Jesus therefore means an active involvement in a transformative process that changes our earth into a place of love, peace and beauty as well as a place of deep spirituality:

The love of God and the love of neighbor – as spelt by Jesus in terms of God's Reign and God's Poor – involves us in His mission of transforming the Earth into what the Creator meant it to be: - a *home with one table*, where the gifts of creation are enjoyed together by all its inhabitants, so that some do not gorge while others starve (I Cor. 11:21); *a temple of worship or a house of prayer*, where Mammon is given no chance to turn it into a 'Den of Robbers' (Lk. 19:46) or an 'Open Market' (Jn. 16); a garden of Delight, where Creation remains an 'enjoyable icon' of the Creator's beauty, which is the desired fruit of wisdom, rather than a 'monstrous idol' of technocracy which is the forbidden fruit of power generating knowledge (Gen. 3:1).[35]

The justice that goes along with the Reign of God cannot be understood solely as an individualistic responsibility but must be recognized as a social and global one.[36]

Poverty According to Buddhism and Christianity: Differences and Similarities

In Buddhism as well as in Christianity we find statements on the two ways in which poverty is lived: as non-voluntary, imposed or poverty by circumstances and as voluntary or self-chosen. In both religions optional poverty is a consequence of following the respective religious path in an eminently consequent way either to reach *Nirvāna, Nibbāna* (Buddhism) as a state where all suffering or ill-being has ended[37] or as active commitment to the realization of God's Reign (Christianity).

Moreover, in both traditions wealth is accepted under specific premises. Buddhism affirms wealth for laypersons if it is firstly gained by adequate means and, secondly, if there is a sharing of wealth in form of *dāna* ('giving'), alms etc. In Christianity riches are accepted if these are shared with God's poor. The true followers or disciples of Jesus are however those who give up all their riches for the poor by circumstance.

If there is already a difference in which wealth is seen in Buddhism and Christianity with regard to laypersons (Jesus lastly calls all who really want to follow him to give up all their wealth), there is a clear distinction in the cognition of the non-voluntary poor. Whereas Buddhism stresses on the point that they are in danger in danger of spiritual and moral poverty, the New Testaments sees them primarily as covenant partners of God who have a liberating mission for all people.

Practical Social Consequences from the Respective Understanding of Poverty

According to David A. Loy, "Buddhism, like Christianity, lacks an intrinsic social theory." Neither Buddha nor Jesus ever spoke "specially about economics in the sense that we understand it now."[38] Nevertheless, starting points for social theories can be found in both religions:

For Buddhism, Loy consults the *Cakkavattisihanada Sutta* as also Premasiri does. Therein Buddha tells the story of a king who, after a time, started "to rule according to his own ideas and did not" any longer "give property to the needy." As a result poverty, stealing and killing was widespread. "The long-term result was degradation of life and social collapse."[39] "The story according to Loy shows than "social breakdown cannot be separated from broader questions about the benevolence of the social order. The solution to poverty-induced crime is not more severe punishment but helping people provide for their basic needs."[40]

But Loy also points out what is not mentioned in the *Cakkayattisihananda Sutta*. Nowhere is anything mentioned that could be formed under the term 'social justice.' On the other hand, the difference between Buddhism and the Abrahamic religions, i.e. Judaism. Christianity and Islam, in understanding and addressing social problems, become clear. Whereas in Christianity there is an emphasis on social justice, this idea is "not important in traditional Buddhism." This does not mean, as the *Cakkavattisihanada Sutta* shows, that "Buddhism is insensitive to the problem of poverty, but emphasis on karma implies a different way" of addressing such problem.[41] As we have already seen above the Buddhist solution is individual *dāna* or giving or generosity. But there are also new tendencies in Buddhism that are addressing social problems on a more structural level in engaging in development and social movements and work. As one example the *sarvodaya* movement[42] in Sri Lanka may be mentioned.[43] The important lesson Buddhism has to teach, facing a growing "world consumerism" that falsely promises happiness and well-being, is according to Loy "the importance of self-limitation, which requires some degree of non-attachment."[44]

But also in Christianity the cognition of poverty as a structural and global problem that needs an adequate answer other than individual charity is not so old. In the Roman Catholic Church, starting with the Latin American Christianity there had been a shift of emphasis "from a definition of charity as almsgiving to an advocacy of social justice through the empowerment of disadvantaged classes. Its intellectual articulation is found in the theology of liberation and its most concrete application in base ecclesial communities."[45] Since then other theologies of liberation have emerged like the Dalit theology or the Minjung theology in Asia. Common to all these theologies is the "articulation of the belief that one's eternal salvation is inseparable from the struggle toward social justice"[46] demanding social and also political activities. The document of Medellon Colombia (1968) put the 'option for the poor' in its central statement. After Medellon the Roman Catholic Church however "withdraws from the more radical implications of the 'preferential option for the poor.'[47]

The change the awareness that not only charity is needed but structural transformation that would lead to social change and betterment in the situation of the poor started in Europe with the Catholic social movements in 19th century. With the Encyclical *'Rerum novarum'* (1891) of Pope Leo XIII also the Church hierarchy accepted that not personal charity but political structural reforms were necessary to answer the problem of the industrial working proletariat. With the social Encyclicals there started also the Catholic social teaching that tries to give an orientation the formation of a just social order. It was only in the middle of the 20th century that Christians slowly became aware of the contrast of poverty and riches in its worldwide dimension. This 'global view' in the Catholic Church was mainly due to Pope John XXIII and the Second Vatican Council (1962-1965) convened by him.[48]

As a conclusion we can state that in both religions, Buddhism and Christianity, there are starting points to understand poverty as a social and structural problem that needs an appropriate answer that has also political implications. This understanding, however, seems to be more developed, elaborated and strived for in Christianity than in Buddhism.

Inter-faith Dialogue with the Poor on Poverty

In both religions, Buddhism and Christianity, we find the ideal of a world where people can live together in peace and harmony, in home-temple-garden as Pieris writes. There is also the recognition in both religions that such a society is not possible when parts of a community are living in great material poverty. Societies, through globalization, through migration etc. become, especially in the West, more and more multi-religious. As a consequence, the different religious communities within a society have to work together in their struggle against non-voluntary poverty. Inter-religious or inter-faith dialogue is one precondition for this collaboration. Only if there is, besides all differences, is a common understanding of what poverty is, its effects, and how it can be overcome can different communities fruitfully co-operate or compete with one another in their struggle against poverty. One aim of inter-religious or inter-faith dialogue on poverty would be to find what common projects could be started to work not only on the level of charity against poverty but also for the structural changes of the respective societies. This dialogue will only be fruitful when it takes place not only on the level of the religious elite and if it takes place not on the poor but with the poor.[49] Pieris says with regard to the possible partners for such a dialogue:

> The religious elite exercise power in the name of religion. They are usually a propertied class. It is very unlikely that they all understand the language of God's Reign in whatever religious idiom it is expressed. Here in our county and elsewhere, we see the institutional leadership of all religions meeting on the same platform. One must first answer this question: when religious hierarchies engage themselves in inter-religious dialogue, what is their dominant concern, the liberation of the poor or the consolidation of their power?

> We must be wary of our association with this class of religious elite. They fear any liberational activity on behalf of the poor. They have access to seats of political power.[50]

According to Pieris, it is the charismatics as people who are 'conspicuous' and who take "their stand outside their religious institutions" who are the "indispensable partners in inter-religious dialogue with the poor."[51]

Conclusion

Coming back to Andreas' question that I have mentioned the beginning of my contribution: "Why does rioting take place always the old city of Hyderabad, where most of the poor live, and not in Banjara Hills, the habitat of the rich?" A Buddhist answer to this question could be: Because involuntary poverty caused by oppression, exploitation and marginalization may lead to spiritual and moral poverty that finds its expression in riots, in killing and crime. To stop such a moral decline of a group, society etc. would mean helping people in providing for their basic needs. A Christian answer to Andreas' question could go: riots etc. take place because the rich people have not exercised their responsibilities for God's poor. The rich people have to give their wealth for the poor to become God's true followers. The riots make clear what is going wrong in a world, society ruled by Mammon.

Even though the cognition of poverty and the significance of the involuntary poor are different in Buddhism and Christianity the practical outcome is similar. Only if a life of dignity, with all basic needs being covered is granted, can a group, society etc. live in peace and harmony. So both religions have to engage in the project of social justice. A precondition of social justice, peace and harmony is a lively dialogue between the different groups involved, i.e. the different religious communities and the different social, cultural ethnic etc. groups. Therefore inter-religious dialogue has to be a dialogue with the poor not on the poor. As an example for such a dialogue let me mention the work of Henry Martyn Institute: International Centre for Research, Interfaith Relations and Reconciliation that, besides academic work and research, is actively engaged in a lively dialogue with the poor of the different local religious communities on a very practical level.

To complete my paper allow me to once more quote Rilke's sentence: "for poverty is a great luminosity from within...." Non-attachment to the world of Mammon or optional material poverty is the kind of poverty that, above all, can lead to spiritual and moral richness. It often goes along with simplicity and modesty which are essential causes of the great shine from within. The poverty Rilke is writing on is not equated with "non-richness" as Rilke clearly states only a few lines above the quoted sentence.[52]

Endnotes

[1] Raner Maria Rilke, *The Books of Hours: The Book of Poverty and Death* (Madison: Hogarth Press, 1961).

[2] David R. Loy, "Shall We Pave the Planet or Learn to Wear Shoes? A Buddhist Perspective on Greed and Globalization," in *Turning Wheel Magazine*, 4, http://www. bpf.org/tsangha/loy-globo.html (February 9, 2006).

[3] "Poverty," http://wordnet.princeton.edu/perl/webwn (February 9, 2006).

[4] N. Krieger, "Poverty," www.hsph.harvard.edu/thegeocodingproject/webpage/ monograph/glossary.htm (February 9, 2006).

[5] "Poverty," http://en.wikipedia.org/wiki/Poverty (February 9, 2006).

[6] Loy, "Shall We Pave the Planet or Learn to Wear Shoes? A Buddhist Perspective on Greed and Globalization," in *Turning Wheel Magazine*, 4.

[7] The author employs 'sic' to identify exclusive terms.

[8] P.D. Premasiri, "Religious Values and the Measurement of Poverty: A Buddhist Perspective," in *Values, Norms and Poverty, A Consultation on WDR2000/01: Poverty and Development*, 3, http://www. Wor ldbank.org/prem/poverty/wdrpovertyjoburg/ (February 9, 2006).

[9] A.B. Ananda Maitreya, "The Blessings of Household Life 2/2," in *Buddhist Monthly Magazine* (Singapore), 1, http:// www.dw.com cantant/09.hmm (March 8, 2006)

[10] Premasiri, "Religious Values and the Measurement of Poverty: A Buddhist Perspective," in *Values, Norms and Poverty, A Consultation on WDR2000/01: Poverty and Development*, 2.

[11] Laypersons have to follow five rules (*sikkhāpada*) while those choosing a "homeless life" should follow ten basic rules, including the rule of not accepting gold or silver (10 rules).

[12] Premasiri, "Religious Values and the Measurement of Poverty: A Buddhist Perspective," in *Values, Norms and Poverty, A Consultation on WDR2000/01: Poverty and Development*, 2.

[13] Maitreya, "The Blessings of Household Life 2/2," in *Buddhist Monthly Magazine*, 1.

[14] Maitreya, "The Blessings of Household Life 2/2," in *Buddhist Monthly Magazine*, 1.

[15] Maitreya, "The Blessings of Household Life 2/2," in *Buddhist Monthly Magazine*, 2.

[16] Frank Usarski, "Armut/Reichtum, Buddhismus," in *Ethik der Weltreligionen*, edited by Michael Kicker, Udo Tworuschka (Darmstadt: Wissenschaftliche Buchgesellschaft, 2005), 32.

[17] See for example, Dīgha Nikāya 33.

[18] Premasiri, "Religious Values and the Measurement of Poverty: A Buddhist Perspective," in *Values, Norms and Poverty, A Consultation on WDR2000/01: Poverty and Development*, 4.

[19] Premasiri, "Religious Values and the Measurement of Poverty: A Buddhist Perspective," in *Values, Norms and Poverty, A Consultation on WDR2000/01: Poverty and Development*, 4.

[20] Premasiri, "Religious Values and the Measurement of Poverty: A Buddhist Perspective," in *Values, Norms and Poverty, A Consultation on WDR2000/01: Poverty and Development*, 2.

[21] Premasiri, "Religious Values and the Measurement of Poverty: A Buddhist Perspective," in *Values, Norms and Poverty, A Consultation on WDR2000/01: Poverty and Development*, 2.

[22] Premasiri, "Religious Values and the Measurement of Poverty: A Buddhist Perspective," in *Values, Norms and Poverty, A Consultation on WDR2000/01: Poverty and Development*, 4.

[23] Premasiri, "Religious Values and the Measurement of Poverty: A Buddhist Perspective," in *Values, Norms and Poverty, A Consultation on WDR2000/01: Poverty and Development*, 4.

[24] Premasiri, "Religious Values and the Measurement of Poverty: A Buddhist Perspective," in *Values, Norms and Poverty, A Consultation on WDR2000/01: Poverty and Development*, 5.

[25] Aloysius Pieris, *God's Reign for God's Poor: A Return to the Jesus Formula* (Gonawila: Tulana Research Centre, 1999), 43.

[26] Mammon means more than only money. In the Old Testament we find the term only in Sir. 31:8. In the New Testament the term has a clear negative connotation.

[27] Pieris, *God's Reign for God's Poor: A Return to the Jesus Formula*, 42.

[28] Erwin Fahlbusch, Jan Milic Lochman, John S. Mbiti, Jaroslav Pelikan, Lukas Vischer, eds., *Evangelisches Kirchenlexikon, Internationale Theologische Enzyklopadie*, vol. 1, 3rd rev. ed. (Göttingen: Vandenhoeck & Ruprecht, 1986), 275.

[29] Pieris, *God's Reign for God's Poor: A Return to the Jesus Formula*, 42.

[30] Pieris, *God's Reign for God's Poor: A Return to the Jesus Formula*, 59-60.

[31] The liberative force of the poor lies in the fact that on the one hand they help all others to realize their love of God as love of the poor and that on the other hand, through this help, they compel others to overcome their selfishness and to renounce Mammon to become disciples of Jesus; see, Pieris, *God's Reign for God's Poor: A Return to the Jesus Formula*, 43.

[32] The phrase "option for the poor" is of relatively recent coinage although the recognition that the poor hold special attention and affection in God's eyes is as old as Christianity. "Roman Catholics began wrestling with issues related to poverty in the Second Vatican Council (1962-65). Catholics in Latin America, who felt

that the work at Vatican II did not go far enough, convened in Medellin, where the emphasis was changed from seeing the poor as the objects of the mercy of the church to seeing them as the subjects of their own history. The actual phrase "preferential option of the poor" did not appear until the 1970s, reportedly used Gustavo Gutierrez in a lecture given in Spain in 1972. Since then the term has been used primarily in liberation and conciliar theological circles but also increasingly in evangelical missiology. The concept behind the term is one that demands a radical paradigm shift. The poor are not to be seen as objects of mercy, but as people who are particularly gifted by God to represent His [sic] justice to the rest of the world. The "option" for the poor is not optional but required by the very nature of God's compassion and incarnation in Jesus. Because Jesus came to preach liberty to the poor, they have an advantage in reading the Scriptures. They are not weighted down with the presuppositions and agendas of the rich and are freer to read and interpret the text as its primary audience. Such reading requires the recognition of structural issues that create and perpetuate poverty and new tools of analysis to understand and change those structures." A. Scott Morean, "Option for the Poor," in *Evangelical Dictionary* of World Missions, Dec. 19, 2000, http://www.missionreview.com/index. php?lockb& view= v&id=3455.27498 (March 6, 2006).

[33] Pieris, *God's Reign for God's Poor: A Return to the Jesus Formula*, 43.

[34] Pieris, *God's Reign for God's Poor: A Return to the Jesus Formula*, 44.

[35] Pieris, *God's Reign for God's Poor: A Return to the Jesus Formula*, 44.

[36] Walter Kasper, ed., *Lexikon für Theologie und Kirche*, vol. v, 3rd rev. ed. (Wien: Herder, 1996), 30.

[37] This is how *Nibbāna* is understood in *Theravāda* Buddhism or *Hīnayāna*. In *Mahāyana*, we find more positive characterisation of what *Nirvāna* means.

[38] Loy, "Shall We Pave the Planet or Learn to Wear Shoes? A Buddhist Perspective on Greed and Globalization," in *Turning Wheel Magazine*, 3.

[39] Loy, "Shall We Pave the Planet or Learn to Wear Shoes? A Buddhist Perspective on Greed and Globalization," in *Turning Wheel Magazine*, 3ff.

[40] Loy, "Shall We Pave the Planet or Learn to Wear Shoes? A Buddhist Perspective on Greed and Globalization," in *Turning Wheel Magazine*, 4.

[41] "The doctrine of karma implies that such unfortunates are reaping the fruit of their previous deeds [of former lives], but this is not understood in a punitive way, and the importance of generosity for those walking the Buddhist path does not permit us to be indifferent to their misfortune. We are expected, even spiritually required, to lend what assistance we can to them." Loy, "Shall We Pave the Planet or Learn to Wear Shoes? A Buddhist Perspective on Greed and Globalization," in *Turning Wheel Magazine*, 5.

[42] George D. Bond, Joanna Macy, and George Doherty Bond, *Buddhism at Work* (Bloomfield: Kumarian Press, 2004).

[43] The ideal of the bodhisattva in Mahāyāna Buddhism brings in other aspects of support for the poor which cannot be taken into account in this paper.

[44] Loy, "Shall We Pave the Planet or Learn to Wear Shoes? A Buddhist Perspective on Greed and Globalization," in *Turning Wheel Magazine*, 9.

[45] William H. Swatos, ed., "Preferential Option for the Poor," in *Encyclopedia of Religion and Society*, 1, http://hirr hartsem.edu/ency/PreferentialOP.htm (March 2, 2006).

[46] Swatos, ed., "Preferential Option for the Poor," in *Encyclopedia of Religion and Society*, 1.

[47] Swatos, ed., "Preferential Option for the Poor," in *Encyclopedia of Religion and Society*, 2.

[48] Josef Senft, "Armut/Reichtum, Katholizismus," in *Ethik der Weltreligionen, Ein Handbuch*, edited by Michael Klöcker and Udo Tworuschka (Darmstadt: Wissenschaftliche Buchgesellschaft, 2005), 40.

[49] This is just the reason why I prefer the expression 'friendship with the poor' to 'the option the poor.' Friendship is founded on mutuality and emphasizes it. The term 'option' can be understood in a very one-sided way: I am the one who has the option and the other is the chosen one. Such a relationship is all too often unbalanced and hierarchical.

[50] Pieris, *God's Reign for God's Poor: A Return to the Jesus Formula*, 76.

[51] Pieris, *God's Reign for God's Poor: A Return to the Jesus Formula*, 77.

[52] Raner Maria Rilke, *The Books of Hours: The Book of Poverty and Death* (Madison: Hogarth Press, 1961).

Inter-Religious Collaboration: The Response of Religions to the Signs of Our Times

Clemens Mendonca

The dreadful Tsunami is a powerful wake-up call to warn that something is going wrong with us and our earth. We observe a change in the rhythm of the earth. But it is not just the Tsunami alone that preoccupies our mind. Equally horrendous events take place almost every day in variant degrees and forms and places, bringing fear and anxiety to the inhabitants of this planet: earthquakes, floods, hurricanes, drastic climatic changes, bird flu, bomb blasts, suicide bombs, terrorist activities,[1] wars and nuclear weapon cruelty of all sorts to the marginalized groups, massacres and destruction of life and property, etc. Human attitude to life itself seems to be languid or lethargic. Hatred and revenge, competition and consumerism. irrational thrust towards materialism, politics of corruption, etc. have become part of our lifestyle. In a nutshell, we are growing accustomed to living in a culture of conflict and aggression. Such destructive culture is affecting not only humans but also our ecosystem, the way we interact with the planet and its resources. Further, it affects our religious ideology – the way we understand God and interact with other religious traditions. In other words, our problems are clearly interconnected. The significant factor in this interconnected problematic is that the measure in which the world is destroyed by humans is the measure in which humans are destroying themselves. Thomas Berry poignantly points out that "the glory of the human has become the desolation of the earth and the desolation of the earth is becoming the destiny of the human."[2]

But this is just one side of the story. The other side is equally important and gives us hope in our moments of despair. Today we experience something like 'world consciousness'[3] for peace, harmony, justice and equality. There is an unmistakable common quest that surfaces among people of good will everywhere: the quest for a healthy world, a healthy environment; the quest for unity in the one human family crossing boundaries of race, color, caste, religion, gender, politics, nations, and continents, and the quest for meaning in life. This is what unites all people of good will today. The same dreadful Tsunami, for example, brought humanity together. It posed a challenge to people all over the world to bear witness to their common humanity. The whole world came together, motivated by one common concern of instilling hope in those despairing lives in whatever way they could. Calamities such as these inspire us to rise above our human-made boundaries and limitations. Common humanity binds us. People all over are gradually becoming aware of their common responsibility towards their fellow human beings, especially in times of grave human and environmental disasters. Consequently, we find movements towards integration and peace. Collaboration and dialogue in such rare occasions become an imperative. However, such ideals of collaboration are always short lived.

The Meeting of Religions: A Vital Necessity

The question now is should we always wait for tragic events to bring us together or are there other alternatives through which we can learn to respect, love, and collaborate with one another in building up one human family, respecting the diversity of cultures and religions, and contributing our might to bring about a harmonious pluralistic living?

In fact, harmonious pluralistic living is not alien to those who live in pluralistic world. Our context is multi-religious and multi-cultural. For those who ingrained with a mono-cultural milieu, experience of pluralism might appear weird and intimidating. But for those who live in a multi-religious and multi-cultural framework, dialogue/collaboration is the order of the day. It happens constantly and unconsciously within our neighborhoods, in schools, colleges and universities, in the place of work, in the circle of our friends, in our own families (in cases of mixed marriages), in the media and in the internet, etc. This is because life is not static but a constant dialogue with the context in which we live and it's socio-cultural, religious, historical, economic and political complexities. Our lives are determined by our context. It is in a context that we experience the stark realities of life, like joys and sorrows, happiness and pain, light and darkness, brokenness and healing, peace and liberation, etc. These are not abstractions but are intimately connected with our lives. Context challenges and shapes our value system and helps us to discover meaning for our existence. Hence, dialogue is rooted in our very being. In other words, our needs are cross-cultural, our problems are cross-cultural and our response cannot but be dialogical.

In such a multi-religious context how do we understand religion, especially the religion of the other? In a multi-religious and multi-cultural context we cannot but speak of religion as inter-religion. Religion is a significant factor in human life because it deals with ultimate questions and problems of life. Raimon Panikkar describes religion "as the quest for the ultimate, as the set of symbols and practices of the human being when confronted with the most definitive questions as the meaning of life and the universe, not just on an intellectual plane but on an existential and vital level. Religion is, in the last instance, a dimension of human life."[4] Again, he calls religion 'the ultimate way', 'eschatodos.' When we give this definition-the way-a specific content, we can describe it in multifarious ways: ultimate way, way to salvation, and, most importantly, the way to peace. Panikkar believes that peace is the homeomorphic equivalent for all other interpretations of salvation. Peace is the "blend of harmony, freedom and justice" that is implicit in every religion.[5] Religion as a way to peace is a way to fulfillment and wellbeing of all, a way to a certain wholeness.

Religion symbolizes a triple relationship. It is earth-bound, i.e. firmly rooted here and now in this world (it is a reality that exists on earth); it is concerned with humans (their wellbeing), and it is a means that brings one in touch with the transcendence (mystery). The movement of religion is the "search of the human for the divine in the cosmic."[6] This is not a mere theoretical definition but follows a phenomenological approach.

The meeting of religions is a vital necessity today because the nature of problems is earth-shattering. Panikkar points out that:

> The political and economic situation of the world today compels us to radical changes in our conception of humanity and the place of humanity in the cosmos. If the change has to be radical and lasting, it also has to transform our ways of thinking and experiencing reality. I am prepared to argue that if there is any solution to the present predicament, it cannot come out of one single religion or tradition, but has to be brought about by collaboration among the different traditions of the world. Hinduism will not survive if it does not face modernity. Christianity will disappear if it does not meet

Marxism. Technocratic religion will destroy itself if it does not pay heed to, say, the Amerindian tradition, and so on. Humanity will collapse if we do not gather together all the fragments of the scattered cultures and religions.[7]

Religions are rooted in cultures and as such they are historically limited. Yet every genuine religion has a goal: to bring about healing and wholeness to all. But as Panikkar points out, being aware of its cultural rooted-ness and because of its historical limitedness no single religion alone has the capacity to bring about universal wholeness. At the same time every religion has its specific and indispensable role to play in realizing this integration.

In short, by whatever name it might be called, religion is a symbol of peace and wholeness. It is a powerful force to transform this world. But transformation will not take place unless religious traditions are willing to come together and cooperate at the local, national and international levels in working for a more just world order, a world order where issues of peace are of the essence. Indubitably, interreligious dialogue and collaboration are not just ideals to be pursued but imperatives for the survival of humans and the planet.

The Pontifical Council for Interreligious Dialogue (PCID) confirms this vital necessity of interreligious collaboration. The PCID points out that interreligious cooperation is no longer an option but a necessity.[8] It expresses the need for dedicated efforts on the part of religious traditions to "examine how, in a world that is increasingly interconnected, we can find new ways to respect our religious differences while forging peaceful bonds based on our common humanity."[9] It also states categorically that "Religion will prosper in this century only to the extent that we can maintain a sense of community among people of different religious beliefs, who work together as a human family to achieve a world peace."[10] In short the PCI brings to limelight the dire need for dialogue and collaboration among diverse religious traditions. The PCID is constantly making great efforts to bring religious traditions of the world together for dialogue and collaboration.

The object of this collaboration should be common concerns. Common concerns are those issues that affect all religious and secular traditions. They are not just individual problems. They should be the meeting points for religious traditions to dialogue and collaborate.[11] Concretely, it means: to work for the wholeness of creation-cosmic commitment; to work for the wholeness of human welfare; to discover spirituality for our times -

i.e., spirituality that takes this world and humans seriously, a holistic and integrated spirituality.

But in order to dialogue and collaborate we need to change our approach. We cannot approach another culture from a mono-cultural stand. A cross-cultural approach is important for dealing with this problem.

A Cross-cultural Approach

Today one can no longer speak of cultures, religions, nations or continents in isolation. Given the contemporary global situation, the 'world' needs to be understood in an intercultural perspective. For, to speak of one global culture is to speak of a monoculture. Culture is meaningful only in an intercultural perspective. But cultures are not universal. They are expressions or the mythos in which religions take their roots, blossom, and flower. "Religion gives culture its vision and culture gives religion its language."[12] That is why we speak of religions from an interreligious context. This is equally true of nations and continents. We need a broader vision of collaboration with one another be it on cultural, religious, national or continental grounds.

Culture means to 'cultivate or till together' (from the root word *colere*). It is "the cultivation of the human and the cosmic soil together."[13] Cultures are not absolute but relative. Panikkar calls this "cultural relativity." Cultural relativity is the "insight that any perception, experience, or knowledge is related to the horizon and dependent on the myth which makes the perception, the experience, or the knowledge possible."[14] Cultural relativity implies that each culture has its own separate criteria of truth according to its own constitutive myth; that these criteria, valid as they are within the mythic horizon of the given culture, are not absolute even within one's own culture. This is because cultures are always evolving they are open and unfinished; that in order to reach some cross-cultural criteria, these cultures have to be elaborated in the encounter of two cultures. Only then can a meaningful interaction take place.[15] In other words, cultural relativity upholds the importance of every culture and every being making its culture obvious and, at the same time, acknowledges the impossibility of absolutizing cultures.

Any attempt to understand a religion, culture or ideology is always laudable. The question is how? First of all, every culture has something in common and something specific.

For example, the earth and its elements are common to all cultures. Birth suffering, thirst, hunger, marriage, death etc., are common to all cultures and traditions. But these common experiences are understood and expressed differently in different cultures and traditions. Every culture has its unique understanding of the same common things. This is the richness of cultures.

The experience of transcendence by whichever name it may be called – thirst for the infinite – is common to all cultures. Again, this thirst for the infinite is understood and expressed differently in different cultures. It is an ontological thirst/search based on an 'existential openness' in humans. Panikkar calls this 'existential openness' faith.[16] This faith is the prerogative of every human being and not the privilege of selected few. It is faith that makes one human.

On the other hand, every culture has a particular perception of a particular thing. This is because our perceptions are conditioned by our myth, religions, education, world views, etc. We perceive things according to our pre-understanding. Something becomes important to us according to our pre-understanding. For example, I have been brought up in a specific culture and this culture has given me a specific understanding of what is truth and what is right. So, too, have others been brought up in their specific understanding of truth and right. All human understanding is relative and conditioned by history. At any given time in history no religious tradition will ever arrive at a full understanding of anything. On the contrary every tradition will always be on the way to understanding absolute truth. Once we understand something of the way the other traditions view reality, we are in a better position to understand our own faith and the faith expressions of others. For this we need to understand understanding! We have to distinguish between information and understanding.

Information and Understanding

We can look at reality (and consequently persons, our world, cultures and religions) from two perspectives: either we look at it from an objective perspective, i.e. from the perspective of information, or from a symbolic perspective, i.e. from the level of understanding. Understanding is different from information.[17]

Information is important for our pragmatic lives. It belongs to the world of perception, the world of the senses, where we can directly or indirectly measure and quantify. It is a world we prove and falsify. Here we concentrate on meaning-unequivocal meaning. Mere information about another person, religion or culture does not lead us to dialogue.

Understanding on the other hand, operates at the symbolic level. It belongs to the world of persons. The world of persons presupposes but goes beyond the senses (information), i.e., understanding is built on but restricted to information. Collecting information about person is different from understanding a person. The former is, to say, a matter of fact but the latter is built on personal relationship. It focuses on the significance of meaning. To understand another other culture and religion is to enter into the mythos of that culture and religion.

Understanding naturally opens us to a third dimension: the dimension of faith, to the world of beliefs. The world of beliefs is the most comprehensive of all since it not only presupposes information and understanding but also opens up to the divine. The door to the divine is faith. Here the concentration is on the meaning in life.[18] Faith makes life meaningful, full of meaning.

In brief, compared to information, understanding is an altogether different proposition because understanding is basically a bridge-building enterprise. It discards the walls of prejudices. It is through understanding that we enter into the world of the other. But understanding is not the first step towards engaging in genuine dialogue. It is the other way round: it is dialogue that helps promote understanding. When instead of dialoguing we become disputatious, no understanding will ever occur. The spirit of disputation, unlike that of discussion and clarification, is foreign to dialogue.

Universe of Faith and Pluriverse of Beliefs

Understanding leads us to the mythos of another tradition, another culture. Mystery is present in every culture and tradition. These traditions are the colors of the rainbow that touch one another and constantly interact. Through this interaction we perceive that a search for Unity in diversity is possible. It is in this diversity that one discovers one's full identity. For example from a Christian point of view we speak of One Centre, i.e. One Mystery which draws all things to itself. We live, move and have our being in this Mystery (universe of faith). At the same time, this One experienced differently and expressed differently in different culture (pluriverse of beliefs).

Christian beliefs are the Christian experience of that One Mystery expressed in Hebrew, Greek, and Roman cultures. Today they need to be experienced and expressed in other cultures too. Our tendency is to impose our credo on other cultures. Now we are gradually realizing that the same Mystery at work in Jesus is also at work in other cultures.

Interreligious Dialogue and Collaboration

The Catholic Church from the time of the Vatican II, with its Decree on *Nostra Aetate*, has been gradually opening itself up in the direction of dialogue. The openness of the Church has also occasioned interreligious dialogues at various levels. Hence we have today The Pontifical Council for Interreligious Dialogue and The Congregation for the Evangelization of Peoples. The Council insists on the constructive and positive interreligious relationship between various religious traditions in order to enhance mutual enrichment and understanding. It recommends a fourfold dialogue:[19]

a. The dialogue of life, where people strive to live in an open and neighborly spirit, sharing their joys and sorrows, their human problems and preoccupations.

b. The dialogue of action, in which Christians and others collaborate for the integral development and liberation of people.

c. The dialogue of experience, where persons, rooted in their own religious traditions, share their spiritual riches, for instance with regard to prayer and contemplation, faith, and ways of searching for God or the Absolute.

d. The dialogue of theological exchange, where specialist seek to deepen their understanding of their respective religious heritages, and appreciate each other's spiritual values.

What is Interreligious Dialogue?

In dialogue we may disagree (perhaps because we do not understand!) but we certainly do not refute the positions espoused by the other! Dialogue does not mean that we agree with whatever the dialoguing partner says or what we ironically give up our own position. If this were so, dialogue would be a farce, not a genuine sharing. In this regard we could take a cue from what the Pontifical Council for Interreligious Dialogue (PICD) said about its methodology a few years ago in its self-introduction.

> Dialogue is a two-way communication. It implies speaking and listening, giving and receiving, for mutual growth and enrichment. It includes witness to one's faith as well as openness to that of the other. It is not a betrayal of mission of the Church, nor is it a new method of conversion to Christianity. This has been clearly stated in the encyclical letter of Pope John Paul II 'Redemptoris Missio.' This view is also developed in the two documents produced by the PCID: The attitude of the Catholic Church towards the Followers of Other Religious Traditions: Reflection on Dialogue and Mission (1984), Dialogue and Proclamation (1991).[20]

Before entering onto an interreligious dialogue certain misunderstandings need to be clarified. According to Panikkar, in interreligious dialogue there is no merging of religious traditions. The aim is not merging of world's religions into universal religion. Nor is it to arrive at a total agreement between religious traditions. Instead the ideal foreseen by interreligious dialogue is to foster communication between diverse religious traditions and different cultures of the world in order to bride the gulfs of mutual ignorance and misunderstandings, giving people the chance to speak their own mythical language, to share the richness of their faith experience. He points out that there may be moments when some may reach this ideal communion, but this does not imply a reduction of the rich variety of religious experiences into a single system or tradition.[21] Indeed it is an experience of the arrival of a new Pentecost, a genuine quest for an integrated spirituality, a spirituality that crosses cultural, mythical and religious boundaries in order to realize the fullness of human destiny.

Interreligious dialogue is also a means of purification of religions. For example, in the face of fundamentalism, fanaticism, religious communalism and interreligious wars that are becoming a common phenomenon of our time, interreligious dialogue plays an important role in showing what religion truly is.

Finally, dialogue is a spiritual quest, a school of humility which teaches us that no one is self-sufficient, that there are no monopolies in this wide world where the sun shines for the sinner and for the just alike. Dialogue itself is not a means to get to the other but a means to discover myself in greater depth; a means of going out into the whole world, of meeting that alienated human being.[22]

However we must keep in mind certain prerequisites before entering to dialogue. Panikkar gives us certain guidelines:

Firstly, one must be deeply rooted in, convinced of and be faithful to one's religious tradition. Remaining loyal to one's own tradition does not mean obeying blindly without a critical judgment of the beliefs and doctrines that have handed down by a religious tradition. It is not just a mechanical repetition of rituals. Instead tradition in its real sense means "continuation of growth." That which is handed over in a tradition for future generations is the "crystallized experience of what has happened" long ago in a particular context. It can become stagnant and mechanical if it does not cater to the changing situation of the recipients. In fact, tradition has within itself an inner dynamism of growth, open to change to suit the needs of the receivers. A tradition that remains unchanged over the years has no relevance for changing generations and so is bound to degenerate into a dead symbol. In such a case it cannot be called a tradition.[23]

Secondly, one must be genuine and be able to understand rightly the traditions of others. We must not violate other traditions; they must be interpreted according to their own self-understanding: we have no right to interpret the religious beliefs and faith of other religious traditions from our perspective. Doing this would be great violation of these traditions. Violating these traditions is equal to absolutizing one's own religion. This means that we are called to enter and share in the same myth and its beliefs, sacred as they are to their believers.[24]

Thirdly, one must also be open to the new, that is, to listen to the Spirit and be open to its guidance.

Fourthly, we need to avoid aggression and insensitivity. Our whole project of dialogue will suffer if we are aggressive and insensitive in dealing with other religious tradition. Concretely our work is to unite and not to divide, to discern not to destroy, to heal and not to hurt. Our path is the path of love (Cf. I Cor. 13).

Interreligious Collaboration

The contemporary situation of common concerns beckons diverse religious traditions to come together. No genuine religion can consciously abide by or follow the ideology of any oppressive system. Interreligious dialogue must take upon itself this responsibility of making our people aware of the dangers of these oppressive systems. This entails a triple task: reflection and analysis of the situation in which we find ourselves, a deepening awareness of what such a situation does to us in the depth of our being, and an effort towards handling this situation. In other words, together the religions should read the signs of the times in order to understand what is really going on behind the grave human, ecological and religious problems of our times. The religions should dialogue and share the way they perceive the world in light of their respective revelations. An awareness of the common responsibility in handling these diabolic forces, urging them to joint initiatives, should be the objective of interreligious dialogue and collaboration. For this, all religious traditions need to do some soul-searching. They have a responsibility to criticize, oppose and take their clear stand against these systems and inspire the people to reach their human/communitarian destiny. In this sense every genuine religious tradition has a mission to fulfill in today's world. This mission is to be reconcilers and bridge-builders between God, world and humans. Propagating a doctrine of hatred and cultural superiority would only worsen our situation.

Concretely it means: commitment for justice, peace and the well-being of all, inclusive of the earth. This is, in reality, sharing the Good News of God's Kingdom with the whole of creation. Every religious tradition has its Good News to offer. What is this Good News if not caring for the poor and the downtrodden, bringing comfort, healing and hope to the broken-hearted, freedom to those in bondage, to those who grope in the darkness of ignorance, and proclaiming peace and reconciliation where hatred, revenge and injustice abound in the whole world (Luke 4:18-19). Religions should make brave attempts to work towards this goal. The following statement of Panikkar could inspire us to usher in a new style of life, a life of collaboration to guide us in our praxis of interreligious collaboration: "Our dream is precisely this collaboration between a handful of people of all races, colors, and religions –perhaps the real Christian Pentecost of our era – working together, not only for an improvement of the programmes, or for the relief of others, but for a reform and transformation of the world."[25]

Similarly, the Declaration of the Global Ethic of the World Parliament of Religions in 1993 confirms this responsibility:

The earth cannot be changed for the better unless the consciousness of individuals is changed first, and becomes a consciousness of responsibility in the minds and hearts of the women and men of today. If humankind urgently needs social, economic, and ecological reforms, it needs spiritual renewal just as urgently.[26]

Finally dialogue and collaboration should not be just an isolated event. It has to become a pattern, a life-style for all our religious traditions. Only then can religions become relevant for our contemporary world. This requires a process of awareness. Such process of awareness has to be ushered in through an adequate interreligious faith formation or education.

Conclusion

To substantiate what has been said above, I would like to introduce here our interreligious project called *Maher* that is run by people of goodwill belonging to various religious traditions: Christians, Hindus, Muslims, and Buddhists. It stands as a symbol of the holistic vision. It houses an inter-religious community. The focus of the project is the common concern, i.e. the battered women and street children. In other words, the focal point of the project is on rescuing is on rescuing and rehabilitating abandoned and underprivileged women and on educating them, their children and the society that treats women inhumanly.

There are three categories of women in *Maher*:

a.   Women who have run away from their homes due to mishandling by husbands/in-laws.

b.   Women who are abandoned/battered by their husbands and in laws either because they failed to bring forth sons and bore only daughters or they are childless or the husbands are in love with some other women.

c.   Raped, pregnant young girls whose parents refuse to take them back as their own.

When one woman is abandoned it is one woman's problem. But where women are regularly abandoned it is the problem of the whole society. The mission of *Maher* is to see to the needs of the abandoned women and at the same time to strive for a better future, a better society where the rights of women and children are respected and protected. Hence the material and moral help given to the abandoned women constitutes the centripetal force, and all-round education and development of the villages is the centrifugal force of the orbital movement called *Maher*. This holistic vision is the fruit of the close and on-going cooperation that exists between *Maher* and the Institute for the Study of Religion in Pune (a research center that promotes Interreligious Dialogue). In short, Maher embodies both theory and praxis.

The objectives Maher keeps before it are the following:

a. that women in villages have equal right to live.

b. that men change their basic attitude towards women and consider them not as objects of use but persons to be respected and loved.

c. that men assume serious responsibility for their children and do just leave them to the helpless women and disappear.

Meher is the home where one discovers that we all belong to one Ultimate Mystery. There are no conversions but all are taught to respect one another's religious conditions. No difference is made between people's religion and caste. There is no discrimination on grounds of gender. If there is some preference then it is to uplift the weak, the helpless and the old.

Maher is the entry point through which other surrounding villages are reached for all-round village development programmes: children's project, *balvadis* project, project for mentally disturbed women, income generation schemes, self-help groups for both men and women, non-formal education, open school system for the dropouts in the villages, de-addiction programmes, legal awareness, awareness programmes on the problem of untouchability, awareness programmes on gender sensitivity, superstitions, health and hygiene, environment and sanitation, workshops for youth, leadership training, sanitation educational programme, etc. These are some of the works done in *Maher* with the collaboration of diverse religious traditions. The staff consisting of diverse religious traditions not only collaborates and cooperates but also lives a community life.

Interreligious dialogue and collaboration has a prophetic role to play in today's world. It can not only shun all religious extremism, fundamentalism and communalism but also positively harness the energies of all people of faith and good will to bring about peace and justice that we so earnestly desire. Let me conclude by saying that, ultimately, the mission of every religion is to be the salt of the earth and light of the world. Salt gives not just taste and flavor but is used as preservative. We are called to preserve life, not just human life but life as a whole. We are called to be the lights of the world.

Light dispels darkness of ignorance and oppressive systems. The future of the world lies not in the power of the powerful but in the sacrifice of the simple people, the people of good will. The happiness happens in togetherness, in communion, in justice – justice for children, justice for women and men – who cannot fight for their own rights, who are marginalized on grounds of poverty, caste system, ignorance, gender and religion. The end result of this process is peace with God, humans and the World!

A Guru asked his disciples how they could tell when the night had ended and day begun.

One said, "When you see an animal in the distance and can tell whether it is or a horse."

"No" said the Guru.

Another said, "When you look at a tree in the distance and can tell if it is a neem tree or a mango tree.

"Wrong again" said the Guru.

"Well then what is it?" asked the disciples.

The Guru answered: "When you look into the face of any man and recognize your brother in him and when you look into the face of any woman and recognize in her your sister. At that moment your night has ended and you are in the light of Day. If you cannot do this, no matter what time it is by the sun, it is still night, you are still in darkness."

Endnotes

[1] According to the South Asia Terrorism Portal (SATPL since 1994 over people have died in India alone due to terrorist activities: 23.955 terrorists, 19.662 civilians and 7320 security force personnel. Cf., Avijit Ghosh and Pradeep Thakur, "Terror Feasts on India Worst Victims," *Times News Network*, October 31, 2005.

[2] Thomas Berry, "Teilhard in the Ecological Age," in *Telhard Studies* 7 (1982), 1-33, 9.

[3] C. Murray Rogers, "A New Millenium – Nearly!" in *Hindu-Christian Studies*, 8 (1995) 36-37, 36.

[4] Raimon Panikkar, "The Invisible Harmony: A Universal Theory of Religion or a Cosmic Confidence in Reality?" in *Inter-Culture* 108 (1990), Montreal, 45-78, 65.

[5] Raimon Panikkar, "The Challenge of Religious Studies to the Issues of Our times," in *Nucleus, Reconnecting Science and Religion in the Nuclear Age*, by Scott Thomas Eastham (Bear & Co, 1987), xiii-xxxviii, xxiv-xxv.

[6] F.X. D'Sa, "The Interreligious Dialogue of the Future: Exploration into the Cosmotheandric Nature of Dialogue," in *Vidyajyoti Journal of Theological Reflection* LXI (1997), 693-707.

[7] Panikkar, "The Invisible Harmony: A Universal Theory of Religion or a Cosmic Confidence in Reality?" in *Inter-Culture*, 69.

[8] Symposium on Interreligious Dialogue held in Rome by the Pontifical Council for Interreligious Dialogue, Jan. 16-18, 2003.

[9] Symposium on Interreligious Dialogue held in Rome by the Pontifical Council for Interreligious Dialogue, Jan. 16-18, 2003.

[10] Symposium on Interreligious Dialogue held in Rome by the Pontifical Council for Interreligious Dialogue, Jan. 16-18, 2003.

[11] According to Ali Asghar Engineer "there is no future for pluralist India except in unity between its people of diverse faiths, languages and cultures." Cf. Asghar Ali Engineer, Tribal-Muslim Dialogue," in *Interfaith Interaction*, Digest No. 606.

[12] Collegium with Raimon Panikkar, "Interdisciplinary Seminar of Psychology, Spirituality and Social Justice," Silver Jubilee Celebrations, Sudhana Institute, Lonavla, December 3-5, 1999.

[13] Raimon Panikkar, "Present Day University Education and World Cultures," in *Asian Cultural Studies* "Religious Consciousness and Modern World," edited by M. Uozumi and M. Kasai Mitaka, special Issue 4. 187-198, 194-195; See also R. Panikkar, *Persons of other Faith and Christian Higher Education*, 17.

[14] Raimon Panikkar "Indra's Cunning: The Challenge of Modernity," in *The Indic Experiment*, 75.

[15] Raimon Panikkar "Indra's Cunning: The Challenge of Modernity," in *The Indic Experiment*, 75.

[16] Raimon Panikkar, *Myth, Faith and Hermeneutics* (New York: Paulist Press, 1979), 207-208.

[17] Francis X. D'Sa, Interkulturelle Theologie - Dialog zwischen den theologischen Kultur - Univ. Prof. Dr. Franz Weber & Univ. Prof. Dr. Francis X. D'Sa. Bildungshaus Batschus, Batschunser Theologische Akademie (Btha), 1 Mai - 5 Mai 2000.

[18] Francis X. D'Sa, Interkulturelle Theologie - Dialog zwischen den theologischen Kultur - Univ. Prof. Dr. Franz Weber & Univ. Prof. Dr. Francis X. D'Sa. Bildungshaus Batschus, Batschunser Theologische Akademie (Btha), 1 Mai - 5 Mai 2000.

[19] Dialogue and Proclamation: Reflections and Orientations on Interreligious Dialogue Proclamation of the Gospel of Jesus Christ (Pontifical Council for Interreligious Dialogue and Congregation for the Evangelization of Peoples, 1991), no., 42.

[20] Pontifical Council for Interreligious Dialogue.

[21] Raimon Panikkar, *The Intrareligious Dialogue* (Bangalore: Asian Trading Corporation, 1984), 36-37.

[22] Raimon Panikkar, "Transforming Christian Mission into Dialogue," in *Inter-Culture* 20/4 issue 97 (Fall/October, 1987), 19-27.

[23] Raimon Panikkar, "In Christ There is Neither Hindu nor Christian: Perspectives on Hindu-Christian Dialogue," in *Religious Issues and Interreligious Dialogues*, edited by Wei-hsun Fu & G. E. Spiegler (N.p: n.p., 1989), 475-490,

[24] Raimon Panikkar, "In Christ There is Neither Hindu nor Christian: Perspectives on Hindu-Christian Dialogue," in *Religious Issues and Interreligious Dialogues*, 479.

[25] Raimon Panikkar, "Persons of other Faiths and Christian Higher Education," in *AIACHE Newsletter* XXIV (August-September 1990), 19.

[26] The Document, "A Global Ethic," in *A Parliament of the World's Religions*, Chicago, 1993, 9.

Interfaith Cooperation
and Political Context

Ch. Vasantha Rao and T. Swami Raju

Introduction

We live in a world that is separated into umpteen number of divisions; it has become part of our common language to speak about the first world and the third world, the north south divide, the Orient and the Occident, polarized identities of different philosophical strands, belonging to different religious sects, affiliation to different political parties, caste, class, region do play a part in parochial assertions. Human life has journeyed through a long history making us realize that there are also factors that could unite us irrespective of our affiliations.

The stark realities of the adverse effects in our daily life both in the global and local scenario challenge us of our identities, assertions, belongingness and affiliations, how are we to facilitate life, the quality of life affirming the one humanness and universality of all life. All entities have potentials for destructive as well as constructive may lead to either way of assertions of particularity with consequences being dissentions or on the other hand affirmations of universal outlook with resultant effect being unity, peace and harmony.

Our premise is that there is no peace without justice. Many a times we try to establish peace by all ways and means oblivious of the necessity of catering active justice. It is here that an Inter-faith Co-operation for Fostering Peace in the Context of Divided Affiliations must be explored and executed. Here are a few avenues to begin with.

Inter-faith Co-operation: A Model

Almost all religions take note of the plight of the poor and are concerned about alleviating their poverty. The ancient codes of law such as the Sumerian and Hammurabi Codes show a profound concern for the poor. This is how they have underlined their religiosity and their spirituality. The Biblical codes too show this theological concern for the poor by regulating the social and religious life of the Israelites. The Biblical concern for the orphans, widows and the strangers is noteworthy. These are the *persona miserea* that are part of every society and all communities. They are the ones that lack necessary support in life. They are the ones, who are easily taken advantage of in this competitive world.

The Hindu spirituality facilitates a special concern for the poor and we are time and again reminded of the same with the words '*dana*', and '*darmam*' helping or giving to the poor with an altruistic attitude. The Muslim spirituality gives a strong emphasis on alms giving to the poor making the practice mandatory by making it one of the five pillars of faith.

As much as we have seen and studied at least the three major religions, Christianity, Hinduism and Islam all project a profound concern for the poor. How would it be if the adherents of these religions see this common concern as a universal concern and not confined only to the parameters of their own religious milieu, times have changed and we have come a long way in history. Today we seek an inter-faith co-operation for fostering peace in the context of divided affiliations, we have a good number of examples to emulate a new religious ethos that overcomes particular identities and converges into action for justice thereby perpetuating peace in the society.

Let me share with you a report I heard from a participant at the 78th summer session at the Sattal Christian Ashram. The participant I remember was a woman working with either the CASA or CCC YCC of the north India, she was a qualified doctor in her own discipline of social work and was kind enough to share about the work they were doing in the society, I remember she showed us a video clipping on 'water' and how they were working for making safe drinking water available for the poor people in the remote parts of northern India. Later she shared one event from their ministry, which touched many hearts and inspired most of us to think in a different way and act in such a manner as to foster inter-faith co-operation for establishing a just and health society, which every religion envisages.

She narrated that in one particular geographical area of north India there were many families that were professing Hindus particularly Brahmins. Unfortunately in this community there happen to be many young widows, who were constantly being harassed by the local anti-social elements, the widows were employed but were underpaid and at times were also denied their monthly pay. They had no social support from the community they were living in. They suffered silently since there was no one, who could voice their injustice and redress their issue. Living at different places made them more and more vulnerable in many aspects in their community life.

It was in this context that the Hindu widows together had approached this CCC-YCC organization run by Christians. When the Christians heard the woes of the Hindu Brahmin widows, they were moved with compassion; caste, creed and color were not considered as the criteria and were determined to extend their support and had several rounds of talks with the widows to come to a conclusion of what sort of help was sought by them. Ultimately the widows decided on one thing, which they thought would provide them peace in their life. That request was that all the widows would be provided some accommodation together to live with their families. This was seen a task beyond the capacity of the Christian organization, although they were willing to help the magnitude of the solution seemed a Hercules task ahead of them. The Christian organization was all geared up to building decent accommodation but acquiring land for the purpose was a greatest hurdle, it was at this juncture that a Muslim landlord with deep religious convictions of helping the poor as divine mandate generously donated a piece of land just enough for the purpose. So the Christian organization built house for the Hindu widows on the lands donated by a devout Muslim. A model for celebrating life came into being with the inter-faith co-operation for fostering peace in the community that is torn apart with strife.

Political Division and Inter-faith Co-operation

The above model instills in us a deep faith that religion and religious convictions and inter-faith co-operation will play a major role in the state of Andhra Pradesh, which is threatened by disharmony and violence creating instability in all walks of life.

One of the burning issues now in Andhra Pradesh is 'division of the state' and very particularly political parties are preparing to face bi-elections on this issue during this month. Hence, it is a very sensitive issue and highly problematic to make any judgments either positive or negative especially from religious point of view. Though some religious leaders and gurus, for instance Satya Saibaba[1] and Jitendra Saraswathi,[2] made different claims either in favor or disfavor, they faced bitter resentment from some political parties of both regions silencing them by suggesting it is much better to permit their lives and talks to meditation and contemplation. Keeping the seriousness of this issue in mind this section is focused mainly on the immediate importance and dire necessity of "inter-faith cooperation in the context of divided affiliations".

Previous governments of this state seem more and more unable to fulfill various functions such as ensuring economic development and social justice, and handling different types of serious conflicts. While growing more powerless and unstable, the state also becomes increasingly centralized, authoritarian, repressive and even violent. It moreover fails to prevent, and often even creates or strengthens, all sorts of divisions on the basis of caste, region, language, ethnicity, politics and religion. Opposing groups are thus pitched against each other and lawlessness and violence spread in society. Politics have unfortunately become more fertile ground for money-grabbing, corruption, exploitation, dividing people by politicization of religion and communalization of politics and even criminal activities creating violence, which results in disturbing harmonious co-existence of people of various backgrounds living in peace. In our country, for instance, religion is becoming increasingly 'politicized', and politics 'communalized', hence, communal violence is increased day by day. It is true, indeed, as cited in HMI brochure "In the present context of the state of Andhra Pradesh, the demands from a section of people for the division of the state and subsequent violence in the Andhra Pradesh created disharmony and political instability. Violence and clashes instigated by political and communal groups are also destroying the culture of peace in Andhra Pradesh."

One can argue, in fact, the case of Andhra Pradesh is "communalization of socio-economic and political conflict rather than the politicization of religious conflict." The main reasons for most communal conflicts in our country lie not in religion but elsewhere. Ethnic, caste and religio-cultural identities are indeed manipulated by people with vested interests which seek the legitimization of social, economic and political conflicts under the garb of religion. In consequence, "the greatest threat to communal peace in our country today is the communalization of politics and society. Yet, why is religion misused in this manner? What makes such a phenomenon possible? How is it that the expression of economic or political conflicts takes on a definite communal character and that "the conflicting groups assume a religious identity?" Why are many communalists and rioters actually convinced that they defend or promote their religion? I believe that all religions – Hinduism, Christianity, Islam etc., originally aimed at promoting peace and harmonious living relations, but unfortunately due to either 'politicization of religion' or 'communalization of politics' religious communities are misunderstood as responsible for dividing people and creating communal violence.

The present Andhra Pradesh context is different, which is based purely on politics and political division. It does not understand in terms of purely communal division based on religion. The people of one section of state are demanding for a separate state and it is not only the issue of very recent past but this issue also has been challenging the unity and integrity of people in Andhra Pradesh from the very beginning of Indian independence. Separate state is an outcome of a section of people's aspiration for 'social justice' and 'political equality.' Where there is no justice there is no peace, hence, people are seeking for social justice i.e. equal status in matters of economic, education, employment, political power and social dignity. Keeping this fact in his serious consideration, perhaps, Dr. Rajashekara Reddy (former Chief Minister of Andhra Pradesh) gave much importance to 'overall development' of the people by adopting courageously and implementing sincerely policies/ schemes like *jalayajanm* (irrigation projects), *rajiv arogyasree* (free medical treatment to the poor), *atmabandu*, pension to the aged, scholarships to the poor students and so on which, indeed, helped many to get social justice.

Some political parties misused the aspirations of people for their own political interests and misguided people to agitate against government and irritated them to adopt violent methods creating communal conflicts further dividing people based on geographical region. It is, perhaps, an agitation for socio-economic and political justice rather than religious identity. People of different faiths are living together in all regions of Andhra Pradesh professing and practicing their religion. We need to understand the issue of 'division of state' in Andhra Pradesh from socio-economic-political point of view and seek the role of religion, in such a context of dividing affiliations, to promote better harmonious inter-faith relations. Therefore, what should be the role of religion in general and multi-faiths in particular?

Etymologically, the term 'religion' is derived from the Latin word '*religio*' meaning 'drawing people together' or 'bind together' hence; every religion seeks unity and integrity of community at the same time holistic wellbeing of all members of a community or society. The prophetical teachings of Old Testament, ethical precepts of Jesus in the New Testament and ideals of other faiths are based on 'justice and equality' of human beings, but when this fact is ignored in practice, injustice and disruption of peace prevail in the society, which leads to communal conflicts, tensions, violence and divisions. At this context of 'dividing affiliations' inter-faith co-operation is much needed to foster peace and develop harmonious relations between people of various faith backgrounds.

People of various faiths work together to fight for 'justice and equality' based on fourfold agenda: 1) the basic equality of all humans before God as more important than the things in which they are unequal. All human beings are equal basing common human origin irrespective of religion, race, color, creed, gender and region, therefore, to have equal justice is the right of every human being. 2) a special concern for the poor and by doing justice to eradicate poverty; 3) equal distribution of state resources – land, wealth, employment, political power etc., basing the needs of people; and 4) co-operation in building healthy community fighting against common problems of society like – exploitation, corruption, inequalities, illiteracy, disease and violence as well as working together for the developmental programs of nation and co-operating in social movements for human rights, dalits, women, environment and peace. Government needs to make constructive policies and implement them faithfully to develop and improve living conditions of people – dalits, marginalized, poor and underprivileged, those who have been suffering for centuries under the oppressive structures of society like injustice and inequality, then only peace will prevail and harmonious social relations develop and 'divided affiliations' disappear. Let all of us join our hands together, whether we are Hindus, Jains, Buddhists, Sikhs, Christians or Muslims, to foster peace that unites and binds us as 'one common just human community' having the hallmark of unity in diversity. Shalom.

Endnotes

[1] *Eenadu*, (Hyderabad), Janaury 1, 2007, 1; *Eenadu*, (Hyderabad), March 7, 2008.

[2] *Saakshi*, (Hyderabad), February 17, 2010, 10.

Muslim Understanding
of Hindu Civilization

Reeta Bagchi

As we moved through the last decade towards preceding century, we experience that humankind is transiting to a world order which is global and full of challenges and change. The world has been global since its inception. As thousands of years ago tribes moved across the globe freely. With the laying of territorial boundaries ideas and people were not confined. Later on invasions and conquest furthered the process of interaction. Today migrations and travels have brought the need to develop good relationship with the people of various cultures and religions. It has become now difficult to deal with the people without knowing about their faith and practices. In this context interfaith and intercultural understanding has become essential for everyone. In India historically there have been efforts to bring religious groups closer, considering all faiths have important role to play overlooking the sectarian dogma and ideological disputes. There always existed vital bond of amity and integrity ignoring the differences in cultural practices. There existed diffusion of philosophical, ethical and cultural thoughts of world literatures of different traditions. According to the philosopher Dr. Radhakrishnan: "We are the heirs of the heritage of whole humanity and not merely of our nation or religion."

Existence of diverse religion is an accepted fact that demands tolerance and respect towards others. But in present century the communal forces deny the existence of composite nature of culture. The God of all creation sometimes is taken as a God of one's own community, giving way to fanaticism, instead of universality and catholicity in outlook. This resulted increase in problems like terrorism, war, crimes, injustice, oppression and exploitation. The crisis situation is perceived in every walk of life all over the world. Such situation led some to speculate a clash of Civilization.[1] But such global scenario of negativity could not discourage scholars in every age to face the challenges for the attainment of a just and peaceful world order. They consider that although it is impossible to root out conflicts, yet is well within the reach to make efforts to reconcile in the framework of dialogue to achieve progress, peace and justice. It encourages tolerance and understanding towards other faiths and cultures.

Civilization in India is known for its variety, change and diversity. The varieties were being represented by different communities, indicating multiplicity in behavioral pattern. It included the people of different religions, cultures and languages. Despite diversity there always remain a basic civilizational unity and distinctive composite cultural identity. Every individual and religious group enjoyed individual or group identity. Jawaharlal Nehru asserted in his book *Discovery of India*: "Some kind of a dream of unity had occupied the mind of Indians since the dawn of civilization. That unity was not conceived as something imposed from outside. It was something deeper and within its fold, the widest toleration of beliefs and custom was practiced and every variety acknowledged and even encouraged."[2] It is based on the believe that humanity split in divisions which is necessary as man has to adjust himself in different geographical and historical circumstances.[3] The differences of race and creed are not intended to mark differences but to serve as man's identity.

India witnessed several cultural contacts. The result represents a unique multi-cultural situation derived from different sources. Apart from indigenous growth of diversities, the people of both Aryans and non-Aryans contributed to the formation of the composite culture. Hellenistic, Greeks, Huns, Kushans, Persians, Arabs, Turk-Afghans and others helped in the development of syncretistic tradition. Among them the advent of Muslims was an event of great significance. They ruled over Indian subcontinent for longest period with their concept of equality and justice for all. The historical contact between Islam and Hinduism reveals the fact that during its history, Islam felt the presence of other religions. There had been unpleasant incidents in historical record but in general Muslim scholars, travelers, rulers and others observed tolerance and mutual cooperation in their practices. Due to non-Muslim majority the syncretism in religion and cultural spheres propounded with the aim of socio-political stability. For that the Muslims in India have left behind an era of common cultural traditions. They contributed towards the growth of social, religious and cultural ideals and have shown a great respect in peaceful solutions of issues and problems through dialogue. In eleventh century al-Bīrūnī is known for making Hindu philosophy accessible to Muslims. Saint Kabir introduced the tradition of non-conformity in fifteenth century. Emperor Akbar created a sense of oneness among the diverse elements in Sixteenth century. Dara Shikoh made an attempt towards unique Indian synthesis of composite culture in seventeenth century. The tradition continued even after him attracted Hindu reformists from Ram Mohun Roy to Mahatma Gandhi. Ram Mohun Roy known as the father of Indian renaissance in modern period (nineteenth century) brought reform in India on the basis of his Islamic understanding which he developed during his study at an Indian Madrasa in Patna.

Al-Bīrūnī - A Scholar of Indian Civilization

Al-biruni can be said the first Indologist or scholar of Indian civilization. He was born in Khorasan in Central Asia and was of Persian descent had visited to India in eleventh century as a traveler. He tried to understand the religious and intellectual aspects of ancient India when the studies were not systematized. He went deep to understand the roots of Hindu philosophy, theology and jurisprudence during the time when it was unknown outside India. His observation about India, its culture, creed and social life of the people continue to be held in great esteem throughout the world even today. He interpreted Indian science and thought to the Arabs and Persians. His *Kitāb-ul-Hind*, popularly known as *al-Bīrūnī's India* or '*Indica*' is a rare and first great book on cultural history, religion and philosophy of India from the pen of a Muslim scholar. The book is originally written in Arabic and was never translated in any popular Indian language. It was only in nineteenth century a German scholar Dr. Sachau translated it in English *al-Bīrūnī's India*[4] realizing the importance of this great work. Al-Birunis's book is a storehouse of information about India. It introduced the best of Indian achievements to the world of Islam and later to Europe. The book provides an overview of al-Bīrūnī's humanistic methodology in understanding the religion and philosophy of India, in the section pertaining the religious and philosophical life of India. For this he consulted *Pundits* or the Hindu Sanskrit scholars who were willing to respond to his questions regarding Indian philosophy and religion as well as traditional science. But they were also unable to provide satisfactory information in the absence of any systematic study at that time. For this purpose he got mastery over Sanskrit which enabled him to reach to the original sources of information.[5] He had already studied Greek philosophy which was popular in the early days of Islam in Baghdad. He was struck by many common features of Hindu and Greek philosophy which he has discussed in his book on India. He refers some of the Sanskrit works deal with Greek and Roman astronomy.

Although he had to face many difficulties in getting data as reflected in his book, his aim always remain to give a true picture of India. He tried to present Hinduism in a better light and Hindus as a believer in the unity of God. Although it seems his experience about Hindu society was bitter due to its rigid caste system. His scholarship is evident in his cross-cultural dialogue found in the final chapter of the book. His approach suggests the study of comparative religion which was rare in his time. His mark is valuable in the sense that he followed scientific approach in understanding Hindu religion without any religious prejudice. He accepted philosophy as inseparable constituent of cultural and civilized values and tried to use it to open the path of his investigative understanding.

The Syncretistic Tradition of Saint Kabīr

In medieval India, Muslims followed the practice of peaceful co-existence with non-Muslims principally Hindus. Kabīr the (fifteenth century) mystic was born of a Hindu mother and was brought up by a Muslim weaver. His mystical concept reflects strong Sufi influences. His life and teachings help us understand the tradition of non-conformity in Indian civilization. His voice was that of a downtrodden who rebels openly against social inequalities and injustice and seeks social reordering. His teachings were in the form of poetical verses borrowed freely from Sanskrit and Persian vocabularies. He preached the unity of God and unity of humankind abandoned the division between the two communities—Hindus and Muslims. Modern poet Rabindranath Tagore for whom Kabīr stood as one of the inspiring symbol translated his many poetical verses. In such verses Kabīr says:

Hari is in the East, Allah is in the West,
Look within your heart, there you will find both Karim and Ram.

I and you are of one blood, and one life animates us both.
From one mother is the world born,
What knowledge is this which makes us separate?

The evil influence of this world,
has divided us into innumerable sects.[6]

More than a philosopher Kabīr was a practical teacher. His teachings were
based on devotion (bhakti) acceptable to both Hindus and Muslims.[7] He is
known for the syncretistic tradition. He has accepted cultural co-existence
a natural condition towards cultural assimilation with identity of both the
communities.

Emperor Akbar's Policy of Co-Existence

Akbar the third of the Mughal dynasty (sixteenth century) in India foresaw
an era of universalism and a united world with several religions together.
He was the grandson of Bābar who had won the throne of Delhi in 1526
but was a stranger in India and continued to feel so. Akbar as a warrior had
conquered large parts of India but his aim was more to conquer the heart of
the people. He had a dream of a united India. Akbar's period had experienced
a revolutionary advancement in Europe towards human rights, on the other
the old traditional way in India relying on man's hard labor. It may be due
to the social system practiced was a bar on advancement in India. Akbar
made a sincere effort to define human rights. He followed rational manner
with the aim to bring transformation among the followers of traditional
system. His ideal was the synthesis of old tradition with diverse elements
towards fusion into commonality. Akbar was also known for the spirit of
new inventions which could not spread much due to Hindu practices of
caste, untouchability and exclusiveness. His liberal interpretation of Islam
and the idea of common humanity, the concept of equality of humankind
made powerful appeal especially to those who were denied equal treatment
in Hindu fold. The result was that many conversions took place and majority
was from lower castes. The differences did not disappear but a feeling of
oneness grew. It also made revolutionary change in the mindset aiming
religious synthesis for national integration.

He was surrounded by the ancient civilization and culture of Hindus.
Due to literary renaissance in the age of Akbar, Muslims began to take greater
interest in Sanskrit literature and Hindu philosophy and religion. Akbar
introduced popular Hinduism to the Muslims through translations of the
popular Hindu scriptures like *Mahābharata*, *Ramayana* and the *Atharva-veda*
in Persian. With an enquiring mind he patronized learned *pundits*, eminent
Sufis and Christian missionaries. He built a new capital at *Fatehpur Sikri*

twenty miles from Agra. The tourists from all parts of the world come to see even today. There is a most remarkable though small building *Dīwān-i-Khas*, where the private Hall of Worship (*Ibādat Khāna*) is situated. In this hall every Friday evening Akbar when he returned from his campaigns held a religious session. The representatives from various religions were invited and each by turn described their faith, ideals for righteousness and the ways towards God. All took part in lively debate and Akbar carefully listened to all of them curious to learn something new seeking an answer of the basic problem of humanity. As a Muslim he realized that there is only one God and many paths leading to Him. This was Akbar's concept of Truth that roses are of many kinds and they grow in many lands and numerous are the gardeners but there is only one beauty of the rose whether it is white, pink or yellow. So Akbar said very clearly that all human beings are the children of one God; that human being who benefits others is greatest friend of God; that no individual becomes faithful unless he/she wishes for his/her fellow brothers what he/she wishes for himself/herself. This is the essence of Islam which is essentially a religion of peace. He not only preached but also practiced religious toleration.[8] His later generation accepted the structure and worked within that framework.

Dara Shikoh's Cultural Syncretism

Dara Shikoh the greatest scholar of medieval period is the representative of the unique composite culture of India. Akbar's mantle as a religious seeker fell not on his son Jahangir or his grandson Shahjahan but on his great-grandson Dara Shikoh. He was a profound Muslim and known to the world for his liberal views. His dream was a new-enlightened India of which Emperor Akbar laid the foundation. As he grew he combined in himself the qualities of his two great ancestors Humayun and Akbar. They had the habit of passing more time in acquiring knowledge. He also spent more of his time in the Royal library studying mysticism, philosophy and principles of Sufism. This resulted in publication of many works on Sufism. His faith in Sufism played important role in shaping his mind.

He is known for his effort to bring literary movement which inspired every man of wider outlook, and placed religion on a broader foundation. He had deep interest in the study of Hinduism and Indian philosophy as he believed in syncretistic cultural interaction among people of all faiths. His aim was essentially to define the true spirit of Islam to develop brotherhood against the practices of his time which had developed communal feeling among Muslims and Hindus. He denounced Muslim communal feeling and tried to explore the possibility for common basis. He realized that there is no dispute in 'Holy Book' (*Ahl-i-kitāb*) whether it is Vedas or Quran, or Old and New Testament which have a common faith. He studied Jewish, Christian and Hindu religions with the aim to discover the underlying principles of these religions and harmonizing them with the tenets of Islam. He was convinced to the doctrine of *tawḥīd* or divine unity. He had studied Holy Qur'ān and Ḥadīth under the guidance of Abdul Latif, which helped in intellectual advancement. In his young age he also came in contact with many Hindu and Muslim mystics of liberal thinking. This helped him to grasp the essence of religion through intuitive perception without attaching any importance to the dogmatic formalism. He was influenced by the liberal thought of Sufism and initiated to the Qadri order, which developed a natural revolt against formalism of ritualistic religion. It opened him the path of self-realization, toleration and admiration towards other faiths. His Sufi learning led him to study the well-known works on Islamic and Hindu mysticism. It helped him to understand that the Ultimate Truth is not the exclusive property of any particular or chosen race but it can be found in all religions and at all time. He defined that the two religions i.e. Hinduism and Islam which apparently looked dissimilar, essentially united in their search towards spiritual-realization. The differences are only based on the ground of practices could be reconciled.

He acquired from Akbar the interest in comparative religion, concept of universal brotherhood, humanism and peace. Orthodox Muslims generally regard Hinduism as polytheistic religion, which is against Islamic uncompromising monotheism. That is also the cause of deep rooted hostility among Hindus and Muslims. The Sufis protest this attitude as un-Islamic and follows Unitarianism. The Sufi Islam has been a bridge between Hindus and Muslims in India. Their goal is unification (*tawḥīd*) consists in affirming the unity of God or the realization that nothing exists except God. The soul does not exist independently but becomes one (*fāna*) with the divine that 'he who knows himself [sic] knows his Lord.' This knowledge cannot be received through intellect but it is a divine experience and the basis of human unity. This common divine revelation of Sufism and Bhakti (devotion) tradition of Hinduism was basis to bring reconciliation between Hindus and Muslims.

It followed the belief that 'there are innumerable ways to God that each one seeks Him in his own way'.

In the search for truth, Dara Shikoh met Baba Lal Das Bairagi the Hindu medicant which proved quite enlightening for him. The dialogue with him demonstrates his interest in Hindu philosophy and his spirit of understanding Hindu mythology and other aspects of speculative philosophy of the Hindus. Their discussion focuses several similarities in the teachings of Hindu and Muslim mystics. This made him to consider that there must be a common ultimate source, the root of all monotheism, differences are only in name. He said:--

Here is the secret of unity (tawḥīd), understand it,
Nowhere exist anything but God.
All that you see or know other than Him
Verily is separate in name, but in essence one with God.[9]

It is like pure water, different colors in different vessels i.e. the various religions, which differ only in appearance but completely agree in essence.

Like Akbar, Dara Shikoh patronized learned men from all denominations: saints, theologians, philosophers, poets and mystics of every community— Muslims, Hindus, Christians, Jews and others. But unlike Emperor Akbar, who made an attempt to weld into a political synthesis of divergent creed and different racial elements in India, the approach of Dara Shikoh was from different point of view and that was purely as a seeker of spiritual truth. As Holy Quran pre-supposes diversity in faith and considers it as part of planning.[10] He considers this integral approach of Holy Qur'ān is scientific as well as modern. The same integral approach he finds in Hindu philosophy especially in Advaita Vedānta as it believes that the same self exists in every human being. This thought enables to establish integral relationship with everyone all around. His quest for understanding Hindu religion made to appoint a large number of *pundits* or the learned men from Banaras who helped him to study Sanskrit and Indian philosophy. He is more known for his literary and religious movement in India through his effort towards understanding Hindu philosophy. He translated Upaniṣads, Yoga-Vāsiṣṭha and Bhagavad-Gītā in Persian. It was from the Persian version translated into Latin and French influenced 19th century European scholars. The Latin version was published but the French version remained in manuscript form. He has following popular literary contributions in his effort towards cultural syncretism:

Majma-ul Bahrain (Mingling of the two Oceans)

His sustained research in comparative religion came out in the form of extremely remarkable work known as '*Majma-ul Bahrain*'[11](Mingling of Two Oceans) a work of remarkable merit and originality. It is an anthology of Vedas to which Dara Shikoh declared the Vedas to be heavenly books and in conformity with the Holy Quran. It is based on his belief that there were no fundamental differences between Hinduism and Islam. The work is preserved in Persian. The contents of this work are divided into twenty sections. In each section he shows similarities between the two great traditions—Hinduism and Islam. It is a seminal work in the history of composite culture of India, a comparative exposition of Islamic Sufism and Hindu religious philosophy.[12] It shows Dara Shikoh's belief in unity of religions. He tried to show the identity of Hindu and Muslim doctrines of unity – *Brahmāvidyā* (Indian Pantheism) of Hinduism and the tenets of Holy Quran based on Sufi phraseology. He called it 'a collection of truth and wisdom of two truth knowing groups.' In other words he propounded 'Mysticism is equality.' He tries to bring the points of similarity and identity between Hinduism and Islam to show where these two ocean's mystic thought unite. His constant association and discourse with the Hindus helped him to understand that as regards the ways or means of knowing God, the difference between the Hindus and the Muslims was only verbal i.e. only in terminology, the conflict being one of language and expression. With this view he tried to prove essential harmony between religions.

Yoga-Vāsiḥtha

Yoga-Vāsiḥtha is a rare Sanskrit work on Hindu Gnosticism. It is the work of speculative philosophy delivered by sage Vasistha to his disciple; about real (*sat*) and unreal (*asat*) entity, principles of psychology, faculties of mind and tenets of ethics. As Dara Shikoh was a keen student of Gnosticism he got deeply interested in the study of Yoga Philosophy. He had already initiated himself into the practice of Yoga because of his constant association with *Yogis* and *Sanyasis* of India. Dara Shikoh claimed that he had read a Persian translation of *Yoga-Vāsiḥtha* by Sheikh Sufi. Some of the Sufi physical exercises in the *risala* bear a close resemblance to the Hindu *Tantric* meditation. His own understanding of common elements in Qadri and yogic meditational practices of Hindus encouraged translating *Yoga-Vāsiḥṭha* in Persian. Prof. Qanungo refers Dara Shikoh: He highly recommends *Sultan-ul-azkar*, which is exactly the same process of controlling the mind by the regulation of breath as the *Pranayam* of the Hindus, with the difference that the Hindu *Yogi* sits erect while the Sufi bends forward placing his two elbows on his knees at the time of regulating his breath.'[13] Al-Biruni also had translated into Arabic another work on Hindu Yoga i.e. *Patañjali's Yoga Sūtra* and *Samkhya Sūtra*. Emperor Akbar also had made to translate *Yoga-Vāsiḥṭha*.

Sirr-i-Akbar (the Great Secret)

Dara Shikoh devoted much time finding a common mystical language between Islam and Hinduism. Towards this goal his greatest literary achievement was the translation of 50 Upanishads from original Sanskrit into Persian, under the title *Sirr-i-Akbar*[14] (the great secret). He not only translated words into Persian but also ideas into the framework of Sufism. His translation contains a Sufi view of the Upanishads. Through this he tried to syncretize Hindu and Islamic metaphysics. He accepted the superiority of Hinduism in point of priority of revelation of the Vedas. The Vedic literature consists of four Vedas which is the store house of Indian wisdom and knowledge. The Vedas contain all the secrets of the pure monotheism and mysteries of life which elaborated in the Upanishads, throw light on certain very difficult questions of life. The Upanishads have influenced people all over the world. Dara Shikoh was also a great admirer of its philosophy. It was his thirst for the fullest exposition of oneness of God, brought him to its very fountain head of Hinduism, the Upanishads. It is considered by Hindus the Divine knowledge revealed to the sages. He began to ponder to why the discussion about monotheism is so conspicuous in India and why the Indian mystics and theologians of ancient India do not find any fault with Unitarians. With this query he studied the Upanishads and arrived to the conclusion that the ancient Indian philosophical thought is linked with the monotheistic ideals of Islam. He found that Hindu monotheists have given the clear explanation of this concept. As expressed in Vedantic philosophy:' I am Brahman' or "I am the Truth" (*ana al-ḥaqq*). This was the truth Vedic saint proclaimed. This corresponds to the unity of mankind and in fact unity of all creation. It is the consideration that in spite of plurality there is unity. This is reflected in the first *Surah al-Fatihā*; addresses man as a whole. It can also be ascertained from Holy Quran that there is no nation without a prophet and without a revealed scripture. Upanishads as the interpretation of the Vedas are treasure of monotheism. So Dara Shikoh tried to understand Upanishads thoroughly. He learnt Sanskrit and studied Upanishads in original with the aim to make an exact translation of the Upanishads. Although there were interpretations and commentaries of Upanishads, still he felt it a treasure of knowledge and there were few thoroughly conversant with it even among the Indians. He also wanted to solve the mystery which underlies the Hindu effort to conceal some truth from the Muslims. He states boldly his speculative hypothesis in the introduction of his book, that it is referred in Holy Quran as the *kitāb-ul maknun* or the hidden Book (Holy Qur'ān refers, indeed there is a book which is hidden).[15] This hidden book can neither be the Book of Moses, nor the Gospels. Upanishads could be the hidden Book mentioned in Quran. He comes to the conclusion that in the Upanishads the verses of the Holy Quran are found. The concept of *tawḥīd* can be found in the Upanishads which is the most fundamental doctrine of Islam. That is why he made word to word translation of Upanishads with the aim to remove differences that prevailed among orthodox Muslims.

On this assumption he also tried to understand the mysteries of Holy Qur'ān which according to him is hidden in Upanishads. He never aimed the acceptance of each other's theories and cultural practices but to define that the Truth in both the religions are linked with each other. He restricted to apply Vedantic methods to the explanation of the fundamental doctrines as enunciated in Holy Qur'ān. On the other avoided using Qur'ānic terminology in the explanation of Hindu philosophic terms, in his translation of Upanishads. He only tried to establish harmony between the two creeds of India – Hinduism and Islam. It was also translated into Latin and French. The handwritten manuscript of *Sirr-i-Akbar* by Dara Shikoh is preserved in the library in Ajamgarh (U. P). It begins with *Bismillah-ar-Reḥman ar-Raḥim* on left side and *Ganeshnamah* on the right side with a small figure of Ganesha. The Persian translations of Dara Shikoh were important for the preservation of Hindu doctrines for Hindu themselves. The Hindu translators of the Upanishads refer Dara Shikoh as one of the revivers of Hinduism along with Sankaracharya and Vyasa.

Bhagavad-Gita

The Persian translation of Bhagavad-Gita was made by Dara Shikoh realizing the hidden beauty of Hindu philosophy. The book is termed by Hindus as the core of all the Vedas, Upanishads and other religious books. It is based on the dialogue between Krishna and Arjuna. It is Krishna's advice to Arjuna to fight for the sake of justice. The book is well known for its philosophy. It is a guide in all aspects of human life for the achievement of knowledge, happiness and peace of mind. The book is translated in almost all the languages of the world. Through the Persian translation of Bhagavad-Gita, Dara Shikoh made it to reach to the Muslims. After him *Sufi* teachers in India interpreted Hindu metaphysics and mythology which serve as a basis of the study of Hindu tradition. All the works of Dara Shikoh are the landmark in the spread of composite culture based on inter-religious interaction. It shows him as greatest representative of Indian cultural synthesis. In pursuing his goal he lost the distinction between Mosque and temple. He prays: "Thou art in the Ka'ba at Mecca, as well as in the Hindu temple of Somnath."

Later he was criticized by the orthodox *Maulvis* who puzzled how Islam could be twin brothers. His findings were too radical for Muslim elite. He was criticized for his liberal outlook which he had formed after much study. *Maulvis* refused to accept the concept propounded by him. His thoughts annoyed them for which they issued *fatwa* (decree) against him. Political opponents were looking for an opportunity to remove him. It was fulfilled by his younger brother Aurangzeb a fanatic, who declared him a threat to the public peace and ordered to execute him. His search for truth cost him life on August 30, 1659. Dara Shikoh who fought for just peace became the part of a system of injustice. But up to his last days he continued his policy of *Sulh-i-Kul* (Peace) with an honest approach towards understanding Hindu civilization. His dream shattered by his untimely death. He sacrificed for his effort to bring cultural synthesis through literary achievements. After him the vision of unity was lost in the atmosphere of hatred and rivalry created by the warring sects and religious schools and even today we are living in the atmosphere of religious disintegration.

It shows how the people of other country and community tried to understand the culture and religion of another country and community. Although they had to go through war and other hardship but behind all a patient scholarship continued. That great tradition of inter-religious and inter-cultural understanding is ignored in today's communal politics which has widened gap between two communities. The fanatic and fundamentalists of both the traditions try to create disharmony by denouncing each other and try to prove the truth of their own religion. Positive outlook is the need of the hour to preserve the composite cultural tradition of India. To remove stereotypes about each other, there is need to highlight Muslim contribution

to the development of Indian civilization. In the past their effort improved
the relations of the two communities and helped in removing the social and
religious differences. Their findings are lesson in present day situation of
prevailed misconception among Hindus and Muslims. They stressed upon
inter-community concord. Islam teaches peace on earth and considers conflict
(*fasad*) as worse than murder. The Hindu scripture *Kathopaniṣad* prays for
the wellbeing of all irrespective of any particular religion or community:
"*Saha nāvavatu saha nau bhunaktu saha vīryam karavāvahi...*"(May he
(God) protect all of us together, Let us share the food together, May we
work conjointly with greater energy, May we not hate anyone, Let there be
peace). Understanding and dialogue can create peace among civilizations
and cultures. To borrow the words from Hans Kung, the foremost authority
of interfaith relations: 'There will be no peace among nations unless there is
peace among religions. And there will be no peace among religions unless
there is authentic dialogue among religions'.[16] In present century we need
commitment for positive approach towards other sects and communities.
It is therefore the responsibility of the adherents to promote goodwill and
not to forget the basic ideals of religion.

Endnotes

[1] Samuel P. Huntington, *The Clash of Civilization* (Penguin Book: New Delhi,
1996), 207.

[2] Jawaharlal Nehru, *The Discovery of India* (Oxford University Press, New Delhi,
1993), 61.

[3] Qur'ān: 4.1.

[4] Edward. C. Sachau, *al-Bīrūnī's India* (New Delhi. 1964).

[5] Hakim M. Said, ed., *Al-biruni* (Karachi: Hamdard Academy, 1979), 22.

[6] Rabindranath Tagore, *Songs of Kabir* (New York: Macmillan, 1917), 112.

[7] Tarachand, *Influence of Islam on Indian Culture* (Allahabad: The Indian Press,
1963), 15.

[8] Abdul Majid Khan, "Islam and other Religions and Cultures," in *India and
Contemporary Islam*, edited by Lokhandwala (Shimla: Indian Institute of Advanced
Study, 1971), 97.

[9] Dara Shikoh, *Risala-yi-Haqq-Nama*, 24, 26, cited by Theodore de Bary, ed., *Sources
of Indian Tradition* (New Delhi: Motilal Banarasidas, 1963), 445.

[10] Qur'ān 22:17.

[11] Dara Shikoh, *Majma-ul-Bahrain*, trans. M. Mahfuz-ul-Haq (Calcutta: Asiatic
Society of Bengal, 1929), 5.

[12] K.R. Quanungo, *Dara Shikoh*, vol. I (Calcutta: Vishwabharati, 1953), 220-221.

[13] Qanungo, *Dara Shikoh*, 83.

[14] Dara Shikoh, trans., Sirr-*i-Akbar*, edited by Tarachand and J. Naini (Tehran:n.p., 1957).

[15] Qur'ān LVL. 78-81.

[16] Hans Kung, *Global responsibility: In search of a new world Ethic* (New York:WIPF and Stock Publisher, 1991), xv.

Pluralism, Dialogue and Mission

M.M. Abraham

In today's world it has become almost impossible for any religious community to live in isolation and, therefore, we can no longer be indifferent to other religious groups. For a better world where everyone is free to believe in whichever religion he wants to believe, one has to seek the co-operation of others and try to find ways and means for a durable inter-religious harmony without injuring its interest in particular and the interests of others in general.

Anything less than a sincere desire for co-operation and a mutual application of each other's heritage, along with a conviction of equality of all as human being in the eyes of God, would fall short of the mark of achieving a peaceful world community. The task is difficult; it may be painful and it may even seem impossible; but it has to be done. There is nothing less at stake than the very future of the whole human race. We cannot turn our faces away from the followers of other religions. We have to meet each other, look into each other's eyes with an open heart.[1]

Arnold Toynbee, in his best known monumental twelve volume work *The Study of History* (1934-61), contends that civilizations rather than nations or periods are the most significant unit of historical study. He distinguishes twenty six of them in the history of the world. According to him, humankind could not convert to a 'syncretic' religion, constructed artificially out of elements taken from all the existing religions.[2] He cites the example of the Mughal emperor Akbar's attempt in India, in the early years of the seventeenth century, to create a new composite religion blending elements of Islam, Hinduism, Zoroastrianism, and Christianity, and the attempt of the Roman emperor Julian to reverse the triumph of Christianity in the Roman Empire by building up artificially a pagan counter-church in which he tried to weld together all the non-Christian religions in the Roman Empire. Neither of them ever captured the imagination, the feeling, and the allegiance of humankind. Toynbee asserted that it is notorious that such attempts have failed in the past, and they are also likely to fail in the future, as far as the past is any guide to the future.[3] So it may be expected and also may be hoped that all religions while retaining their historic identities, will become more and more open-minded, and open-hearted towards one another as the world's different cultural and spiritual heritages become the common possession of all humankind.

Religious Pluralism

Religious pluralism has always been a fact in history. In the past various religions existed in isolation from each other without serious encounter. They were almost indifferent to each other as long as they were faced with no serious threats to their existence from others. Today, the situation has drastically changed. There is an increasing awareness of the plurality of religions all over the world, especially in the Christian West. The term is used mainly in two senses. Firstly, it signifies a state of religious diversity within a society, a situation in which various religions exist and develop side by side. Secondly, it refers to a particular kind of response or attitude of an adherent of one religion towards another religion.[4]

It has been customary in recent literature on religious pluralism to distinguish between three broad perspectives on the relation of Christianity to other religions: exclusivism, inclusivism and pluralism. Exclusivism maintains that the central claims of Christianity are true and that where the claims of Christianity conflict with those of other religions the latter are to be rejected as false. Salvation is not to be found in the structures of other religious traditions. Inclusivism, like exclusivism, maintains that the central claims of Christian faith are true, but it adopts a much more positive view of other religions than does exclusivism. Although inclusivists hold that God has revealed himself definitively in Jesus Christ and that Jesus is somehow central to God's provision of salvation for humankind, they are willing to allow that salvation is available even through non-Christian religions. Pluralism deviates from both exclusivism and inclusivism by rejecting the premise that God has revealed himself in any unique or definitive sense in Jesus Christ. To the contrary, God is said to be actively revealing himself in all religious traditions. Pluralism then, goes beyond inclusivism in rejecting the idea that there is anything superior, normative, or definitive about Christianity. All religions are equally legitimate human responses to the same divine reality.[5]

There are clear signs of religious resurgence everywhere. Whether it is in Judaism or Islam or Hinduism in India, or Buddhism in Sri Lanka, or the traditional religions in Africa, dogmas are being questioned and structures are disintegrating but the core of different religions is becoming more alive. Even in socialist states where atheistic propaganda has gone on for many decades there are no signs of religions withering away. The recovery of religious values and their reinterpretation to meet contemporary needs sustain people in their struggles against meaninglessness and provide them with a vision for the future.[6] While the missionary movement planted churches throughout the world, other religions have not disappeared but have taken on new vitality and in some areas have expanded their influence. Ancient religions faced the challenge of western Christianity and culture and have renewed themselves, not by rejecting but by re-appropriating their own traditions. A renewed Hinduism, Buddhism and Islam have started small but highly visible counter missionary movements.

To acknowledge the fact of pluralism means that one cannot take shelter in neutral or objective ground. S. J. Samartha points out that there is no theological helicopter that can help us rise above all religions and to look down upon the terrain below in lofty condescension.[7] One is free to be a Christian; but by the same token his neighbour is also free to have his particular standpoint.

When the Christian Roman imperial government was forcibly closing the pagan temples and suppressing pagan forms of worship in the western part of the Roman Empire, the government ordered the removal, from the senate house of Rome, of the statue and altar of Victory that had been placed there by Julius Caesar. The spokesman of the senate Symmachus opposed this move but was beaten and silenced. Despite his opposition the authorities closed the temple and removed the statues. But, in one of his last pleas, Symmachus has put on record these words: "It is impossible that so great a mystery should be approached by one road only."[8] The mystery of which he is speaking is the mystery of the universe, the mystery of human's encounter with God. To suppress a rival religion is not an answer. The question raised by Symmachus is still alive in world history.

Inter-Religious Dialogue

A.J. Appasamy, a Bishop in the Church of South India during the fifties was one of the many who played a significant role in preparing the way for mutual understanding and respect between Christians and people of other faiths. His approach was positive and practical. He challenged the Christian community to get acquainted with the religious literature of India and appreciate their value and rethink and re-conceive the Christian way of life which was full of elements acquired from the West.[9]

Appasamy engaged himself in collecting and compiling selections from the Bhakti poems of India which he published with useful notes and an introduction under the title *The Temple Bells* (1930). This he wrote at a time when enlightened Christian as well as Hindu scholars were looking into the enormous scope available for meaningful understanding and appreciation of each other's religion. Appasamy challenges his Christian readers by saying:

> If we know a Hindu guru of spiritual power, we should sit at his feet and learn from him...too long have we considered Hindus as people to whom to lecture. Too long have they stood in the outer courts listening to our preaching, hearing our denunciation, resenting our criticism and attacking our argument. In the atmosphere of reverent worship many difficulties will disappear.[10]

Appasamy was consistent in advocating an indigenous Christian theology which could be enriched by Hindu Bhakti thought. Attracted by Hindu theism, he made a lifelong study of Ramanuja and published *The Theology of Hindu Bhakti* (1970). The Bhakti elements in the Upanishads, the Gita, the Bhagavata Purana and the Tamil Saivite and Vaishnavite literatures are dealt with at length in this book. The doctrines of immanence and grace of God together with the related concepts of self-surrender, the missionary zeal and the fellowship motif found in Hindu Bhakti literature appealed to Appasamy and were commended by him for responsible study and reflection by Indian Christians.

Appasamy recognised long ago that mutual complementation and re-conception are possible only when conviction and tolerance go hand in hand. As one who was interested in the blending together of the meditative and action-motivated aspects of Bhakti in the Christian context, Appasamy did show interest in inspiring and encouraging Christian in India to reach the level of contribution in inter-religious affairs. He insisted on Christian cooperation and collaboration for nation building activities and urged them to protest against various kinds of social evils. Appasamy certainly deserves to be regarded as a Christian forerunner and prophet of the emerging inter-faith dialogue in India.

Samartha states:

> A particular religion can claim to be decisive for some people, and some people can claim that a particular religion is decisive for them, but no religion is justified in claiming that it is decisive for all. The Hindus and the Christians have their own particularly distinctive contributions to make to the common quest for truth.[11]

Adherents of other religions are not to be regarded as spiritually lost, in need of salvation through the atoning death of Jesus Christ, but rather as already enjoying a saving relationship with God. To be sure, as Christians we must be faithful to our commitment to Jesus Christ and must engage in 'witness' concerning our fundamental beliefs. But such witness should not have as its goal the conversion of the other person. The time has come for restating the meaning of mission in multi-religious contexts, taking into account the integrity of the other faiths.

Following the lead of Vatican II, Pope John Paul II, in his encyclical *Redemptor Hominis*, affirmed that religion is a universal phenomenon linked with humankind's history and consequently that we should impose no strict limits in its exploration. For John Paul II, openness to other religions is not a betrayal of commitment but often a call to faith. He says:

> The firm belief of the followers of non-Christian religions – a belief that is also an effect of the spirit operating outside the visible confines of the mystical body – can make Christians ashamed at being often themselves so disposed to doubt concerning the truths revealed by God.[12]

Pope John Paul II rejects past references to non-Christians as heathens, pagans or enemies of God. While upholding that Christians must be witness to the special revelation of God in Christ, he calls on them to respect all that the spirit, who 'blows where it wills' (John 3:8), has done in members of other religious faiths through general revelation.

Although Muslims consider themselves in the line of faith of Abraham, many Christians do not consider them as such. However, Pope John Paul II clarified this ambiguity in his discourse to the catholic community in Ankara

(3 December 1979) when he said unequivocally, "They have, like you, the faith of Abraham in the one, almighty and merciful God." In his message to the president of Palestine (23 February 1981) John Paul II referred to Abraham as "to whose faith Christians, Muslims and Jews eagerly link their own." And in Lisbon (14 May 1982) he said: "And Abraham, our common forefather, teaches all Christians, Jews and Muslims to follow the path of mercy and love."[13] Moreover, John Paul II, in his address to young Muslims at Casablanca (19 August 1985), made it explicit that Muslims are not Ishmaelites or Hagarenes to be excluded from the covenant, not heretics or schismatics, but members of a community of faith with Christians.

Attempting to promote dialogue and interfaith harmony during or soon after a conflict, though it has its own limited value, is a frustrating exercise. Communities by now are deeply polarised, confused and uncertain about who can be trusted. Solidarity with another community is often misunderstood as betrayal. Dialogue, thus, is an attempt to help people to understand and accept the other in their 'otherness.' It seeks to make people 'at home' with plurality, to develop an appreciation of diversity and to make those links that may just help them to hold together when the whole community is threatened by force of separation and anarchy.[14]

Dialogue and Mission

According to Mark the purpose of Jesus' coming is to announce the kingdom of God, which is at the centre of Jesus's message and ministry (Mk. 1:15). The reign of God, its nearness and its actual breaking in are the central themes of his preaching (Lk. 4:16-22). Hence the disciples of Jesus today need to see mission as dialogue in the general Asian and particular Indian context of religiosity and human situation. Religious pluralism provides an opportunity for a new united witness to the whole of humanity.

The Indian church cannot be in mission without dialogue. As Samartha says: "Dialogue is not a concept; it is a relationship. Community is not a concept; it is people, men and women, sharing the meaning and mystery of human existence, struggling together in suffering, hope and joy."[15]

Such a dialogue in community or a dialogue of life takes place in markets, street corners, during festivals and holy days. It needs to be extended to humanitarian projects as an effective weapon against crises in community and society. Thus, people, their world, and their problems are the starting point of dialogue.

Dialogue is inevitable because everywhere in the world Christians are now living in a pluralistic society. It is urgent because all humankind are under common pressures in the search for justice, peace and a hopeful future and all are faced with the challenge to live together as human beings. It is full of opportunity because Christians can now as never before, discover the meaning of the Lordship of the church in a truly universal context of common living and common urgency. Dialogues, designed to get to the deepest levels of commitment and directed to the most serious exploration of common action are, therefore, a clear human demand at this hour of human history.

In the context of dialogue with people of other faiths, which demands genuine openness on both sides, the Christian is free to bear witness to the risen Christ, just as his partners of another faith are free to witness to what is most important in his own existence. Peter's words to Cornelius are significant: "truly I perceive that God shows no partiality, but in every nation anyone who fears him [sic] and does what is right is acceptable to him" (Acts 10: 34-35). God is at work among all humankind and God speaks to a Cyrus and a Cornelius and bids them to do God's will.[16]

Each Christian community involved in dialogue is thus in a particular situation and has a specific partner or partners. Since however, at the same time, it is part of the universal church, it is involved in the calling of the whole church to work for the unity of mankind. For this reason, Christians have a responsibility to seek dialogue at the world level, as well as in regional groups and in particular localities.

In seeking this positive relationship the fact has to be faced that there are those Christians who fear that dialogue with people of other faiths is a betrayal of mission. There are people of other faiths who suspect that dialogue is simply a new tool for mission. If the fears of such Christians are to be allayed it would seem that the suspicions of people of other faiths are to be justified. There should be understanding of mission which neither betrays the commitment of the Christian nor exploits the confidence and the reality of people of other faiths.[17]

For a Christian, faith involves both relationship to God through Jesus Christ and a way of understanding God, humankind and the world. The Christian understanding and working out of dialogue will therefore be on the basis of that relationship and that understanding. Hence dialogue with people of other faiths will be understood and practised by Christians as part of the experiment of faith and as a living out of faith. We seek to place the faith of Christians and the mission of the church in a positive relationship to the faiths of other people and the commitment to mission which they may draw from their respective faiths. The mission of the church stems from and is concerned with the activity of God for the salvation of the whole world.

The positive recognition of world religions as ways of salvation and the call to collaborate with their followers is a great shift in the church from conquest to dialogue. This dialogue is understood as an attitude of life and love, and as a way of sharing our vision and mission. In the context of cultural and religious pluralism, including tribal religions, "Dialogue is a pilgrimage towards the fullness of life and truth, through mutual communication, which demands a deep commitment to one's own faith and genuine openness to that of the other."[18]

A believer's dialogue with another believer becomes a dialogue with another religious community. Such a meeting between believers cannot be a mere theological or spiritual exchange without a living witness of involvement. Hence these encounters with various religious paths not only deepen and strengthen our faith but also pave the way for inter-religious co-operation for social change.[19] It is at any rate clear that the relation of the Christian faith to people of other faiths, and the continuing of the Christian mission to and among people who also believe they have a mission will require much sensitivity, exploration and reflection.

Dialogue, therefore, is clearly part of mission and is to be undertaken within the context of God's mission. All missions in fact require this approach of openness to and respect for the other. This respect must involve our openness to the other including being open to the realities and possibilities of his mission to us. Hence dialogue cannot either be a new tool for old forms of mission which involve dominance, or a dishonest means of getting into contact with a view to a conversion which does not take the other partners seriously. Nor can it be a betrayal of the Christian mission. For dialogue between Christians and people of other faiths, being understood within the context of God's mission to all humankind, stems from love and is seeking the fruit of love. True love never only gives. It is also concerned always to receive. For love is a relationship and a power of mutual respect. Love therefore is concerned always with the reality, the freedom and the fulfilment of the other.[20]

Religions are the result of an on-going dialogue between God and the human person. Christianity is a religion which has at its core this divine-human dialogue expressed in Jesus, who in turn dialogued with his situation and transformed it. Jesus began a movement to continue this dialogue and transformation which we call the church (Matt. 16:18). The call of the church is to love in the midst of pluralism, understanding the work of the Holy Spirit in the church and the activity of God's spirit among people of different religious traditions and ideological persuasions.

Dialogue is at the core of missionary activity, which attempts to bring about God's plan for humankind's communion with him and the unity of all peoples of the earth, as Paul explains (Eph. 1: 1-10). Taking up the suggestion of Karl Rahner that in Vatican II the church is becoming a world church with the awareness of a community-in-Diaspora which is everywhere. Michael Amaladoss speaks of a paradigm shift in the theology of evangelization: "The theology of evangelization is undergoing a Copernican revolution, under the impact of a positive experience of other religions. The centre of the framework is shifting from the Church to the Kingdom."[21]

The WCC central committee at its 1979 meeting at Kingston commended dialogue as one way in which Jesus Christ can be confessed in the world today. In the same year Pope John Paul II said, "It is my hope and my desire that commitment to dialogue ... should be strengthened throughout the church, including the countries where there is a Christian majority."[22] And the Pope instructed the Indian Bishops: "The lord calls you, especially in the particular circumstances in which you are placed, to do everything possible to promote Dialogue according to the commandment of the church."[23]

One of the theological insights of second Vatican Council is that God's salvific presence penetrates all cultures and human realities, and is not found only in the visible church. This positive view of other religions permeates the Vatican documents especially those dealing with the modern world, ecumenism and world religions. In the last document Christians are exhorted to dialogue and to collaborate with followers of other religions for "the catholic church rejects nothing of what is true and holy in these religions. She has a high regard for the manner of life and conduct, the precepts and doctrines which....reflects a ray of that truth which enlightens all."[24]

Dialogue is only possible if we proceed from the belief that we are not moving into a void that we go expecting to meet the God who preceded us and has been preparing people within the context of their own cultures and convictions. God has already removed the barriers; his spirit is constantly at work in ways that pass human understanding. We do not have in our pocket; he accompanies us and also comes towards us. We are not the "haves" standing over against spiritual "have not's." We are all recipients of the same mercy, sharing in the same mystery. We thus approach every other faith and its adherents reverently, taking off our shoes, as the place we are approaching is holy.[25] Both dialogue and mission can be conducted only in an attitude of humility.

An inter-religious spirituality provides an appropriate platform for people of different religions in our country to work together to bring about a human social order that is in the spirit of Christ's vision of the Kingdom of God. In this kingdom, rivalry, conflict and exclusivism that so often mar the relationship among followers of different religions today have no place. It is our Christian task and responsibility to promote and accelerate the process of the emergence of such an inter-religious spirituality, the breeding ground of which is the existing religious pluralism itself.

Endnotes

[1] Ziaul Hasan Faruqi, "Ways and Means of Inter-Religious Harmony and Reconciliation," in *The Bulletin* ii/4 (October-December, 1979): 4.

[2] Arnold Toynbee, *Christianity Among the Other Religions of the World* (New York: Charles Scribner's Sons, 1957), 83-112, quoted by Owen C. Thomas, ed., *Attitudes Towards Other Religions* (London: SCM Press Ltd., 1969), 166.

[3] Toynbee, *Christianity among the Other Religions of the World*, 166-167.

[4] P.S. Daniel, *Hindu Response to Religious Pluralism* (Delhi: Kant Publication, 2000), 13-14.

[5] Harold A. Netland, *Dissonant Voices* (England: Apollos, 1991), 9-10.

[6] Gerald H. Anderson, ed., *Christ's Lordship and Religious Pluralism* (New York: Orbis Books, 1983), 21.

[7] Anderson, ed., *Christ's Lordship and Religious Pluralism*, 29.

[8] Toynbee, *Christianity among the Other Religions of the World*, 171.

[9] T. Dayanandan Francis, *A.J. Appasamy: A Christian Forerunner of Inter-Religious Dialogue in India* (Madras: The C.L.S, 1991), 1.

[10] Francis, *A.J. Appasamy: A Christian Forerunner of Inter-Religious Dialogue in India*, 4-6.

[11] S.J. Samartha, *Courage for Dialogue*: Ecumenical Issues in Inter-religious Relationships (Maryknoll: Orbis Books, 1982), 153.

[12] Ovey N. Mohamed, *Muslim-Christian Relations* (New York: Orbis Books, 1999), 59.

[13] Mohamed, *Muslim-Christian Relations*, 60.

[14] S. Wesley Ariarajah, *Not Without My Neighbor* (Geneva: W.C.C Publication, 1999), 14.

[15] Joy Thomas, "Dialogue as Mission," in *Dimensions of Mission in India*, edited by Joseph Mattam (Bombay: Saint Paul Society, 1995), 118.

[16] S.J. Samartha, ed., *Living Faiths* (Geneva: World Council of Churches, 1971), 34.

[17] Samartha, ed., *Living Faiths*, 36.

[18] Thomas, "Dialogue as Mission," in *Dimensions of Mission in India*, 112.

[19] Samartha, ed., *Living Faiths*, 37.

[20] Samartha, ed., *Living Faiths*, 38.

[21] Thomas, "Dialogue as Mission," in *Dimensions of Mission in India*, 116.

[22] Vatican Secretariat Bulletin, nos. 41 & 42, April 28, 1979.

[23] Thomas, "Dialogue as Mission," in *Dimensions of Mission in India*, 111.

[24] Thomas, "Dialogue as Mission," in *Dimensions of Mission in India*, 112.

[25] David J. Bosch, *Transforming Mission* (New York: Orbis Books, 1995), 484.

The Ultimate Experience: The Ways of the West and the East

Raimon Panikkar

'Religious Experience' is a common topic of today's concern. The Ultimate Experience is the title of this study. If both topic and title do not say the same, they are at least so closely related; that the latter is religious almost by definition and most probable also religious experience is to be considered as ultimate, even if it allows for other types of experiences. In order to expose with a certain order the core, and obviously only the core, of the question, we shall consider, first the meaning of experience; second, with ultimate can possible mean in the case and thirdly, some of the different ways of expressing it. If I were to follow a more congenial way of putting the problem, I would simply say: the Myth, the Logos and the Spirit.

The Problem of Experience – The Myth

Prolegomena

The question about the nature and value of experience arises at the very moment when we begin to think about our experience. But then we no longer experience: we think, or simply we remember. Or even more generally expressed: the awareness of an experience is not the experience. And even more: an experience cannot be experienced. Experiencing, unlike thinking, does not allow for self-reflection. That is its strength and its weakness at the same time. This implies that the talk and the reflection about experience have necessarily to be non-experiential.

By experience we may understand any immediate contact with reality. Or, again, experience is that opening of the human being by which the distance between the subject and the object tends asymptotically to zero. The perfect experience would be that experience in which this distance is actually zero: no difference, no distinction whatsoever between the experiencing subject and the experienced object.

For the sake of situating the place of experience in human life and not with the claim of stating a full-fledged anthropological theory, we may assume that man has three organs, or groups of organs, relating him with reality: the senses, the intellect and another peculiar faculty, which we may call the mystical consciousness. All there are forms of consciousness, i.e., openings or windows on to reality.

The sensuous consciousness relates us by means or our sense organs, to what we could call the material part of reality. The intellectual consciousness opens us up to the intelligible world, to that web of relations which give consistence to the material world and which we cannot equate with mere matter. The mystical consciousness identifies us in a very special way to the very reality which it opens up to us. With whatever name we may like to describe these facts there seems to be no doubt about the existence of these three stages of consciousness. Whatever interpretation we may give to the reality opened up in each case there would not seem to be much disagreement in saying that those three degrees of consciousness are ultimately not independent windows but three dimensions of one and the same primordial consciousness, of which the sensual, intellectual and mystical consciousness are different forms. In other words, consciousness may be the window relating us to reality, only if seen from our particular perspective. Otherwise, consciousness may be described as the common, light, reality itself, which the window allows to go in and out.

Now, both reductionisms are equally one-sided at that reducing reality to the mere subject, thus denying the objective sphere and that of reducing reality to mere objectivity, thus, ignoring the subjective world. The senses are not only 'knowing' instruments, they are also acting tools. This is to say that they are also part of the same reality which they disclose. The intellect is not only a knowing mind either; it is an acting will also. This is to say that the intellectual web of reality is not just a private property of the individual, but a common feature in which others participate. The mystical consciousness is not mainly a source of knowledge for somebody, but an aspect of reality itself, which discloses itself when it becomes patent to a particular subject.

There is no need to interpret what has been said so far in an epistemic realistic sense: it has meaning and validity also within other epistemologies and within more than one metaphysical system. We do not affirm here that reality is or whether those human experiences have objective truth or not. We only offer a general pattern capable of being accepted by many different cultural and philosophical backgrounds.

What has been stressed however is a Unitarian character of this trinity, i.e., the fact that any human act of consciousness has to a greater or lesser degree the three above mentioned dimensions. When we call a human act a sensory activity or an intellectual action or a mystical awareness we are actually abstracting, i.e., considering only one aspect of a more complex and tri-Unitarian fact, which includes all in one the sensual, the intellectual and the mystical.

In the light of this we may call consciousness 'that bridge between the two shores of reality, the subject and the object.' This bridge connects these two shores by means of one of the three ways of that unique bridge: an upper level of a sensorial two-way-traffic between subject and object: a deeper intellectual level, predominantly a one-way track from the object to the subject, and the very columns of the bridge itself connecting the two shores in an all-embracing manner. On the first level we act; on the second we understand; on the third we are. What has been just said does not exclude the view that the bridge is actually more real than the two shores—or even that it is the whole reality.

Whereas the concept of consciousness may be used to stress the overall character of this process of discovering reality and the supra-individual aspect of the same phenomenon, the concept of experience stands for the peculiar distinctive feature of the individual taking part in that process. Whereas consciousness is something in which we share, experience is something peculiar to and particular to every one of us. We may almost say that by definition experience is the individualistic and peculiar way of sharing in a given state of consciousness.

With these clarifications we may now proceed to our task of describing what can be understood by ultimate Experience.

The Empirical, the Experiment and the Experience

The history of human civilisation could be considered under the perspective of one or the other of these three variations of the same basic concept, the basic concept being personal realisation or, following the common etymological root, the attempt at integrating ourselves into reality by passing through whatever process is needed.[1] We could call them *kairological* moments, for obviously there is no question of considering them as chronological divisions.

There is a first period in the history of humankind and one is tempted to say that there is equally a first period in the development of human consciousness, historical and personal, in which given data are uncritically assumed and taken as bare facts. That which is given, especially what is given to our senses, is taken as real. The empirical here does not mean only sense-knowledge. The philosophically uncritical mind takes equally for granted, that what appears to it is a given. And the mystical vision is also unreflective. It is the ecstatic vision, the overwhelming presence of the object, with forgetfulness about the subject: it is the awareness of presence without the cloud of self-awareness. In religion, philosophy and art we could substantiate this period recalling the beginnings of almost any culture.

The second moment is represented by the predominance of the experiment. A certain doubt about the value of the objectivity has crept in; human has become more conscious about himself/herself and realizes that he/she cannot leave the external subject untouched and unreflected upon. The doubt has to be checked by abandoning the passive attitude of the contemplator and taking a more active and aggressive approach; the experiment, the trial, the test, the intervention in the object itself. It is the period of the critical awareness. This is felt on all the three levels of consciousness. The experimental sciences make their appearance. In order to know what a thing is, mere observation is not considered enough. But the experiment is not limited to the object alone; it is also performed on the subject itself. Men begin to analyse the human mind and the whole spiritual organism. To the physical experiment in the natural sciences corresponds the internal experiments of critical philosophy and the psychological introspection of the mystics. The European Renaissance offers us a typical example: We have here a flourishing of experimentation on the three levels of consciousness. Not only the human body and the celestial bodies are examined, but also the human mind and spirit are submitted to the scrutinizing process of experimentation. There is one and the same wind blowing in Leonardo de Vinci, Luther, St. Theresa, Galileo and Descartes, the quote only a few names from very different fields.

The third moment is the obvious result of the same continuing process. Human has lost confidence in his first empirical data; he/she asks for criteria of truth, of verification and is ready to accept only that which sees for himself/herself. But the experiment is still too impersonal, too objective, and too reliant on the objective methods of the experiment or it requires still a certain confidence in shell, awareness and judgements of others. Human will not be satisfied until he/she experiences it by himself/herself. Only individual experience cannot err; only if he makes the experience for himself will he be convinced that such is the case.

The empirical is pure objectivity; the experiment blends the object with subjectivity; the experience abolishes any kind of objectivity not assumed and integrated in the subjectivity. Anybody today asking for an experience of whatever kind, biological, psychological, scientific or religious is saying that he does not care for objectivity or for how others judge, see or sense things. He has to have an individual involvement which is only possible if the experience is there. One cannot have an experience by proxy.

The Myth

Experience implies in consequence not only the in transferable and individualistic contact with the experienced object but it excludes also any type of intermediaries, which would be a third party making the experience impossible and reverting it to an experiment, which is always done by means of instruments. This implies, further, that any experience worthy of the name excludes and consciousness of any distance between the object and the subject. That the object is no longer envisaged as such, but as totally united with or plunged into the subject.

The difference between knowing about pain or God or love and experiencing pain, God or love is obvious. My ideas about any object may be correct, checked, changed and eventually abandoned as inaccurate or wrong. There is a distance between the subject and the object, which permits such modifications in the object without endangering the subject. Not so with any experience, as long as it is my experience. When I experience pain it is no doubt possible that I am in pain, even if I am convinced that there is no external or organic cause or mental reason for it. I can doubt whether to make this or the other choice as long as I am guided by anything short of experience. I may have to ponder and decide according to common sense, reasons instincts or the like as long as I do not have an experience which renders any further doubt or hesitation impossible. But when experience dawns, it is incontrovertible. There is no real dialogue possible between experiences.

What we have to underscore here is its mythical character, which amounts to recognizing its primordial and irreducible nature. Any experience, sensory, intellectual or mystical is in fact, a myth. It performs, to begin with the same function and it presents the same structure.

One of the functions of myth, as the function of experience, is to allow us to stop somewhere and thus to rest in our quest for the foundations of everything. Otherwise there would be a *regressus in infinitum* (process of going back endlessly). You cannot go beyond a myth as you cannot go beyond experience without destroying them. That is to say, that what you really transcend is for you no longer a myth or an experience, but a mythological content or a remembrance of an experience. If you could go beyond them they would lose the immediacy which is part of their own essence and there would be neither myth nor experience. Both do not allow for further explanation. The moment you explain a myth it ceases to be such; the moment you explain an experience it is no longer an experience. Both do not allow for *becauses* and *therefores*, they are ultimate. Any demythologization destroys the myth as any explanation destroys the experience. Both, myth and experience are taken for granted when they are actually taken as myth and experience. If one feels the need for some justification they have ceased to be what they were. Neither mythic consciousness nor experiential consciousness allows room for critical self-awareness. They are at opposite poles. If metaphysics implies self-awareness and if philosophy is critical knowledge, then both myth and experience are neither metaphysics not philosophy; but perhaps these both latter rely on and are based on the former pair.

Both myth and experience present the same structure. In the myth as in the experience, there is no distance between the subject and the object. You are in the myth as you are in the experience. You live in them or rather you *live* them. You believe in the myth as you believe in the experience, without being aware in both cases in that you really believe i.e. you believe in them, but you do not believe that you believe in them. Both present a kind of similar receding structure, i.e., they altogether disappear when challenged or endangered. When visited by the logos that questions their validity or asks for their justification, they simply *retrocede*, they recede to a deeper level, and to another region still untouched be the invading light of the critical reasons or the rational mind. The relations between science and religion offer us constant examples of those strategic retreats.

Our main concern, however, is not to draw a sketch of their resemblances, but to point out the fact that among the many myths, experience is one of them and probably one of the most important and invariant ones.

No myth can be explained without being explained away, Mythology, if it were understood as the analysis or even justification of the myth by the logos, would be a contradiction in terms, because it would destroy the very myth it wants to explain. Another thing altogether is the telling of the myths, the '*mythes logein*' over against the 'mythology'. Here the original connection between word and myth is brought again to light and the mythical roots of language appear in the very telling of myths.

What we can do in our particular case is then to tell the myth of the experience, i.e., the story of the human being believing that he/she has direct contact with reality, that he/she can participate not only in the ontic celebration of beings, but also in the ultimate worship of Being, that he/she has an immediacy which vouches for a direct contact with the real and that therefore once he/she has reached the experiential level he/she can stop and rest. The myth of experience is another more subtle form of the myth of heaven and of the celestial paradise; it is sophisticated form of the myth of the ultimate.

It goes without saying that myths do not need to be overcome. Even when we overcome one myth, another one creeps in its place, though perhaps at a deeper level. What really goes on in that so popular nowadays process of demythologization is simply a dynamics of trans-mythologization, a kind of mythical metamorphosis, where obsolete and anachronistic myths give place to more modern and up-to-date myths. These new myths, obviously, like the old myths, for those who believed in them, are not seen as myths by the new believers.

We may sum up this first section by saying that any experience is to be considered ultimate because experience means immediate contact with the real and thus there is no possibility of going beyond it without destroying the experience.

The Quest for the Supreme Experience – The Logos

The Loss of the Subject

Human history, both collective and personal, proves that what at one certain period was considered to be ultimate or immediate, later on was discovered to be mediate and thus, neither final nor ultimate. Innocence is lost at the moment when one is deceived. What then is the value of experience once you cannot have the conviction that experience is going to be the last one, the final and definitive one? In other words, what happens to experience once it is demythologized? The process is worth analysing. No experience which is genuinely an experience can have any criterion of its validity and authenticity outside itself. Any experience is self-validating or it is not an experience at all.

Now we have two logical possibilities. Either we say that the experience is the same, even when we see it changing, or we appeal to the historical dimension of man. In the first hypothesis the change is said to have taken place in the interpretation of the experience, but not in the experience itself. In the second hypothesis we have to pay the price of abandoning any possible objective criterion. In other words, either we say that the experience is a temporal, and thus everlasting, though our interpretation depends on the cultural degree, the historical moment. Etc., or we affirm that the experience is intrinsically temporal which amounts to saying that human, and eventually the whole reality, is essentially temporal.

The first hypothesis has the obvious difficulty of stating a fact for which there is no direct evidence whatsoever; it is an a priori derived from a certain world view; the second hypothesis has the inconvenience that it seems to fall into a total anarchy, for there seems to be no guarantee that the human experiences are going to offer any coherence and continuity along the temporal line. There is no reason why what is experienced today as positive, as valuable and as immediately evident is not going to appear tomorrow as utterly untenable.

Is there any way out of the dilemma of a timeless rigidity of everlasting values and a chaotic revolution of sheer relativism? The quest for the ultimate experience seems to be relevant here. If this is the case, we shall have another example of how the apparently most abstract and theoretical speculation can have practical and concrete relevance. Are we not asking ourselves, among other questions whether there is no middle way between a Maoist way of constant revolution and the liberal or capitalistic solution of unchanging abstract principles which take care of themselves if only allowed to develop unhindered? We are asking whether this middle way exists without being either a betrayal or a compromise.

But before embarking on such problems we should go back to our philosophical analysis of human experience.

Let me ask myself the simple question: when do I begin to doubt the validity of my experience? If our description of what an experience is correct, there can only be one answer: I doubt about the validity of my experience, only when I cease to have that experience, as long as I have an experience I cannot doubt it. I begin to doubt when I begin to wonder whether what I am having is an experience or not. This occurs in the first place when I realize the experience as experience, for then I am no longer having the pure experience. When the experience becomes aware of itself as an experience it ceases to be an experience, and becomes a reflective consciousness of the experience that I am having. The experience of prayer, like the experience of pain, like the experience of intellectual evidence, like any real experience of love, is incompatible with the awareness that I am having that experience. In other words, when the logos enter into the experience so as to make possible the sort of self-awareness which is peculiar to the intellect, the experience is no longer pure experience.

Let us imagine that we are having an aesthetic experience contemplating the beauty of a landscape. The moment that I become aware that I am having such an experience or that it is through the eye, that I am seeing and having that experience I have lost the real experience: I have become aware of an intermediary which I did not consider before. Rather, there was no intermediary until I become conscious of there being one. The intermediate image in my retina through which I see is at the same time the means that separates that which it unites. In a word, no critical awareness is capable of being an experience, because it belongs to the essence of criticism to be conscious of itself.

We could prolong and deepen this analysis, but its thrust is already visible. The main question now is that of so many cultures and religions: Is there any possible experience which does not allow for such destructive self-awareness? Could there be an experience in which the self that experiences is the same as the experience itself?

We could try to formulate this question in all its universality by asking whether it is possible to have the experience of the self itself i.e., of the I, the ultimate subject of any experience. We have already seen that in any real experience the object is lost. The ultimate experience would be that experience in which the subject is equally lost.

We should not, at this stage, commit the methodological mistake of trying to describe such an experience by relying on a particular interpretation of its contents, say in a theistic world-view, for instance. We have to remain on purely formalistic grounds.

Yes, we may perhaps describe it by leaning on a particular tradition in as far as the terminology goes, but without implying any allegiance to that particular way. If I see the landscape or smell the flower or think the thought or will the action or understand the situation, I may have an experience of those objects when they merge into me so that there is no longer any distinction. But there is always the possibility of coming back, as certain mysticism would say, because, whereas in the experience the object is lost in the subject, this latter one is not lost, nor is the identification total in either direction that of the object to the subject and that of the subject to the object. How can I see (understand, discover) that by seeing (understanding, discovering) which all the rest becomes seen (understood, discovered)?

By what would one know the knower? The difficulty is clear: You cannot see the seer of seeing; you cannot think the thinker of thinking. How can you know the knower? That knower which you might eventually know, by this very fact would no longer be the knower but the 'known'—by you.

To be sure, there is one way by which this question may be answered. Undoubtedly not by knowing the knower or understanding the understander, but by being oneself the knower and understander. This is the only way in which the experience cannot cancel itself, not by mere reaching identification with the object experienced but becoming the experience itself, the knower, the understander.

The supreme experience is neither supreme not experience. It is not supreme, because it is not the superior or the first one among many. It is not experience either because there is no subject experiencing an object. Not only the distance between the two is zero, there is no remnant of any 'support' in either side. The union means here an ontic explosion (of both).

The Experience, its Expression and Interpretation

We should not too easily assume that the supreme experience or any experience for that matter is totally independent of its expression or that its interpretation is equally irrelevant to the experience itself. Even if this be the case it would not be an evident case.

It is one of the most common affirmation regarding this type of problems to repeat time and again that the authentic experience is ineffable, that those who know do not speak and those who speak do not know, that those who understand do not understand it and those who do not understand it do understand it; the experience which utters itself tells a lie, the experience which can be named is no longer the real experience, etc.

First of all, we have to remark that to assert that something is unspeakable does not need to mean that any way of pointing to it is a contradiction. It may be that no words can communicate what is, but not all communication needs to be verbal. To affirm that some reality is unthinkable amounts to recognising that thinking does not exhaust the realm of being. To assert that the ultimate experience goes beyond being, because it has left all being behind, amounts to confessing that beings are a relative reality that the spatial metaphor of the 'beyond' is pointing towards a real leaving behind all reality, if the words are interpreted in their thrust and not in their meaning.

Secondly, we have to become aware of the implications of the dichotomy between the experience and its expression. We understand by expression the manifestation of the experience, i.e., its first emanation ad extra, its first result, as it were, so that the act of the experience could not be said to be solipsistic act with no repercussion or irradiation outside itself. It is there that the place and function of memory becomes central for an integral anthropology.

And finally we must also distinguish the expression from its interpretation, this latter being the intellectual explanation of the experience as it is understood by our intellect.

If we accept those three degrees of consciousness mentioned earlier, we can easily see an interesting correlation between each one of these three stages. On the one side, there is a correlation between, the interpretation and the intellectual consciousness. The expression of manifestation of experience would correspond to the sensorial consciousness. We may understand by this latter not only the traditional sense organs but our whole body complex, so that the manifestation of the experience does not need to be a word or even a sound but may be the more primordial expression of it in our whole body, in our terrestrial and temporal life. The experience itself would then correspond to what we called the mystical consciousness. If this were the case, we would then have also met the difficulty of the so-called ineffability of the real experience. It would be inexpressible in terms of our sensorial and intellectual consciousness but it would correspond to mystical consciousness which evidently does not translate itself in any other form or take any other name, being itself the act which gives name and form to everything.

But be this as it may, we ought not to distinguish so much as to break the ultimate unity of reality. We should not lose sight of the underlying unity between the three stage of consciousness, and the three modes of realisation: the experience, the manifestation and its interpretation. It is here that we should introduce that concept which seems to be an adequate carrier of all the burden of the three worlds: the *symbol*.

By way of summary, we may state that the symbol stands for the whole of reality as it appears and manifests itself in the manifold way of its structure. A symbol is precisely the thing, but not the "thing in itself," which is an abstraction of the mind, but the thing as it appeals, as it expresses and manifests itself. The symbol of a thing is neither another thing nor the "thing in itself" but the very thing as it manifests itself, as it is in the world of beings., in the epiphany of the 'is'. Contemporary philosophy speaks of the ontological or transcendental difference, that of beings and their entity, of the theological or transcendent difference, that of God and beings, including even the so-called widely ontological or, 'transcendentable' difference, that of beings along with their entity and Being. We could, analogously, introduce here the *symbolic* difference, as the *sui generis* difference between the symbol and its reality. The symbol is not another reality, it is not another thing, nor the thing as we may imagine that it is in a non-existent ideal realm, but it is the thing as it really appears, as it really 'is' in the realm of beings. The symbol is nothing but the symbol of the thing, that is (subjective genitive), the peculiar mode of being that very thing, which outside its symbolic form is not and cannot be; because, ultimately, being is nothing but the symbol of its self. To be able to discover the symbolic difference, i.e., to discover me as symbol of myself, or, in other words, to realize that my existence is one of the real symbols of the I, (certainly not of my ego), could perhaps be said to be one of the ways to reach the supreme experience.

The Supreme Experience
If all that has been said so far makes some sense, the supreme experience will be synonymous with pure consciousness and pure consciousness will stand for reality inasmuch as only consciousness makes room for the plurality of the sense-experience and the multiplicity of the intellectual-experience without tainting the oneness of the mystical-experience. Consciousness and consciousness alone, allows the harmonious blending between the many and the one: the many states of consciousness and the fact of being conscious of the multiplicity does not make consciousness multiple; on the contrary it reinforces, as it were, its primordial oneness.

The supreme experience would then be that experience which is so identified with reality itself that it is nothing but the same reality. It is not the highest among the experiences; it does not experience anything. It recovers the lost innocence in a way that is not even comparable to the original one. The original innocence had no knowledge of good and evil, nor properly any experience of the manifold in its excruciating diversity, division and tension; it was a kind of blessed ignorance, what we still today call innocence. The recovery of innocence is properly speaking not a recovery, but a creation, a state, which cannot be called new, because it does not substitute an old or decrepit state for another "new" one, but 'discovers' the ever-lasting, i.e., ever-changing 'newness' of reality.

The supreme experience is not an experience either in the sense in which we may use the word in all other cases. Not only is the object lost, but also the subject is no longer there as substratum of basis for the experience. No human can have pure consciousness. It would be no longer pure if it has a foundation in any subject. It cannot be self-consciousness either, if we understand by this any type of reflective consciousness upon the self. We could call it rather self-unconsciousness, precisely because it is mere consciousness: awareness that it is not aware that it is aware, an infinite ignorance.

One way of describing the supreme experience with the minimum of philosophical assumptions could perhaps take the following form.

Let us begin with any experience, with perhaps the simplest of all of them: I am touching an object. I am having the branch of a tree in my hand: I am pressing and caressing it, I may like to bite it and to smell and taste it eventually. My thinking is absent for the moment and my mystical awareness also. I am lost in that contact with a piece of nature. This is a sensual experience. But this experience does not last for ever. Perhaps an impertinent fly disturbs me in my 'distraction', or a fleeting thought crosses my mind, or my body reminds me of the hour. I still want to remain in communion with that branch, but I have discovered, first, that neither the object nor the subject were pure, total and exhaustive. The branch is not the whole tree and much less the whole of nature; my hands and all my senses are not the whole of my being and much less the whole of all the other possible subjects. I would like to cling to my branch and I may begin to mediate upon it, to concentrate not only my senses but also my mind and even my will upon the branch. If I succeed, I may reach another type of experience in which the moment I may be identified with the branch and if I am lost deep enough in the branch my identification may not stop at the branch, which I may no longer experience as branch, but with a great part of nature, with the whole vegetal life eventually. For a moment there may be identification between me and the whole nature. It is not the branch that I touch, but the whole natural world that I embrace.

But my experience does not need to stop here. It may grow in both directions, in the loosing of the object until reaching also the other pole of the totality, as it were. Perhaps with the branch it may become a little difficult, but surely not impossible. I may have to leave the woods and throw the branch away, but I may equally go back to the branch though now no longer as branch but as the whole tree and the entire wood and the universe in its totality, which I cannot touch with my hands, not feel with my sentiments, but somehow enter with my whole being, a concrete mirror and reflection of the whole. I may lose myself in such an experience and perhaps more than one expert will tell me that I have had an experience of nature mysticism.

But this is not all. We may assume that I believe in a personal God. This would allow for another type of experience, which some may call the vision of God. But I do not need to assume, for my general description, that I am a theist or an atheist and I am convinced that the experience may be the same, even if its interpretation differs.

The contact with the branch may be so intense and profound that what I am in contact with is not a bundle of electrons with the configuration of a branch, but that primordial matter in which all material things have their share. Now entering in immediate contact with this primordial matter, I am also in immediate contact with the very ground of being which gives consistency and existence to that primal matter. Some may call it God, some may not. In any case I am in direct contact with the ultimate reality of that branch, which has to do ultimately with the same reality of everything. We may differ in the use of the word reality, we may disagree inasmuch as I may think that the reality that matters is the distinctive and not the uniting factor, but there is an experience there, which as such, i.e. without any claim at metaphysical interpretations, reaches those very boundaries of reality.

This is not yet the supreme experience, because it still has to grow into the total universalization of the subject having that experience. Until now I have been *carried away*, as it ware, being lost, or in the object, or the object is lost for me, but I have not yet been *carried above* me, such that there is no longer a 'me.' If by concentrating myself on the branch, (disregarding now other possible requirements according to different schools) I can lose myself totally in the entire universe, I need the action of the ultimate reality of the branch upon me, i.e., I need the opposite thrust, in order to totally lose myself, my ego and realise that the subject of the experience is no longer my senses or my mind or my mystical awareness, but something which overwhelms and overcomes me (about which I can speak only from remembrance later on) which does but allow room for saying in any way that the experience is mine. In theistic terms I am no longer 'seeing' the branch or the universe, but 'creating' it, calling it into existence because it is no longer my ego which does it but the divine I in which my person is merged and with which my person is united, or however we may prefer to express this process. This would be the threshold of the supreme experience. The explanations i.e., the interpretations may come afterwards. One thing may still be added: the manifestation of the experience is something which can be detected: it is something which totally transforms my life. The manifestation will not be my words or my recital of the experience, but the expression will be incarnated in my own life, it will crystallise in my experience and be visible to those who may care to look.

This is the threshold of the supreme experience we said. In other words, it has been the supreme experience for the time being. The person who has had such an experience will 'come back' to what mortals call the ordinary life. The supreme experience once it has taken hold of a person has transformed that person totally and he/she cannot be the same as before. It is a process of death and resurrection. That person will perform the ordinary acts of human life as any other moral will do. He/she will not feel distracted by his/her ordinary life, because there is no incompatibility of domains, the supreme experience not belonging to the domain of psychology. Nevertheless it is understandable that most of the mystical school dealing with these problems distinguish a double degree even at this point: the supreme experience compatible with the moral life in the visible structures of space and time and that other supreme experience in which time and space have completely been integrated into the experience itself.

But we cannot say much more, and even we have said already too much before proceeding to a certain typology of the manifestations of the supreme experience.

The Ways of the East and of the West

The spirit

The Eastern and Western Values

East and west have been separated for such a long time misunderstanding each other and living worlds apart that it is understandable that certain inertia in our ways of looking at things may obscure the fact that in 1970 East and West begin to be no longer what has been traditionally described under these two almost magical names.

East and west cannot be considered, to begin with, as purely or mainly geographical features. Not only because already long ago it was discovered that the earth is round, so that all depends on the perspective one adopts, but also because actually those geographical differences are minimal today and to be found in any relatively big geographical unit.

East and West cannot be said to be *historical* concepts either. The history of the peoples of the world is no longer an isolated his story and the destiny of the West may well be dependent on the battles taking place in the East and the future of the East may depend on the policy of the West. There are no longer closed eastern and western histories. For the first time in the world human history is the history of humankind.

Cultural distinctions also fade away or are expressions of not yet totally overcome oversimplifications and ignorance. Not only is the typical Western spirit to be found outside the West, but also the traditional Eastern way of looking at things is gaining more and more ground in the Western latitudes. There is not a single cultural difference which could be said specifically Eastern or Western – surely neither logic, nor mysticism, nor technology, science or metaphysics.

Also, the *philosophical* idiosyncrasies cannot be divided into Eastern and Western ways of thinking or philosophizing. The East and the West as well are too vast and variegated; to allow for overstatements regarding special features in the philosophical outlook on life. The times in which it could be said that a certain feature is peculiar with exclusivity to the East or to the West are over.

Even religious divisions can no longer be credited to East and West. In spite of the still heavy burden of the past, hardly any religion today can be identified with a particular east-west dichotomy. Most of the religions of the world were born in one place and flourish in another and hardly any religion today would identify itself with one particular continent. It is hard to say whether Christianity is more Jewish then Greek or Roman, whether Buddhism is more Indian than Chinese or even Islam more Arabic than Asian, or even for that matter Judaism more Palestinian than Babylonian, eastern European, Spanish or whatever.

Is there, thus, no meaning at all to speak of the ways of the East and those of the West? I do not believe it to be so. There is still a deep significance, perhaps the deepest, and it will seem that only if they are understood as anthropological categories do East and West have their place, justification and value.

In every human being there is an East and a West as any human being is in a certain way androgynous, only with the normal preponderance of one of the two aspects of the human. It would be monstrous if the world would be becoming geographically and culturally one and the human persons would still remain isolated, unconcerned and without that symbiosis, which is the only hope to more than one world problem today. But the cross-fertilization is possible because the human being has within himself/herself already the seeds of both values. In every one of us there is a West and an East. Every human person has an orient, a horizon, always beyond and behind, where the sun rises and which he never reaches, a dimension of hope, a dim sense of transcendence, a matutinal knowledge (*cognitio matutina*) as some tradition would have said. Every human being has likewise a dimension of West, of maturity, where the sun sets, where the values materialize, where the concreteness has the upper hand and faith is felt as a necessity, where the shapes and forms become relevant and the evening knowledge (*cognition vespertina*) represents the most coveted value, discovering the value of the immanence in the things themselves.

We could go on indefinitely, but this may suffice to apply it to our problems. The burden of our tale being that any inter-religious and inter-human dialogue i.e., any exchange among cultures has to be proceeded by an intra-religious and intra-human dialogue, i.e., an internal conversion within the person. We can only bridge the gulf between so many abysses, between East and West in this case, if we realise the synthesis and the harmony within that microcosm of ourselves. The chasm is within us; but also its remedy.

Four Archetypes of the Ultimate

We cannot go on forever avoiding the problem of the contents and overlooking the different ways in which the supreme experience has been described in the different schools and traditions. But then we must be aware of the limitations of any particular description. It is here that a study from the point of view of the History of Religions should prove fruitful and enlightening. Only very tentatively I may submit the following typology, based not so much on the perhaps too much school bookish divisions between religions or culture but along the lines of what has been said before of East and West as anthropological categories. If examples are drawn from the great religious traditions of mankind this should not contradict what we have been saying, but simply witness to the fact that certain emphasis are easier to find among certain people than others.

I repeat once for all that I do not intend to describe any religious spirituality in particular or deny that within a given religion there are no other trends of thought or even affirm that this typology is a typology of religions. I speak of four archetypes of the human being, though they may be more visible in one place or time than in another one. Moreover, a visible trend of our times is to find more and more each one of the four archetypes within the fold of one and the same religion.

It seems that the human spirit in its effort at understanding and expressing the supreme experience has stressed either the transcendence or the immanence of it. In the first group we find again two definite tendencies: the tendency stressing the transcendence and the tendency stressing the immanence. The former is typical of the Semitic religions: Judaism, Christianity and Islam. The letter could be said to form the Hindu type and could be represented by the bundle of religious traditions which circulate under the name of Hinduism.

The group more inclined to emphasize the immanence could equally be divided into two: the one underscoring the transcendent character of the immanence and we think of Buddhism and the other laying the accent on the immanent aspect of the same immanence, and here we would see the Chinese religious tradition and curiously enough the modern secular spirit also.

The following scheme sums up what we would like to sketch equally very briefly:

Ultimate Experience

Transcendence		
	Transcendent	Yahweh – Theos – Allah – Father Masculine –Sanctity Distinction
	Immanent	Brahman – Mother Feminine – Negation Absorption

Immanence		
	Transcendent	Neuter – Nirvana – Sunya Impersonal Realisation of the Universe
	Immanent	A Personal – Secular – Kamic Acceptance of human Condition – Service to the World-Order

The transcendent Transcendence

Its attitude is markedly masculine. Force, Power, Glory are some of its attributes. Be it Yahweh, the Christian Theos or Allah, this God is eminently Father and thus creator and evidently outside the world: he is transcendent in such an absolute way that he mainly creates, looks after and judges the world. He does not mix with the world as it were. The supreme experience is to see this glaring light face to face. Of course, there is the softening effect of the Christian Incarnation like the more mellow tones of the *kabbala*, the Hasidic spirituality and Sufism, but we have already said that we are trying to describe anthropological archetypes more than to elaborate a typology of religions.

God is the saint and holiness means here separateness, lofty segregation. God is utterly transcendent and it is this very transcendence which gives God the sovereign freedom to deal with humankind.

The supreme experience is here ultimately not possible for human. It is exclusively reserved for the transcendent God. We can at most be united with this supreme by love or knowledge according to the theological trends of different schools. The only possible supreme experience for human cannot in any way represent an escape from the human condition. It has to be on the human scale, concrete, personal and it must preserve our peculiarities. At the same time it has to save us from our limitations. It has to throw us into the arms of the Absolute, but the distinction between both is zealously guarded.

The Immanent Transcendence

The attitude is here visibly feminine. Brahman is equally transcendent, though not because Brahman is distant, different and above, but precisely because Brahman is below, common, the mere condition and basis of any existence without being itself any existence. Brahman is transcendent because of its own and proper immanence. So immanent that it has no consistence or its own, as it were. It does not even know that is Brahman. This would jeopardise its immanent transcendence, it would then have the necessary distance for any knowledge and could not be so radically immanent to the world. It is the matrix, the yoni, more like a mother nurturing from below rather than commanding from above. It does not lead, but sustains.

The supreme experience would consist accordingly in being immersed in Brahman; not perhaps to become Brahman, which would posit a certain activity alien to its utter passivity, necessary for its immanent transcendence, but in discovering the Brahman that is in me or that I am. The supreme experience is not so much one of keeping with one's own human condition sticking to a name and form which are only passing and provisional, but to experience the totality, to be the totality from that angle of 180 degrees, or degree of 300 degrees embracing all that is. This way is a negative path of denying all individuality and all differences. One of the criteria of the authenticity of the genuine experience consists in checking whether the candidate has lost fear of disappearing and losing himself, or if he still sticks to his little ego.

The Transcendent Immanence

The panorama here changes radically. The attitude is no longer masculine or feminine, but rather neuter (*ne utrum*), neither masculine not feminine and yet somehow personal in the non-anthropomorphic sense of the term. There is so radical an immanence that only by transcending all that is built on it can one reach the ultimate. One has to reduce to ashes everything which one can conceive or think of, even every idea or imagination of being has to disappear in order that pure nothingness, (Śūnya) may emerge, not evidently as something and much less as something else, but as the non-emergence of anything. Nirvana is the supreme experience and is the experience which is no experience at all and at once has realised that *saṃsāra* is *nirvāna*, i.e., that there is no transcendence other than the immanence, and thus that only by transcending the immanence itself can human somehow fulfil their life.

The supreme experience is obviously here not the experience of another and not even an experience different from any other of the human experiences. It is underlying all of them and can be reached only by quenching all desire of transcending the human condition. Yet, precisely because this human condition is a negative experience, the negation of it, without wanting to transcend it, is the only way to salvation, to nirvana. The human experience is reached neither by seeing God in all things (first way) nor by seeing all things in God (second way, though expressed in rather foreign terms to this second way), but refusing to divinize anything within the range or our experience. The best criterion to know that one has not got the supreme experience is when one affirms or even doubts whether he has got it. The supreme experience is that there is not such a thing as supreme experience. And yet realising this is what opens us up to the real liberation.

The Immanent Immanence

The attitude here is radically terrestrial. The immanence has not to be transcended. If the three other attitudes were, in a personal or impersonal way, still recognizing that the sphere of the immanence has to be somehow corrected, transcended, this attitude does not recognize any escapism of the factual human condition. There is no way out of it. There is no other world than this world and it is of no use in sublimating our longings and desires or projecting our dreams outside the realm of sober verification. Kami in Japanese means God for the Shinto, but also above, up, of anything for the matter that is superior to human in any trivial way. Traditional Chinese religiousness will not allow to introduce any other factor in the human situation in order to handle it. Religion is ultimate unconcern.

The supreme experience is that of the sage full of the knowledge of the trickeries and depths also of the human heart. The supreme experience is to renounce any extrapolation and to plunge into the real situation of the world without transcending it, not even negatively.

Modern secular spirituality by pragmatically refusing to speculate about any other experience outside the range of the world could also be adduced as an example of this attitude. In the concrete it finds the universal and the immanent, in the given, there is all that is needed...

The Spirit

Is there any possible way of finding certain equivalence to such variegated views and opinions? Is the unity of the family of man only a biological factor or a utopian dream? Am I so right that the others are wrong? Nations are at war one with another, religions consider themselves incompatible; philosophies contradict one another and not the human experience, when trying to overcome all pettiness of the systems and ideologies, there appear divergences as deep as any other human reality. Was not the drive towards experience one in order to overcome the discrepancies of sentiments and the divergences of opinions? If there is no other ulterior judge than our personal experience must one give up all hope for a peaceful understanding of one another thus preparing the way for new forms of imperialism and world dominion, for otherwise there seems no other way of bringing certain coherence and harmony to mankind? If after two world wars and with several minor, but no less horrible, wars still ravaging men today, we cannot trust much in pure reason and particular ideologies, does human experience supreme or not, offer any better starting point?

All these questions are for from theological and they constitute a real challenge to any authentic theology and philosophy if these disciplines are to be more than mere barren and devitalized brain-juice for the dumbfounding of those men who are still sensitive and sensible. We should not expect everything from philosophy or theology and we must beware of false messianisms, but the one extreme does not justify the other.

Is there any way of understanding and somehow accepting the manifold human experience and even of integrating the variety of expressions of the ultimate experience? If we can give a positive answer to this tantalizing query we shall not have solved the problems of the world, but shall have contributed in a very positive and efficacious way to their solution. At least we shall have removed one of the subtlest obstacles: lack of mutual confidence because of lack of understanding. This lack of understanding is the cause of considering the other wrong with all the consequences of this assumption.

On the other hand, it would be a negative and lethal service to philosophy and a betrayal to humankind if, led by a sentimental and good desire of mutual understanding, we were to blur the issues and to preach harmony and convergence when there is none.

To put it quite bluntly: if there is a God and this is the only possible hypothesis for a fully human and meaningful life, even if we respect the right of the others or acknowledge their good faith, we shall not be able to consider full citizens of academic of culture, religion or humankind all those who deny such a personal God. Or the other way round: if there is no God and the idea of God is still the 'hang up' of an obscurantist epoch totally incompatible with an enlightened and non-sectarian and fanatical existence, all those who still go on hanging on to such superstition are, to say the least, parasites of society and the greatest obstacles for a better world. We should not minimize or banalize the issue under the guise of academic etiquette.

An investigation into the ultimate experience cannot bypass this challenge. Briefly but pointedly, I would like to elaborate the direction of my answer.

First of all, as the previous analyses may have already suggested, the shift in emphasis from objective values to the experiential truth can only be judged as a positive step toward a more mature conception of the whole and complex human situation. Orthodox cannot be the supreme value.

Secondly, the distinction between agnostic or sceptical relativism and a realistic relativity seems to be important. The former being a dogmatic attitude emerging out of a reaction against another monolithic dogmatism; the latter being the recognition that nothing is absolute in this relative world of ours, that all depend on the constitutive and intrinsic relationship in which all things are, for isolation and solipsism are the product of particular human hubris. The brotherhood of human is not only an ethical imperative.

Thirdly, and this is what we should draw from the foregoing analyses, human experience is not reducible to one single denominator and furthermore the logos element in it is an important factor, which even has the power of veto nothing against reason can be accepted, but which is not the only power in human not his highest endowment: not only can everything not be put into words or concepts, but not even all here on earth is logos.

A real philosophical and theological endeavour today has to integrate in the task not only the exigencies of the logos, but also the realities of the myth and, last but not least, the freedom of the spirit.

Endnotes

[1] *Perao* and *peiran* in Greek, both at the basis of our three words, come from the root *per* (*cf. pl-parami*) meaning to conduct, to pass through, to test. Cf. the latin *porta, peritus, periculum*, the German (from where erfahren), the English fare, ferry, etc. The empirical is the proven reality, because it has passed through our senses; the experience is the same reality submitted to our testing and trying capacities: experience is again the same reality which has already passed through.

An Inquiry into the Communicational Structures of the Early Sangha and King Ashoka's Edicts:[1] A Model to Tackle Religious Diversity

Martin Repp

Introduction

This study attempts to clarify the question of how early Buddhism responded to the challenge of religious diversity. For this purpose the term religious communication will be applied as heuristic tool. This problem has two aspects, namely the diversification of the early sangha (monastic community) itself, i.e. its growth into different schools, and the relationship of the sangha (or individual schools) to other religious groups. Although two basically different issues are involved, a method which analyses the forms of religious communication allows investigating both as related to each other. It can be shown that basic forms and structures of intra and inter-religious communication are quite similar, even though there are some modes of communication which are characteristic of either internal or of external forms of communication. Thus, an analysis of communicational structures allows viewing as interrelated seemingly different issues: the attitude of the early sangha to other religious groups, such as Brahmin and Jainas, and the inner-Buddhist tensions evolving into schisms.

Although the present study treats a historical problem of intra- and inter-religious communication in the early sangha, the subsequent development of Buddhism shows that this issue continued to play a significant role throughout its history until today. Thus, its continuous diversification through splits posed the important question of how to establish a unity of the sangha. Apart from this intra-Buddhist problem, inquiries into the problem of communicational structures in religious diversities are relevant today. In an age of so-called globalization, contemporary religious pluralism causes serious social tensions and political conflicts. This situation suggests historical investigations in the hope of identifying previous models of solving the problem of religious diversity and maintaining peace within religions, among religions, in society and between different cultures and countries. This issue is prominent at the very time this article is being written. A Danish newspaper and a Norwegian magazine have published cartoons of Muhammad which have provoked the anger of many Muslims worldwide, triggered economic boycotts of Danish products, evolved into international diplomatic rows, and resulted in threats to attack and kill Danish and Norwegian people.[2] This intercultural and interreligious conflict is not a singular case of intercultural and interreligious miscommunication, for it has been paralleled by the cases of Salman Rushdie and Theo van Gogh.

This study first provides an introduction to how Shakyamuni and the early sangha dealt with religious diversity inside and outside their community. Next, the first Buddhist king, Ashoka, and his model of solving the problem of religious plurality will be treated. Finally, a few examples of how this issue was dealt with in the subsequent development of Buddhism will be mentioned in order to provide some cases for comparison.

Sakyamuni and the Early Sangha

This section first treats Sakyamuni's advice for communication with outsiders, especially with critics, and then it provides a brief introduction to the communicational process occurring in schisms within the early sangha.

According to the *Digha-nikaya*, Sakyamuni gave his disciples the following advice concerning how to respond to hostile communication initiated from outside the sangha:

> Brethren, if outsiders should speak against me, or against the Doctrine, or against the Order, you should not on that account either bear malice, or suffer heart-burning, or feel ill will. If you, on that account, should be angry or hurt, that would stand in the way of your own self-conquest. If, when others speak against us, you feel angry at that, and displeased, would you then be able to judge how far that speech of theirs is well said or ill?[3]

This quotation addresses two forms of communication, first external criticism of the Threefold Treasure (Buddha, dharma and sangha) and the monks' reaction, and second the internal communication of believers, namely the feeling of anger and its relation to the search for religious liberation. What is of particular interest is that both forms of communication, those with the outside and those occurring inside a practitioner, are here immediately connected with each other. In other words, criticism from outside should not lead the follower to respond likewise because such attitude and behaviour may become an obstacle for attaining the ultimate goal of awakening. In this way, interior and exterior forms of communication are closely interrelated. For pursuing the religious way, Sakyamuni's advice discourages retaliation against criticism which could unleash a chain of conflicts, but instead encourages overcoming such communicational problems between the self and the other.

Sakyamuni seems to have personally incorporated this rule, since, according to the *Majjhima-nikaya*, "the reverend Gotama, while he was being spoken to so offensively and with such insinuations, never changed colour nor did his countenance alter."[4] In the *Digha-nikaya*, we read: "Putting away slander, Gotama the recluse holds himself aloof from calumny."[5] Apart from this 'negative' side, the positive aspect of Sakyamuni's kind of communication, or his ethos of conversation, is expressed as follows: "Putting away lying words, Gotama the recluse holds himself aloof from falsehood. He speaks truth ..."[6] At another place, this ethos and its opposite are named "righteousness" and "unrighteousness of speech."[7]

Such an ethos of communication is maintained also in the rules of the sangha which names the transgressions of speech. For example, the *Patimokkha* ("Bond"), an early collection of monastic discipline to enhance the unity of the sangha,[8] contains the following statements: "In abusive speech there is an offense entailing expiation."[9] "In slander of a *bhikkhu* there is an offense entailing expiation."[10] The same rules apply for *bhikkhunis*.[11]

Next is the question of how communicational processes occurred in internal divisions of the early sangha. Buddhist tradition portrays *Devadatta* as the one who attempted to break up the unity of the sangha already during Buddha's life-time. According to the *Vinaya-pitaka (Suttavibhanga)*, he suggested to other disciples: "Now we, your reverences, will make a schism in the Order of the recluse Gotama, a breaking of the concord."[12] This case then was taken as reason to establish the general monastic rule prohibiting schisms.[13] It is maintained that "the Order is harmonious, on friendly terms, not quarrelsome, it dwells comfortable under a single rule."[14]

However, according to Buddhist tradition, soon after Gotama's death (ca. 480), his followers already had to convene an assembly or 'council' (*samgiti*) in order to discuss, and thereby attempt to resolve, opposing views concerning the rules (*vinaya*).[15] About a hundred years later, a conflict arose concerning the question whether monks should accept gold and silver from lay followers. The majority ruled that this was to be rejected.[16] Not long after that, dissent arose concerning the nature of an *arhat*, his 'dignity and prerogatives.' (Lamotte 1988: 274). According to Vasumitra's *Samayabhedoparacanacakra*, during the reign of Ashoka, monks convened and "discussed five theses (*pancavastu*) which had been presented by heretics" (Lamotte 1988: 276; cf. 274 f). As the conflict could not be resolved, a schism evolved. Consequently we hear: "Thus, for the first time since the Buddha, two schools came into being, one known as the *Mahasamghika*, the other as *Sthavira*."[17] The *Mahasamghika*, the 'majority,' had proposed a liberal understanding of the *arhat*, while the *Sthavira*, the 'elders,' defended rigorous principles.[18] It is interesting to note that according to later sources, the decision was made by "majority vote." When Ashoka asked Mahadeva, the leader of the *Mahasamghika*, "for advice in order to settle the quarrel," the latter "told him that, according to the Vinaya, it is the majority which prevails in controversies."[19] From that time onwards, conflicts continued in form of debates, and after having convened various subsequent assemblies, schisms within the Buddhist community occurred again and again.[20] After such events, the respective opponent was declared to be a 'heretic.' Such frequent debates, originally aimed at resolving conflicts in order to maintain the unity of the sangha, in the end proved to be inconclusive and instead only finalized a schismatic process.

There were a number of reasons for these conflicts and schisms in the early (and later) Buddhist community. First of all, after Sakyamuni's death, there was no person serving as unifying authority for the sangha.[21] Next, Buddha's teachings, as it was first orally transmitted and then compiled and edited into texts and collections, were not that homogenous, but rather contained divergent and even contradicting teachings. This resulted in different interpretations of the teaching. Also the personality of individual teachers played a role in the tendency towards diversification of the sangha and of the dharma. The numerical growth and geographic spread of the sangha without central authority was a significant factor as well. Apart from these factors, also cultural, social, economic, and political reasons may have played a role in such a development.

Returning to the monastic rules, the *Patimokkha* states concerning schism in the sangha as follows:

> Should any *bhikkhu* attempt to cause schism in a united sangha or should he persist having undertaken and having taken up a legal process conducive to schism, that *bhikkhu* is to be spoken to by the *bhikkhus* thus, 'Do not, venerable sir, attempt to cause schism in a united sangha; do not persist having undertaken and having taken up a legal process conducive to schism. Let the venerable one be at peace with the sangha; for the sangha, united, in agreement, not disputing, having a united recitation (of the *Patimokkha*), etc.), lives comfortably.' And should that *bhikkhu*, being spoken to thus by the *bhikkhus*, persist in the same way (as before), that bhikkhu is to be admonished by the *bhikkhus* up to the third time to give up that (course of action). If, being admonished up to the third time, he should give it up, that is good. If he should not give it up, this entails a formal meeting of the sangha.[22]

The same rule applies for *bhikkhunis*.[23] According to Pachow and Mishra[24] "the function of the *Pratimoksa-Sutra* is to govern the conduct of the *bhikhus* is to maintain peace and unity in the Order ..." In its introduction we read: "As long as the *Pratimoksa Sutra* is not destroyed among the Chapter of the bhikhus, so long shall the true Dharma and the unity remain in the Sangha."[25]

However, the following of rules, such as control of speech and avoiding schism, has yet another dimension. The introductory section of the *Pratimoksa Sutra* states: "Having heard the *Pratimoksa* which was promulgated by the Blessed one and which is capable of freeing us from the troubles of this world, the wise control their six sense-organs completely and thus put an end to births and deaths."[26] Among the six sense-organs are the ear, the tongue and the mind. Their activities also influence the process or hindrance of religious liberation. Thus, control of speech, listening and thought do not only concern the unity of the sangha, but are of 'soteriological' relevance.[27] Drawing such a connection between religious liberation and communication conforms to Sakyamuni's teaching, as outlined above.

Ashoka

According to the historiography of the outstanding Buddhist philosopher Nagarjuna (ca. 150-250 C.E.),[28] early Buddhism developed as follows: "When the Buddha was in this world, there was no opposition to the Law. When he had disappeared, and the Law was recited for the first time, it was still as when the Buddha was alive. One hundred years later, King Asoka convened a great assembly of the quinquinnial (*pancavarsaparisad*) and the Great Masters of the Law debated.[29] Because of their differences, there were distinctive sects (*nikaya*), each having a name and each of which was subsequently to evolve."[30]

In the light of the previous section, the first two sentences of this quotation portray an idealized picture of the early sangha. The subsequent part, according to Nagarjuna, indicates King Ashoka's concern about sectarian striving and the unity of the sangha. Ashoka (r. ca. 263-232) was the first king in the Mauryan Dynasty[31] who converted to Buddhism and promoted its missionary endeavours widely.[32] During the time of his reign, schisms in the Buddhist community apparently had become such a social and political concern that he had to convene Buddhist monks for debate with the purpose to create concord among them. However, according to this record, this form of intra-religious communication did not reach its goal of securing the sangha's unity, but resulted in further splits and diversification in early Buddhism.

Contemporary sources confirm that Ashoka was deeply concerned with the unity of the sangha since he promulgated edicts with clear warnings against schism.[33] For example, the inscription of the Samchi Pillar treats the division of the sangha as follows:

"The *Samgha* both of monks and of nuns is made united as long as (my) sons and great-grandsons (shall reign, and) as long as the moon and the sun (shall shine). The monk or nun who shall break up the *Samgha*, must be caused to put on white robes[34] and to reside in a non-residence.[35] For my desire is that the *Samgha* may be united (and) of long duration."[36]

The same direction is expressed in the edict of the Sarnath Pillar which reads:

"... the *Samgha* [cannot] be divided by any one. But indeed that monk or nun who shall break up the *Samgha*, should be caused to put on white robes and to reside in a non-residence. Thus, this edict must be submitted both to the *Samgha* of monks and to the *Samgha* of nuns."[37]

Apart from the unity of the sangha, maintaining peace among different religious groups in his country was also of deep concern for Ashoka. First of all it is noteworthy that he was Realpolitiker enough not to ignore the fact of the existing religious diversity, but to grasp it and make it the starting point of his political discourse. This is expressed in Ashoka's Rock Edict No. 7 (Girnar) as follows:

> "King Priyadarsin [Ashoka], Beloved of the gods, wishes that all sects [save pasmda] should dwell everywhere. He wishes them all self-control and purity of sentiment.[38] But the people are of diverse inclinations and of diverse passions."[39]

Here, Ashoka first acknowledges the fact that (in the translation by Hultzsch 1977:14) "men possess various desires (and) various passions," which not only creates social and religious diversity, but may trigger serious tensions and conflicts in a country. Next, however, he advices his people of diverse religious convictions to exert "self-control and [to cultivate] purity of mind" in order to counterbalance the centrifugal force of diversification. At the end of this edict, Ashoka is more explicit concerning the virtues he expects his subjects to cultivate, namely "self-control, purity of mind, gratitude and firm devotion."[40] The word 'gratitude' signifies the attitude of appreciation for Ashoka's patronage of various religious groups.[41] And the word 'firm devotion' indicates that he did not expect his subjects to water down religious convictions and differences in order to reach social harmony, but to maintain these commitments. Moreover, he seems to imply that these commitments play a positive role in maintaining social peace as long as self-control, sincerity and gratitude are exercised.

This edict addresses the interior forms of communication, such as passions and desires on the one hand, and self-control and purity of mind on the other. In another edict Ashoka proceeds to depict exterior forms of communication as disrupting (centrifugal) or unifying (centripetal) factors. The most important edict for our concern here is Rock Edict No. XII (Kalsi) which reads:

> King Priyadarsin, Beloved of the gods, honours all sects[42] of recluses or householders with gifts and by various modes of honouring.[43]

But the Beloved of the gods does not mind either the offering of gifts or honouring so much as that there should be growth of all sects in the essence of things (*saravadhi*).

The growth in the essence of things is, of course, of various kinds. The root of it, however, is this, namely the control of speech (*vaciguti*), intending that there may be no honouring of one's own sect or condemnation of other sects without point, or that condemnation on this or that point may be light, or even that other sects should be honoured in this or that form.

In so doing, one greatly increases (the fame of) one's own sect, and also renders service to other sects.

In acting otherwise, one digs the grave for one's own sect, and also does harm to other sects.

Whosoever honours one's own sect or condemns other sects, (does so) all due indeed to devotion to one's own sect, intending, 'I will glorify my own sect.' But again in acting thus, by far the more they injure their own sect.

(So) concord [*samavaya*] is good, intending that they will hear one another's doctrine.[44]

Such indeed is the wish of the Beloved of the gods that all sects may be well-informed [*bahusruta*] and possessed of a good tradition [*kalyanagama*]. ...[45]

Ashoka argues here along two lines. For practical reasons, I begin with the second one in the order of discourse. His argument is as follows: If one honours the own school only, while condemning the other, "one digs the grave for one's own sect, and also does harm to other sects." To paraphrase this, although having a seemingly good intention of promoting one's own school, such partial behaviour results in the damage not only of the other side, but also of one's own group. According to Ashoka's opinion, the damage caused to one's own school even surpasses the damage of the other which, of course, contradicts one's original intention. Arguing in such a way, he urges the members of the various schools to restrain their speech, which implies a certain degree of impartiality. Such self-imposed restrained speech may be called a moderate way of both appreciating one's own school and of distancing oneself from another one.[46] On the other hand, Ashoka names not only the negative consequences of unrestrained talk, but also the positive effects of moderate speech, when stating: In so doing, one greatly increases (the fame of) one's own sect, and also renders service to other sects. In short, while the partial behaviour of honouring and slandering is damaging both sides, moderate ways of talking benefit both equally.

Analysing the replacement of the first mode of human behaviour by the second one, as Ashoka suggests, we may say the following. He observes the fact that his religious subjects being involved in verbal competition or dispute does not, as expected, achieve victory for one side and defeat for the other, but causes only mutual damage to both. Thus, he declares their expectations as illusory. Instead he suggests replacing the 'victory or defeat' mechanism by that of a 'win-win' and 'lose-lose' as a new model for social communication. Since human beings naturally tend towards (in his view, futile) competition, such a form of behaviour should be replaced by an alternative model of interaction. Such a new form of communication does not seem to be a natural behaviour, but needs to be taught and cultivated. In contrast to the fact of competitive behaviour, this kind of friendly communication is envisaged as a desired goal. For this reason, the part of the edict dealing with this issue appears in form of a moral admonition. Which is the decisive turning point that allows Ashoka to argue for a replacement of competitive forms by conversational modes of communication? Since he argues here from the point of view of mutual benefit and mutual damage, it seems that the Golden Rule (acting in mutual responsibility) is the ethical principle underlying his admonition. And its background is clearly the concept of *karma* that is to consider the consequences of one's own deeds.

Next, turning to the first line of Ashoka's argumentation, the expression "restraint of speech" again plays a crucial role. Here he first states: "there should be growth of all sects in the essence of things. The growth in the essence of things is, of course, of various kinds." The edict itself does not explain the expression 'essence,' but leaves it somehow open.[47] What it says is only, first, that the schools should grow in this essence, and, second, that the nature of such growth is diverse. The first issue implies that religious schools are no static entities but should be dynamic in their development. Further, as the word 'should' indicates, this development in the direction towards the 'essence' is desirable or necessary. And this again presupposes that there is a basic tension, or a gap, between the status quo of an existing religion and an 'essence,' whatever that may be. In other words, this first issue indicates that religious groups should not remain fixed in their *status quo* by assuming to have attained the ultimate goal already or realized the full truth, but they should continue in their endeavour to search for realization of certain potentialities as a continuous religious process.

The second issue defines the process of growth as being diverse. One might assume that the monarch would have condemned religious diversity right from the beginning because it was sectarian tensions that caused trouble for the country. This, however, is in this sentence not the case, since Ashoka not only recognizes, but affirms the existing diversity of religious groups and convictions. This conforms to the previously quoted edict where the diversity of personal inclinations of human beings is acknowledged. Now, in Rock Edict No. XII, Ashoka even encourages religious diversity as a growing, continuous process. At the same time, he also defines the direction, or the subject, of such a process as 'essence.'

Regarding the word 'essence,' there are considerable differences in the translations. While Hultzsch[48] renders the expression with "promotion of the essentials of all sects," Schneider[49] translates it with "Wachstum im Wesentlichen bei allen Religionsgemeinschaften," and Barua[50] with "growth of all sects in the essence of things." This poses the problem whether "essence" is defined by an object, such as the essence of a school (Hultzsch) or the essence of things,[51] or whether it is not clearly defined by an object (Schneider).[52] Thus we are confronted with the following alternative interpretation of this statement in the edict: Does Ashoka expect from the religious groups to grow further in their own individual essence, or to grow in a kind of universal essence which comprises religion and the rest of reality? The Stele Edicts Nr. VI and VII speak of a growth in the *dhamma*,[53] that is, his people should grow in morality. Since Ashoka (according to the respective situation) uses *dhamma* in the two meanings of civil morality and of religious teaching, very likely 'growth' in Rock Edict No. XII means that each religious group should grow in its own *dhamma*.

Next, Ashoka proceeds to explain that the 'root' for such diverse growth in one's *dhamma* is the 'control of speech.' What does he mean by that? First, when introducing the metaphor of the root, he refers to the problem of the relationship between unity and diversity. After first having affirmed the religious diversity, he counterbalances it with the simile of the root symbolizing a fundamental unity. Ashoka now identifies this basic unity as 'restraint' or 'control of speech.' This kind of talk is, as he stated, of mutual benefit for both sides, as opposed to the mutual damage caused by uncontrolled forms of communication. Thus, self-controlled speech not only fosters the development of opposing schools mutually, but (as root) their growth in their own religious group as well.

The second reason for the controlled speech being the root for the religious development in sound diversity becomes clear from a statement towards the end of Ashoka's discourse where he says: "concord is good, intending that they will hear one another's doctrine." Here again, the theme of unity (in diversity) is taken up by the word "concord," and this is followed by the expression "hearing (the teachings, the *dhamma*, of other schools)." Thus, controlled speech is here not only supplemented by listening, but first of all creates space where one is enabled to listen to each other's teachings. In contrast, uncontrolled, polemic, or aggressive talk is not only expression of a basic unwillingness to listen, but creates a bad atmosphere and thereby prevents listening to opponents. Whereas uncontrolled speech obstructs friendly forms of communication and triggers or perpetuates polemic discourse, controlled speech enables friendly communication and fosters concord by intentional listening to one another. Thus, controlled speech and intentional listening create concord in a social unit which is characterized by an affirmed diversity. It is remarkable that Ashoka does not only stress the necessity of controlled speech for the peace of society, but, at the same time, that of intentional listening to each other. By means of such listening, members of the different schools become 'well-informed.' They may learn from each other about matters which are unfamiliar up to now, but which may become significant for their continuous growth in their dhamma which again occurs in 'various kinds.'

Along this line of reasoning, Ashoka combines the intra-religious benefit of controlled speech and listening with the social benefit of 'concord.' This matter becomes clear in the subsequent passage where he talks about 'fruits' which supplements the simile of the 'root' from the beginning of the edict. Ashoka states toward the end of the edict: "And this is the fruit of it, (viz.) that both the promotion of one's own sect takes place, and the glorification of morality."[54]

Thus, moderate talk and listening in inter- and intra-religious communication form the roots, which 'downwards' enable continuous growth in the essence and 'upwards' foster diversification in the branches. The branches bear especially two kinds of fruit, namely the prosperity of the various religious groups and that of morality (*dhamma*)[55] for the benefit of the public. In such a way, moderate speech and listening to one another contribute not only significantly to the diverse development of religious groups themselves, but by maintaining concord and fostering morality (*dhamma*), diverse religious groups serve the society and a whole country. Ashoka's edict concerning the self-imposed, self-controlled forms of inter-religious communication maintains a balance between the religious freedom and political responsibility of the various religious groups.

In order to encourage religious groups to exercise self-controlled speech and to cultivate listening to each other, according to this edict, Ashoka employed civil servants in the whole country.[56] Thereby, he did not leave the problem of religious diversity and concord completely to the individual efforts of religious groups and their leaders, but additionally he considered the necessity of such government supervision as part of his political responsibility. Thereby, this edict strikes another balance, namely that between autonomous self-control of religious groups and political rule.

This is, as I would call it, Ashoka's ingenious model of solving the problem of the relationship between religious diversity and unity as far as they concern society and state. In his edict, he first realistically acknowledged and affirmed the diversity of religious quest and sectarian development. However, in order to prevent such centrifugal movements from endangering the peace, he counterbalances this tendency by the centripetal forces of controlled speech and intentional listening. Here we see what an important role certain forms of communication play for the public good. Since human beings do not necessarily behave in the desired way, these forms of communication, though being elementary, have to be intentionally cultivated. This edict was promulgated for precisely such reason and purpose.

In conclusion of this section, we may state two observations. The first one is that Ashoka's moral admonitions for cultivated forms of communication among his religious subjects fits perfectly with Sakyamuni's rules for self-control of mind, ear and tongue. This means that the ethos of Ashoka's edicts is not an alien law, forcefully applied to the subjects from outside, but concurs perfectly with the rules established at least in the sangha, if not in other religious groups as well. The second observation is that King Ashoka's handling of the problem of religious diversity is also of particular significance insofar as the ethos of intra-Buddhist and inter-religious communication appears here for the first time on a political level.

Examples from Subsequent Buddhist History

The continuous process of diversification in Buddhist history posed constant challenges of communication to the sangha. One example may serve as illustration of this fact, namely the Lotus Sutra. Probably the deepest split occurring in the history of the sangha was that between 'Hinayana' ('Small Vehicle', Theravada) and 'Mahayana' ('Great Vehicle'). It is presumed that Mahayana developed during the 2nd century C.E.[57] The Lotus Sutra, a representative sutra of this tradition, explicitly treats this issue of how to maintain religious unity in the diversity of Buddhist schools. First, this sutra acknowledges the fact that there are 'three vehicles' (*trini yanani*) which differ in their path to reach the ultimate goal of liberation. There is the 'vehicle of the listeners' (*sravaka yana*), who wish "to follow the dictate of an authoritative voice ... to acquire the knowledge of the four great truths, for the sake of their own complete Nirvana."[58]   Next, there is the 'vehicle of the *pratyeka buddhas*' (*pratyeka buddha yana*), who desire "the science without a master ... [who want] to learn causes and effects for the sake of their own complete Nirvana."[59]   Finally there is the 'great vehicle' of the 'Bodhisattvas Mahasattvas' (*bodhisattva yana*), who are "desirous of the knowledge of the all-knowing, the knowledge of Buddha" and who engage themselves "for the sake of the common weal and happiness, out of compassion to the world at large, both gods and men, for the sake of the complete Nirvana of all beings."[60]

Then the Lotus Sutra offers a solution for the problem of unity in such diversity by stating that the Tathagata does teach "no other vehicle but the Buddha-vehicle to full development. He does not teach a particular Nirvana for each being; he causes all beings to reach complete Nirvana by means of the complete Nirvana of the Tathagata."[61] The Buddha-vehicle (*buddha yana*) is the 'one vehicle' (*eka yana*) which contains the three vehicles mentioned above since its goal is not manifold but one, the attainment of nirvana. According to the Lotus Sutra, the diversity of the three vehicles results from the diversity of beings because these vehicles respond to their different individual needs in various ways:

"I [Buddha] reveal the law in its multifariousness with regard to the inclinations and dispositions of creatures. I use different means to rouse each according to his own character. Such is the might of my knowledge."[62]

In another passage of this sutra, this problem is treated in a conversation between Buddha and his disciple Kasyapa as follows: "There are not three vehicles, Kasyapa; there are but beings who act differently; therefore it is declared that there are three vehicles."[63] Thereupon Kasyapa asks: "... for what reason then is the designation of disciples (*sravakas*), Buddhas and Bodhisattvas kept up in the present time?"[64] The Buddha responds with a parable according to which vessels are of the same nature, but the "diversity of the pots is only due to the substances which are put into each of them." Thereupon Kasyapa asks the next question: "Lord, if the beings are of different disposition, will there be for those who have left the triple world one Nirvana, or two, or three?" Buddha clarifies: "... all laws (things) are equal."[65] Thereby he maintains the unity of the different vehicles in the one common goal.[66]

The Lotus Sutra provides yet another model to maintain such unity. In response to the problem of how the tension between diversity and unity can be mediated, it introduces the crucial term *upaya*, or skilful means.[67] Accordingly we read: the Buddha "preaches the law by able devices ... with due regard to the different dispositions and inclinations of creatures whose temperaments are so various. All his preachings of the law have no other end but supreme and perfect enlightenment, for which he is rousing beings to the Bodhisattva-course."[68] The sutra considers the teachings of the three vehicles as skilful means.[69] An important achievement of this term is that it avoids a negation of the variety of teachings; instead it affirms diversity, including that of 'Hinayana.'[70]

In summarizing the Lotus Sutra's treatment of the problem of diversity and unity, we arrive at the following model: (1) The one Tathagata teaches the one vehicle which is the Buddha vehicle. (2) In response to the variety of beings, the three vehicles were taught as means to attain liberation from suffering and death. (3) The ultimate goal of liberation is the one nirvana. Thus, there is the unity of the Tathagata in the beginning and that of nirvana in the end. In between are the diversities of the three vehicles and the skilful means occasioned by the diversity of human beings. The variety of the vehicles is subsumed under the concept of skilful means.[71] This concept makes it possible to understand the three vehicles as being essentially united in the one Buddha vehicle.

Thus, the Lotus Sutra sees the unity clearly in the beginning (Tathagata)[72] and the end (nirvana), and the diversity of the major existing Buddhist groups stretched in between. As a term for the different forms of communicating the dharma by adapting to a variety of situations or persons, the concept of skilful means (being themselves communicational processes) makes it possible to perceive the three vehicles in their unity as the one Buddha vehicle. The Lotus Sutra basically provides two models for the problem of keeping religious diversity unified: The first consists of the proposition of metaphysical concepts such as the Tathagata, nirvana and the Buddha vehicle, and the second of communicational modes, namely the three vehicles and the various skilful means which concern concrete Buddhist soteriology.

What is interesting for our inquiry here are a few observations based on the comparison with the previous findings. The Lotus Sutra deals with intra-Buddhist diversities, whereas in the above quoted sutras and edicts the relationship between early Buddhism and other religious groups is also treated. It may be safe to say as well that in intra-Buddhist discourse, such as the Lotus Sutra, metaphysical concepts are employed in order to define the unity of the sangha, because they form a common basis for various groups. However, in relation to non-Buddhist groups – as long as there are no metaphysical concepts which may serve as common basis – only communicational models can function as factors to establish peace among them, as we saw in Ashoka's edicts.

Conclusion

The process of diversification of the sangha and the accompanying quest for unity continued until modern times. For example, David Hewavitarne (1864-1933), better known as Anagarika Dharmapala, founded the Bodh-Gaya-Mahabodhi-Society 1891 in Colombo which became the first international Buddhist organization. Its aim was to make Bodh Gaya the centre of Buddhism and to unite Buddhists from all countries.[73] On the other hand, Japanese new Buddhist groups established in the 20 C.E. are recent examples for the on-going diversification process. Thus, both centripetal and centrifugal movements continue to play significant roles within Buddhism, even though one gains the impression that throughout history the latter has outweighed the former. This is true also for other religions. What is this power which drives the continuous process of diversification in the history of religions? European philosophy viewed this matter in a generalized way and called it *principium individuation* is being at work in any being on earth. King Milinda, presumably being at an intersection between East and West, asks: "what is the reason that men are not all the same ...?" (Horner 1969: 89) We cannot lift this mystery, but we can ask what it may be that keeps divergent tendencies in the world of religion and society together. This study suggests that the solution to this problem basically consists of cultivated forms of communication.

In history, there were also other ideas considered to solve the problem of unity in diversity. The European Enlightenment, for example, employed the concept of 'tolerance' in order to maintain diversity in religion and thought. At least since Rhys Davids (1972: 4 ff, first edition 1881), this term has been also applied to the attitude of the early sangha and of Ashoka towards other religious groups. Many authors have followed such interpretation[74] and today this kind of 'orientalism' has become a common place. However, upon a more thorough investigation, it seems questionable whether this interpretation fits the subject properly. There are several reasons for such doubt. First, this term is not a historical term originally used in this particular context, but a historiographical term, derived from a different context, and then applied to earlier times and other geographical places. Such interpretative procedure becomes problematic when the subject under scrutiny proves to differ significantly from the interpretative term. This is here the case, as the following considerations show. Second, Ashoka certainly 'tolerated' a variety of religious groups. However, he was more than only tolerant since he actively supported them through his patronage. Third, on the other hand, he did less than 'tolerating' these groups because he issued imperial edicts demanding that they followed certain rules of conduct and abstained from deviating behaviour.

As Barua[75] has pointed out, there was also a 'co-operative side' in Ashoka's strategy. He even enforced his policy by employing officials in the country charged with overseeing this.[76] Fourth, the term tolerance signifies a certain attitude. However, this study of the sangha and Ashoka's edict has shown that it was not only a matter of attitude (certainly, 'sincerity' played a major role), but more a certain communicational behaviour that was considered to be the main factor for fostering peace within and among religions as well as in the country. Finally, tolerance signifies one-way guidance from political authority down towards diverse subjects. Ashoka's edicts, however, are based on a mechanism of mutual exchange, as his patronage and respect for religious groups on the one hand, and their required behaviour of cultivated communication (i.e., their responsibility and contribution for the common good) on the other show.

At this point, it may be critically asked whether it is adequate to use the term 'communication' itself in the Buddhist context since it is of European origin. Here is no sufficient space to discuss this problem in a satisfactory way. Only a few remarks may serve as hints for future discussion. First, societies and religions in East and West consist of human beings talking and listening to each other. Second, the aspect of mutual exchange (in Japanese *koryu, kokan*) signified by the word communication, indicates that it is not only applicable for verbal, but also for non-verbal and other forms of mutual exchange. This is expressed, for example, in the Japanese rendering of the word as *kotsu* (traffic). In the Buddhist context, the basic concept of such mutual exchange extending beyond verbal forms (but also including them) is probably *pratitya samutpada*. It means that all phenomena come into being and exist by mutual causation and conditioning. Such a concept was brought to perfection in the Kegon Sutra which illustrates the interrelatedness with the simile of Indra's net. This symbol signifies that everything in the cosmos is interconnected with each other in mutual exchange. At this point, it may be critically contented that a major difference between Buddhist and Christian thinking is that the former denies the existence of individual substance, while the latter affirms this. After all, the concept of "communication" seems to presuppose the existence of at least two individual entities. I doubt whether such a simple comparison adequately renders the rich traditions of both religions, but refrain from discussing it further. Here it is suffice to say that we are talking about issues which the Buddhist tradition recognizes as 'worldly' or 'relative truth.' Therefore, at least for the time being, I presume, it may be allowed to apply the term communication also in the context of Buddhist history.

In order to apprehend the specific role of communication, a brief comparison may be at place. In history also another common pattern in attempts to solve the problem of overly strong diversity in a community is to be found. This is the attempt to employ ideas or ideologies as unifying factor. Recent examples from the 20th century are Communism, Nazism and Fascism. In comparison, we observe that Ashoka did not offer a unifying ideology, such as a metaphysical concept or a political idea, as the unifying bond for religious diversity. Instead, he considers controlled speech and intentional listening as the factors which maintain concord in all diversity. His communicational model is, in my view, a really significant contribution to the question of how diverse groups can maintain concord in a bigger community.

As mentioned before, the process of diversification consists of centrifugal movements. These are accompanied also by centripetal tendencies. According to this study, cultivated forms of communication played in Buddhist history such a centripetal role. Above, the inherent tendency towards continuous diversification was called *principium individuations*. Accordingly, in order to name the force which counterbalances the divergent tendencies of the principle of individuation, I would suggest introducing here the term *principium communicationis*. It was probably no incident that the Latin words *communicatio* and *communio* are not only etymologically related to each other. A community consists of, and exists in, various ways of communication. Communication establishes, constitutes and maintains a community. Thus, cultivated forms of communication can bind together a broad variety of individuals or groups, without the fear that those entities feel threatened in their individual identity. Such fear, of course, is to be found in the case of "rough talk," polemical or aggressive forms of communication.

This study has shown the importance of human forms of communication for religion and society. The cases treated here demonstrate what a huge difference it makes whether one choses polemic or cultivated forms of communication considering the results. The actual relevance of this matter is demonstrated by the aforementioned violent conflict surrounding the publication of cartoons of Muhammad. An analysis of its communicational structures on the basis of Ashoka's admonition makes the sad affair understandable. By stressing only the right of freedom of expression, the editors apparently neglected the old European tradition that freedom always includes responsibility in respect to others.[77] One conclusion from this study is that the topic of communicational forms requires much more attention from religionists, educators, scholars, journalists and politicians.

Endnotes

[1] This article was first published in the journal *Shinshu-gaku* (Journal of Studies in Shin Buddhism, Ryukoku University, Kyoto) No. 114 (2006), 1-33 and is reprinted here

with kind permission. I would like to thank my colleague Prof. Dr. Galen Amstutz for kindly correcting the English of this article. The present version is revised.

[2] For an analysis see my article "The Caricature of Caricatures" – Communicational Strategies in the Danish Cartoon Conflict, *Japanese Religions* 31/2 (2006): 120-162.

[3] T. W. Rhys Davids, trans., *Sacred Books of the Buddhists - Dialogues of the Buddha*, part I (London: Luzac & Company, Ltd. [1899], 1956), 3.

[4] Lord Chalmers, trans., *Further Dialogues of the Buddha*, vol. I, in *Bibliotheca Indo-Buddhica* no. 44 (New Delhi: Sri Satguru Publications [1927], 1988), 179.

[5] Rhys Davids, trans., *Sacred Books of the Buddhists - Dialogues of the Buddha*, 4.

[6] Rhys Davids, trans., *Sacred Books of the Buddhists - Dialogues of the Buddha*, 4.

[7] Chalmers, trans., *Further Dialogues of the Buddha*, 203-205.

[8] John Clifford Holt, *Discipline: The Canonical Buddhism of the Vinayapitika* (Delhi: Motilal Barsidass, 1981), 39.

[9] William Pruitt, ed., *The Patimokkha*, translated by K.R. Norman (Oxford: Pali Text Society, 2001), 47.

[10] Pruitt, ed., *The Patimokkha*, 47.

[11] Pruitt, ed., *The Patimokkha*, 195.

[12] I. B. Horner, trans., *The Book of the Discipline* (London: Luzac & Company Ltd., 1949), 296.

[13] Horner, trans., *The Book of the Discipline*, 299.

[14] Horner, trans., *The Book of the Discipline*, 300, cf. 305. The expression 'single rule' signifies the authority of the Pratimokkha rules.

[15] Andre Bareau, "Der indische Buddhismus," in *Die Religionen Indiens III Buddhismus – Jinismus – Primitivvolker*, Die Religionen der Menschheit Bd. 13 (Stuttgart: W. Kohlhammer Verlag, 1964), 20. Scholars have scrutinized the historicity of this and subsequent 'councils.' What seems sure is that these meetings were no general councils, as the connotation of this term may suggest, but rather 'local synods' in which not representatives of the whole sangha came together for deliberation but those of various schools. Erich Frauwallner, "Die buddhistischen Konzile," *Zeitschrift der Deutschen Morgenländischen Gesellschaft* Bd. 102, 1952, 258 ff. It seems also safe to say that most of these meetings ended in a schism that is in the establishment of new schools. For a discussion of this problem and recent literature, see also Holt, *Discipline: The Canonical Buddhism of the Vinayapitika*, 41-44.

[16] Bareau, "Der indische Buddhismus," 21 ff.

[17] Lamotte 1988: 276. Shortly before this statement, Vasumitra writes: "In those days [of King Ashoka's rule], the great sangha was divided into schools and diversified the Law.

[18] Bareau, "Der indische Buddhismus," 70.

[19] Lamotte 1988: 278; cf. 279. For settling a legal process pertaining the sangha, the *Patimokkha* also mentions the "decision of the majority." Pruitt, ed., *The Patimokkha*, 109.

[20] For an overview of early councils and schisms, see, Bareau, "Der indische Buddhismus," 20-23; 69-77; for a more detailed study of the sources, see Lamotte 1988: 271-292.

[21] Bareau, "Der indische Buddhismus," 69; Lamotte 1988: 62-65. According to the famous Chinese pilgrim Xuangzang (Hsuantsang, 596/602-664), when he visited the Ashokan stupa where the Mahasanghika canon was said to have been compiled, he stated, "While the Tathagata was alive, we all had one and the same master; now that he is deceased, we are cast aside like strangers. In order to display our gratitude to the Buddha, we must compile a Dharmapitaka." (Lamotte 1988: 286).

[22] Pruitt, ed., *The Patimokkha*, 17.

[23] Pruitt, ed., *The Patimokkha*, 137-139.

[24] W. Pachow and Ramakanta Mishra, eds., *The Pratimoksa-Sutra of the Mahasanghikas* (Allahabad: Ganganatha Jha Research Institute, 1956), 5.

[25] Pachow and Mishra, eds., *The Pratimoksa-Sutra of the Mahasanghikas*, 51.

[26] Pachow and Mishra, eds., *The Pratimoksa-Sutra of the Mahasanghikas*, 49.

[27] "The Sramana and the Brahmanas who have shila cross over (the sea of world-sufferings)," Pachow and Mishra, eds., *The Pratimoksa-Sutra of the Mahasanghikas*, 49.

[28] This passage may also be a gloss by his translator Kumarajiva (405 C.A.). Lamotte 1988: 291).

[29] For a description of the quinquinnial festival, a formal imperial offering (*dana*) to the Buddhist community, see Strong 1989: 91-96; 256-269. The debate among the monks was apparently held at the occasion of such a festival.

[30] Lamotte 1988: 292.

[31] The Mauryan Dynasty (B.C.E. 315-180) united India for the first time after the invasion of Alexander the Great and his retreat.

[32] For the studies of Ashoka and his legend; see, e.g. Radhakumud Mookerji, *Asoka* (Delhi: Motilal Banasidass [1928], 1972); E. Hultzsch, *Inscriptions of Asoka*, Corpus Inscriptorum Indicarum Vol. I. (Tokyo: Meicho-Fukyu-kai [1925], 1977); Strong (1989).

[33] E. Hultzsch, *Inscriptions of Asoka*, 159-164; Benimadhab Barua, trans., *Inscriptions of Asoka*, 2nd ed. (Calcutta: Sanskrit College [1943], 1990), 36 ff.

[34] That is, to return to the life of a householder or become adherent of another religious tradition. Cf. Barua, trans., *Inscriptions of Asoka*, 36.

[35] This is a residence other than a Buddhist monastery. Barua, trans., *Inscriptions of Asoka*, 36.

[36] Hultzsch, *Inscriptions of Asoka*, 161.

[37] Hultzsch, *Inscriptions of Asoka*, 161 ff.

[38] By referring to self-control and restraint of speech of Rock Edict XII; Barua, trans., *Inscriptions of Asoka*, 131, explains this expressions as "that kind of self-restraint which enables the adherents of different sects to learn one another's doctrine."

[39] Barua, trans., *Inscriptions of Asoka*, 8.

[40] Hultzsch, *Inscriptions of Asoka*, 14.

[41] Rock Edict No. XII.

[42] Schneider (1978: 115) translates "Religionsgemeinschaften."

[43] This occurred especially during quinquinnial festivals, when the Buddhist community formally received imperial offerings (*dana*).

[44] In his translation Schneider (1978: 115) provides an interpretation that differs from the renderings by Barua and Hultzsch: "Daher sind Versammlungen gut, damit sie voneinander den Dhammha sowohl horen as befolgen."

[45] Barua, trans., *Inscriptions of Asoka*, 12; Hultzsch, *Inscriptions of Asoka*, 43 translates this passage as follows: King Devanampriya Priyadarshin is honoring all sects: ascetics or householders, with gifts and with honors of various kinds. But Devanampriya does not value either gifts or honors so (highly) as (this), (viz.) that a promotion of the essentials of all sects should take place. This promotion of the essentials (is possible) in many ways. But its root is this viz. guarding (one's) speech, (i.e.) that neither praising one's own sect nor blaming other sects should take place on improper occasions, or (that) it should be moderate in every case. But other sects ought to be honored in every way. If one is acting thus, he is promoting his own sect considerably and benefiting other sects as well. If one is acting otherwise than thus, he is both hurting his own sect and wrongdoing other sects as well. For whosoever praises his own sect or blames other sects – all (this) out of pure devotion to his own sect, (i.e.) with the view of glorifying his own sect, - if he is acting thus, he rather injures his own sect very severely. But concord id mysterious, (i.e.) that they should both hear and obey each other's morals. For this is the desire of Devanapriya, (viz) that all sects should be both full of earing and pure in doctrine ..." See Hultzsch, *Inscriptions of Asoka*, 21 for a translation of a similar rock edict in Girnar.

[46] According to the *Digha-nikaya*, Sakyamuni tells his disciples not only to react in a restrained way towards criticism from outside (as quoted above), but he urges them also to be moderate in respect to praise: "... brethren, if outsiders should speak in praise of me, in praise of the Doctrine, in praise of the Order, you should not, on that account, be filled with pleasure or gladness, or be lifted up in heart. Were you to be so that would stand in the way of your self-conquest. When outsiders speak in praise of me, in praise of the Doctrine, in praise of the Order, you should acknowledge what is right to be the fact, saying: 'For this or that reason this is the fact, that is so, such a thing is found among us, in us.'" (Rhys Davids 1959: 3).

[47] Barua, trans., *Inscriptions of Asoka*, 146 explains *saravadhi* (growth of substance or essence) as follows: *sara* is first of all a botanical term, but also a religious term, as it is used here.

[48] Hultzsch, *Inscriptions of Asoka*, 43

[49] Schneider (1978: 115).

[50] Barua, trans., *Inscriptions of Asoka*, 12.

[51] In his explanation of the term (and by referring to Rock Edict No. IV), Barua, trans., *Inscriptions of Asoka*, 146 states that for Ashoka, "piety and virtue (*dhamma, sila*) constitute the *sara* or essence of all religions." Here, Barua replaces "all things" as the object of essence by "all religions." He further identifies the essence as piety and virtue (*dhamma, sila*).

[52] The word "bei" is here remarkably vague because it leaves open whether "Relionsgemeinschaften" are the agents of growth in essence, or whether they are the object of essence.

[53] Barua, trans., *Inscriptions of Asoka*, 33.

[54] Hultzsch, *Inscriptions of Asoka*, 43; cf. 22; Barua, trans., *Inscriptions of Asoka*, 12 translates this sentence as follows: "And this is the result of that, namely, an increase in the fame of one's own sect as well as glorification of the doctrine." Schneider (1978: 117) translates: "Und dies ist die Frucht ebendessen: dass sowohl Wachstum der eigenen Religionsgemeinschaft stattfindet als auch Glorifizierung des Dhaṃma."

[55] For studies of Ashoka's use and understanding of this term as public moral (or moral law), see Mookerji, *Asoka*, 69-78; Hultzsch, *Inscriptions of Asoka*, xlvii-lv; Schneider 1978: 156-160.

[56] Barua, trans., *Inscriptions of Asoka*, 12; Hultzsch, *Inscriptions of Asoka*, 43. The task of these officials was to distribute gifts among the different sects and honor them, "to encourage the to restrain their speech with a view to the practice of tolerance," and "to persuade them to co-operate with one another for their growth in essential matters of religion and enable them to be well-informed and possessed of a sound tradition." Barua, trans., *Inscriptions of Asoka*, 147.

[57] Hajime Nakamura, *Indian Buddhism: A Survey with Bibliographical Notes* (Hirakata: Kansai University of Foreign Studies Publication, 1980), 151.

[58] H. Kern, trans., *The Saddharma-Pundarika or The Lotus of the True Law* (Dehli: Motilal Banarsidass Publishers [1884], 1989), 80. According to Mahayana, this vehicle of listeners or disciples of the Buddha, who understand the four noble truths and become *arhat*, designates Hinayana.

[59] Kern, trans., *The Saddharma-Pundarika or The Lotus of the True Law*, 80. According to Mahayana, this vehicle of understanding the twelve links of causation and becoming a self-enlightened Buddha also designates Hinayana.

[60] Kern, trans., *The Saddharma-Pundarika or The Lotus of the True Law*, 80. According to Mahayana, this vehicle of becoming a bodhisattva and working for the awakening not only of one self, but also of others, designates its own self-understanding.

[61] Kern, trans., *The Saddharma-Pundarika or The Lotus of the True Law*, 81.

[62] Kern, trans., *The Saddharma-Pundarika or The Lotus of the True Law*, 54.

[63] Kern, trans., *The Saddharma-Pundarika or The Lotus of the True Law*, 128.

[64] Kern, trans., *The Saddharma-Pundarika or The Lotus of the True Law*, 129.

[65] Kern, trans., *The Saddharma-Pundarika or The Lotus of the True Law*, 129.

[66] According to another passage, those who hear Buddha's law "shall all of them reach supreme, perfect enlightenment." Kern, trans., *The Saddharma-Pundarika or The Lotus of the True Law*, 42.

[67] For a study on this concept, see Michael Pye, *Skillful Means: A Concept in Mahayana Buddhism* (London: Duckworth, 1978), 18-83.

[68] Kern, trans., *The Saddharma-Pundarika or The Lotus of the True Law*, 72. As illustration for the function of *upaya* serves the famous parable of the burning house; see, Kern, trans., *The Saddharma-Pundarika or The Lotus of the True Law*, 72-76.

[69] Kern, trans., *The Saddharma-Pundarika or The Lotus of the True Law*, 75.

[70] Cf., Pye, *Skillful Means: A Concept in Mahayana Buddhism*, 30.

[71] The Lotus Sutra considers the teachings of the three vehicles as skillful mean; see, Kern, trans., *The Saddharma-Pundarika or The Lotus of the True Law*, 75.

[72] The Tathagata teaches the 'one vehicle,' and there is no second or a third vehicle. Kern, trans., *The Saddharma-Pundarika or The Lotus of the True Law*, 40ff.

[73] Heinz Bechert, "Die Erneuerung des asiatischen und die Entstehung des abendländischen Buddhismus," in *Die Welt des Buddhismus*, edited by Heinz Bechert and Reinhard Gombrich (München: Verlag C.H. Beck, 1984), 276.

[74] See e.g. Hultzsch, *Inscriptions of Asoka*, xlviii, first ed. 1925; Barua, trans., *Inscriptions of Asoka*, 146 ff., first ed. 1943; and Mookerji, *Asoka*, 64-68, first ed. 1928. Though the latter first praises the breath of "a lofty spirit of toleration" in Ashoka's edicts (p. 65), he then arrives at a more nuanced and realistic evaluation of this matter (pp. 65 ff. 68).

[75] Barua, trans., *Inscriptions of Asoka*, 146 ff.

[76] Mookerji, *Asoka*, 68, even states concerning Ashoka's 'fear of schism' and his countermeasures: "His intolerance towards dissent or schism was only due to his desire to nip it in the bud before it was too late: the intolerance could be commended if it had anticipated, and ad not followed, the schism."

[77] Luther's famous *Liberty of a Christian*, or the juridical concept of negative freedom (freedom from ...) paired by the positive term (freedom for ...), are only two examples. Since some years, retired statesmen attempt to supplement the United Nation's Charter of Human Rights by a Charter of Human Responsibilities.

Toward an Interfaith Encounter: Islamic Perspective

Safia Amir

The Need for Interfaith Perspective

In a world drawn inexorably close together by the demands of globalisation, it is becoming increasingly important to develop an interfaith perspective. The convergence of faith communities makes it imperative to build bridges of reconciliation and peace across not only religions, but even cultures and civilisations. Genuine interfaith dialogue and cooperation is a significant way of bringing the world together, leading to the creation of a harmonious environment needed to build a world of peace, justice and prosperity for all. At a time when the world has become a global village, the destiny of all of humankind is inextricably bound together, whether it is about the fight against deadly disease like AIDS, the outbreak of pandemics, widespread ecological degradation, or the dangers of a nuclear holocaust.

In the vitiated political climate in India, it is all the more necessary for its various faith communities to work together to promote probity and ethical values in public life. In fact, because they are plagued alike by problems like the erosion of moral values, communalism, poverty and unemployment; and equally impacted by social evils like excessive materialism, exploitations of weaker sections, caste discrimination, dowry, female infanticide, drug addiction and alcoholism they need to work together to combat these common dangers. In such a multi-religious and multi-cultural society, ethics affords one of the most important modes of interfaith communication and co-operation.

It is necessary for various faith communities to engage with each other through dialogue and interaction, in order to dispel prejudices, clear doubts, minimize suspicions, built trust, and come to a better understanding of other's ideology. Since the foundation of all religions rests on ethics, it is best suited to being made the basis for their co-operation and convergence. In a world torn by strife and conflict, and in an age when exclusivist religious ideologies are threatening to hijack the process, the best way to advance our understanding of the other's faith is by appealing to the spirituality, compassion, ethical values, and respect for all, that are common to all religious traditions.

Ethics in the Qur'ān and the Sunnah

The Qur'ān is essentially a book of ethics, setting out an exemplary code of human conduct. The essential purpose of the Quran is to enable human to live at peace with themselves, and the external world, so the humankind might live together, in the words of Muhammad the Prophet as a "Family of Allah (Bukhārī), or as "a fold, every member of which shall be a keeper or shepherd unto each other, and be accountable for the welfare of the fold" (Bukhārī). Thus Islam aims at developing in human a sense of inward peace operating for peace among humankind, peace which will keep them company in the life hereafter as well. The stress is on the perfection of the individual through which the perfection of society is to be sought. As a messenger has said, "respect the ways of Allah and be affectionate to the family of Allah." The qualities of kindness purity, chastity, love, affection, truth, neighbourliness, tolerance, forbearance, forgiveness, trustworthiness, justice, mercy, the honouring of commitments, and other such virtues need to be cultivated in the interests of one's inward peace, and of peaceful relations between human to human. To live thus is to live in Islam, which in itself mean 'peace' that peace which is attained by surrendering to the will of Allah.[1]

Islam has always been a champion of religious pluralism: as the last of the Semitic and Abrahamic faiths, it is inherently inclusive, recognising all previous prophets in the tradition, and their books and religious teachings. In fact in the Qur'ān the Prophet is asked to appeal to the People of the Book in the name of their shared belief in monotheism, to come to an agreement to renew their common commitment to it (Qur'ān 3:64).

The Qur'ān explicitly states that the existence of multiplicity of religions is as per the will of Allah "for each we have planted a divine law and a traced-out way. Had Allah willed He [sic] could have made you one community." Further, this diversity of religious tradition is also a trial for humankind (Qur'ān 5:48). It also states categorically that "there is no compulsion in religion (Qur'ān 2:256). Religious dialogue, according to the Qur'ān must be civilized and cultured (Qur'ān 29:46).

The Qur'ān repeatedly underlines the common origin in humankind, which is the basis for their universal brotherhood (Qur'ān 4:1 and Qur'ān 49:13). This is also borne out by the Messenger's sermon during his farewell pilgrimage and numerous other aḥadīth or traditions (Abu Dawūd: 1508; Aḥmad ibn Ḥanbal: 1880). Since the whole humankind as one family, they must cooperate in worldly affairs, irrespective of their religious affiliations. Honouring this common bond of humanity over and above religious difference is the only way forward for their peaceful co-existence in the world.

Therefore in its moral and ethical teaching Islam does not differentiate between Muslims and others: Qur'ān commands regarding the sanctity of human live (Qur'ān 5:32; 6:151), justice and equity toward all (Qur'ān 5:8; 16:90), the merits of charity (Qur'ān 2:272), and the prohibition of social evils like slander, ridicule, back-biting, suspicion and spying (Qur'ān 49:11-12), apply not only to Muslims, but to others as well.

In like manner there are many aḥadīth in which the Messenger upholds the inviolability of the right to life, honour and property of a non-Muslim citizen of a Muslim state (Bukhārī: 3166; Abu Dawūd: 3035) and the rights of neighbours, irrespective of their religious affiliation. We get detailed picture of religious tolerance in practice from the sunnah of the Prophet.

Muslim Attitude towards Indian Religions: A Historical Perspective
Within the Arabian Peninsula, the early Muslim community was born in the midst of local Christians, Jews, polytheist and some Sabians. Later, as the Arab Muslims expanded outside the peninsula, into a large part of the then known world, they came into contact with their religious communities as well, such as the Zoroastrians, Buddhists and Hindus. Thus, being exposed to the world's religions from the very early times, and in keeping with their quest for knowledge, catholicity of spirit, or missionary zeal, Muslim historians, travellers, people of letters, theologians and jurists, attempted

to study, an thus understand their beliefs and ways: ibn Ḥazm, al-Bīrūnī, ash-Shahrastānī, al-Masʿūdī and Ibn Khaldūn are some of the famous names in the field, who are "considered as forerunners of the modern study of religion." As a result of their endeavours, Muslims recognised the greatness of other contemporary civilisations in South Asia and the Far East, which provoked much more interest than Christian Europe. The *Fihrist* of ibn al-Nadīm, written around 900 C.E. "shows to what extent Muslim culture was interested in the outside world ... and is a work to which the modern discipline o the history of religions is indebted."[2]

As a result Muslims have always, even in the medieval period, accepted the reality of religious pluralism, in being conscious of followers of various religions living side by side in one universal world. They thus followed "the idea that all believers are deeply united through their belief in the One God and the existence of a shared, primordial, monotheistic religion."[3] Particularly those immersed in Islamic mysticism were much more open to and tolerant of those belonging to other religious traditions, and believed in peaceful co-existence for all, on the basis of their acute consciousness of shared ethics and a common humanity.

Islam first came to India through Arab traders who visited and later settled on its southern coast. In the North, it came through travellers, traders, missionaries and the conquest of Sindh by Moḥamed bin Qāsim. Parts of north India were ruled at first intermittently, by conquerors like Muḥammad and Maḥmud Ghaznavi; later Muslim rule was established for six and a half centuries over large parts of the subcontinent by the Delhi Sultanate, followed by the Mughals. These Muslim rulers followed an enlightened policy of benevolence and co-operation towards their non-Muslim subjects and peaceful co-existence of all faith communities was the accepted norm of the day.

India has always been a meeting-ground of religions and cultures, and the medieval period was no different. Even as the armies of Maḥmud of Ghaznavi were ravaging Indian cities in almost annual forays, the scholar al-Bīrūnī was writing his invaluable *kitāb tarikh al-hind*, which was competed in 1030 C.E. Born in 973 in Khwarizm (modern Khiva), he established himself as a historian and student of comparative religion by writing a detailed and important work on the religions and institutions of ancient people, quite early in life. Around the year 1020 or so, he was brought to India by Sūltan

Maḥmud during one of his campaigns, where al-Bīrūnī spent many years in the company of Hindu pandits, learnt Sanskrit, and studied their religion and culture from them personally, from their texts, and through inquiry and personal observations. The resultant work is remarkable for its fairness and impartiality, and as an attempt to reach a true understandings and faithful conclusions, based on the Hindus' own rendering of their belief. No wonder it is said that "his attitude toward other religions betrays openness and inquisitive that testify to a modern mind in search of universal truth." He also came to the conclusion that "Greeks and Hindus also knew God as One," but through philosophy and mystical experience.[4]

Abū al-Māli's *kitāb bayān al-adyān* written around 1900 C.E. in Ghana, is the earliest Persian work in the field of comparative religion. In it he praises the Hindus highly "for their refinement and wisdom." In medieval Muslim theology, "the Barahima (Brahmins) were described as those accepting reason and believing in one God (*muwaḥḥidah*) but rejecting prophecy." The unknown author of the *kitāb al-bad' wa al-tarikh*, written around 965 suggests that the monotheistic Barahima (Brahmins) revere one god who sent an angel to them in human form." Another author al-Gardizi who died around the year 1060 describes two Hindu sects "in purely monotheistic terms."[5]

About the year 1125 C.E. ash-Shahrastānī of Khurasan wrote the famous *kitāb al-milal wa al-nihal*, which went on to become a classic, and in which, among other religions, he has studied the Hindus (Brahmins, Vaishnavas and Shaivas), and the Buddhist. He believed that Sabianism is mentioned in the Qur'ān along with the People of the Book, because it was situated somewhere between monotheism and polytheism, being a deviation from the former. In fact, by presenting Hinduism "as a form of the more or less admissible Sabianism" al-Shahrastani tries to "legitimize" the thought and worship of the former. He reasoned that real idolaters were those who worshipped human-made idols, like pagan Arabs, whereas the Vaishnavas and Shiavas "venerate Vishnu and Shiva as Spiritual Beings who were incarnated … as a consequence they cannot be called idolaters in a strict sense of the word." Similarly, those Hindus who worshiped the sun and the moon were like the Sabians star worshippers, "which is a grade lower, but still not idolatry." At the same times "he gives a fair treatment of Buddhism about which Muslim communities at the time could not have known much."[6]

Rashīd al-din (d. 1318 C.E), the author of the world history named *Jāmi'* *al-tawārīkh*, is also flexible in interpreting Hinduism. This positive attitude towards Indian religions became all the more pronounced when Muslims began ruling over parts of the subcontinent. As per the Mālikī and Hanafī schools of jurisprudence, the "Hindus were not considered as polytheist (*mushrikūn*) in the strict sense." They could thus be accorded the status of *dhimmīs* by the Muslim rulers of India, and the protection that was due to them as such. During the Mughal period of Indian history positive Muslim views of Indian religions would gain further currency.[7]

Indian 'Ulamā and Religious Co-existence

In the modern period, the **'ulamā** of India were in the forefront of the first war of independence fought against the British in 1857. Even after its failure they did not give up the struggle against the foreign government. In fact the scholars associated with the Dār al 'Ulūm at Deoband believed that it was the religious duty of the Indian Muslims to co-operate with their fellow-countrymen of other faiths to oust the tyrannical government of an alien country. Scholars like Mawlānā Husayn Ahmad Madani and Abul Kalām Āzād tried to demonstrate that the Muslims of India, by virtue of being natives of this country, partook of an inalienable composite nationalism along with their non-Muslim compatriots, and should, on these grounds, undertake joint action with them for their common good, without compromising their religious principles in any way.[8] The model that was most frequently invoked in support of this argument was the Prophet's *Mithāq-i madīnah* or the Constitution of Madīna, in which it was expressly stated that in all worldly matters which did not go against their faith, the Muslims of Madīna were one nation (*'ummat-i wāhidah'*) with its Jews and other inhabitants.[9] Thus the model espoused was not the passive one of merely peaceful co-existence, but a far more active one of joint action and co-operation for the common good.

Today, after more than sixty years of shared nationhood, it behoves the various faith communities of modern India to work together for their common good on the line of shared ethical and mutual cooperation. As for Muslims, the Qur'ān guides them by asking them to help one another in righteousness and pious duty, not in sin and transgression, and to be ever mindful of their duty to their Lord (Qur'ān 5:2). It also urges its followers not to hesitate in being kind to those non-Muslims who have not fought them on account of their region, for Allah love those who are just (Qur'ān 60:8). And finally, it teaches Muslims the loftiest ethical principle: that of repelling evil by good, which is sure to make friends out of sworn enemies (Qur'ān 41:43).

Endnotes

[1] Syed Abdul Latif, *Principles of Islamic Cultures* (Madras: University of Madras, 1961), 31-35.

[2] Jacques Waardenburg, *Muslim Perceptions of Other Religions: A Historical Survey* (New York: Oxford University Press, 1999), 23, 25.

[3] Waardenburg, *Muslim Perceptions of Other Religions: A Historical Survey*, 24.

[4] Waardenburg, *Muslim Perceptions of Other Religions: A Historical Survey*, 26-29.

[5] Waardenburg, *Muslim Perceptions of Other Religions: A Historical Survey*, 30, 34-35.

[6] Waardenburg, *Muslim Perceptions of Other Religions: A Historical Survey*, 29-30, 34.

[7] Waardenburg, *Muslim Perceptions of Other Religions: A Historical Survey*, 34-35.

[8] Safia Amir, *Muslim Nationhood in India: Perceptions of Seven Eminent Thinkers* (New Delhi: Kanishka Publishers, 2000), 153, 183.

[9] Amir, *Muslim Nationhood in India: Perceptions of Seven Eminent Thinkers*, 158, 185.

The Challenge of
Religious Pluralism and the Indian Context

K. P. Aleaz

Inter-religious relations in the emerging contemporary pluralist geo-political context of India is not healthy or encouraging as violence against Christians has erupted in certain pockets, because of the Christian violence against the gospel of God in Jesus. In this paper we analyse the patterns of this Christian violence against the gospel. Actually religious pluralism is a blessing for mutual enrichment of religious experiences. There is a need for us to experience the gospel of God in Jesus in the line of such a vision, rather than perpetuating violence against the gospel.

Christian Violence against the Gospel

When we think of the challenge of religious pluralism and the Indian context it would be good if we Christians do not forget the following two contentions I have: (a) Conversion by Christian churches is understood by many people in India only as proselytizing through the use of force, fraud and inducement or allurement, which is nothing but a Christian violence against the gospel of God in Jesus. (b) Another aspect of the Christian violence against the gospel being committed in India relates to the projection of Christianity as a foreign religion supposedly by Christians. It is such a Christian violence against the gospel such as these which are the causes for recent violence against Christians in India.

In the recent past, tense and violent relations between Hindus and Christians in India were generating their own heat as Hindu nationalist groups such as the Viswa Hindu Parisad, Bajarang Dal, Rastriya Swayam Sevak Sangh and the Bharatiya Janata Party hail a new 'Hindu Renaissance.'

It should be noted that the current crisis in Hindu- Christian relations reproduces fundamental disagreements and divergent perceptions already manifest in India since the early 19th century. The two issues in focus are conversion and the foreign character of Christianity.

The Hindu nationalist voices regard conversion as an act of one individual upon another as an object. Conversion occurred largely by means of fraud or inducement. Hindutva exponents maintain a strong link between the activity of proselytizing Christians and the abandonment of ancestral faith by converts to Christianity. The conversion activities undertaken by Christian churches in India are understood by the Sangh Parivar as proselytizing activities. The Supreme Court Judgment on the Orissa and Madhya Pradesh Bills on freedom of religion in 1977 understood conversion by Christians as proselytizing: 'There is no fundamental right to convert another person to one's own religion because if a person purposely undertakes the conversion of another person to his religion, as distinguished from his effort to transmit or spread the tenets of his religion, that would impinge on the 'freedom of conscience' guaranteed to all the citizens of the country alike'. Freedom for 'propagation' granted by Articles 25 (1) does not mean conversion understood as proselytizing.

The freedom of religion bills passed by the different Indian States understood Christian conversion as proselytizing. For example the object of *Orissa Freedom of Religion Act, 1968* is stated thus: 'To provide for prohibition of conversion from one religion to another by the use of Force or Inducement or by Fraudulent means and for matters incident thereto'. *The Madhya Pradesh Dharma Swatantrya Adhiniyam, 1968* also gives the statement of objects and reasons as: 'The Bill seeks to prohibit conversions by use of force or by allurement or by any fraudulent means'. The object of the *Arunachal Pradesh Freedom of Religion Act, 1978* again is stated as to provide for prohibition of conversion from indigenous faith to any other faith by use of force or inducement or by fraudulent means and matters connected therewith.

The Orissa Act defines 'force' and 'inducement' in the following way: 'Force' shall include a show of force or a threat of injury of any kind including threat of divine displeasure or social excommunication. 'Fraud' shall include misrepresentation or any other fraudulent contrivance. 'Inducement' shall include the offer of any gift or gratification, either in cash or in kind, and shall also include the grant of any benefit, either pecuniary or otherwise. In the Madhya Pradesh Act also 'force' and 'fraud' are defined as in the Orissa Act. Allurement is explained as offer of any temptation in the form it (i) gift or gratification either in cash or in kind; (ii) grant of any material benefit, either monetary or otherwise. The Arunachal Pradesh Act again is very similar to the other two Acts in the definition of terms of the objects. The statement of objects and the definition of the key terms in it of these Acts thus clearly show that conversion by Christian churches is understood by many people in India only as proselytizing through the use of force, fraud and inducement or allurement which is nothing but a Christian violence against the Gospel of God in Jesus.

Such a Christian violence against the gospel of God in Jesus in the second half of the 20th c. has to be understood as a continuation of the violence committed by the Christian missionaries from the beginning of the 19th c. or even before. For example, the activities of many of the Christian missionaries were found intolerable to Raja Ram Mohan Roy and in 1821 he had the following words of criticism:

> During the last twenty years, a body of English gentlemen, who are called missionaries, have been publicly endeavouring, in several ways, to convert Hindus and Musulmans of this country into Christianity. The first way is that of publishing among the natives various books, large and small reviling both religions, and abusing and ridiculing the Gods and Saints of the former; the second way is that of standing in front of the doors of the natives or in the public roads to preach the excellence of their own religion and the debasedness of that of others; the third way is that if any native of low origin become Christian from the desire of gain or from any other motives, these gentlemen employ and maintain them as a necessary encouragement to others to follow their example.

The Bengali language newspaper *Samacar Chandrika* established in 1822 by Bhabanicaran Bandhyopadhyay, the secretary of the Dharma Sabha became a mouthpiece for religiously conservative Hindus in Calcutta and it had regular exchanges over religious issues with *Samacar Darpan* edited by J. C. Marshman, one of the Serampore missionary trio. From Bandhyopadhyay's perspective, missionaries in Bengal routinely resorted to outright fraud, coercion, and material inducement in order to win converts. His paper produced evidences for such a claim. It consistently presented converts to

Christianity as apostates from Hindu society – traitors who had taken refuge with foreigners (e.g. October 4, 1830).

In the nineties of 19th c. another prominent Indian, Swami Vivekananda had the following to say in a lecture delivered to the Western audience: "You train and educate and clothe and pay men [sic] to do what? To come over to my country to curse and abuse all my forefathers, my religion, and everything." They walk near temple, and say, "you idolaters, you will go to hell." But they dare not do that to the Mohammendans of India: the sword would be out. But the Hindu is too mild; he smiles and passes on and says, "let the fools talk." Or to quote Mahatma Gandhi to know the Christian missionary methods in the first half of the 20th c.: "I am not against conversion. But I am against the modern methods of it. Conversion nowadays has become a matter of business, like any other. I remember having read a missionary report saying how much it cost per head to convert and then presenting a budget for the 'next harvest.'"

These few examples show that in the 19th and the first half of 20th c. most of the Christian missionaries had a negative imperialist attitude to other religious faiths in India. The way in which they perceived their faith in relation to other faiths i.e., in their theology of religions, the missionaries maintained exclusivism. It is amazing to note that in spite of such a negative attitude from the Christian missionaries; these and many other Hindu leaders were influenced by Christ and his ideals to reform their own religious faith and society. We can identify an acknowledged Christ of Indian Renaissance. It is also amazing to note that in spite of such a Christian violence against the gospel of God in Jesus being continued all through the 20th c. India, still today there are lakhs and lakhs of unbaptized believers in Jesus who is admitted and a survey showed for example that around 10% of the Hindu population of Chennai are unbaptized believers in Jesus.

The second aspect of the Christian violence against the gospel being committed in India relates to the Christian projection of Christianity as a foreign religion. It should be noted that Mahatma Gandhi developed a dislike for Christianity (but not for Christ) because the missionaries abused at street corners Hindus and their Gods; and also they encouraged the converts to eat beef, drink liquor and to have European costume. He said: "Unfortunately, Christianity in India has been inextricably mixed up….with the British rule. It appears to us as synonymous with materialistic civilization and imperialistic exploitation by the strong white races of the weaker races of the world. Its contribution to India has been therefore, largely of a negative character." To quote again: "I have never been able to reconcile myself to the gaieties of the Christmas season. They have appeared to me to be so inconsistent with the life and teaching of Jesus." Further Gandhiji has said: "It is a first class human tragedy that people of the earth who claim to believe in the message of Jesus whom they describe as the Prince of Peace, show little of that belief in actual practice."

Why did Babasaheb B. R. Ambedkar and his Mahar community reject Christianity and get converted to Buddhism? As we know, he was much impressed by the message of Christ. But the churches created by the Christian Missions produced 'a different feeling' in him. He saw the Christian Missions as an instrument of de-socialisation as conversions to Christianity was making Christians of 'outcaste' origin selfish and self-centred. To quote: "They do not care a snap of their finger what becomes of their former caste associates so long as they and their families, or they and the little group who have become Christians get ahead. Indeed their chief concern with reference to their old caste associates is to hide the fact that they were in the same community. I do not want to add to the number of such Christians." Ambedkarji thought that conversion to Christianity would denationalize the Depressed Classes; would strengthen the hold of British imperialism in India.

The Viswa Hindu Parishad today hold the same allegation that Christian Missions are not just converting but denationalizing the people and therefore they urge that the Constitution be amended to outlaw 'foreign priests' and 'propagation by foreigners' (15th Jan. 1999). The Sangh Parivar maintains that because of its wealth, its alliance with international educational organizations, and its favourable treatment by the Western media, Christianity is a powerful source of Western influence in India (6th Feb. 1999). The adoption of Hindu style of worship, terminology, community living and so forth by Christians appear to them nothing other than a more sophisticated version of the same fraud that had been perpetrated for generations upon unsuspecting Indians in order to convert them to the foreign religion Christianity.

Therefore, we Indian Christians have to look forward to a future when instead of committing violence against the gospel, we will enable the gospel to emerge the hermeneutical context of India. The gospel of God in Jesus emerging from within India would be India's own gospel with new insights and meanings, and not something foreign. Also, such a gospel experience would mean one's own conversion and not proselytizing through the use of force, fraud and inducement or allurement.

Conclusion

Christian violence against the gospel of God in Jesus which is the cause for recent violence against Christians in India can be eliminated in terms of an Indian understanding and experience of the gospel of God in Jesus emerging from the context of pluralist faith-experiences.

Proselytizing a person through the use of force, fraud and inducement or allurement by another person has to end at the earliest and genuine conversion meaning one's own acceptance of the discipleship of Jesus has to take place in India. Genuine conversion is exclusively in terms of a personal inward experience. The person who has such an experience, may or may not change his/her outward religious 'label', as per his/her own conscience. Genuine conversion is always a double conversion. That is, in the very conversion to Jesus in India, there is a conversion to the religio-cultural context of India, effecting thus a double conversion and this hinds to the possible relational convergence of religious experiences. If the gospel of God in Jesus has to emerge from the hermeneutical context of India, we can rightly say that Indian Christians are in a process of converting to the Indian religio-cultural context. The Indian religio-cultural context will decide the content of the gospel of God in Jesus for India. The gospel is not pre-formulated, but is in the process of formulation. The faith-experience of the Indian Christian is not pre-formulated, but is in the process of formulation through the guidance of Hindu and other religious experiences. Living as a community with the people of other faiths becomes a reality in terms of such a vision and its practice.

Spirituality for Interfaith Thinking: A Hindu Perspective

Reeta Bagchi

In present century the world is transiting through scientific and technological advancement promoting material prosperity in human lives all over the world. Despite material prosperity the quest for spirituality has grown more and human looks to religion for spirituality enlightened blissful life and traditional wisdom. The spiritual component of religion is the real element which develop divine attribute in the individual personality with a view of attending higher goal of life. Human has unique inner faculty which inspires him/her to evolve from a lower level to a higher level of consciousness. It contributes to the attainment of perfection by eliminating the dichotomy between human's external and internal life, between his material and the spiritual advancement.

Every religion is a treasure house of spiritual wisdom. Different religions of the world contribute in their own way to the transformation of primitive human into a civilized one. The precepts of religions bind the soul with God showing the path leading to a spiritual state that is peaceful, disciplined and moral. It recognizes the divine spark within each individual and stresses upon the essential unity of humankind by improving her personal and social life and the culture of civilization. In this age of global integration of human community religion is being looked upon as a science of spirituality which tries to understand interfaith relationship.

Ethics, religion and spirituality are synonymous terms in common parlance as they coexist in the elevation of human's consciousness. While religion is more socially organized, spirituality is more inward looking to one's own spirit or self. It is religion in practice and spirituality in principle.

Spiritualism purifies hearts and promotes wisdom. It integrates the total personality of a human – physical, vital, intellectual, emotional and spiritual. It is the spiritual consciousness of every human being that raises human to blessedness and true freedom. A righteous and virtuous life is the backbone of spiritual progress of human and society. The enlightened human becomes aware of the harmonious world order and a more humane civilization.

Spiritualism is above dogmatism, obscurantism and fundamentalism. These are sectarian and dogma bound exterior aspect of religion which stress on forms, ritualism and code of conduct that binds its adherents to a rigid and complex religio-social system. These externals of religion appeal to emotions rather than to the rational mind, stresses in preserving the outer forms rather than pursuing the inner spirit of religion. Such belief system has several dimensions: ritualistic, ceremonial, mythological etc. Such orthodox institutionalized religions translate transcendental spiritual universal truth into dogmatic form hidden below symbols and ritualistic practices. The dogmatic aspect of religion represents darker side of religion which is rigid, narrow and intolerant. It covers the intrinsic spirit with selfish motives, works through elaborate organizations of priesthood, temples and other procedures. It does not agree to the synthesis of religions. This aspect of religion has been the cause of many violent conflicts in the religious history of humankind. Even in present century one experiences such religiosity in practice. On the other hand spiritualism has potentialities to unite. While the former attitudes divide the society, spiritualism enlightens vision and understanding of humankind. It guides its adherents towards spiritual wisdom through values, duties and responsibilities towards unity of all human being irrespective of race and religion. The quality of human life is determined by the ethical culture.

The greatness and continuity of Indian civilization lies in its achievement in the field of spirituality. It has characteristics to combine, assimilate and harmonize. It gives opportunity to know the people of other faiths. The result can be seen that the various cultures and religions have flourished together in this land and contributed towards Indian way of life. All the religions help in developing the universalistic outlook of commonness against exclusiveness of the particular tradition. Indian religious practices elevated generation with their precepts. Spirituality or mystical charm has always drawn people from all over the world to India. That sense of religion is not based on dogmas, sects or names but a means of spiritual realization, in the sense of seeing

God and serving him in all human beings. According to it all the externals of religions, rituals, priesthood and temples are intended to a waken faith and source of spiritual enlightenment following the inner law of the spirit.

Spirituality in Hinduism

Hinduism owns a vast treasure of spiritual wisdom to awaken the human being to transcendental mystery and the way to its attainment. Mystical ideas have universal appeal and this can be traced to the scriptures. It guides human on the basis of righteous action aiming towards perfection. It enables human to go beyond images, rituals to experience the ultimate reality which is one. Traditional Hinduism speaks of universal spirituality: 'Truth alone triumphs' (*satyameva jayate*). Hindu scriptures records varieties of spiritual experiences based on the collective wisdom of great seers and sages in different periods of time. It provides freedom to its adherents to choose the belief system that suits him/her best.

Rig-Veda expressed the concept of mankind as a single family – *vasudhāiva kutumbakam* (Rig-Veda 1.191.2). It further says: "Common be your action and achievements, common be your thoughts and intentions, common be the wishes of your hearts, so may there be union amongst you" (Rig-Veda 10.192). The morning and evening prayers are universal and for all irrespective of caste, community or religion – "May all be happy, May all be free from pains and sorrows. May other thoughts integrate in the minds of people" (*sarve sukhino bhavantu, sarve bhavantu niramaya, sarve bhadrani pasyantu, ma kashid dukha bhag bhavet*). The Vedic message was that the truth is one, sages call it in various names (*ekam sad vipra vahudha vadanti*). Ramakrishna repeated the same – *yato mat tatho path*. Each religion is accepted as valid path for the attainment of perfection, variously suited for human to different temperament, capacities and attitudes. The Hindu Scriptures emphasize on friendly evaluation of the doctrines and practices of other faiths. The aim is to bring what is best in different religions – Yajurveda says, "*a no bhadra kritavo yantuvishvataha* (Let the noble thoughts come from all sides)." The Indian culture, its philosophy, values, literature, art and architecture and socio- political system is based on multi-sided spirituality.

The unity of being is stressed in the Upaniṣad. It says: 'All variations are matters of mere words and names' I. IV. 4. It formed the basis of Vedanta and provided a practical philosophy of spiritualization of human life and its goal. The spirituality is expressed in literatures written in Sanskrit the most ancient language of India. It has been a common language of rich literary and spiritual culture of India. The languages of various ethnic groups of diverse origin eventually merged. Its successor Hindi and other regional languages played significant role in promoting the understanding of rich spiritual culture of India.

Sometimes it is believed that truthfulness and other spiritual values are one's personal matters. But spirituality involves all social relations. Gandhi says, "There is not a single virtues which aims at or content with the welfare of the individual alone. In the same way there is not a single offence which does not directly or indirectly affect many others besides the actual offender. Hence a virtuous life is the concern of whole community as well as of the whole world." The divine virtues override all social stratifications and distinctions mankind encompasses a vast area pertaining to family, civil society, democratic polity and religious code and conduct. It provides physiological, psychological and social bonds with integration in national and international levels. These are sings of acceptance of integrated life.

Hinduism has set forth the pursuit of *Dharma* (religion), *Artha* (wealth), *Kāma* (Enjoyment) and Moksha (liberation) as the goal of life. It suggests that there is a need for harmony of temporal and spiritual aspects of life because the worldly life is the gateway to the spiritual life. Today there is separation of spiritual values and activities of life. There is a great need of spiritualization of religious, social, economic and political life. Law of selfless action (*nishkāma karma*) directs human to spirituality. The highest aim of humankind is realizing that spirituality to attain liberation (moksha). Yoga system has played as important role in the evolution of spiritualism. Different Yogas – *Asanas, Dhyāna, Dhārana* and *Samadhi* are recommended for physical and psychological wellbeing of all practitioners. A process of spiritual discipline enables human to discover the inner self which is considered immortal. Hindu scriptures exhort human to recognize one's potential and conquer oneself by overcoming anger by love, evil by good, greed by contentment and falsehood by truth to seek redemption universally (*sarvamūkti*).

The acceptance of diversity is inherent in the pluralistic tradition of India. It accommodates a vast variety of precepts for our spiritual journey. Diversity in society reflects diversity of temperaments. That is the reason that there are many sects and movements. The religious pluralism help in interfaith understanding. It believes in the harmony of all religions. The different religions are considered as pathways to the same common goal. Harmony of religions are not uniform, it is a harmony in diversity. It is not based on a mere intellectual understanding, but is to be discovered by realizing spiritual consciousness of divinity of all souls. All are in the spiritual quest for salvation. In the vision of cosmic unity, human and nature are sustained by essential oneness of whole creation.

Earth, water, fire, air, plants, animals etc. are seen to be enveloped in the cosmic whole by a hidden power – universal consciousness. According to Upanishad, "Life is a homogenous organic whole contained in every expressions of life" (*ishavasya idam sarvam yatkinchajagatyam jagat—Isopaniṣad-*1). It shows respect to all living beings including trees, rivers, rocks and water for a positive and healthy life.

The spiritual leaders and saints have delivered the message of peace, brotherhood and co-existence. They stressed upon understanding and harmony with people of different cultures and faiths. Philosopher saints like Kabīr, Chaitanya, Gurū Nānak and others were based upon the assimilation of communities. In the 19th century Ram Mohan Roy guided socio-political reform with the concept of spirituality. In the 20th century we found that Gandhi in his constructive programme giving the first place to interfaith understanding.

East-West Dialogue

Foundation of interfaith thinking was laid in Chicago (1893) with the establishment of 'World Parliament of Religions' where leaders, saints and sages of world religious congregated and evolved a methodology of synthesis of religious and spiritual values for peace and progress. It was an effort to create a global dialogue of faith communities. It led to the series of conferences under the title of 'Parliament of world religions.' It attracted different organizations from all over the world to bridge the gap between faith communities by sharing spiritual values of each other's religions on the way towards understanding.

Swami Vivekananda was the first cultural ambassador and an exponent of universal principles. He represented Hinduism with global mission towards building bridges between India and the west. It opened a new chapter in East-West dialogue to create a borderless world. He interpreted Hindu philosophy and Hindu way of life to develop understanding of Indian cultural heritage to the western people. West realized that they have to learn much from Indian ethos and spirituality. On the other hand India learnt from the West the science and technology including western ideas of individual freedom, social equality and justice leading to humanism. He shared his vision for an end of violence and fanaticism in the name of religion. According to him there is nothing that has brought man more blessing than religion. In his message in Chicago he said, "Secularism, bigotry and its horrible descendent fanaticism have possessed this beautiful earth. These have filled the earth with violence drenched it with human blood, destroyed civilization and brought nations to despair. Had it not been there, human society would have been more advanced than now. Religion does not live in sects, societies or doctrines but it consists in self-realization."

Humankind continues to face suffering due to communal disharmony. It promotes bitterness, misunderstanding and hatred among adherents of different religions. Now such ideology has come to an end filled with a new hope. But this hope has not been fulfilled fully. The vision is there and we must try to achieve the goal. Universal values are inherent in every religion of the world but they need to be clearly articulated in terms of contemporary knowledge of the global society. The spiritual ideals of peace, love, synthesis and harmony are more relevant in the present century.

Christian Spiritual Resources for Christian-Muslim Relations

Victor Edwin, S.J.

Introduction

Christianity and Islam are both monotheistic religions. Belief in one God is of fundamental importance for Christians and Muslims. Both faiths share in a common search for the will of God. However, there are differences in their concept of God. Thus Christianity and Islam are distinctly two different religions each with its own religious and social history. Their faith-convictions, along with the social, cultural, and political situations in which they live, shape the way they understand and interact with each other. The positive exchanges between Christians and Muslims have helped both the groups of believers. The negative interactions have taught them, at least some of them, to avoid falling into negativity. It is heartening to see that both Muslims and Christians continue to open up avenues for better understanding of each other's faith and engage with each other in common tasks for the betterment of humanity.

The Christian sources for relations with Muslims are many and varied. The Bible, especially the Gospel, inspires Christians to love and serve the neighbour, especially one who is in need. No one is outside the realm of God's merciful love. Consequently, for a Christian no one should be an "outsider." Following the Gospel paradigm, many mystics and theologians searched for ways and helped others to enter into fruitful conversation with Muslims. History is full of such examples.

In their paper, I will focus on the lives of a few Christians who, inspired by their faith, engaged in fruitful conversation between Christians and Muslims. Their lives and their contributions are inspiring for all time.

We shall reflect on a great mystic, St Francis of Assisi (d.1226), and a great theologian, St Thomas Aquinas (d.1274), to get guidance for a fruitful interaction between Christians and Muslims. Then we shall give some attention to the witness of Charles de Foucauld (d. 1916), Henri Marechal (d. 1957) and Louis Massignon (d. 1962) who lived close to our time. Their lives and teachings are spiritual resources for Christians, who reach out to Muslims today.

It is important to state the reason for choosing these scholars and mystics for our attention. Francis of Assisi is universally known for his prayer for peace. His city, Assisi, was chosen by the Blessed Pope John Paul II for the meeting of the leaders of different religious traditions. They gathered there in 1987 to pray for peace in the world. Francis met Muslims and preached to them, although briefly. He has some insightful instructions for his brothers about Muslims.

The second figure in our narrative is Aquinas. He was a theologian par excellence. His contribution is vast in every field of philosophy and theology. He is one of the greatest theologians of all time. This great theologian has a number of very interesting things to say about Islam and Muslims.

The other three men lived among Muslims and chose to imitate Christ in their life with them though different ways. Their lives become models for meaningful interaction with the followers of Islam.

Francis and Aquinas

Francis and Aquinas lived in an historical context of the power struggles between Christian and Muslim rulers. In Spain a number of Muslim kingdoms had fallen to the Christian kings. In North Africa a few new Muslim dynasties came to power at their time. Intermittent wars and military expeditions between them were common. In the East, the situation was not better. The Crusader states steadily lost ground under pressure from the Muslim rulers of Egypt. These struggles between Christians and Muslims resulted in the purging of a large number of Muslims from Spain and a similar elimination of Christian rulers in Asia. This situation gave rise to an image of Christian Europe facing a Muslim Asia across the Mediterranean and in North Africa.

While these changes were taking place in Muslim lands, Europe was experiencing cultural and spiritual awakening. European scholars were rediscovering their Greek heritage largely through translations from the Arabic. Universities were established in many European cities. Latin was the lingua franca of the scholarly world. Many scholars under the influence of Muslim philosophers such as Averroes favoured the Aristotelian system of thought rather than the Platonic paradigm since the Aristotelian system was pragmatic and more favourable to new sciences.[1] An intense curiosity in science affected theology too. Theology was expanded to take new approaches. Christian scholars strove to bring about a Christian synthesis of the new explorations then in progress. In other words, Christian Europe was searching for a new identity. In this search unfortunately all evil to be repudiated was projected on to Islam, a symbol of all that was "un-Christian." European scholars portrayed Islam as falsehood and a deliberate perversion of truth. They showed Islam as a religion of violence that was spread by the sword. They saw it as a way of self-indulgence and licentiousness, inspired by Satan and founded by an anti-Christ (Muḥammad). Scholars say that this projection was not deliberate but instinctive: for, Europeans had practically no objective information about Islam and Muslims. At the same time an interior reform swept the Church. Poverty as a value was emphasised in religious life. Many mendicant orders were formed. This was the context in which both Francis and Aquinas lived.

Francis: No Condemnation of Muḥammad or Islam

It needs to be emphasised today that Francis began a new chapter which stood in contrast to the earlier attitudes of condemnation. This new attitude was to approach Muslims with love, not condemning them as followers of a false religion. He felt that God himself was calling him to a new missionary presence among Muslims. The word 'presence among Muslims' needs to be emphasised. With this attitude Francis was keen to go and preach among Muslims either in Syria or Morocco. However, he could not go because he did not enjoy good health. It was the time (1217) when the fifth Crusade was launched. Francis joined the crusader camp at Damietta (Egypt). However, his intention was not to enter into any armed conflict, but to find an opportunity to preach to Muslims. He sought and got permission to go to the Muslim camp. He spent a few days preaching to Caliph al-Mālik al-Kamil. While he was in the Muslim camp he even offered to go through trial by fire to prove the truth of Christianity. Though no one would approve this trail of Francis, the Caliph admired his courage, zeal and detachment.

Francis' attitude towards Islam could be seen from the First Rule he wrote for his Order in which he made reference to Islam. It is worth reproducing it here.

> The Lord said: Behold I am sending you out as sheep among wolves. Be therefore as prudent as snakes and as simple as doves (Matthew 10:16).
>
> Consequently, if some brethren, under God's inspiration, desire to go among Saracens (Muslims) ... let them ask permission from their superior, and if he thinks they are fit to be sent, let him grant them permission, putting no obstacle in their way ... The Brethren who go there may adopt two sorts of behaviour in the Spirit. One is that of avoiding disputes and controversies, submitting instead to every human authority for the sake of the Lord (1 Peter 2:13) declaring them [selves] to be Christians.
>
> The other, when they discern it to be God's will, is to proclaim the word of God, (inviting people) to believe in the Almighty God, Father, Son and Holy Spirit, Creator of all, in the Son who is Saviour and Redeemer, (calling them) to be baptised and become Christians, for "no one can enter the kingdom of God unless he is born of water and the Spirit" (John 3:5) ...
>
> And let all the Brethren, wherever they are . . . remember that they gave up their persons and their bodies for the sake of our Lord Jesus Christ ... for the Lord says: "Whoever loses his life for my sake will save it for eternal life" (Luke 9:24)

There are different dimensions in the new approach that Francis explored. What strikes one first is that he did not attack Islam and Muhammad as a false faith or false prophet. This in itself is a ground-breaking attitude. Secondly, Francis presents Christianity in the best possible way and thus he invites the Muslims to the Christian faith.

According to tradition the Sultan's final words to Francis included a request "pray for me, that God may reveal to me the law and the faith that is most pleasing to him." It is said that during the interval of peace (Fifth Crusade) Francis spent several days with the Sultan. One of the lesser known legendary accounts of Francis' encounter with the sultan records that Francis was deeply affected by the regular call to prayer of *mūezzin*, that he even write a *Letter to the Rulers of the People*, requesting them to send at a "town crier" a some other signed as a call to prayer.[2]

He visualised two 'ways' of mission among Muslims. The First is to simply live among Muslims as a Christian brother. Perhaps like leaven in the dough! This we could say is a 'witness of life': living an authentic Christian life among Muslims. The Second Way is if it is God's will, they are to preach Jesus and his message and invite his listeners to baptism, which according to the theology of his times, was necessary for salvation. The 'First Way' does not necessarily lead into the 'Second Way.' They are two different modes of being among Muslims as Christians, who love them and care for them. Discernment is crucial for both these modes of mission: presence and preaching. God's will should be done. That remains paramount. There should not be any condemnation of Islam and Muhammad.

This was a fresh approach as against the use of polemics. This approach emphasise the centrality of God's role in conversion of Muslims to lead to baptism in the Christian Church. The missionary has to live an authentic Christian life. Francis must have expected martyrdom for himself or for his brethren who would be missionaries among Muslims. The Rule seems to indicate this. However, his expectation of martyrdom was very different from some examples of Christian martyrdom where Christians seem to have provoked their own deaths.

For example, there is the shocking instance of the two Cordovan Christians, a priest by the name of Eulogius and a lay person named Paul Alvarus. They responded to the situation of living under Muslim rule in a provocative way. This strange behaviour came to be called in history the Spanish Martyrs Movement (850-860).[3] Both Eulogius and Paul Alvarus considered Islam as the precursor of the coming of the anti-Christ. They developed this view when they looked at the Bible for guidance especially the book of Daniel. They abused Muḥammad and called for conversion of Muslims to Christianity. Both these actions made one liable to suffer capital punishment in a Muslim ruled State. Despite warnings Eulogius and Paul Alvarus continued to provoke Muslims to abandon Islam and adopt Christianity. They were put to death. Their 'martyrdom' inspired more Christians follow their ways. In those ten years, between, 850 to 860 around 50 people were executed by the Muslim authorities. It is said that their 'martyrdoms' were etched in the memory of the Western European peoples and continues to influence negatively their opinion of Islam.[4]

The Cordovan 'martyrs' called upon themselves capital punishment by their sheer determination to precipitate an ugly confrontation between Christians and Muslims by abusing Muhammad, Francis was ready to give up life for mission by living an authentic Christian life of love among Muslims. He visualised a mission life among Muslims as giving witness to Jesus in a loving way, without attacking the faith of Muslims.

Aquinas: Invitation to a Common Ground

Aquinas wrote his *Summa Contra Gentiles* (SCG), most probably at the request of Raymund of Peñafort (d. 1275) a member of the Dominican Order in which Aquinas was a member, as a hand book for those who are missioned among Muslims. Aquinas had some knowledge of Islam as he was brought up in Sicily. He acquired a rather accurate knowledge of Islam from the writings of fellow Dominicans (Raymund of Peñafort and Raymond Marti (d.1284) and the writings of John of Damascene (d. 753) and Peter the Venerable (d. 1156).[5]

Aquinas recognised that the Christian faith involves mysteries which, though not irrational, are above reason. Consequently he affirmed that arguments *to prove* Christian faith to Muslims are fruitless. Because, Muslim can counter-argue to show that Christian arguments are insufficient. Moreover, they might think that the Christian faith is based on weak arguments. Such thinking would confirm Muslims in error, declared Aquinas. Consequently, he suggested that natural reason could be a common ground where both Christians and Muslims could meet. He stated that Muslims would accept moral and philosophical reasons.

The SCG reveals his approach towards Muslims. This book has four sections. (1) God in Himself [*sic*], (2) God in His [*sic*] creative activity and creatures, (3) The way to God: moral life, and (4) The Christian Mysteries: the Trinity, Incarnation, Sacraments and Beatific Vision. Aquinas states that only the first three sections alone should be used in relation with Muslims. For the truths that are discussed in the first three sections could be known by reason alone. The last part is strictly for Christians. Since the Christian mysteries cannot be discussed through intellectual proofs, because they involve revelation, they can only be presented to those who are prepared to receive the Christian faith. One can see immediately that the contents are not polemical. Muslims were not attacked in this document. The focus is that from the platform of natural reason Christians can show Muslims that the Christian faith is not contrary to reason. The implication is that faith is a gift from God. It cannot be forced upon the other through rational arguments. In SCG and as well another document (*de rationibus fidei contra saracenos*), Aquinas advocates a similar view as discussed above. He also stated that the Bible should not be used in conversation with Muslims since they do not accept its validity.

Three basic principles for relations with Muslims emerge from the spiritual treasures of these two great Christian saints. First, never condemn Islam or Muhammad. Such condemnation is not only fruitless but it is a counter witness to the love of Christ. In Christ all flesh has seen salvation. Second, discernment is crucial. Missioners should always remain attentive to the whispers of the divine in their listening hearts. Doing God's will is paramount in the mission among Muslims. Third, don't try to prove mysteries of the Christian faith through rational arguments, since they are above reason. Simply show from the common ground of natural reason that the Christian faith is not irrational but above reason. These three gems are timeless treasures, even for today for furthering Christian-Muslim relations. These will continue to remain golden rules for interreligious conversations.

We make a leap from the 13th century to the 19th century. The next set of three men is missioners among Muslims. They definitely reflected the first way of Francis. They lived among Muslims as 'witnesses to Christian life.' What is new in their approach? They consciously imitated a specific dimension of the life of Christ. So, their mission was to imitate Christ amidst Muslim brothers and sisters.

Charles De Foucauld: Living the Mystery of the Incarnation

De Foucauld discerned his vocation to live among Muslims as their brother and fellow servant, with esteem and friendship for them. Foucauld wanted to live in simple silence – a silent presence in the midst of Muslims adopting their way of life as Christ adopted human nature in the Incarnation. This is the model Francis proposed as the 'First Way.' This specific dimension of Foucauld's vocation to live in silent presence amidst Muslims is a powerful example of reversing the negative attitude of Christians for Muslims. Gaudeul notes that in such vocations God is calling Christians to make the Muslim world and its culture their home. Paraphrasing the words of '"The Church in the Modern World' (Vat. II) one can say that the joys and sorrows of Muslims are mine." Christians in solidarity with Muslims emerges as a distinct form of vocation.

Muslims know Jesus as he is presented in the Qur'ān. However, the Foucauldian dimension of Christian vocation may invite a Muslim to learn more about Christ as faith in Jesus is being lived out in sacrifice by a Christian who dwells in proximity and in solidarity with Muslims. In the same way, a Christian may learn the deeper dimensions of the spirituality of Muslims. A mutually enriched Christian and Muslim will be able to live their vocations as Christian and Muslim in a much more authentic sense.

Foucauld's life and mission touches an important dimension of dialogue that is very relevant to dialogue in Asia. The Asian bishops consider dialogue to be threefold: (1) dialogue with the poor, (2) dialogue with cultures and (3) dialogue with religions. Each of these dimensions calls for missioners to live an 'enfleshed life' among people of other religions. To my mind, the most challenging form of dialogue seems to be the dimension of solidarity with the poor. Foucauld lived as a servant attending to the aspirations and hopes of the poor Muslims in the Sahara desert. Foucauld is a great model of dialogue with the poor. In the spirit of Foucauld, Christians should not hesitate to enter into dialogue with Muslims by drawing upon the strong prophetic traditions of the Bible. We may refer to the teachings of the Old Testament prophets and their voice for the voiceless and the teaching of Jesus that called for solidarity with the poor and marginalised.

Henry Marchal: Freedom to follow God's Call

Marchal believed only God can convert human persons. God alone can enter into the soul of men and women directly and move them according to His will. Missionaries among Muslims, he insisted, should never use arguments, influence, or pressure to *convert* Muslims to Christian faith. This is not conversion but proselytising. Each person is moved by the Spirit in different ways. The missionary has to discern with the others and understand the work of the Spirit in their lives. As a Jesuit, I cannot but recognise a key insight of St Ignatius here. Ignatius would tell those who guide others in the Spiritual Exercises to be docile to the Spirit of God and to discern how the Holy Spirit is guiding the retreatant and make explicit what is implicit in the guidance of the Spirit. This insight of Ignatius has been appropriated here.

Marchal deepens his understanding of conversion. First, Conversion to God is the conversion each human person has to exercise in his/her life. This is necessary for salvation, although 'God' may appear as a call to commitment to justice and love.

Some may be called to conversion to Christ. It is an invitation to a personal friendship with the Lord. It is a call to be with Him and to go to the world to share Him with others.

God may call some to Christian community. One gives up one way of life and accepts another way of life in a faith community that is marked by Christian baptism. This freedom to change one's religion has been under severe stress in many Muslim countries where Christians are minorities. The Catholic Church's teaching is very clear and it is expressed in the Vatican II document on human dignity. Human dignity is linked to human conscience. The freedom to follow one's conscience is a human right and the dignified way of living. Any force exerted on the human conscience destroys one's dignity. Religious freedom is not only the freedom to worship according to one's faith; it is also the freedom to choose one's religion according to one's conscience. This is one of the critical elements in the dialogue with Muslims that should be clearly stated.

Louis Massignon: A Call to Suffer with Jesus for Muslims

Massignon was a scholar of Arabic and Islamic mysticism. He lived a life of religious indifference before converting to the Catholic faith. He regained his Christian hope when he was cared for and cured by a Muslim family in Bagdad when he had fallen ill. He became a professor of Arabic and Sufi thought at 'College de France' Paris.

Massignon experienced harmony in the face of differences that exist in the world. He recognised that this harmony is brought about by secret keys or links that connected persons and events. The beauty of symphony where different voices are blended together give us a glimpse of differences in oneness and oneness in differences. Similarly Massignon observed the religious figures and Prophets from different religions, complement and complete one another to produce harmony in the world.

Massignon recognised that God can make use of Islam to draw men and women to himself in marvellous ways. He affirmed that this was not due

to 'Christian influence.' It is only due to the presence of the Spirit of Christ
that people are brought closer to God in and through Islam. In his opinion
Islam should be judged by the fruits of the Spirit that are found within
Islam itself and not by the limitations found in the lives of some Muslims.

Massignon guided many to enter into Muslim homes and Muslim lives
and learn from them the values of Islam. In other words he discovered that
a Christian should enter into the lives of Muslims in order to understand
Muslims. He was convinced that when Christians experience their hospitality,
they in turn will be able to provide hospitality for Muslims. In short, cordial
relationships are at the heart of positive Christian-Muslim relations. In
mutual relationships and hospitality a Christian can "become all things to
all men" [sic] (1 Co 9:19-22).

Massignon carries these reflections a little further. While contemplating
the mystery of Christ offering himself on the Cross for humanity ... he
experienced himself among an 'invisible community' that offers their lives
to the Father for Muslims, for their salvation in union with Christ crucified
for all people.

What does this vision encourage one to do? It says that a Christian
who is called for a mission among Muslims must be in solidarity and in
communion with Muslims so that his/her struggles become meaningful.

Conclusion

What do we draw from our Christian spiritual resources for Christian-Muslim
relations? The first guideline is that we live in an era of dialogue and not
of debates and arguments. In Christian relations with Muslims there is no
space for any condemnation of Islam or of Muhammad. Arguments and
debates are not only futile exercises but they go against the spirit of Christ.
Christ came to save the world, not to condemn it.

The second guideline which is often missed is the solidarity with the
anawim of Allah. This is an important element of all Christian Muslim
relations. Christians should joyfully draw from the strong emphasis of the
Christian tradition on love for and solidarity with the poor, especially poor
Muslims. It also includes working in specific programs with Muslims for
the betterment of the poor at large.

Discernment is the key to Christian-Muslim relations. This is the third guideline that we recognise in reflecting on the life of these illustrious Christian saints and mystics. It involves first and foremost affirming the presence of God and His Spirit in the lives of Muslims and doing the will of God in our lives as Christians in relation with Muslims.

The fourth guideline is developing a real respect for freedom of conscience. We need to support the freedom of each individual to follow a religion according to one's conscience. Coercion to do anything that goes against the conscience of a person is not only against his/her human rights, but against her/his dignity.

The willingness to suffer for Muslims is the final and mystical guideline of relationships with Muslims. This demands one to live as *alter Christus* among Muslims. In this the Christian vocation is tested and purified and Christians are made worthy of Christ.

Endnotes

[1] It is well documented that before the 13th century Greek science was very much in the hands of Arab scholars, who developed different aspects of it, thereby keeping Aristotle's science very much alive. These Greek treasures that were preserved in Arabic were translated into Latin, including the works of Aristotle. Once Aristotle became known, the thinkers of the West noticed its superiority over Plato's. A number of points showed this superiority particularly in empirical sciences. First, Plato considered the world of ideas as the real world, whereas the world of material reality was only shadow. For Aristotle the material world was real, made up of matter and form. Secondly, while Plato underestimated the importance of observation in the study of nature Aristotle considered observation necessary. According to Aristotle there is nothing in the intellect that does not pass through the senses first. It must be added that Plato emphasised the importance of mathematics in the study of physical nature, whereas Aristotle discouraged mathematics in the study of nature. In this respect, Aristotle was not helpful to science, while Plato was.

[2] Cf. Varghese Manimala, *Toward Mutual Fecundation and Fulfilment of Religion* (Delhi: Media House and ISPCK, 2009), 393-394.

[3] H. Goddard, *A History of Christian-Muslim Relations* (Edinburgh: Edinburgh University Press, 2000), 81.

[4] R.W. Southern, *Western Views of Islam in the Middle Ages* (Harvard: Harvard University Press, 1962), 16-25; A. Cutler, "The Ninth-Century Spanish Martyr's Movement and the Origins of Western Christian Mission to the Muslims," in *Muslim World* 55 [1965], 321-39; J. Waltz, "The Significance of the Voluntary Martyrs' of

Ninth-Century Cordoba," in *Muslim World* 60 [1970], 143-159 and 226-236; H. Goddard, *A History of Christian-Muslim Relations* (Edinburgh: Edinburgh University Press, 2000), 84.

[5] It will be interesting to note all these men have different kinds of ideas about Islam and the approach to Muslims. John of Damascus (d. 753) treated Islam as a heresy. He believed that the Qur'ān was an ignorant imitation of the Bible. Peter the Venerable suggested that Islam should be studied from its sources. He encouraged Christians to meet Muslims not with weapons but with reason and love. Raymund of Peᴁafort, wanted to avoid the danger of intolerance and syncretism. He showed a certain measure of openness towards Muslims. Raymond Marti, a Catalan, was well acquainted with the works of Arab philosophers and the greatest theologian of the Muslim world, al-Ghazālī.

Buddhism and Islam:
Inter-Religious Dialogue on Ethics

G.N. Khaki and Shabir Ahmad Mugloo

Introduction

Inter-religious dialogue has today become an advanced discourse and practical form of engagement geared to promoting harmonious relations among people of different faiths. Its contribution to peaceful cosmopolitan civilization, cultural advancement and the promotion of communal harmony and co-existence is noteworthy.

The contemporary world presents special challenges and opportunities for interaction between different communities. Globalization, on the one hand, and the reorganization of special ethnic and local identities, on the other, creates the risk of violent conflict as well as the hope of constructive cooperation. Religious leaders play a special role in these interactions. Relations between people of different religions can determine whether the future of humanity will involve a great clash of civilizations or a successful inter-civilizational dialogue. The chaos, confusion, conflict, disharmony and fear that abound in the contemporary world have played an important role in promoting awareness of the need for inter-religious dialogue for peace. Such dialogue can open the doors of ideological contact and communication between followers of different faiths.

In this paper, an attempt has been made to shed light on inter-religious dialogue based on ethics shared by Buddhism and Islam. Both religions have a universal ethical code. Buddhism and Islam, the paper shows, have different approaches to ethics. Yet, both the religions are at par with each other on addressing ethical issues because there is a commonality of ethics between the two.

Definition of Ethics

Ethics is the science of highest good. It is the science of the supreme ideal of human life. Ethics, also known as moral philosophy, is a branch of philosophy that involves systematizing, defending and recommending concepts of right and wrong conduct. The term comes from the Greek word 'ethos', which means 'character'. Ethics seeks to resolve questions dealing with human morality, concepts such as good and evil, right and wrong, virtue and vice, justice and crime.

Mackenzie defines ethics as "the study of what is right or good in human conduct", or "the science of the ideal involved in human life."[1] In this definition, ethics has been accepted as the study of both right and good. *Rectus*, the Latin word from which 'right' has been derived, means 'straight' or 'according to law'. 'Good' comes from the German *gut*, meaning that which is useful for the supreme good. In this instance, 'good' is that which leads to the supreme good. 'Good' is taken to mean an end, and not a means to an end. The *Cambridge Dictionary of Philosophy* states that the word 'ethics' is "commonly used interchangeably with 'morality' [...] and sometimes it is used more narrowly to mean the moral principles of a particular tradition, group or individual."[2]

Ethics aims at systematic knowledge. Therefore, ethics is a science. Every science is concerned with a particular sphere of nature. As a science, ethics has its own particular sphere. It deals with certain judgments that are related to human conduct. It deals with the systematic explanation of rightness or wrongness in the light of the highest good of human.

Ethics is a normative science. It is concerned with what ought to be done, rather than what the case is. It differs from positive science. A positive science, natural science or descriptive science is concerned with what is. It deals with facts and explains them by their causes. In positive science, there is no question of judging its objects in any way. But ethics does not deal with fact. Rather it deals with value. Therefore, it is clear that ethics is concerned with judgments of value, while positive science deals with judgments of facts. That is why ethics is not a positive science.

Normative ethics deals with standards or norms by which human actions are judged to be right or wrong. Ethics is concerned with the nature, object, faculty, and standard of moral judgments. Moral judgments are accompanied by moral sentiments, e.g., feelings of approval and disapproval, remorse and the like. Moral judgments are also accompanied by the sense of duty; 'oughtness' or moral obligation. The aim of ethics is to define the nature of the highest good of human as a member of society. It investigates the nature of the *summum bonum*, which is the highest personal good and the highest social good. It is the root of all moral distinctions. These notions of rightness and wrongness of conduct are derived from it. This is the theoretical aim of ethics. Although ethics is not a practical science, it deduces concrete duties and virtues from the notion of the supreme good, which may guide humans in the regulation of their conduct.

Ethics from Buddhist Perspective

The world today is in a state of disorder, and deeply-cherished ethics are being upturned. The forces of materialistic skepticism have turned their dissecting blades on the traditional concepts of what are considered as humane qualities. Yet, people who are concerned for the future of humankind will concern themselves with leading and promoting an ethical life. In this regard, ethical values from different religions, including Buddhism, can be exceedingly helpful. They can contribute importantly to an 'inter-religious dialogue of life.'

Buddhist ethics are traditionally based on the Buddha's enlightenment. Moral concepts in Buddhism are elaborated upon either in the scriptures or in the traditions of Buddhism. According to traditional Buddhism, the foundation of Buddhist ethics for laypeople is the five precepts: no killing, stealing, lying, sexual misconduct, or intoxicants. To become a Buddhist, or to affirm one's faith in the Dhamma as taught by the Buddha, a layperson is encouraged to vow to abstain from these negative actions. The precepts are not formulated as imperatives, but, rather, as training rules that laypeople undertake voluntarily to practice.[3]

In Buddhist thought it is believed that the cultivation of *dāna* (generosity) and ethical conduct will themselves refine consciousness to such a level that rebirth in one of the lower heavens is unlikely, even if there is no further Buddhist practice. There is nothing improper or un-Buddhist about limiting ones aims to this level of attainment. The Buddha provided some basic guidelines for acceptable behavior that are part of the Eightfold Path. The initial precept is non-injury or non-violence to all living creatures, from the smallest insect to humans. This precept defines a non-violent attitude toward every living thing. The Buddhist view is that moral behavior flows naturally from mastering one's ego and desires and cultivating loving-kindness and compassion. This teaching is expressed in the well-known Four Noble Truths.

The uniqueness of Buddhist ethics lies in its many outstanding qualities. It is all-embracing and comprehensive, without being impractical or impossible to follow. It is free from taboos relating to diet, dress, behavior etc. It serves the needs of the worldly as well as those of the recluse. It is useful to the rich and to the poor; to the powerful as well as to the powerless. Buddhist ethics are the threshold for those who wish to pursue the Buddha's path to enlightenment and the end of all suffering.

Buddhist ethics differ from other ethical systems when analyzed in detail. In this regard, Manohar Bhardwaj remarks,

> It [Buddhism] no doubt contains an excellent ethical code, which is unparalleled in its perfection and altruistic attitude. It deals with one way of life for the monks and another for the laity. But Buddhism is much more than an ordinary moral teaching. Morality is only the preliminary stage on the path of purity and is a means to an end, but not an end in itself. The base of Buddhism is morality, and wisdom is its apex.[4]

Morality in Buddhism is essentially practical, in that it is only a means leading to the final goal of ultimate happiness. On the Buddhist path to emancipation, every individual is considered responsible for his own fortunes and misfortunes. Each individual is expected to work out his own deliverance by his understanding and effort. Buddhist salvation is the result of one's own moral development and can neither be imposed nor granted to one by some external agent. The Buddha's mission was to enlighten human as to the nature of existence and to advise them how best to act for their own happiness and for the benefit of others. Consequently, Buddhist ethics are not founded on any commandments which men are compelled to follow.

Ethics from Islamic Perspective

Every religion lays great emphasis on the ethical aspects of human conduct, each in its own unique way. Generally, there is great commonality between different religions as far as moral and ethical questions are concerned. In fact, to mould a moral character is the most fundamental function of religion *per se*. All other functions are subsidiary to this. But it is also true that each religion has unique way of doing this and that each puts differing emphasis on different aspects of morality. Islam, like all other religions, has its own ethical values and moral concepts, which are universal as well as specific to Islam.

The basic sources of the disciplinary code in Islam are the Qur'ān and the Ḥadīth (traditions). A Muslim's concept of discipline and ethics is to be formulated on the basis of the guidance revealed in the Quran and the practice of the Prophet Muhammad. The ethical code as stated in the Quran and practiced by the Prophet covers a person's entire life, from the dining table to the deathbed, from the cradle to the grave. In short, no sphere of life is left out from the application of the moral principles of Islam. This ethical code is termed in Arabic as *Ādāb al-Islam*. Ādāb is an Arabic term meaning 'custom.' It denotes a habit, etiquette, a manner of conduct derived from people considered as models.

Given its importance for a healthy society, Islam supports morality and matters that lead to it. The Guardian and Judge of all deeds is God Himself. The most fundamental characteristics of a true Muslim are held to be piety and humility. The guiding principle for the behavior of Muslim is meant to be 'virtuous deeds.' This term covers all deeds, not just acts of worship. Muslims must be in control of their passions and desires. It cannot be stressed strongly enough that Islam is not a mere belief system, nor a 'religion' in the commonly-understood sense of the term. Rather, it is what in Arabic is called a *dīn*. Dīn is a total frame of reference, a complete system and way of life which embraces the entirety of human's existence. Islam does not separate what pertains to 'religion', such as acts of worship, from what pertains to human interaction and mundane or 'secular' life. Consequently, there is no fragmentation or division within the personality of the ideal Muslim caused by the splitting of life into two distinct and opposed compartments or by applying different rules or criteria to different parts of life. The same God-given laws and standards govern all aspects of life, and all of an individual's actions are considered in Islam as worship in the broad sense of the term if they are done with the sincere intention of pleasing God, in keeping with God's injunctions.

The Qur'ān says:

It is not righteousness that ye turn your faces to the East and West , but righteous is he who believeth in Allah and the last day and the Angels and the Scripture and the prophets; and giveth his wealth , for love of Him, to kinsfolk and to orphans and the needy and the wayfarer and to those who to ask, and to set slaves free; and observeth proper worship and payeth the poor-due, and those who keep their treaty when they make one, and the patient in tribulation and adversity and time of stress. Such are they who are sincere. Such are the God fearing.[5]

This verse teaches us that righteousness and piety are based on true and sincere faith. The key to virtue and good conduct is a strong relationship with God, Who sees all, at all times and everywhere. He knows the secrets of the hearts and intentions.

The Qur'ān defines and sets the standards of social and moral values for Muslims. Thus, it says:

Do not make [as equal] with Allah another deity and [thereby] become censured and forsaken. And your Lord has decreed that you not worship except Him, and to parents, good treatment. Whether one or both of them reach old age [while] with you, say not to them [so much as], 'uff' and do not repel them but speak to them a noble word. And lower to them the wing of humility out of mercy and say, 'My Lord, have mercy upon them as they brought me up [when I was] small'. Your Lord is most knowing of what is within yourselves. If you should be righteous [in intention] - then indeed He is ever, to the often returning [to Him], Forgiving. And give the relative his right, and [also] the poor and the traveler, and do not spend wastefully. Indeed, the wasteful are brothers of the devils, and ever has Satan been to his Lord ungrateful.[6]

Islam is a comprehensive way of life, and morality is one of the cornerstones of Islam. Islam has established some universal fundamental rights for humanity as whole, which are to be observed in all circumstances. To uphold these rights, Islam has provided not only legal safeguards but also an effective moral system. Whatever leads to the welfare of the individual or the society and does not oppose any maxims of the religion is considered as morally good in Islam, and whatever is harmful is considered as morally bad.

Need for Inter-Religious Dialogue on Ethics

Every religion shares certain basic ethical and moral teachings for reducing human problems. John Hick claims that all religions propose salvation as the actual transformation of human life from self-centeredness to reality centeredness.[7] Inter-religious dialogue on ethics is a deep listening to different truth-claims and learning about each other's ethical and religious beliefs and practices. Ideally, participants in such dialogue strive to put today's global problems of humanity at the center and to listen to each problem with loving-kindness and compassion, which are stressed in all religions.

There is a long history of relations between Islam and Buddhism. These two major religions came into contact first in Central Asia and in South-East Asia. The first encounter between Islam and Buddhism took place in the middle of the seventh century in Eastern Iran, Persia, Transoxiana, Afghanistan and Sindh.[8] The historical interaction between Islam and Buddhism is an eloquent testimony to the fact that it is only through understanding, tolerance and mutual respect that fruitful dialogue can be established between religions and cultures. Islam and Buddhism share some common values that could form a strong basis for dialogue between adherents of these two religions. Compassion and mercy, love and kindness towards living beings, patience and forgiveness, tolerance and generosity are some of the important values emphasized by both Islam and Buddhism. *Ar-Raḥman* – the Merciful, and *Ar-Raḥim* – the Compassionate, stand for two important attributes of Allah. His love and mercy find their manifestation in the entire creation. The Qur'ān says: "My Mercy encompasses everything."[9]

Compassion and mercy are also central to Buddhist ethics. Buddhism places much emphasis on *mettā* (loving kindness), *karunā* (compassion), *muditā* (sympathetic joy), and *upekkhā* (equanimity) as means of avoiding resentment. According to the Buddha, love and compassion are be generated only in a mind that is free from anger and hatred.

Islam and Buddhism are different from each other in terms of their doctrinal and metaphysical understanding of the cosmos. The followers of both religions have existed in diverse social relationships to each other for centuries in several parts of the world. This co-existence has led, in some cases, to adopting an attitude of 'live and let live' towards each other. There have, however, also been instances of violence between these two communities. Upon inquiry, one finds that in most cases, such violence was caused by non-religious factors, such as ethnicity and economics, rather than simply religious or doctrinal differences. It is also important to note that throughout history, Muslims and Buddhists have been instrumental in promoting close bonds. There have been several such interfaith initiatives to bring Muslims and Buddhists together in recent years, too. For instance, in 2002, a conference under the title "A Dialogue on Peace: Islamic and Buddhist Perspectives" was held in Los Angeles. In May 2003, a conference was sponsored by UNESCO, The Museum of World Religions, Global Family for Love and Peace, and the Elijah School for the Study of Wisdom in World Religions, in Paris, bringing Buddhists and Muslims to dialogue in global ethics and good governance. In October 2013, a conference under the theme "Compassion as Common Ground for Understanding between Buddhism and Islam" was held at Thailand's Mahidol University. It was organized by the Centre for Buddhist-Muslim Understanding in Bangkok. In his address Dr. Imtiyaz Yusuf, Director of this Centre, remarked,

> Compassion was chosen as the 'unifying theme' in the conference because it goes to the heart of religious, ethical and spiritual traditions required to heal a polarized world and counter the voices of extremism, intolerance and hatred. Compassion encourages religious adherents to assert their common humanity to work together for a better world and move beyond dogmatic and philosophical differences.[10]

The major obstacle to dialogue between Buddhism and Islam is theological. However, there are commonalties between Buddhism and Islam that can serve as foundations for constructive interfaith dialogue. Both religions have similar perspectives on proper action and the value of inter-religious dialogue that can contribute to greater inter-religious understanding and respect. Both religions stress peace and justice. Both have common ethical values that could contribute to the development and prosperity of humanity in the world in general.

Conclusion

Engaging in inter-religious dialogue is for everyone, whether ethically-concerned academics, religious personnel or 'lay' people. The basic ethical values in both Buddhism and Islam provide a basis for practical inter-religious dialogue, values such as sincerity, equality, patience, self-criticism, trust, sympathy, empathy, loving-kindness and open-mindedness. Buddhist-Muslim dialogue may be sometimes difficult, but it is becoming increasingly necessary as tensions between Muslims and Buddhists worldwide escalate.

Buddhist-Muslim dialogue on ethics has been receiving increasing attention in recent years, with several conferences being held for the purpose of mutual understanding between adherents of Buddhism and Islam. Although these two religions may be divided by complex theological questions, inter-religious dialogue focused around morality, ethics and values can be an extraordinary avenue for inter-cultural change and understanding between Buddhists and Muslims.

Endnotes

[1] J.S. Mackenzie, *A Manual of Ethics* (London: University Tutorial press, 1956), 1-4.

[2] *Robert Audi, Cambridge Dictionary of Philosophy (New York: Cambridge University Press, 1995), 49.*

[3] See the discussion in *Damien Keown, The Nature of Buddhist Ethics (London: Macmillan, 1992).*

[4] *Manohar Bhardwaj, Philosophy of Buddhism (New Delhi: Cybertech Publications, 2010), 67.*

[5] Qur'ān *2:177.*

[6] Qur'ān 17:22-27.

[7] *John Hick, Dialogues in the Philosophy of Religion (London: Macmillan, 1991), 31.*

[8] For details, see, *Alexander Berzin, Historical Survey of the Buddhist and Muslim Worlds (Oxford: Oxford University Press, 2010), 11.*

[9] Qur'ān 7:156.

[10] Imtiaz Muqbil, "First Conference to Promote Buddhist-Muslim Understanding as Key to ASEAN Integration," (September 18, 2013), http://www.travel-impact-newswire.com/2013/09/first-conference-to-promote-buddhist-muslim-understanding-as-key-to-asean-integration/#axzz33ppnppn66 *(February 5, 2014).*

Muslims Approaches to Interfaith Dialogue: The Authentic and the Apologetic

Adis Duderija

Introduction

This article was prompted by my attendance in an inter-faith dialogue at Perth, W. Australia. I found it a welcome development that a local group of Imams have been involved in organizing an inter-faith event. This is especially so given the fact that their attendance at events organized by 'my' interfaith group (which was found 4 years before this particular event), apart from one notable exception (an imam who probably is not the member of the council of imams in question), was virtually non-existent. Nevertheless, according to one of the 'traditional' imams, whose talk I will utilize to discuss some broader issues pertaining to Muslim approaches to inter-faith dialogue as inter-faith dialogue was 'a burning issue' of huge socio-political and religious significance.

I would like to analyse the imam's (who has a significant following and is seen as 'progressive' by many young people) speech in relation to the question of an authentic vs. apologetic approach to inter-faith dialogue. An authentic approach I define as one that deals with the reality of the complex nature, diversity and at times mutually exclusive strands of what constitutes a religious tradition with the attendant issue of who has the power and authority to 'canonise' and interpret that very tradition. It is an approach which evaluates religious tradition holistically, contextually and in a historically sensitive manner. An apologetic approach, on the other hand, strives to score an ideological point in most cases but importantly it is also a one dimensional approach and an understanding of the religious tradition based on selective utilisation of tradition that suppresses certain aspects of it and privileges others, an approach which is at best semi-contextualise and not attune to the historical circumstances in which the tradition unfolded.

Islam, according to the imam in question, by the virtue of its very doctrine (*'aqīdah*) has a very 'inclusivist' approach to inter-faith, although God recognises one *din* (Arabic term roughly translated as 'religion' or 'way of life') by which the imam implicitly assumes that that din is the historical religion of Prophet Muhammad. According to the imam this inclusivism is attested by the Islam's doctrinal principles of unity of God's Message, the very meaning of Islam/Muslims, the unity of Prophethood and the historical truth of Islam's 'tolerance' of non-Muslim religions based on the Qur'ānically founded principle of non-coercion in religious belief (*lā ikrāha fid -dīn*, Qur'an 2:256) bestowing upon non-Muslims the right to worship in freedom.

Now this all sounds nice and 'beautiful' in the world of late modernity (or post-modernity) but it is not so much what the imam did say that I am critical of but of the things he did not say that I find problematic.

Firstly, he did not mention that one part of the 'mainstream' Sunni Islamic doctrine is the notion of successive nature of Prophethood which was fulfilled and completed by prophet Muhammad which renders all other existing traditions a priori as 'incomplete' , 'corrupted' or 'deviant.' Hence, this translates into an argument that as Muslims, there is nothing we can learn from 'them.' In this respect let me mention that before the imam in question was to speak a Christian representative was speaking on the issue of inter-faith dialogue from a Catholic perspective and based on the behaviour of another younger imam (engaging in talk with someone else) as well as the imam in question (coming late and leaving the room a number of times) - one could clearly see this attitude of "you have nothing of importance to say" manifesting itself by their poor listening and inattention as to what the Christian speaker had to say.

Secondly, the way Islamic historical experience of dealing with the religious other was presented gave an impression that it represented the pinnacle of 'tolerance' (the term being used similar to how it is in toxicology, to indicate how much of something one can 'tolerate' before it starts having adverse effects) that must forever be emulated and cannot be surpassed. This brushes aside more problematic evidence, for example in contemporary Saudi Arabia, in relation to issues of non-permissibility of restoration of existing churches and the erecting of new ones or the ban on public practice of non-Muslim faiths, including proselytising, and the non-existing option of choosing to opt out of Muslim faith (or if you do it, you would attract capital punishment, albeit as a last resort not often put into practice). All of these practices and laws are an organic and mainstream component of pre-modern Islamic law, however, none of it was mentioned by the imam and I have significant doubts that he was not aware of this facet of the Islamic tradition.

Thirdly, the imam did not mention other problematic components of the Islamic tradition on the question of the religious other, especially the Hadith literature. Given his external appearance with the emphasis on the first-long beard and trimmed moustache, he must be aware of it. According to several Ḥadīth, the Prophet had commanded Muslims to distinguish themselves from the 'Jews' (and Christians) by adopting the above and other practices. This commandment, if 'authentic', is not interpreted in a context of the political animosity between the 7th century Madīnan Muslims, whose very existence was under threat, and some Jewish tribes at a particular pointing history, but is interpreted as a universal principle of a 'devout' and 'pious' Muslim who keeps the Prophet's sunna.

In what follows I outline the view of the religious 'other' as embodied by a contemporary Muslim school of thought that I have elsewhere described as neo-traditional salafism (NTS) and its implications for IFD.

Texts on the View of the Religious 'Other' based upon NTS Approach to Interpretation of and Qur'ān and Sunna

NTS is a contemporary Islamic school of thought. Among the most influential exponents of NTS are contemporary Middle Eastern Muslim scholars Al-Albanee (d. 1999 CE), Bin Baz (d. 1999 CE) and Al-Madkhalee (1931–). Although the majority of the theoreticians behind NTS are of Saudi Arabian background or have lived in the Saudi Kingdom, the proponents of NTS school of thought are well entrenched in many parts of the Muslim clerical (and non-clerical) establishment.

The influence of the NTS Middle Eastern scholars is felt not only across the Middle East but also North Africa, South Asia, and, due to easier and faster communications, in major Muslim communities living in the United States, Canada, Australasia and the United Kingdom, where their ideological sympathizers have established their own publishing houses and websites.

This is where the works of the Middle Eastern NTS scholars are translated into, among others languages, English. In the western context, NTS scholars include personalities such as Jamal Zarabozo and Dr. Bilal Philips. Although the Middle Eastern NTS scholars write exclusively in Arabic, their western colleagues write in English.

NTS interpretation of the Qur'an and Sunna is heavily textualist, generally eschews reason (apart from a very limited recognition given to analogical reason) and they completely conflate the concept of sunna what that of an 'authentic' Ḥadīth as defined by early Muslim Ḥadīth scholars.

For the purposes of this article, one important part of the NTS worldview that needs to be highlighted is their subscription to the concept of *al wala' wal bara* which is considered by the proponents of NTS as a fundamental part of the Islamic belief *('aqīdah)*. Because of its centrality to NTS thought and its important implications on how NTS construct their views of the religious Self and the religious 'Other', it requires more elaboration.

Al-wala' lexically means alliance with, loyalty to, friendship, showing preference for and associating with one of the parties engaged in a conflict. *Al-bara'*, on the other hand, is its antonym, meaning severance, to walk away or distance oneself from or to be free of obligation from something or someone. The concept has pre-Islamic Arabia tribal conflict–alliance dynamics origins and historically has been interpreted differently by different Muslim groups. Its power lies in the ability of those who share the same understanding of the concept to make strong bonds of loyalty and brotherhood between themselves and, on the basis of piety and purity claims, disavow and create boundaries between themselves and all others who do not subscribe to the same understanding of this concept.

Such a view of *al wala' wal bara* and the above NTS Qur'ān-Sunna hermeneutic have important implications on how NTS Muslims construct the religious Other. In what follows I present some evidence NTS Muslims use to construct a very exclusivist and antagonistic nature of the relationship between the Self and the other which has important implications on their approach to IFD.

Qur'ānic Verses

Qur'ān 2:120

Never will the Jews or the Christians be satisfied with thee unless thou follow their form of religion. Say: "The guidance of Allah that is the (only) guidance." Wert thou to follow their desires after the knowledge which hath reached thee then wouldst thou find neither protector nor helper against Allah.

Qur'ān 3:118

O ye who believe! Take not into your intimacy those outside your ranks; they will not fail to corrupt you. They only desire your ruin: rank hatred has already appeared from their mouths; what their hearts conceal is far worse. We have made plain to you the Signs if ye have wisdom.

Qur'ān 5:51

O ye who believe! Take not the Jews and the Christians for your friends and protectors: they are but friends and protectors to each other. And he amongst you that turns to them (for friendship) is of them. Verily Allah guideth not a people unjust.

Qur'ān 9:5

But when the forbidden months are past, then fight and slay the Pagans wherever ye find them, an seize them, beleaguer them, and lie in wait for them in every stratagem (of war); but if they repent, and establish regular prayers and practice regular charity, then open the way for them: for Allah is Oft-forgiving, Most Merciful.

Qur'ān 3:85

If anyone desires a religion other than Islam (submission to Allah) never will it be accepted of him; and in the hereafter he [sic] will be in the ranks of those who have lost (All spiritual good).

Qur'ānic exegesis has documented the context behind these verses and *sūrahs* (chapters). Broadly speaking at the time of revelation of these verses, and the larger chapters (*surah*) they are embedded in, the small Muslim population residing in Medina was under constant threat for sheer survival. The threat was both internal and external. The internal threat came from those that the Qur'ān on numerous occasions addresses as *munāfiqūn* or religious hypocrites who cooperated with the external sources of threat and attempted to sabotage the Muslim community from within. The external threat, apart from the Makkan tribe of Quraysh, was also, in particular, increasingly felt from the side of Jewish tribes living in the outskirts of Madīna. These tribes at first signed a joint peace treaty, known as "The Constitution of Madīna", with and swore allegiance to Muhammad. According to this document all of the inhabitants of the city where considered as one community (*ummah*) whose religious difference was respected, as attested and endorsed by the Qur'ān.

Furthermore, this document stipulated that between Muslims and Jews there is to be sincere friendship, and honourable dealing, not treachery. All the signatories of the document were also to help against whoever suddenly attacked Medina. However, as Muslim community grew in numbers and strength and became more 'self- reliant' and 'self-conscious', these Jewish tribes withdrew their support and started to openly cooperate and conspire with the Makkans against the Muslim community. As such they broke the constitutional agreement outlined in the 'Constitution of Medina' document by committing treason. This inevitably prompted responses on behalf of the Qur'ān and Prophet as to how Muslims ought to deal with these tribes/individuals.

In this context, the execution of one Jewish tribe and that of the expulsion of another are often used as examples to buttress the claim that Muhammad's policies and that of the Qur'ān reflect certain exclusivity. That above quoted verses are, indeed, contextually embedded, and are not universal in nature is born out of the fact that the Qur'ānic discourse pertaining to Jews and Christians not only contains a large number of conciliatory verses. Muhammad's actions against the Jewish tribes from Medina were not motivated by any sense of religious exclusivism but were result of irresolvable civic tensions that had no bearing on the Qur'ān's position on religious pluralism." Furthermore, Karen Armstrong, a non-Muslim catholic nun, asserts in this context asserts that after the events of expulsion and execution of two Jewish tribes in question, the "Qur'ān continued to revere Jewish prophet's and to urge Muslims to respect the people of the Book. Smaller Jewish groups continued to live in Medina, and later Jews, like Christians, enjoyed full religious liberty in Islamic empires."[1]

In relation to the Qur'ān 3:85 verse, Faird Esack argues that while in the pre-classical or early stages of Islamic thought it was considered to afford salvation to groups outside the Muslim community, it was much later, when the exegetes had recourse to more sophisticated exegetical devices such as that of theory of abrogation (*naskh*) were used to "secure exclusion from salvation for the other."[2]

Furthermore, in the case of Qur'ān 9:5, its specific rather than general nature is not only based upon the contextual considerations but also grammatical ones. The use of the definite article in the verse limits the content of the verse to specific tribes addressed is not to be understood as universally prescriptive and normative.

Hadith

The reflection of the above context is also found in many *aḥadīth* reportedly going back to the Prophet, in which the emphasis on the difference between Muslims, on the one side, and Jews and Christians, on the other, and thus the creation of a reactionary identity is noticeable. Here are several examples:

Narrated Abū Hurrairah, The Prophet said, "Jews and Christians do not dye their hair so you should do the opposite of what they do." (Ṣaḥīḥ Bukhārī, 7.786)

Narrated Abdullah ibn Amr ibn al-'As: Allah's Messenger (peace be upon him) said, "He does not belong to us who imitates other people. Do not imitate the Jews or the Christians, for the Jews' salutation is to make a gesture with the fingers and the Christians' salutation is to make a gesture with the palms of the hands." (Tirmidhī, 4648, classified as weak).

Narrated Abū Hurrairah: Suhayl ibn Abū Salih said: I went out with my father to Syria. The people passed by the cloisters in which there were Christians and began to salute them. My father said: Do not give them salutation first, for Abū Hurrairah reported the Apostle of Allah (peace be upon him) as saying: Do not salute them (Jews and Christians) first, and when you meet them on the road, force them to go to the narrowest part of it. (Abū Dāwūd, 5186)

Narrated Abu Hurrairah: The Prophet (peace be upon him) said: Religion will continue to prevail as long as people hasten to break the fast, because the Jews and the Christians delay doing so. (Abū Dawūd, 2346)

Ibn Abbas reported: "The Messenger of Allah fasted on the day of 'Āshūrah and ordered the people to fast on it. The people said: 'O Messenger of Allah, it is a day that the Jews and Christians honour.' The Prophet said, 'When the following year comes – Allah willing – we shall fast on the ninth.' The death of the Prophet came before the following year." This is recorded by Muslim and Abū Dāwūd.

It is not difficult to understand that, the above given verses and narrations, reportedly going back to the Prophet, if taken *prima facie* and without taking into account the above-sketched historical circumstances and the background behind the Revelation would result in construction of a very negative view of the religious 'other' which would be considered as normative. This is exactly so in the eyes of those Muslims who follow NTS interpretational model of Qur'āno-Sunnatic teachings characterised by marginalisation of contextual background on the nature, content, understanding, interpretation and objective of the above Qur'ānic injunctions and Hadith texts. Additionally, the interpretational proclivity to generalise/ universalise these contextually-based injunctions, which is another feature of NTS approach to interpretation of Qur'āno-Sunnatic teachings, would result in application of these verses to all Muslim, Christian and Jewish communities living during and after the Prophet's death. NTS atomistic or segmentalist approach to textual evidence (which does not systematically consider all the textual evidence on a particular theme in order to develop a coherent and holistic view, alongside the taking of recourse to the principal of abrogation or *naskh* as espoused by classical Islamic legal theory) is also responsible for the development of this view. Additionally, the NTS *ḥadīth-dependent* Sunnah hermeneutic render the above-quoted *aḥadīth* as normative, thus religiously binding. Thus, based on the delineating features of NTS methodology, verses that appear to inspire intolerance are wilfully misrepresented in an attempt to overpower the essential and overarching message of the Qur'ān: one of toleration.

In addition to the above there are several Qur'ānic verses and a number of *aḥadīth* which when taken out of their original context described above and applied de-contextually impact upon the view of the religious other and thus reinforce a particular type of religious identity construction *vis-à-vis* the religious other as they emphasise the tension and enmity that existed between Muslims and Jews and Christians during the early Madīnan community. Here we consider several of those.

Qur'ānic Verses

Qur'ān 5:82

Strongest among men in enmity to the believers wilt thou fined the Jews and Pagans...

Qur'ān 9:29

Fight those who believe not in Allah or the Last Day nor hold that forbidden which hath been forbidden by Allah and His apostle nor acknowledge the religion of truth (even if they are) of the People of the Book until they pay the *jizya* with willing submission and feel themselves subdued.

Ḥadīth

Narrated Abdullah ibn Umar: Allah's Apostle said, "You (i.e. Muslims) will fight with the Jews till some of them will hide behind stones. The stones will (betray them) saying, 'O Abdullah (i.e. slave of Allah)! There is a Jew hiding behind me; so kill him.'" (Bukhārī, 4. 176)

Abdullah ibn Mulaika narrates: Aisha said that the Jews came to the Prophet and said, "As-Sāmu 'Alaikum' (death be on you)." 'Aisha said (to them), "(Death) be on you, and may Allah curse you and shower His [*sic*] wrath upon you!" The Prophet said, "Be calm, O 'Aisha! You should be kind and lenient, and beware of harshness and *fuḥsh* (i.e. bad words)." She said (to the Prophet), "Haven't you heard what they (Jews) have said?" He said, "Haven't you heard what I have said (to them)? I said the same to them, and my invocation against them will be accepted while theirs against me will be rejected (by Allah)." (Bukhārī, 8.57)

The conflictive nature of these verses and *aḥadīth* texts, again if considered from the NTS interpretational perspective can have very grim implications and provide a religious foundation for a purely oppositional, conflictive Muslim identity construction *vis-a-vis* the religious Other. This is particularly evident in the following statement by Abou El-Fadl who, in this context asserts,

> The puritan worldview is bipolar – on the one end there is Islam which represents the unadulterated good, and on the other end are non-Muslims, who represent evil. Relying on the writings of some classical jurists, the puritans advocate a theology known as *al-wala' wa al-bara'* (the doctrine of loyalty and disassociation) which states it is imperative that Muslims care for, ally them with, and befriend only Muslims. Accordingly, Muslims may

ally themselves with or seek the assistance of non-Muslims only for limited and identifiable purposes. Muslims should do so only if they are weak and in need, but as soon as Muslims are able to regain their power, they must regain their superior status...The fact that non-Muslims are not Muslim is seen as a moral fault ...[3]

This type of mentality and approach to Jews and Christians, for example, is promoted by a NTS scholar Albani (d.1999) who considers that Prophet forbade to initiate greetings with Jews and Christians and that Muslims should not develop genuine, human-based relationships with non-Muslims. He based his decisions upon a complete decontextualize approach to a couple of isolated *aḥadīth*.

As such this NTS approach and methodology engender a construction of a religiously exclusivist self *vis-a-vis* the Religious Other which a *priori* completely undermines their capacity to engage in meaningful dialogue.

This begs the question as the why the imam did not mention this aspect of the Islamic tradition that we as Muslims need to acknowledge and deal with in a methodologically sound and historically sensitive and honest manner, especially if we want to promote inter-religious understanding. Sweeping things under the carpet and pretending that they are not there is not only apologetic but also 'politically' and morally incorrect.

The Religious Self and the Other in the Qur'ān and Sunnah: The Importance of Context

Before examining the question of the Religious Self and the Religious Other in the Qur'ān and Sunnah, more needs to be said about the revelatory environment in which the revelation and the Prophet's embodiment of revelation took place. The revelatory environment relates to the question of the identity of the Self and that of the other, especially in the Madīnan period. Not only was it primarily in Medina that Muḥammad's message—and, therefore, the Muslim identity—became more 'self-conscious,' but also the Madīnan model of the Prophetic and early Muslim community is considered by many Muslims worthy of emulation in many respects, including that of the relationship with the (religious) Other. Furthermore, even a cursory examination of the Qur'ānic content (and, therefore, of the Prophet's legacy) was organically linked to this context, especially the dimension of the Qur'ānic content bearing on the relationship between Muslims and the religious 'Other.'

Several general points need to be considered in attempting to understand, from a religious perspective, the concept of the identity of Self and Other as understood during the Prophet's time in light of the Qur'ān and the Prophet's embodiment of it.

First, the context behind the emergence of the Prophet Muḥammad's message in 7th century Hijaz was such that it took place alongside already well-established religious communities, most important of which were, apart from the pre- Qur'ānic paganism, Judaism, Christianity, and Hanifiyyah. The Qur'ān describes several instances of the Muslim community's attitude toward the non-Muslim Other and vice-versa.

Second, the Qur'ānic attitude (and Muḥammad's conduct) toward the non-Muslim Other is highly contextual in nature and, therefore, possibly ambivalent. Also, during much of the Muslim community's 'formative period' in Medina, a climate of friction and hostility between the Muslims, on the one hand, and the *mushrikūn*, large Jewish tribes, Christians, and hypocrites (*munāfiqūn*), on the other, prevailed, under which Muslims were constantly concerned about the survival of their community, which often took a reactionary, antagonistic stance *vis-à-vis* the religious Other. Montgomery Watt describes the circumstances and motives behind the relationship between Muslims and non-Muslims, especially between the Prophet of Islam and the Madīna Jews:

> In Muhammad's first two years at Medina the Jews were the most dangerous critics of his claim to be a prophet, and the religious fervour of his followers, on which so much depended, was liable to be greatly reduced unless Jewish criticisms could be silenced or rendered impotent ... In so far as the Jews changed their attitude and ceased to be actively hostile, they were unmolested... [4]

This is attested to by the Qur'ān itself. The context-dependency of the scriptures toward the view of the (religious) Other (and, by implication, the religious Self) lead Jacques Waardenburg to assert that "Looking back at the interaction of the new Islamic religious movement with the existing religious communities, we are struck by the importance of socio-political factors."[5]

Besides the socio-political factors, religious ideas were also significant, since the Qur'ānic progressive consolidation of Islamic religious identity is inextricably linked with the religious identity of the Other, notably of Jews and Christians. The aspects of religious identity's continuity and commonality with other faiths in the Qur'ān are intertwined with those of the emergence of, and the emphasis on, the Muslim identity's originality and distinctiveness. Thus, the religious aspects of, and interactions between various religious communities in the Qur'ānic milieu led to the genesis of the construction of religious identity of Muslims and played a very important role in its construction.

In his study of the extent of the Prophet Muḥammad's and the Qur'ān's emphasis on confessional distinctiveness, Donner has demonstrated that, in the Islamic scripture and in early Islam, "the community of Believers was originally conceptualized independently of confessional identities," and that

> It was only late—apparently during the third quarter of the first century A.H., a full generation of or more after the founding of Muhammad's community—that membership in the community of Believers came to be seen as confessional identity in itself when, to use a somewhat later formulation of religious terminology, being a Believer and Muslim meant that one could not also be a Christian, say, or a Jew.[6]

Donner adduces a substantial amount of evidence to support the argument that. Qur'ānically, (some) Jews and Christians would qualify as *mu'minūn* (believers) besides the *muslimūn* (those who submit to God).[7]

Another significant trend in the 'historicity' of the development of the Muslim religious Self was the gradual but ever-growing religious self-consciousness of the Prophet of Islam and its early community. Whilst attempts to find common ground and syncretism featured more frequently during the earlier periods of Muḥammad's life, later periods stressed "features constituting specific identity and what distinguished one [i.e. Muslims] fundamentally from others."[8] Whereas pluralism was an essential foundation of Islam, exclusivism was a later addition. In the centuries following the Revelation, the original pluralist impulse that prompted the Constitution of Madīna was usurped by politically motivated factions who propounded exclusivist interpretations of the Qur'ān in order to justify warfare and territorial expansion. Writing about the context of the early Muslim view of the Byzantines in the days of Prophet Muḥammad, A. Shboul echoes this observation by saying that the attitudes of the Muslims developed from sympathy and affinity, reflected in the early Qur'ānic verses, to awe and apprehension of Byzantium's military power, scorn of Byzantine wealth and luxury, and, finally, anticipation of open antagonism and prolonged warfare.[9]

Jews and Christians were eventually recognized by Islam as recipients of previous revelations (*ahl-Kitāb*) and were awarded by it the status of protected/secured minorities (*dhimmīs*).

Another point to be considered in relation to the question under examination is the Qur'ānic concept of a *Hanif/Millat Ibrahīm*. Qur'ānically, this notion may be called the primordial, monotheistic Irreligion based on the belief in the One, True God as embodied in Abraham's message (Arabic *Millat Ibrāhim*) considered as the universal belief system. It is, however, unclear, whether the Prophet of Islam himself identified 'historical Islam' "as the only or merely one possible realisation of the primordial religion, the Hanifiyyah, on earth."[10]

Lastly, an 'Islamocentric view' of Muslim perceptions of the religious Other stems from a certain interpretation of the Qur'āno-Sunnatic teachings. This view is based upon the premise that the Qur'ān is a source of empirical knowledge of the religious Other that is to be applied universally, a historically and without regard to context.

It is important to keep in mind that this apologetic approach is not restricted to issues of inter-faith only but is particularly evident in relation to the question of the role and the status of women in Islam.

Conclusion

If we as Muslims wish to engage in inter-faith dialogue in an authentic way, rather than in an apologetic manner, we have a moral responsibility to deal with all of the aspects of our inherited tradition – the good, the bad and the ugly – if we are to enhance and appreciate our understanding of our own tradition as well as that of the other. Only in this way are we going to be meaningfully engaged and ready to be transformed through and by the Other for the better.

Endnotes

[1] Karen Amstrong, *Muhammad: A Western Attempt to Understand Islam* (London: Orion, 1991), 207.

[2] Farid Esack, *Qur'ān, Liberation and Pluralism: An Islamic Perspective of Interreligious Solidarity against Oppression* (Oxford: One World, 1997), 163.

[3] Khaled M. Abou El Fadl, *The Great Theft: Wrestling Islam from the Extremists* (N.p.: Harper Collins, 2005), 206.

[4] W. Montgomery Watt, *Muhammad at Medina* (Oxford: Clarendon Press, 1956), 217.

[5] Jacques Waardenburg, *Muslims and Others – Relations in Context* (Berlin: Walter de Gruyter, 2003), 99; Jacques Waardenburg, "World Religions as Seen in the Light of Islam," in *Islam: Past Influence and Present Challenge*, edited by A.T. Welch and P. Cachia (Edinburgh: Edinburgh University Press, 1979), 245-276.

[6] F. Donner, "From Believers to Muslims: Confessional Self-Identity in the Early Islamic Community," *Al-Abhath* 50-51 (2002-2003), 12.

[7] Donner, "From Believers to Muslims: Confessional Self-Identity in the Early Islamic Community," 17-24, 28-34.

[8] Waardenburg, *Muslims and Others*, 44. Some traditions reportedly going back to the Prophet stress largely the distinctive and uniqueness of the Islamic religious identity.

[9] A. Shboul, "Byzantine and the Arabs: The Image of the Byzantines as Mirrored in Arabic Literature," in *The Formation of the Classical Islamic World: Arab-Byzantine Relations in Early Islamic Times*, vol. 8, edited by M. Bonner (Farnham: Ashgate Variourum, 2004), 235-260.

[10] Qur'ānic verses such as 5:48 seem to present the existence of religious plurality as a manifestation of God's will.

Spirituality and Interreligious Relations: Pope Francis and M. Fethullah Gülen

Leo D. Lefebure

Spirituality and interreligious relations are intimately intertwined. The values of the spiritual life in both the Christian and the Muslim traditions can inform and enhance interreligious relations, but this contribution cannot be taken for granted. Muslims and Christians have had a long and varied history of relationships, not all of them peaceful. In various contexts, Muslims and Christians have debated with each other, fought with each other, and sought to convert each other; they have also lived together as neighbours, traded with each other, made alliances together, studied together, and learned together. In recent decades and at the present time, there are continuing conflicts in many areas, but there have also been increasing efforts to draw Muslims and Christians together in relationships of mutual respect and cooperation. Two influential leaders who seek interreligious harmony are Pope Francis and M. Fethullah Gülen. For both leaders, authentic spiritual life calls for simplicity, concern for the poor, intercultural cooperation, and respectful attitudes towards followers of other religious paths. There are obvious points of difference between the Christian and the Muslim paths, but today I would like to focus attention on the areas of convergence.

Two Lives of Service and Dialogue

Jorge Mario Bergoglio was born in Buenos Aires, Argentina in 1936 to parents who had emigrated from Italy. As a young man, he worked part-time while going to school and so came to know the life of working families. He later entered the Society of Jesus and studied for the priesthood.[1] When he became a bishop, he chose as his motto the Latin phrase, '*miserando atque eligendo*,' (by having compassion and by choosing). It is a reference to Jesus calling St. Matthew, who was a tax collector, to be his disciple. One may think of the famous painting by Caravaggio in the Church of St. Louis of the French in Rome, where Matthew has his hand on money on the table as Jesus dramatically points to him calling him to another way of life. Later in his life, Bergoglio recalled an influential conversation he had with a priest when he was just 17 years old, which shaped his vocation to the priesthood: "That was how I felt that God saw me during that conversation. And that is the way he wants me always to look upon others: with much compassion and as if I were choosing them for him; not excluding anyone, because everyone is chosen by the love of God. . . . It is one of the centrepieces of my religious experience."[2]

M. Fethullah Gülen was born a few years later, in 1941 in Erzurum in eastern Turkey. He has long been a major leader of Muslims in Turkey and around the world, inspiring his followers in *Hizmet* (Turkish: 'service') to devote their time and energies to spiritual endeavours. While Gülen does not have an episcopal motto, the motto of Pope Francis describes experiences that are central to Gülen: the compassion of God, and God's call to humans to follow God's path. The traditional Turkish phrase that Gülen selected as the title for an anthology of his writings may be taken as analogous to a motto: *'yasatmak icin yasamak'* (living so that others may live; the title of the English translation was shortened to so that others may live).[3] This value is also dear to Pope Francis.

Both leaders have long lived lives of simplicity, and both are suspicious of ostentation in the spiritual life. Cardinal Bergoglio abandoned the elaborate episcopal residence in Buenos Aires for a simpler abode and used public transportation instead of a chauffeur. He has spoken passionately about the plight of the world's poor as a scandal that cries to heaven. Even though both men are famous, neither man wishes to be the centre of major attention; instead both point attention to the central message of his religious tradition. Gülen comments, in words that could also apply to Pope Francis: "By itself, fame is hypocrisy, an attractive honey that poisons hearts. It makes people slaves of others."[4] Neither figure has ever married. Each has dedicated his entire life to the search for spiritual values and the benefit of humanity.

Jorge Bergoglio and Interreligious Dialogue

Jorge Bergoglio's interest in and commitment to shaping healthy interreligious relations began long before he was elected as pope. For a number of years, Rabbi Abraham Skorka and Jorge Mario Cardinal Bergoglio, the Archbishop of Buenos Aires, engaged in a series of wide-ranging conversations, becoming friends in the process. After a number of exchanges, the rabbi and the cardinal decided to share their conversations with the broader public in their joint book, *On Heaven and Earth*. In a true conversation, the speakers seek the true, the good, the beautiful and the holy. The participants are open to being transformed in the exchange because dialogue is not simply a defence of previously formulated positions.

To introduce the notion of dialogue, Rabbi Skorka quotes Proverbs 20:27: "God's candle is man's [*sic*] soul which reveals the innermost parts of his being." He comments, "In its most profound sense, to have a conversation is to bring one's soul nearer to another's in order to reveal and illuminate his or her core. When a dialogue reaches this level of magnitude, one becomes aware of what he or she has in common with the other person."[5]

In response, Cardinal Bergoglio evokes an image from the facade of the Cathedral of Buenos Aires that depicts Joseph and his brothers in the book of Genesis, noting that "Decades of misunderstandings converge in that embrace." In the image, there is both weeping and also the poignant question of whether Joseph's father still lives. The Holy Qur'ān also recounts the narrative of Joseph, and thus Joseph is a figure of importance for Jews, Christians, and Muslims. The biblical narrative describes the estrangement between Joseph and his brothers, but the climax of the story is the moving moment of their reconciliation in Egypt. This stands as an image of hope for all followers of the path of Abraham.

Bergoglio finds in the image of Joseph an invitation to establish a 'culture of encounter,' and he offers a beautiful description of dialogue:

> Dialogue is born from a respectful attitude toward the other person, from a conviction that the other person has something good to say. It supposes that we can make room in our heart for their point of view, their opinion and their proposals. Dialogue entails a warm reception and not a pre-emptive condemnation. To dialogue, one must know how to lower the defences, to open the doors of one's home and to offer warmth.

Gülen has offered a very similar vision of dialogue: "Interfaith dialogue is a must today, and the first step in establishing it is forgetting the past, ignoring polemical arguments, and giving precedence to common points, which far outnumber polemical ones."[6]

In discussing the variety of religions, Skorka views the diversity of religious paths as arising from the different experiences of individuals: "A religion is formed when a common denominator is found as these different experiences are shared," and he quotes the prophet Amos 9:7: "Are you not like the Ethiopians to me, O Israelites? — Oracle of the LORD — Did I not bring the Israelites from the land of Egypt as I brought the Philistines from Caphtor and the Arameans from Kir?" Bergoglio responds that God makes Himself [sic] felt in the heart of each person. He also respects the culture of all people. Each nation picks up that vision of God and translates it in accordance with the culture, and elaborates, purifies and gives it a system. Some cultures are primitive in their explanations, but God is open to all people. He calls everyone. He moves everyone to seek Him and to discover Him through creation.

M. Fethullah Gülen and Interreligious Dialogue

Like Abraham Skorka and Jorge Bergoglio, Fethullah Gülen has long been a strong advocate of interreligious respect and dialogue. Like Skorka and Bergoglio, Gülen sees dialogue as a search for the truth, not a drive to dominate:

> Debate should not be for the sake of your ego, but to enable the truth to appear. When we look at political debates in which the only thought is to beat the other person, there can be no positive result. For the truth to emerge in a debate of ideas, such principles as mutual understanding, respect, and dedication to justice cannot be neglected. As a Qur'ānic rule, this can only take place in a good environment for dialogue.[7]

Like Bergoglio, Gülen acknowledges differences among religious traditions, but he stresses the values that are held in common:

> Regardless of how their adherents implement their faith in their daily lives, such generally accepted values as love, respect, tolerance, forgiveness, mercy, human rights, peace, brotherhood, and freedom [are] exalted by religion. Most of them are accorded the highest precedence in the messages brought by Moses, Jesus, and Muḥammad, as well as in the messages of Buddha and even Zarathustra, Lao-Tzu, Confucius, and the Hindu scholars.[8]

Like Bergoglio, Gülen is aware of the long history of conflict between Christians and Muslims, tragically enduring into the present. Because of this, he acknowledges: "This historical experience leads even educated and conscious Muslims to believe that the West is continuing its 1,000-year-old systematic aggression against Islam and, even worse, with far more subtle and sophisticated methods. Consequently, the Church's call for dialogue meets with considerable suspicion."[9] In response, Gülen insists on recognizing the advances that have been made in mutual understanding: "In the West, some attitudinal changes can be seen in some intellectuals and clerics toward Islam. I must particularly mention the late [Louis] Massignon, who referred to Islam by the expression: 'the faith of Abraham revived with Muhammad.' He believed that Islam has a positive, almost prophetic mission in the post-Christian world."[10]

Gülen goes on to cite Pope Paul VI and the Second Vatican Council, who expressed respect for Muslims and acknowledged truth and holiness in Islam. Gülen strongly endorsed the call of the Second Vatican Council for interreligious cooperation and dialogue. The statements of Pope Paul VI and the Second Vatican Council established the basic framework for respect, dialogue, and cooperation between Muslims and Catholics. The entire ministry of Jorge Bergoglio as priest, bishop, and pope builds on this foundation of interreligious respect, and he has continued this work as pope. These shared assumptions create a framework for a strong convergence of concerns between Bergoglio and Gülen.

Pope Francis

On March 13, 2013, the Conclave of Cardinals of the Catholic Church elected Jorge Mario Cardinal Bergoglio, the Archbishop of Buenos Aires, Argentina as the 266th Pope, bishop of Rome, and successor to St. Peter. For the first time in history, the newly elected pontiff chose to be called Francis, a name with significant resonance for the poor and for interreligious relations, particularly with Muslims. In response to questions, Vatican spokesman Fr. Frederico Lombardi, S.J., clarified that the new pope chose this name in honour of St. Francis of Assisi. Francis was known as 'Il Poverello' (the little poor one) because of his affection and concern for the poor and his simple lifestyle.

Francis of Assisi has a special significance for Muslim-Christian relations because he visited Sultan al-Mālik al-Kāmil at Damietta in Egypt during the Fifth Crusade, seeking peace in a time of conflict. It was to Francis's hometown of Assisi that Pope John Paul II invited the leaders of the world's religious traditions to come to pray for World Peace in October, 1986, an unprecedented gathering.

When Cardinal Bergoglio was elected Pope, the Muslim community of Buenos Aires rejoiced. The *Buenos Aires Herald* reported on March 14, 2013 that Sheij Mohsen Ali and CIRA (Islamic Centre of the Republic of Argentina) Secretary General Dr. Sumer Noufouri praised Pope Francis's 'pro-dialogue' nature: "He always showed himself as a friend of the Islamic community. He visited the At-Tauhid Mosque (located) in the neighbourhood of Floresta and the Arab-Argentine Ali Ibn Abi Talib School strengthening our relations."

For the celebration of Ramadan in 2013 Pope Francis decided to send the annual message from the Vatican to the worldwide Islamic community as his own personal greeting, as a sign of the importance that he places on Muslim-Catholic relations. I would like to cite his words:

To Muslims throughout the World

It gives me great pleasure to greet you as you celebrate 'Id al-Fitr', so concluding the month of Ramadan, dedicated mainly to fasting, prayer and almsgiving ...

This year, the first of my Pontificate, I have decided to sign this traditional message myself and to send it to you, dear friends, as an expression of esteem and friendship for all Muslims, especially those who are religious leaders. ....

Turning to mutual respect in interreligious relations, especially between Christians and Muslims, we are called to respect the religion of the other, its teachings, its symbols, its values. Particular respect is due to religious leaders and to places of worship. How painful are attacks on one or other of these!

It is clear that, when we show respect for the religion of our neighbours or when we offer them our good wishes on the occasion of a religious celebration, we simply seek to share their joy, without making reference to the content of their religious convictions.

Regarding the education of Muslim and Christian youth, we have to bring up our young people to think and speak respectfully of other religions and their followers, and to avoid ridiculing or denigrating their convictions and practices.

> We all know that mutual respect is fundamental in any human relationship, especially among people who profess religious belief. In this way, sincere and lasting friendship can grow.[11]

All of these concerns are shared and endorsed by Gülen, who has also strongly emphasized the importance of education of young people to respect other religious traditions.

Gaudium Evangelii and Gülen's Vision of Islam

On November 24, 2013, Pope Francis issued an Apostolic Exhortation, the first of his Pontificate, and the first major statement of his program. Commentators around the world picked up selected themes for discussion and debate. While popes routinely issue Apostolic Exhortations, particularly after a synod of bishops has met in Rome, it is rare and perhaps unprecedented that an Apostolic Exhortation has aroused such interest beyond Catholic borders. The great theme of Pope Francis's exhortation is expressed in the title: *Gaudium Evangelii*, the Joy of the Gospel, which is our response to God's coming into our lives. Time and time again in this document, the themes emphasized by Pope Francis are very close to the teachings of Gülen.

At the beginning of the Apostolic Exhortation, Pope Francis sets forth a warning that the great danger in today's world, pervaded as it is by consumerism, is the desolation and anguish born of a complacent yet covetous heart, the feverish pursuit of frivolous pleasures, and a blunted conscience. Whenever our interior life becomes caught up in its own interests and concerns, there is no longer room for others, no place for the poor. God's voice is no longer heard, the quiet joy of his love is no longer felt, and the desire to do good fades. This is very similar to Gülen's perspective on materialism as the dominant danger to religions today. Gülen states: "At the root of the problem is the materialist worldview, which severely limits religion's influence in contemporary social life."[12] Gülen further warns against a consumerist mentality:

> Compared with previous centuries, people may well be wealthier and enjoy more convenience and comfort. However, they are trapped in greed, infatuation, addiction, need, and fantasy much more than ever before. The more they gratify their animal appetites, the more crazed they become to gratify those appetites ...

> Those who spend their energy pursuing ephemeral material advantages waste both themselves and all the nobler, truly human feelings in the depths

of their being. They no longer possess the serenity coming from belief, the tolerance and depth of spirit enabled by knowledge of God, or traces of love and spiritual joy.[13]

Joy

Francis laments that too often Christians do not witness to the joy and beauty of the Gospel. He calls for evangelization not by proselytization by attraction through living lives of joy and beauty. Francis warns: "There are Christians whose lives seem like Lent without Easter." "Joy adapts and changes, but it always endures, even as a flicker of light born of our personal certainty that, when everything is said and done, we are infinitely loved." Zephaniah promises that God will rejoice over us as at a festival, and so Pope Francis tells us evangelizers should not look like they are coming from a funeral. Again Gülen's perspective is rather similar. The Sufi tradition, which has influenced Gülen greatly, has long rejoiced in the love of God. Gülen comments on the importance of *Surur* (Rejoicing):

> Meaning joy and delight, *surur* (rejoicing) is a kind of contentment that embraces a person from both within and without. Even though every conscience feels it differently, what is common in the rejoicing felt by every one of those who rejoice is that breezes of intimacy come from the true Friend at different wave-lengths, invading the human inner world. Lovers of God are made aware of rejoicing with the fragrance of meeting Him [sic] the loyal with the faithfulness in their hearts, and the heroes of nearness to Him [sic] with sentiments of certainty.[14]

For Pope Francis, the basis of the Catholic Church's mission is the love of God that comes to us a sheer gift and offers us friendship with God, who brings us beyond ourselves, frees us from our narrowness and self-absorption. Francis invokes the ancient principle: "Goodness tends to spread." The classic Latin phrase was *bonum diffusivum sui*. He quotes the document issued by the Fifth General Conference of the Latin American and Caribbean Bishops in Aparecida, Brazil, in 2007: "Life grows by being given away, and it weakens in isolation and comfort. Those who enjoy life most are those who leave security on the shore and become excited by the mission of communicating life to others." This for Pope Francis is the most basic principle of Christian spiritual life.

Again, there are similarities to the views of Gülen, who sees all creation as the overflow of the goodness of God and understands Islam as proclamation of the goodness of God and an invitation to others to share in God's bounty. Gülen comments on the importance of perceiving creation through love:

> Here love is identical with perceiving the whole universe, and its contents and events, as a continuous interconnected flux and loving it. Those who find this true love pursue neither wealth nor fame; rather, they find peace in the flames of their love and see their beloved's face amid the ashes of their own existence burned away. They are on an uninterrupted journey from the valleys of 'self-annihilation in the existence of God' to the heights of 'attainment to permanence through permanence of God.'[15]

Gülen also uses the image of 'overflowing' to describe the spiritual life:

> Only those who overflow with love will be able to build the happy and enlightened world of the future. Their lips smile with love, their hearts brim over with love, their eyes radiate love and the most tender human feelings— such are the heroes of love who continuously received messages of love from the rising and setting of the sun and from the flickering light of the stars.[16]

Mission

According to Pope Francis, the Christian life is nurtured by two aspects: memory of grace received and reading the signs of the times. Christians retell the narratives of grace in light of our present situation and then invite others to a delicious banquet. Again, Gülen has a very similar approach from the Islamic tradition, recounting teachings of the Qur'ān and narratives of the Prophet and applying them to the present world.

Francis states frankly that the pope cannot carry out this mission alone. The pope in principle cannot do this for the entire world: "Nor do I believe that the papal magisterium should be expected to offer a definitive or complete word on every question which affects the Church and the world. It is not advisable for the Pope to take the place of local Bishops in the discernment of every issue which arises in their territory. In this sense, I am conscious of the need to promote a sound 'decentralization.'" The pope calls for clarifying and strengthening the role of conferences of bishops. The Church is called to be oriented to mission to others, going forth, not oriented to self-preservation, and he echoes Pope John Paul II's warning against 'ecclesial introversion.'

While Gülen does not hold an institutional position of authority comparable to that of the pope, he is warmly revered by millions of Muslims, and his words carry tremendous weight. He similarly encourages Muslims to use their resources to interpret the present situation of the world and to discern where God's will is to be found. He does not try to resolve every issue around the world, but exhorts Muslims to be creative in discerning what is needed in different settings.

Francis calls for renewal and reform on multiple levels, beginning with the call to renew each parish. He calls bishops to foster missionary communion, at times going before their people, at times being with them in their midst, but also at times letting the people go first: "he will have to walk after them, helping those who lag behind and— above all— allowing the flock to strike out on new paths." Francis challenges each bishop to have "a desire to listen to everyone and not simply to those who would tell him what he would like to hear." Gülen has also encouraged frankness in dialogue and urges his followers to be thoughtful and resourceful.

Francis calls for a conversion of the papacy and the central structures of the Catholic Church. He recalls that Pope John Paul II had issued *Ut Unum Sint* (That They May Be One), inviting proposals on new ways to exercise the Petrine Ministry in ways that would be helpful ecumenically. Pope Francis starkly admits: "We have made little progress in this regard." He calls for the central structures to serve the local churches and warns: "Excessive centralization, rather than proving helpful, complicates the Church's life and her missionary outreach." Gülen also calls for major reforms from Muslims. He even asserts: "In my opinion, an Islamic world does not really exist. There are places where Muslims live. They are more Muslims in some places and fewer in others. Islam has become a way of living, a culture; it is not being followed as a faith."[17]

Remembering the past is ambiguous; it can be a wonderful resource, but it can also hinder future developments. Pope Francis calls to abandon the attitude that says: "'we have always done it this way.' I invite everyone to be bold and creative in this task of rethinking the goals, structures, style and methods of evangelization in their respective communities." Gülen similarly challenges Muslims not simply to repeat patterns of the past but to apply the values of Islam in new ways in a changing world.

Francis calls us to reach out to everyone without exclusion, stressing what is beautiful, grand, appealing, and most necessary. He recalls that Thomas Aquinas taught that mercy is the greatest of all virtues and should be at the centre of the presentation of the Gospel. Francis calls us to be like the

Prodigal Father in the parable. He tells us that "the Church is not a tollhouse; it is the house of the Father, where there is room for everyone, with all their problems." Francis is insistent on this theme: "Everyone can share in some way in the life of the Church; everyone can be part of the community, nor should the doors of the sacraments be closed for simply any reason ... The Eucharist, although it is the fullness of sacramental life, is not a prize for the perfect but a powerful medicine and nourishment for the weak."

Mercy is also a central virtue in Islam. The Holy Qur'ān repeatedly addresses God as "a religion of universal mercy."[18] He explains: "Life is the foremost and most manifest blessing of God Almighty, and the true and everlasting life is that of the Hereafter. Since we can deserve this life only by pleasing God, He sent Prophets and revealed Scriptures out of His Compassion for humanity."[19] Gülen further comments: "Mercy was like a magical key in the Prophet's hands, for with it he opened hearts that were so hardened and rusty that no one thought they could be opened. But he did even more: he lit a torch of belief in them."[20]

Pope Francis proclaims that the Church has a mission to all, especially to the poor. Francis repeats to all of us what he used to tell the priests and people of Buenos Aires: "I prefer a Church which is bruised, hurting and dirty because it has been out on the streets, rather than a Church which is unhealthy from being confined and from clinging to its own security." He notes that the call of Jesus echoes through the centuries to us: "Give them something to eat" (Mk 6:37).

Economic Justice

Francis also reflects on the economic structures that perpetuate poverty. He questions why we worry more about the stock market going down by a few points than about the poor who die on the streets. He recalls the commandment not to kill as a call to safeguard the value of all human life. Francis applies this commandment against an economy of exclusion and inequality, stating: "Such an economy kills." He questions: "Can we continue to stand by when food is thrown out while people are starving?" He warns against the globalization of indifference and the idolatry of money as a new golden calf. Francis sets forth the basic principle: "Money must serve, not rule!" We can think of the image of Matthew the tax collector with his hand on the money, while Jesus calls him to another life.

Gülen stresses the social implications of Islam as he asserts:

> The Islamic social system seeks to form a virtuous society and thereby gain God's approval. It recognizes right, not force, as the foundation of social life ... If human beings are considered as a whole, without disregarding the spiritual dimension of their existence and their spiritual needs, and without forgetting that human life is not limited to this mortal life and that all people have a great craving for eternity, democracy could reach the peak of perfection and bring even more happiness to humanity. Islamic principles of equality, tolerance, and justice can help it do just this.[21]

Despite the stern warnings against dangers, Francis rejects pessimism, recalling the words of Pope John XXIII in opening the Second Vatican Council in October 1962, looking beyond the predictions of gloom to the hope: "In our times, divine providence is leading us to a new order of human relations." It is this hopeful note of confidence in God's grace that shapes Francis's message. Gülen stresses the centrality of hope in his Islamic perspective: "People live in perpetual hope and thus are children of hope. At the instant they lose their hope, they also lose their 'fire' of life, no matter if their physical existence continues. Hope is directly proportional to having faith."[22]

Francis reflects on the implications of the Incarnation: "The Son of God, by becoming flesh, summoned us to the revolution of tenderness." Francis stresses the dignity of baptism as the foundation of our identity and the mission of lay people in transforming the world. He calls on all Christians to:

> listen to young people and the elderly. Both represent a source of hope for every people. The elderly bring with them memory and the wisdom of experience, which warns us not to foolishly repeat our past mistakes. Young people call us to renewed and expansive hope, for they represent new direction for humanity and open us up to the future, lest we cling to nostalgia for structures and customs which are no longer life-giving in today's world.

When Christians are confronted by formidable obstacles, Pope Francis offers words of encouragement: "Challenges exist to be overcome! Let us be realists, but without losing our joy, our boldness and our hope-filled commitment." In similar tones, Gülen tells us: "If life is viewed through the window of He Who Has Given Life, then hope is the dynamic of action that does not face. It is nourishment for those who do not think continuously of themselves, but rather of others, for those who find true happiness in the happiness of others and for those who find a life in bettering the lives of others."[23] Gülen states: "People live in perpetual hope, and thus are the children hope ... Having hope is directly proportional to having faith."[24]

Pope Francis reflects on the teaching of the Second Vatican Council that the Church is "a people advancing on its pilgrim way towards God. She is certainly a mystery rooted in the Trinity, yet she exists concretely in history as a people of pilgrims and evangelizers, transcending any institutional expression, however necessary." He is directing our attention to what is really important, and that is not the hierarchical institutional structure of the Church; what really matters is the presentation of the joyful message of the life, death, and resurrection of Jesus Christ.

The Role of Religious Traditions and the Diversity of Cultures

In considering the question of what is the role of the Church, Pope Francis cites the teaching of the Second Vatican Council that the Church is "the sacrament of the salvation offered by God." A sacrament is a concrete, outward sign of transforming grace. The Church is an instrument God uses to share grace with us. As Pope Francis makes clear, this means the Church is not the exclusive locus of salvation. "The salvation which God has wrought, and the Church joyfully proclaims, is for everyone. God has found a way to unite himself to every human being in every age. He has chosen to call them together as a people and not as isolated individuals." God saves us in and through our relationships; God calls us as a people, but this is not an exclusive club. Pope Francis proclaims: "Jesus did not tell the apostles to form an exclusive and elite group." Christians are called to be signs of this to the world. "This means we are to be God's leaven in the midst of humanity ... the Church must be a place of mercy freely given, where everyone can feel welcomed, loved, forgiven and encouraged to life the good life of the Gospel."

Similarly, Gülen calls Muslims to be signs of the mercy and compassion of God to the entire world. Gülen offers a description of the ideal that Muslims are called to live: "The most remarkable feature of those who have devoted themselves to the bestowal of God's consent and to the ideal of loving and being loved by Him is that they never expect anything— material or spiritual— in return. Things like profit, wealth, cost, comfort, etc., things to which people of this world pay great attention do not mean much; they hold no value, nor are they considered as criteria."[25] Gülen elaborates: "Since they devote themselves completely to making people love God and to being loved by God, dedicating their lives to enlightening others, and, once again, because they have managed to orient their goal in this unified direction, which in a sense contributes to the value of this ideal, they avoid divisive and antagonist thoughts, such as 'they' and 'we,' 'others' and 'ours.'"[26]

Pope Francis stresses the diversity and richness of cultures. "Grace supposes culture and God's gift becomes flesh in the culture of those who receive it." This sets up a call for rejoicing in variety: "The history of the Church shows that Christianity does not have simply one cultural expression … In the diversity of peoples who experience the gift of God, each in accordance with its own culture, the Church expresses her genuine catholicity and shows forth the 'beauty of her varied face'" (quoting John Paul II, *Novo Millennio Ineunte* 40). He reiterates the theme: "When properly understood, cultural diversity is not a threat to Church unity." The content of the Gospel is not to be identified with any particular cultural expression: "We would not do justice to the logic of the incarnation if we thought of Christianity as monocultural and monotonous … it's the gospel's content (that) is transcultural."

Gülen also recognizes and respects the diversity of cultures. He said that

Culture is an important resource that must be used by those seeking to develop their community in the most beneficial and appropriate way … The existence of distinct and unique cultures does not mean that there can (or should be) not be any intercultural exchange of ideas and people. Rather, it means that each culture should demand a 'visa' from a foreign cultural element seeking entrance.[27]

Pope Francis knows that cultures are not static: "Culture is a dynamic reality which a people constantly recreates; each generation passes on a whole series of ways of approaching different existential situations to the next generation, which must in turn reformulate it as it confronts its own challenges." Thus even when the Christian faith has long been expressed in a particular culture, the people "also transmit the faith in ever new forms." This is not a process only for the elites, for professional theologians. Much of this happens in popular piety, and the principal agent in it all is the Holy Spirit. Popular spirituality advances "more by way of symbols than by discursive reasoning." Pope Francis exhorts: "Let us not stifle or presume to control this missionary power!" Gülen similarly exhorts Muslims to proclaim the message of Islam in ways appropriate for the contemporary world.

Pope Francis wants to set a fundamentally positive tone: "To understand this reality we need to approach it with the gaze of the Good Shepherd, who seeks not to judge but to love. Only from the affective connaturality born of love can we appreciate the theological life present in the piety of Christian peoples, especially among their poor." At the centre is what Pope Francis describes as "the fundamental message: the personal love of God who became man, who gave himself up for us, who is living and who offers us his salvation and his friendship." We never master this mystery, and Pope Francis marvels: "the message is so rich and so deep that it always exceeds our grasp." Gülen similarly acknowledges that true knowledge of God (ma'rifa) recognizes its limits. He comments: "Knowledge of God sometimes becomes a source of wonder and astonishment for an initiate, as has been said, 'One who knows the Truth becomes dumbfounded and tongue-tied.'"[28] Gülen affirms: "Ma'rifa is a special knowledge that is acquired through reflection, sincere endeavour, using one's conscience and inquiring into one's inner world." He elaborates: "The acknowledgment that *the inability to perceive Him [sic] is the true perception*, excellently expresses the inability of anything limited to perceive Him and the imperceptibility of the One Who is Infinite. The same meaning is exquisitely expressed in the saying, *we are unable to know You, O Known One, as knowing you truly requires*."[29]

Pope Francis wants Catholics to take risks: "But if we allow doubts and fears to dampen our courage, instead of being creative we will remain comfortable and make no progress whatsoever. In this case we will not take an active part in historical processes, but become mere onlookers as the Church gradually stagnates."

Interreligious Relations

Pope Francis situates the mission of the Church in the context of fostering respectful and friendly relations with other religious traditions. He affirms the special bond between Christians and the Jewish people because of our common heritage: "We hold the Jewish people in special regard because their covenant has never been revoked, for 'the gifts and the call of God are irrevocable'" (Rom. 11:29). He deplores the past hostility in this relationship: "The friendship which has grown between us makes us bitterly and sincerely regrets the terrible persecutions which they have endured, and continue to endure, especially those that have involved Christians."

Pope Francis strongly supports interreligious initiatives in the context of seeking peace and the flourishing of life for all: "An attitude of openness in truth and in love must characterize the dialogue with the followers of non-Christian religions ... Interreligious dialogue is a necessary condition for peace in the world, and so it is a duty for Christians as well as other religious communities." Francis endorses the interreligious attitude commended by the Catholic bishops of India of "being open to them, sharing their joys and sorrows."

Francis explains the hoped-for result of such an attitude of openness:

In this way we learn to accept others and their different ways of living, thinking and speaking. We can then join one another in taking up the duty of serving justice and peace, which should become a basic principle of all our exchanges. A dialogue which seeks social peace and justice is in itself, beyond all merely practical considerations, an ethical commitment which brings about a new social situation.

Francis stresses the importance and the transformative power of listening: "Efforts made in dealing with a specific theme can become a process in which, by mutual listening, both parts can be purified and enriched. These efforts, therefore, can also express love for truth." Francis is aware of the important differences among various religious traditions and does not wish to ignore or minimize them: "A facile syncretism would ultimately be a totalitarian gesture on the part of those who would ignore greater values of which they are not the masters. True openness involves remaining steadfast in one's deepest convictions, clear and joyful in one's own identity, while at the same time being 'open to understanding those of the other party' and 'knowing that dialogue can enrich each side'" (quoting Pope John Paul II). Regarding how to handle the disagreements among different religious traditions, Francis, like Gülen, stresses honesty, mutual respect, and trust.

Pope Francis expresses his respect for Muslims in words that echo the themes of Gülen: "Many of them also have a deep conviction that their life, in its entirety, is from God and for God. They also acknowledge the need to respond to God with an ethical commitment and with mercy towards those most in need." Francis emphasizes the importance of good relationships between Christians and Muslims: "We Christians should embrace with affection and respect Muslim immigrants to our countries in the same way that we hope and ask to be received and respected in countries of Islamic tradition." Francis acknowledges the difficulties in relations in many settings and advises: "Faced with disconcerting episodes of violent fundamentalism, our respect for true followers of Islam should lead us to avoid hateful generalizations, for authentic Islam and the proper reading of the Koran are opposed to every form of violence." Gülen has forcefully condemned all acts of terrorism, insisting that "real Muslims cannot be terrorists."[30] He has also issued a similar call to Muslims to respect and embrace Christians with affection and respect.

According to Pope Francis, the grace of God that Christians experience in Jesus Christ can nurture and shape the lives of followers of other religious paths as well. Christians do not have a monopoly on grace and can learn from other traditions: "The same Spirit everywhere brings forth various forms of practical wisdom which help people to bear suffering and to live in greater peace and harmony. As Christians, we can also benefit from these treasures built up over many centuries, which can help us better to live our own beliefs." Gülen, like Pope Francis, views all religions as being rooting in God's love. He has stated that

> the very nature of religion demands this dialogue. Judaism, Christianity, and Islam, and even Hinduism and other world religions accept the same source for themselves, and, including Buddhism, pursue the same goal. As a Muslim, I accept all Prophets and Books sent to different people throughout history, and regard belief in them as an essential principle of being Muslim. A Muslim is a true follower of Abraham, Moses, David, Jesus, and all other Prophets. Not believing in one Prophet or Book means that one is not a Muslim. Thus we acknowledge the oneness and basic unity of religion, which is a symphony of God's blessings and mercy, and the universality of belief in religion.[31]

Francis also reaches out to those who do not belong to any particular religious tradition: "As believers, we also feel close to those who do not consider themselves part of any religious tradition, yet sincerely seek the truth, goodness and beauty which we believe have their highest expression and source in God. We consider them as precious allies in the commitment to defending human dignity, in building peaceful coexistence between peoples and in protecting creation." Francis trusts that reflection on ethics, art, and science and about the human search for transcendence can serve as "a path to peace in our troubled world."

Despite all the difficulties facing the global community, Francis encourages us: "Challenges exist to be overcome! Let us be realists, but without losing our joy, our boldness and our hope-filled commitment." Mary is a figure warmly venerated by both Catholics and Muslims. She is the only woman for whom a *sura* (chapter) of the Holy Qur'ān is named; she has been hailed as a bridge between the two traditions. Pope Francis closes the Apostolic Exhortation with a prayer to Mary, and I would like to close this essay by quoting a portion of it:

> Mary, virgin and Mother,
> You who, moved by the Holy Spirit,
> Welcomed the word of life
> In the depths of your humble faith;
> As you gave yourself completely to the Eternal One,
> Help us to say our own 'yes'
> To the urgent call, as pressing as ever,
> To proclaim the good news of Jesus ...
> Give us a holy courage to seek new paths
> That the gift of unfading beauty
> May reach every man and woman ...
> Mother of the living gospel,
> Wellspring of happiness for God's little ones,
> Pray for us. Amen. Alleluia!

Endnotes

1 Andrea Tornielli, *Francis: Pope of a New World*, trans., William J. Melcher (San Francisco: Ignatius Press, 2003); Paul Vallely, *Pope Francis: Untying the Knots* (London: Bloomsbury Continuum, 2013).

2 Jorge Mario Bergoglio, quoted by Vallely in Vallely, *Pope Francis: Untying the Knots*, 28.

3 Fethullah Gülen, *So That Others May Live: A Fethullah Gülen Reader*, edited and translated by Erkan M. Kurt (New York: Blue Dome Press, 2013), viii.

4 Quoted in Foreword, Ali Ünal and Alphonse Williams, eds., Advocate *of Dialogue: Fethullah Gülen*, trans. Ali Ünal (Fairfax, VA: Fountain), i.

5 Jorge Mario Bergoglio and Abraham Skorka, *On Heaven and Earth: Pope Francis on Faith, Family, and the Church in the Twenty-First Century*, trans. Alejandro Bermudez and Howard Goodman, edited in Spanish by Diego F. Rosemberg (New York: Image), viii.

6 Fethullah Gülen, "Interfaith Meetings and Activities," in *Advocate of Dialogue: Fethullah Gülen*, edited by Ali Ünal and Alphonse Williams, trans. Ali Ünal (Fairfax, VA: Fountain), 244-245.

[7] Gülen, "Interfaith Meetings and Activities," in *Advocate of Dialogue: Fethullah Gülen*, 259.

[8] Gülen, "Interfaith Meetings and Activities," in *Advocate of Dialogue: Fethullah Gülen*, 242.

[9] Gülen, "Interfaith Meetings and Activities," in *Advocate of Dialogue: Fethullah Gülen*, 243.

[10] Gülen, "Interfaith Meetings and Activities," in *Advocate of Dialogue: Fethullah Gülen*, 245.

[11] Francis, "Message of Pope Francis to Muslim throughout the World for the End of Ramadan ('Id al-Fitr)," http://www.vatican.va/holy_father/francesco/messages/pont-messages/2013/documents/papa-francesco _20130710_musulmani-ramadan_en.html (July 10, 2013).

[12] Gülen, "Interfaith Meetings and Activities," in *Advocate of Dialogue: Fethullah Gülen*, 241.

[13] Fethullah Gülen, "Religion and Society," in *Advocate of Dialogue: Fethullah Gülen*, edited by Ali Ünal and Alphonse Williams, trans. Ali Ünal (Fairfax, VA: Fountain), 106.

[14] M. Fethullah Gülen, *Key Concepts in the Practice of Sufism: Emerald Hills of the Heart*, trans. Ali Ünal (Somerset, NJ: The Light, 2004).

[15] Gülen, "Religion and Society," in *Advocate of Dialogue: Fethullah Gülen*, 107-108.

[16] Fethullah Gülen, *Toward a Global Civilization of Love and Tolerance*, translated by Mehmet Ünal, Nagihan Haliloglu and Mükerrem Faniküçükmehmedoglu, and edited by Jane Louise Kandur and Hakan Yesilova (Somerset, NJ: Light), 91.

[17] Gülen, *Toward a Global Civilization of Love and Tolerance*, 185.

[18] Fethullah Gülen, *Essays, Perspectives, Opinions*, rev. ed. (Somerset, NJ: Light, 2004), 55.

[19] Fethullah Gülen, "The Individual and Human Rights," in *Advocate of Dialogue: Fethullah Gülen*, edited by Ali Ünal and Alphonse Williams, trans. Ali Ünal (Fairfax, VA: Fountain), 126.

[20] Gülen, "The Individual and Human Rights," in *Advocate of Dialogue: Fethullah Gülen*, 126-127.

[21] Gülen, *Toward a Global Civilization of Love and Tolerance*, 224.

[22] Gülen, "Interfaith Meetings and Activities," in *Advocate of Dialogue: Fethullah Gülen*, 297.

[23] Gülen, *Toward a Global Civilization of Love and Tolerance*, 233.

[24] Gülen, *Toward a Global Civilization of Love and Tolerance*, 226.

[25] Gülen, *Toward a Global Civilization of Love and Tolerance*, 100.

[26] Gülen, *Toward a Global Civilization of Love and Tolerance*, 100.

[27] Gülen, "Religion and Society," in *Advocate of Dialogue: Fethullah Gülen*, 89.

[28] Gülen, *Key Concepts in the Practice of Sufism: Emerald Hills of the Heart*, 137-38.

[29] Gülen, *Key Concepts in the Practice of Sufism: Emerald Hills of the Heart*, 136.

[30] Gülen, *Toward a Global Civilization of Love and Tolerance*, 179.

[31] Gülen, "Interfaith Meetings and Activities," in *Advocate of Dialogue: Fethullah Gülen*, 242.

Nostra Aetate – 50 Golden Years

A New Style of Relationship with Believers of Different Religions

Teresa Joseph FMA

Nostra Aetate, the landmark Vatican document marked 50 Golden Years on October 28, 2015. During the last 50 years, this document has been studied, discussed and put into praxis at interfaith and inter-religious groups across the globe, often promoted and coordinated by the Pontifical Council for Interreligious Dialogue. Archbishop Felix Machado[1] was under-secretary of that Council from 1999-2008, reflecting on the importance of the document as it marked 50 years he affirmed: The Second Vatican Council's declaration *Nostra Aetate*, which reshaped the Catholic Church's relationship with people of other faiths, has been a blessing to Indian Church. "Vatican II for us in Asia, and particularly in India, has been God's grace because I cannot imagine how we could live our Christianity with the kind of world today, if it were not for the revolutionary opening up – *aggiornamento* – of the Second Vatican Council," Archbishop Machado told Vatican Radio.[2]

Nostra Aetate (NA) means 'In Our Time.' It is the Declaration on the Relation of the Church with Non-Christian Religions of the Second Vatican Council. This declaration was promulgated on October 28, 1965 by Pope Paul VI. *Nostra Aetate* is the landmark Vatican document that launched a historic new positive dialogue between the Catholic Church and the Jewish people. *Nostra Aetate* significantly[3] changed the Catholic teaching about non-Christian religions, "*Nostra Aetate* remains to this day a litmus test for the implementation of the conciliar vision as a whole, so pervasive in

Catholic thought are the challenges it raised and still raises for Christian teaching and preaching."[4]

The Structure of the Document: Declaration *Nostra Aetate*

The historical context of *Nostra Aetate* – it represents one of the first items taken up on the agenda of the Second Vatican Council, yet was one of the last documents to be approved by the Council.

> The document was originally intended to be a lengthier one put out on its own. Then it was thought to attach it to the statement on ecumenism. The final compromise was to include it in a statement on 'Non-Christian Religions' in general. Thus it was that the Council Fathers took up the issue of dialogue with Islam, Hinduism, Buddhism and the native traditions, in a real sense, in order to take a positive approach to Judaism.[5]

The beginning and development of *Nostra Aetate* can be dated back to October 20, 1958 when Angelo Roncalli was elected Pope John XXIII. On September 18, 1960, he directed Cardinal Augustin Bea, S.J., president of the Secretariat for Promoting Christian Unity, to prepare a draft declaration for the upcoming council on the relations between the Church and the Jewish people. Regardless of John XXIII's desire, it was not clear whether the proposed statement should be a free-standing document, part of the planned constitution on the Church, part of an ecumenical text on Christian unity, or, as ultimately happened, be contained within a declaration on the Church's relations with all the other religions of the world. The process of bringing *Nostra Aetate* to birth was a prolonged and difficult labour. On October 28, 1965 the declaration was officially promulgated after a final, overwhelmingly favourable vote of 2221 bishops for and 88 against.

A Summary of the Document

Nostra Aetate 1

This precious document begins with "In our time, when day by day mankind [*sic*] is being drawn closer together, and the ties between different peoples are becoming stronger, the Church examines more closely her relationship to non-Christian religions." In this declaration, the Church considers what people have in common and what draws them to fellowship. There is a unique oneness that is acknowledged and recognized such as one is the community of all peoples, one their origin, for God made the whole human race to live over the face of the earth. One also is their final goal, God. God's providence, goodness and saving design extend to all until that time when in the Holy City, the nations will walk in God's light are well presented. The expectations of people from various religions are expressed clearly in this paragraph. Human beings expect from various religions answers to the unsolved riddles of the human condition and the fundamental questions of life.

Nostra Aetate 2

Throughout centuries, there is found among various peoples a certain perception of that hidden power which hovers over the course of things and over the events of human history, some recognize a Supreme Being, of a Father. And this perception and recognition penetrates the lives of people with a deep religious sense. How different religions have contemplated and expressed the divine mystery is clearly expressed in this paragraph.

The Hindus and Buddhists are specially mentioned. The Church's attitude towards other religions emerges strongly here:

> The Catholic Church rejects nothing that is true and holy in these religions. She regards with sincere reverence those ways of conduct and of life, those precepts and teachings which, though differing in many aspects from the ones she holds and sets forth, nonetheless often reflect a ray of that Truth which enlightens all men [sic].Indeed, she proclaims, and ever must proclaim Christ 'the way, the truth, and the life' (John 14:6), in whom men [sic] may find the fullness of religious life, in whom God has reconciled all things to Himself [sic]

Nostra Aetate 3

This paragraph speaks on how the Church regards with esteem the Muslims. The core values of their belief and religious practices are enumerated. The Church has acknowledged the quarrels and hostilities that have arisen in the course of time between Christians and Muslims and therefore an appeal is made "to forget the past and to work sincerely for mutual understanding and to preserve as well as to promote together for the benefit of all humankind social justice and moral welfare, as well as peace and freedom."

Nostra Aetate 4

This paragraph marks an important milestone in the history of Jewish-Christian relations. The Church as a result of her search into the mystery of the Church remembers "the bond that spiritually ties the people of the New Covenant to Abraham's stock." Although section 4 of the Declaration concerning Jews and Judaism is fairly brief, each phrase was repeatedly discussed and refined by the Council. The chapter has proven to be tremendously influential. *Nostra Aetate* repudiated the long-standing 'deicide' charge by declaring that "Jews should not be spoken of as rejected or accursed as if this followed from Holy Scripture." This refutation of any notion of a divine curse upon Jews was an explicit reversal of an assertion held universally by Christians for more than a millennium.

Nostra Aetate stressed the religious bond and spiritual legacy shared by Jews and Church. It acknowledged the Jewishness of Jesus, his mother, and the apostles, and recognized Christianity's debt to biblical Israel. This has become foundational in later Catholic ecclesiastical and theological writings. John Paul II wrote movingly that "Jesus also came humanly to know (Israel's scriptures); he nourished his mind and heart with them, using them in prayer and as an inspiration for his actions. Thus he became an authentic son of Israel, deeply rooted in his own people's long history."

Nostra Aetate strongly implied that God and Jews abide in covenant. *Nostra Aetate's* implicit recognition that Israel abides in a perpetual covenantal relationship with God has subsequently been made fully explicit. John Paul II repeatedly taught that Jews are "the people of God of the Old Covenant, never revoked by God."

Nostra Aetate 5

In this paragraph we find the Church offering a kind of guideline on how we need to treat in a brotherly and sisterly manner every human person. The reason for this way of dealing is: every person is created in the image of God. Any discrimination against men and women are reproved by the Church because it is foreign to the mind of Christ. The human dignity of the person and the rights flowing from it are brought to light here. "Following in the footsteps of the holy Apostles Peter and Paul, this sacred synod ardently implores the Christian faithful to "maintain good fellowship among the nation" (1 Peter 2:12), and, if possible, to live for their part in peace with all human, so that they may truly be sons of the Father who is in heaven.

A Positive Evaluation of the Religious Traditions

The approval of *Nostra Aetate* in October 1965 by the bishops of the Second Vatican Council set in motion a dynamic process of dialogue that continues to engage the Church even today. It is a teaching about the relation of the Church to people who belong to other religious traditions, with special attention to Jews (the longest section of the Decree), Muslims, Hindus and Buddhists.

What are the positive points which the Council acknowledges about these religious traditions? The search for answers to the unsolved questions of life is common to humanity. And for these answers human beings turn to various religions. The fundamental questions that deeply challenge men and women are: What is man? What is the meaning and the aim of our life? What is moral good, what is sin? What is suffering and what purpose does it serve? Which is the road to true happiness? What are death, judgment and retribution after death? What, finally, is that ultimate inexpressible mystery which encompasses our existence: whence do we come, and where are we going? (*Nostra Aetate* 1). The Hindus, the Buddhists, the Muslims and the Jews find answers to their profound questions in ways that are typical of their religious tradition.

Hindus explore the divine mystery and express it in myth and philosophy; they seek release from the trials of life by asceticism, meditation and recourse to God in confidence and love.

Buddhists live a way of life in which they can attain a state of perfect liberation and reach supreme illumination, either through their own efforts or with divine help.

Muslims worship the one, merciful and almighty God; they learn to submit themselves to God's decrees, venerate Jesus as a prophet, revere the Blessed Virgin and await judgment and the rewards of heaven.

Jews are linked by spiritual bonds to the Church, Israel is the olive tree on which Gentile branches have been grafted; Jews remain very dear to God because God does not take back his gifts and promises to them.

What is the Basis of these Positive Evaluations?

These positive evaluations are grounded on the fact that throughout human history there is a universal 'awareness of a hidden power': it is this awareness that the Council suggests comes to expression in the teachings, ethics and rites of the world's religions. What are the religions of the world? It is as though the religions of the world are ways in which human beings express and channel their orientation towards God the Creator, ways in which the 'one community' of humanity moves towards God who calls all to share his life.

The Unsurpassable Self-Gift of God in the Person of Jesus Christ

God's creative action within the human community needs to be brought into loving contact with the supreme moment of God's self-giving revelation in the person of Jesus Christ, the Word made flesh and the unsurpassable sign of hope, whom God bestows on humanity as its Lord and Saviour. The Council is aware of this point and it is important to highlight the Council's approach to other religions. It is not a relativist approach: it does not say that all religions are of equal validity and merit. It is willed by God as effective communications of his reality to different peoples at different times and places. Modern Catholic reflection on world religions highlight that religions can only be understood in relation to Christ. The Council has made it clear that everything must be understood in relation to God's unsurpassable self-gift in Christ and, indeed, can only be understood in relation to this supreme moment.

It is important to bear in mind that while rejecting nothing of what is true and holy in these different religions, and greatly esteeming the precepts and doctrines of these religions which reflect a ray of truth enlightening all, the Council proclaims Christ as the one in whom "people find the fullness of their religious life." This generous acknowledgement of the divine action in the diversity of religious traditions also surfaces in Vatican II's Decree on Missionary Activity, *Ad Gentes* (AG), which recognizes the presence of the "seeds of the Word" in the cultures of the world and points to "the riches which a generous God has distributed among the nations" (*Ad Gentes* 11). The Dogmatic Constitution on the Church, *Lumen Gentium* (LG), similarly points to the good that is "found sown" not only "in minds and hearts," but also "in the rites and customs of peoples" (*Lumen Gentium* 17). *Nostra Aetate*, in other words, brings into explicit focus important themes which occur in other conciliar decrees and which are part of Catholic Christianity's gracious acknowledgement of the blessings bestowed by God on humanity and the world.

Dialogue with Other Religions: Part of the Church's On-going Pilgrim Journey

Today, dialogue and dialogue with people of other religions is the Church's very style of life and mission. It is very much part of the Church's on-going pilgrim journey. And what *Nostra Aetate* sets in motion is the very development of an account of the Church's mission in which dialogue with other religions becomes part of Catholic reality. This is something very original. The question we need to ask today is: how is the process of dialogical engagement forging ahead? How much are we attentive to the on-going dialogue which God sustains with every man and woman in the person of Jesus of Nazareth?

During the pontificate of late Pope John Paul II the dialogical engagement with other traditions which *Nostra Aetate* initiated in the Church became a major feature of Catholic life. His courageous initiative of inviting the leaders of world religions to Assisi, the various other interreligious encounters he has promoted and his personal encounters with various religious leaders across the globe bear testimony to his untiring work in the field of dialogue with members of other religions. It is very instructive to identify some of the features of the reception of *Nostra Aetate* in the official teachings of the Church during the notable pontificate of John Paul II. In his encyclical *Redemptoris Missio* (RM), John Paul II presented dialogue with other religions as an integral feature of the Church's evangelizing mission which does not stand in tension with the Church's obligation to proclaim Christ: In the light of the economy of salvation, the Church sees no conflict between proclaiming Christ and engaging in inter-religious dialogue. Instead, she feels the need to link the two in the context of her mission *ad gentes*. These two elements must maintain both their intimate connection and their distinctiveness; therefore they should not be confused, manipulated or regarded as identical, as though they were interchangeable (*Redemptoris Missio* 55).

Essential Quotes

The Church examines more closely her relationship to non-Christian religions. In her task of promoting unity and love among men, indeed among nations, she considers above all in this declaration what human have in common what draws them to fellowship, *Nostra Aetate*, 1.

From ancient times down to the present, there is found among various peoples a certain perception of that hidden power which hovers over the course of things and over the events of human history; at times some indeed have come to the recognition of a Supreme Being, or even of a Father. This perception and recognition penetrates their lives with a profound religious sense, *Nostra Aetate*, 2.

The Church, therefore, exhorts her sons, that through dialogue and collaboration with the followers of other religions, carried out with prudence and love and in witness to the Christian faith and life, they recognize, preserve and promote the good things, spiritual and moral, as well as the socio-cultural values found among these human, *Nostra Aetate*, 2.

Since in the course of centuries not a few quarrels and hostilities have arisen between Christians and Muslims, this sacred synod urges all to forget the past and to work sincerely for mutual understanding and to preserve as well as to promote together for the benefit of all humankind social justice and moral welfare, as well as peace and freedom, *Nostra Aetate*, 3.

In company with the Prophets and the same Apostle, the Church awaits that day, known to God alone, on which all peoples will address the Lord in a single voice and serve him shoulder to shoulder, *Nostra Aetate*, 4.

Since the spiritual patrimony common to Christians and Jews is thus so great, this sacred synod wants to foster and recommend that mutual understanding and respect which is the fruit, above all, of biblical and theological studies as well as of fraternal dialogues. NA, 4

We cannot truly call on God, the Father of all, if we refuse to treat in a brotherly way any man, created as he is in the image of God, *Nostra Aetate*, 5.

No foundation therefore remains for any theory or practice that leads to discrimination between man and man or people and people, so far as their human dignity and the rights flowing from it are concerned, *Nostra Aetate*, 5.

There are significant Post-Conciliar Documents of the Magisterium and Documents of the Pontifical Council for Inter-religious Dialogue and the Congregation for the Evangelization of Peoples related to Dialogue.[6]

Catechetical Guidelines on the Topic

Nostra Aetate brought in the Church a remarkable change in her relationship[7] with people of other religions and with the Jewish people. We must realize the changes this document has fashioned in the wider Christian community.

A new awareness for a more realistic presentation of the New Testament texts has come in the Church. Most Catholic teachers, whether familiar with the actual text of *Nostra Aetate* or not, are aware that one must be cautious not to present the New Testament texts in such a way as to impute collective guilt on the Jewish people, then or now, for the death of Jesus, since this charge lay at the heart of the 'teaching of contempt' which rationalized so much persecution of the Jewish people with Christendom in the past.

It is a must to get to know the two passages from the 1985 *Notes on the Correct Way to Present Jews and Judaism in Catholic Preaching and Teaching* issued by the Holy See to mark the 20th anniversary of *Nostra Aetate*. The first states: "The history of Israel did not end in 70 C.E. It continued, especially in a numerous Diaspora which allowed Israel to carry the whole world a witness — often heroic — of its fidelity to the one God and "to exalt Him in the presence of all the living" (Tobit 13:4), while preserving the memory of the land of their forefathers at the heart of their hope (e.g., Passover Seder).

The second passage, invites us to look toward the future, i.e., toward that divinely ordained end of history which, we believe, defines the significance of the present age of history: In underlining (as Catholic teachers and Preachers) the eschatological dimension of Christianity we shall reach a greater awareness that the people of God of the Old and the New Testament are tending towards a like end in the future: the coming or return of the Messiah — even if we start from two different points of view. Attentive to the same God who has spoken, hanging on the same word, we have to witness one same memory and one common hope in God who is the master of history.

Over the years, the Church in India has become more and more aware of her responsibility to dialogue with all peoples and cultures. In her catechetical mission, the Church has taken keen interest to pay particular attention to interreligious dialogue.

Catechesis provides a privileged opportunity to train the Catholics of our responsibility to work together for social justice, respect for the rights of persons and nations, and for social and international reconciliation. Going beyond simple dialogue, we can train Catholics to work together for peace and harmony with people of all religions.

Questions based on the Life Situation

How do I relate to people of other religions in my concrete context?

Every Christian disciple is called upon to proclaim the Good News of Jesus Christ. How am I able to understand and relate 'proclamation of the Good News' with 'Inter-religious Dialogue' both of which are integral expressions of the mission of the Church?

What ways do I privilege to facilitate inter-religious dialogue? Witnessing? Dialogue of life? Sharing of Spiritual Experiences? Contribution of material? Any other?

Questions for Discussion on the Document

What is meant by the word *Nostra Aetate*?

What are the positive points that *Nostra Aetate* mentions about people of other religions?

What is the role of religions according to *Nostra Aetate*?

What are the points that unite Jews and Christians?

What is the purpose of dialogue?

What contribution can you make to build a future of trust, understanding and working together to build a world of peace?

Action Plan

Liturgical Life: Our life of prayer is a constant dialogue with Jesus. What more can I do to make my life a dialogue of love with Jesus the supreme gift of the Father?

Community Life: Dialogue with our brothers and sisters – How can I live the spirit of dialogue in daily life?

Moral Life: How can I (as priest, religious, layperson) actively participate in dialogue with people of other faiths and religions?

Missionary Life: How do I understand "mission of dialogue and proclamation of the Good News" in the concrete situation in which I live?

How to Move Forward: Establish Genuine Dialogue and Build up Communities of Peace and Harmony

We must go back and re-examine our understanding of common concepts from the point of view of the other.

We must become active listeners as suggested by Carl R. Rogers the psychological and social scientist. A non-judgmental listening followed by timely verification by the listener on whether or not what was heard and repeated accurately reflects what was said.

In the process of understanding the 'Jesus event' the Christians need to make sure that they accurately understand how Jews interpret key ideas, notions and concepts without adding a Christian interpretation. The Jews need to investigate how Christians read Hebrew Scriptures and understand how those Scriptures might be used to explain the 'Jesus event.'

To cultivate genuine dialogue among Jews and Christians and with people of other religions and move towards a path of peace and wholeness to learn to see others with new eyes.

A transformation in self-understanding through genuine interreligious dialogue.[8] Past experiences have demonstrated that interreligious dialogue is a positive challenge as it actually leads participants to a deeper understanding of their own tradition as a result of being asked new questions or of viewing their own tradition from the other's perspective. It is the universal experience of those who have been involved in dialogue beyond a superficial level that their own identities as Jews, Christians or Buddhists have been enhanced by the dialogue. They are not the same Christians or Jews or Buddhists that they were before experiencing dialogue, but they understand themselves to be more committed and discerning Christians or Jews or Buddhists. This transformation in self-understanding can be expected to continue to evolve in this Century.

50 Golden Years – The Spirit of *Nostra Aetate* Penetrates the Indian Landscape

The *Declaration on the Relationship of the Church to Non-Christian Religions* (*Nostra Aetate*) is one of the treasures the Council has gifted to the Church and the World at large. This article highlights how the spirit of *Nostra Aetate* is penetrating the Indian landscape. India has a plurality of religions and the Indian subcontinent is the birthplace of many religions: Hinduism,

Jainism, Buddhism and Sikhism. From the earliest times, India as accepted other religions: Christianity, Judaism, Islam and Zoroastrianism. The tribal religions too are present in India.

The Church's New Attitude to Religions

To grasp the Church's new attitude to religions, we have to turn to *Nostra Aetate* which says,

> The Catholic Church rejects nothing that is true and holy in these religions. She regards with sincere reverence those ways of conduct and of life, those precepts and teachings which, though differing in many aspects from the ones she holds and sets forth, nonetheless often reflect a ray of that Truth which enlightens all human. Indeed, she proclaims, and ever must proclaim Christ "the way, the truth, and the life" (John 14:6), in whom human may find the fullness of religious life, in whom God has reconciled all things to Himself.

Dialogue and Collaboration as a Style of Life

The Church today has no other way than that of relationship and dialogue. She therefore exhorts her sons and daughters that the dialogue and collaboration with the members of other religions needs to be carried out with love, prudence and in witness to Jesus. It is in the spirit of relationship and in dialogue that the friends of Jesus can recognize, preserve and promote the spiritual, moral and socio-cultural values found among our brothers and sisters of other religions.

Variety of Initiatives

From educating clergy, religious and laity in the theory and practice of interreligious dialogue to an on-going dialogue of daily life and commitment, a variety of initiatives are carried out in the Church in India to make dialogue and collaboration a true style of life. The training programs in interreligious dialogue for priests, religious, laity, college youth and teachers are conducted in different parts of India and in the Archdiocese of Bombay, a One Year Training Program for teachers and catholic adults called BIRD – Basics in Interreligious Dialogue is by now well known. In Amravati, as suicide by the farmers are the highest a Seminar for farmers with 7 scientists on how to better farming saw 250 farmers actively participating.

There are interfaith and interreligious seminars on values, training in modern Indian spirituality, on the spirituality of Tagore, on the spirit of fasting, on peace and harmony etc. International Symposiums on water and on the significance of life and death in major religions united together various people to come together and share their views and enhance each other.

Building up of Rapports

It is important to focus attention on the very title of the document we are revisiting: The *Declaration on the Relationship of the Church to Non-Christian Religions* (*Nostra Aetate*). Here, the aspect of Relationship has to be highlighted. The whole and sole aim of the Declaration is to come to know and appreciate believers of other religions and to knit and strengthen relationships. Truly, the spirit of *Nostra Aetate* has made its journey in the Indian soil thanks to the tireless efforts and commitment of the Nuncios, Cardinals, Archbishops, Bishops, Priests, Religious and Laity of our motherland. This has come across very forcefully in two of the Interreligious Dialogue Study Seminars that the CBCI Office for Dialogue and Desk for Ecumenism has organized at Agra region (10th-12th March 2013) and in the Western region (18th-19th June 2013). The dialogue of life, the dialogue of action, the dialogue of theological exchange and the dialogue of religious experience has and is indeed playing a significant role in our country.

The Four Interdependent Forms of Dialogue

Dialogue and Proclamation (DP) is an authoritative document issued in 1991 by The Pontifical Council for Inter-religious Dialogue and the Congregation for the Evangelisation of Peoples. *Dialogue and Proclamation* offers the fullest authoritative treatment of the delicate issues raised by the Church's commitment to dialogue which *Nostra Aetate* proposed. This document goes on to identify four interdependent forms of dialogue by which this dimension of the Church's life is to be expressed:

The dialogue of life: where people strive to live in an open and neighbourly spirit, sharing their joys and sorrows, their human problems and preoccupations.

The dialogue of action: in which Christians and others collaborate for the integral development and liberation of people.

The dialogue of theological exchange: where specialists seek to deepen their understanding of their respective religious heritages, and to appreciate each other's spiritual values.

The dialogue of religious experience: where persons, rooted in their own religious traditions, share their spiritual riches, for instance with regard to prayer and contemplation, faith and ways of searching for God or the Absolute (*Dialogue and Proclamation*, 42).

The aim of dialogue is directed, *Dialogue and Proclamation* says, towards "a deeper conversion of all toward God," and thereby has its own validity. In dialogue Christians and others are invited to deepen their religious commitment, to respond with increasing sincerity to God's personal call and gracious self-gift which, as our faith tells us, always passes through the mediation of Jesus Christ and the work of his Spirit (*Dialogue and Proclamation* 40).

Praxis of Interreligious Dialogue

Have you heard of an Interreligious colony? Make a trip to Amravati, stop at the Interreligious colony, you will find 45 houses built for the homeless people. Did anyone tell you that at old Goa during the feast of St. Francis Xavier, teachers and students from different schools and religions are invited to participate and are offered good input session and that this creates an image of living in harmony? Did you know that a Hindu girl who took poison was rushed in two minutes to the hospital driving 3 kilometres by Fr. K.V. Joseph msfs? "You brought her on time otherwise she would have been gone" said the doctor. May be your mind and heart are ready for an interreligious retreat and are still searching how to go about it. Prerana, Bangalore already had Interreligious retreats, Fr. Ronnie Prabhu and his team can accompany you.

Want to taste a bit of what the theological exchange is all about, then the right spot to choose is the seminary of Goa where world religions is part of the philosophy curriculum, the seminarians are sent to visit the Hindu families during their festivals, and the Hindu brethren long for such visits reports Frs. Caetano Fernande and Simeao Fernandes. Have you ever been part of those who visited the prisons with people of other religions? Did you know that on Christmas day most Hindus and Muslims visit the Cathedrals and lot of miracles take place? At Rajkot it really happens narrates Fr. Stanly. In Ahmedabad, on Christmas Day, after the Eucharistic Celebration, there is common supper for all states Fr. Kuriachan Paul. Mr. Shilesh from Ahmedabad joyfully speaks about the book titled *Parvamuth* published with the help of representatives from various religions for use in schools and other places.

In Pune, according to Fr. Lui Heredia, on Christmas Day evening initiatives on peace, good will and harmony is a regular feature. The Moving Crib with stopover at prominent places and banners and flyers at permanent places attracts everyone's eyes. In the words of Fr. S.M. Michael, renowned sociologist and an expert in interreligious dialogue, the 4 levels of dialogue are promoted in each parish of the Archdiocese of Bombay. The much expected special gathering before Christmas where His Eminence Oswald Cardinal Gracias calls for a meeting with the major religious leaders deserves special mention here.

In the Western region there are Parishes that have an interreligious dialogue cell and the members of the Parish Council are given training on interreligious dialogue. Spread the perfume, spread the Good News, seminars and researches, net working with Catholic Sabha and interreligious dialogue forum, news media – message on Good Friday, Christmas etc. and at social front – empowerment, building the rapport with people are all taking place in the Western and other regions too. Commenting on the rich sharing that took place at the Western Region interreligious dialogue Directors meet, His Grace Archbishop Felix, chairperson CBCI Office for Dialogue and Desk for Ecumenism remarked: "I am very happy to know about the great amount of good being done in the Western Region. This meeting gave me an opportunity to get to know the interreligious and ecumenical initiatives in the different dioceses."

Spread the Perfume

It is the faith experience, encounter with Jesus that is at the heart of relationship. It is a faith experience that has gone through a fruitful period of gestation thus finding suitable concepts for a meaningful communication. The lived experience of faith, the process of gestation and the communication prepares the ground for stronger relationships with believers of other religions. *Fides et Ratio* no. 2 uses *"diakonia* of truth" a "marvellous expression to say dialogue." Inter-religious dialogue is all about building up relationships and spreading the perfume of the Good News and getting to know more deeply the believers of other religions. "To live Christianity better is the greatest challenge that interreligious dialogue offers" as the spirit of *Nostra Aetate* continues to blow and glow in the Indian landscape moulding minds and hearts.

Endnotes

1 Archbishop Felix Machado has been elected (March 2010) to lead the Indian Bishops (CBCI) in promoting interreligious dialogue and national harmony in India. In 2011 Archbishop Machado was elected Chairperson of Ecumenism for the Catholic Conference of Bishops of India (CCBI). In 2013 Archbishop Machado was elected Chairman of the Office for Ecumenism and Interreligious Dialogue of the Federation of Asian Bishops' Conferences (FABC).

2 Vatican Radio (October 30, 2015).

3 Teresa Joseph, *Nostra Aetate* – Faith Kit No., 6 NBCLC, Bangalore, 2013.

4 Eugene J. Fisher, "*Nostra Aetate*: Transforming the Catholic-Jewish Relationship: A Catholic Perspective," http://www.adl.org/main_Interfaith/nostra_aetate.htm?Multi_page_sections=sHeading_2 (Novem- ber 8, 2012).

5 "*Nostra Aetate*: Transforming the Catholic-Jewish Relationship: A Catholic Perspective," (November 8, 2012).

6 Vatican Council II, Declaration *on Religious Freedom Dignitatis humanae* (DH0 n. 1-15 (December 7, 1965), in *EV* /1, 1042-1086; John Paul II, Encyclical *letter Redemptoris Missio* [RM] n. 1-92 (December 7, 1990), in *EV*/12 (1992), 547-732; John Paul II, *Encyclical Letter Fides et Ratio* [FR] n. 1-108 (September 14, 1998), in *Enchiridion Encicliche* (*EE*)/8, Bologna, Dehoniane 1998, 2375-2600; John Paul II, *Apostolic Exhortation, Ecclesia in Asia* (November 6, 1999) n. 1-51, in *Insegnamenti di Giovanni Paolo II*, 22/2, Città del Vaticano, Libreria Editrice Vaticana, 2002, 734-840; John Paul II, *Apostolic Letter Novo Millennio Ineunte* [NMI] n. 1-59 (January 6, 2001), in *Insegnamenti di Giovanni Paolo II*, 20/1, Città del Vaticano, Libreria Editrice Vaticana, 2003, 87-127; The Pontifical Council for Inter-religious Dialogue and the Congregation for the Evangelisation of Peoples, *Dialogue and Proclamation* (DP), an authoritative document issued in 1991.

7 Teresa Joseph, "The Spirit of *Nostra Aetate* Penetrates the Indian Landscape," in *Examiner* (Oct 26-Nov 01, 2013), 6-7.

8 Teresa Joseph, "Milestones in the Indian Church, The 12th General Body Meeting of the Catholic Council of India and the 1st National Convention of Small Christian Communities," in *Examiner* (December 07-13, 2013), 10-11.

The Qur'ānic and Prophetic Model of Inter-Religious Dialogue

'Āshaq Ḥussain

Introduction

The root of the word dialogue (from the Greek *dialogos*, from *dia*, across, and *legein*, to speak) tells us that it is the effort to share meaning with someone. By intercultural or interfaith dialogue we mean a conversation between different individuals or groups whose purpose are simply honest engagement and increased mutual understanding. Dialogue is a conversation on a common subject between men, communities or religions. It is a fundamental element of communication to generate bilateral or multilateral relationship. It is a means of talking together to remove all hurdles and barriers to sort out mutual problems to develop cordial relationship and understanding and to learn and help one another, in order to lead better and happier life. Dialogue is of significant importance for those who wish to live out their faith in the modern world. Dialogue is a natural manifestation of our humanness, as both the Qur'ān and the life of the Prophet make clear. The Qur'ān tells us that the fundamental oneness of all human beings and their ethnic and linguistic plurality together enable us to engage with and understand one another: "People, We created you all from a single man and a single woman, and made you into races and tribes so that you should get to know one another..."[1]

The exemplary life of Prophet Muḥammad show that he was a model of positive engagement with those around him before he was called to be a prophet, since before that time he was known as al-Ṣādiq al-Amīn, 'the truthful and the trustworthy.' Thus at that time he positively engaged with others not in obedience to the revealed word of God (Qur'ān) but in obedience to the norms of God's creation – the innate disposition (*fiṭra*) with which God endowed all human beings.

The Qur'ānic Basis of Dialogue with the People of the Book and Non-Muslims

In a dialogue, no idea can be imposed on the other side. In a dialogue one should respect the independent identity of the other side and his or her independent ideological and cultural integrity. Only in such a case, can dialogue be a preliminary step leading to peace, security and Justice.[2] Dialogue is an essential strategy for meeting, understanding, valuing, learning and living together in peace.[3] It begins when people meet. It depends upon mutual understanding and mutual trust. Dialogue makes it possible to share in service and it becomes the medium of authentic witness.[4] Dialogue is not negotiation or polemics occurring among civilizations nor does it simply result in the satisfaction of personal interests of both parties as is the case with negotiations, whereas, polemics is the controversies.[5] Allah has mentioned frequent cases of dialogue between His Messengers and their opponents in Qur'ān and has advised Prophet Muḥammad to engage in dialogue with the pagans.[6] Prophet Muḥammad started spreading his message with dialogue and argument. Dialogue is based on freedom and free will. There are many verses in the Qur'ān on the issue of dialogue with People of the Book: "Say, 'People of the Book,' let us arrive at a statement that is common to us all: we worship God alone, we ascribe no partner to Him, and none of us takes others beside God as lords."[7]

Without doubt, this verse commands the Prophet and therefore the Muslims to establish relations with People of the Book and to unite around common issues. In a way, it draws a framework for dialogue. Common issues around which we can come together may be principles of faith such as faith in God, prophets and the afterlife, principles of practice such as abstinence from adultery, gambling or drinking, or temporal political, social, cultural or economic issues. The fact that the Prophet did not bring up points of conflict in his interactions with People of the Book, did not enter into combative debates with them and sought engagement with them through the Madīna Charter and political and military treaties such as *Ḥudaybiyyah* and *Khaybar* confirms that he carried out the Qur'ānic command in letter and spirit: "People, We created you all from a single man and a single woman, and made you into races and tribes so that you should get to know one another. In God's eyes, the most honoured of you are the ones most mindful of Him: God is all knowing, all aware."[8]

The diversity among humankind mentioned in *Surah Ḥujurāt* is mentioned with a comprehensive affirmation that its purpose is that different groups and individuals are thereby enabled to know each other. So it can be said that the verse no.13 in *Surah Ḥujurāt* encourages us to explore this diversity of ethnicity, culture and faith, engaging respectfully with different groups. The verses concerning difference of faith can be understood as encouraging Muslims (i) to accept that some individuals and groups will not believe in your faith however much you may desire them to; (ii) to live with the resulting differences in compassion and acceptance; (iii) to explore each other's faith and religion with respect and in an attempt to understand one another; (iv) to wait patiently until God explains what people have differed about and why. The Qur'ān's commanding or commending engagement with non-Muslims on the basis of justice, kindness, civility and courtesy, regardless of whether they are People of the Book, is embodied in the Prophetic Sunnah. The examples of the Prophet   encourage Muslims to engage in peaceful relations and dialogue with other groups, not limited to Christians, Jews and Sabians. These examples will be explored further in a later chapter. Here it must suffice to remind readers of the shining example of the Madīna Charter or Constitution, which the Prophet   discussed, agreed and signed with the Jews and polytheists of Madīna .

Prophet's Approach to Dialogue

The Prophet Muḥammad's practice embodied the Qur'ānic teaching. He did not treat all non-Muslims, or indeed all Jews, or all Christians, in the same way, indiscriminately, as if responding only to their being non-Muslims or to their particular confessional identity. Prophet, who had boundless tolerance, lived together with the People of the Book in Madīna and found common agreement points even with the people who say they are Muslims but cause conflicts and with the seditious souls who want to play people with clean consciousness off against each other almost everywhere and showed tolerance to them. He even gave his shirt as a shroud for Abdullah b. Ubay b. Salūl, who acted as an enemy towards him throughout his life, when he died and upon request our Prophet agreed to perform the *janāzah* (death) prayer for him. Thereupon Ḥazrat 'Umar reminded him that Ibn Salūl was a hypocritical person by listing the evils he had committed against the Prophet throughout his life that it was not appropriate to perform the prayer and pray for him. Prophet   pointed out the 80th verse of Chapter *at-Taubah*: "Whether thou ask for their forgiveness or not, (their sin is unforgivable): if thou ask seventy times for their forgiveness, Allah will not forgive them) and said my Lord let me free about this issue."[9]

Therefore if it is necessary, I will ask more than seventy times for his forgiveness. Then the 84th verse of chapter *at-Taubah* was sent down by Allah and the definite judgment was made: Nor do thou ever pray for any of them that dies, nor stand at his grave. Therefore there is no being similar to him nor any message presented to humanity similar to his. Therefore it is impossible for those who try to follow this Guide of Salvation, who is the best example, to think differently.

The relationship of the Prophet with Christians in Makkah, which is the cradle of Islam, started in a friendly way from the beginning. When he signed a treaty with the Najrān Christians, he was at war with the Makkan pagans at the same time. Similarly, when the Jews of Banū Qurayzah were punished for violating the Madīna Charter upon the judgment of the arbitrator whom they themselves had approved, he maintained the treaty with Banū Nazīr, another Jewish tribe. He did not consider all the People of the Book as enemies. If he had done so his approval of practices such as marrying women from among them or sharing their food would be inexplicable. Rather, those social exchanges, alongside everyday commercial engagements, are a strong argument that for Muslims, the norms for how non-Muslims are regarded and treated do not derive from their values or their identity, but from their actions and how those actions are perceived in different political contexts.

The religion of Islam which has been delivered to humanity by Prophet Muḥammad for eternal peace in this life and hereafter is a religion which puts great emphasis on brotherhood and equality. The Prophet's life was spent in dialogue with atheists, idolaters and People of the Book. Treaties, friendly relations and commercial partnerships are all facets of this dialogue. His examples, in this area as in every other, are precious treasures for Muslims, who accept him as a model and a guide.

The Prophet recognized justice and honour in non-Muslim groups and individuals and entered into friendly relationships with those who displayed these qualities. The Muslims suffered severe persecution and torment at the hands of Makkan idolaters in the early period of Islam. The Prophet suggested to those who wanted to escape this persecution, which could amount to murder when Muslims refused to convert back to their ancestors' religion that they should temporarily migrate to Abyssinia. The Prophet explained his preference for Abyssinia as follows: "There is a king who loves justice and in whose territories nobody is oppressed."[10] The king (Najāshī) that the Prophet described as one who did not persecute, Ashama ibn Abjar, was a Christian. The Prophet entered into trade relationships with People of the Book. At the time of his death, a person of Madīna belonging to the Jewish faith was in possession of a shield belonging to the Prophet, which he had given as surety for a debt.[11] This shows that the Jewish people in Madīna traded freely with their Muslim neighbours, and that the Prophet himself traded with his Jewish neighbours. Further, he actively protected the rights and freedom of People of the Book, honoured those beliefs and traditions that he shared with them, and treated them with courtesy and respect. He visited the religious schools of the Jews (Beit Midrash) from time to time to ensure that there were no restrictions on their freedom to learn and teach their religion. When a delegation of Christians from Najran came to negotiate a pact with the Prophet he courteously allowed them to pray in the mosque which lasted the whole day.[12]

It is a well-known fact that the Muslims prayed towards Jerusalem for 17 months before God appointed the Ka'ba as the direction of Muslim prayer. This shows the importance of Bayt al-Maqdis in Islam, demonstrating the significance of beliefs and traditions shared with the People of the Book. In addition, the Prophet preferred to resemble People of the Book rather than the idolaters in mundane matters that were not explicitly stipulated by the divine will. For example, he let his hair down over his forehead like People of the Book in opposition to the idolaters' practice of parting their hair over the forehead.

The peace treaties signed between the holy Prophet and different groups of His enemies in order to put an end to hostilities represent another angle. Islamic state remained loyal to all these treaties in practice so long as other parties did so. Islam considers breach of promise a grave and unforgivable sin.[13] To discuss these treaties thoroughly will go beyond the limits of this paper. Therefore, we mention just a few points here.

The treaties signed by Prophet of Islam were a trilateral comprehensive one between Muslims of Madīna, Jews living in the vicinity, and the polytheists. The main goal of these treaties was to establish peaceful coexistence between all those who lived in Madīna.[14] The content of these treaties shows that Islam recognized the rights of all non-Muslims of any category even the polytheists. Muslims never resorted to suppression or elimination of communities that rejected Islamic faith. Peaceful coexistence, fair treatment, and compassionate conduct were matters of principle to Muslims.

According to the Madīna Charter, those different tribal, ethnic and religious groups who were signatories formed one 'ummah,' that is a common political, economic, legal, military and social entity within which they could co-exist peacefully while retaining their respective identities. This Charter, which is similar, in structure, to a federation, guarantees peace, security, freedom, equality, justice and communal life founded on basic universal human values to all the signatory groups. It is possible to ground all the terms of the agreement in the Qur'ān. It is noteworthy that political scientists today sometimes turn to the Madīna Charter as a resource and model in their search for new political administrative models suited to the changing and developing world. The Madīna Charter has also been the subject of many doctoral dissertations.

Thus, the Madīna Charter provides an invaluable model of a system safeguarding the rights and freedoms of all and thereby providing a safe environment in which peace, co-operation and trust, and perhaps ultimately friendship and fellowship, can develop.

The Charter demonstrates the Islamic desirability of just and harmonious interfaith and intercultural relations. It points to the possibility of relationships of peace, co-operation and trust, of friendship and fellowship, between people of different faiths and cultures belonging to one 'ummah.' It gives an inspiring and practical example of the kind of legal and political provisions which make these relationships possible by enshrining religious freedom, equality and the rule of law as fundamental principles. In short, it affirms the personal and social goals of dialogue activities and provides guidance on the conditions in which these goals may be achieved. The Charter, which was first proposed and subsequently implemented and supervised by the Prophet, is one of the most important sources of Islamic support for interfaith and intercultural dialogue.

Prophet Muḥammad's friendliness towards the Jews is an example of brotherhood. Muḥammad Haykal writes:

Muḥammad achieved an operational Muslim unity. Politically, it was a very wise move destined to show Muḥammad's (SAW) sound judgment and foresight. We shall better appreciate its wisdom when we learn of the attempts to divide *al-Aws* against *al-Khazraj*, and *al-Anṣār* against *al–Muhājirūn*. The politically greater achievement of Muḥammad was his realization of a unity for the city of Yathrib as a whole, his construction of a political structure in which the Jews entered freely into an alliance of mutual cooperation with the Muslims. How the Jews gave Muḥammad a good welcome in the hope of winning him as an ally. He too, returned their greeting with like gestures and sought to consolidate his relations with them. He visited their chiefs and cultivated the friendship of their nobles. He bound himself to them in a bond of friendship on the grounds that they were Scripturists and Monotheists. So much had Muḥammad defended the Jews that the fact that he fasted with them on the days they fasted and prayed towards Jerusalem as they did increased his personal and religious esteem among them. Everything seemed as if the future could only strengthen this Muslim-Jewish friendship and produce further cooperation and closeness between them. Similarly, Muḥammad's own conduct, his great humanity, compassion, and faithfulness, and his outgoing charity and goodness to the poor, oppressed and deprived as well as prestige and influence which these qualities had won for him among all the people of Yathrib, all these enabled him to conclude the pact of friendship, alliance and cooperation in the safe guarding of religious freedom throughout the city. This covenant is one of the greatest political documents which history has known. Such an accomplishment by Muḥammad at this stage of his career and never been reached by any Prophet Jesus, Moses and all the Prophets that precede them never went beyond the preaching of their religious messages through words and miracles. All of them had left their legacy to men of power and political authority, who came after them, it was the latter that put their powers at the service of those messages and fought, with arms where necessary, for the freedom of the people to believe. Christianity spread at the hands of the disciples of Jesus and after his time, but only in extremely limited measure. The disciples as well as their followers were persecuted until one of the kings of the world favoured this religion, adopted it, and put his royal power behind its missionary effort. All other religions in the East and the West have had nearly the same history, but not the religion of Muḥammad. God willed that Islam be spread by Muḥammad and that the truth be vindicated by his hand. He willed Muḥammad to be Prophet, statesmen, fighter, and Conqueror, all for the sake of God and the truth with which he was commissioned as Prophet. In all these aspects of his career Muḥammad was great, the exemplar of human perfection, and the typos of every realized value.[15]

The covenant of Madīna concluded between *Muhājirūn* and *Anṣār* on one side and Jews on the other, was dictated by Muḥammad. It was the instrument of their alliance which confirmed the Jews in both their religion and position in society, and determined their rights as well as their duties.

Thus, it can be said that whereas the Prophet's charisma may have dissipated after his demise, his knowledge, piety, and spiritual legacy have inspired different groups of Muslims to emulate his outstanding examples. The profound characteristics of the Prophet have left an indelible mark on the consciousness of the Muslims. The Qur'ān itself bears the perfume of the soul of the person through whom it was revealed. As the great philosopher poet 'Allāmah Iqbāl said: "You can deny God but you cannot deny the Prophet."[16]

Conclusion

It can be argued from the preceding discussion that Islam regards peaceful dialogue as a primary principle; it is enough to study the circumstances under which Islam considers war legitimate. They include defence against aggression, eradicating anarchy, rescuing the oppressed, defending territory, and facing warmongers who break their promises or agreements and contracts. The purpose of Islam is to bring about divine revolution, to invite people to the worship of God, to strive for a society in which spiritual, ethical, and human values are cherished. Islam advocates an atmosphere where peace, tolerance, love and well-wishing is the order of the day — an atmosphere where controversies are resolved without the use of violence. This is the desired world of Islam and such a world can be established only through peaceful dialogue. The truth is that Islam is based on monotheism, with regard to God; and on peaceful dialogue, with regard to methodology. This is the essence of Islamic teaching. No other way is possible in Islam.

Endnotes

[1] The Holy Qur'ān, 49:13.

[2] Muḥammad Khatami, *Islām Dialogue and Civil Society* (New Delhi: Centre for Persian and Central Asian Studies, School of Language, 2003), 14.

[3] Martin Forward, *Inter-Religious Dialogue: A Short Introduction* (Oxford: One World Publications, 2007), 3.

[4] Forward, *Inter-Religious Dialogue: A Short Introduction*, 3.

[5] Augus Stevenson, *Oxford English Dictionary* (New York: Oxford University Press, 2002).

[6] Muḥammad Munir Ghazban, *Political Conduct of Muḥammad*, vol. 1, translated by Omar Qaderi (Tehran: Ehsan Press, 2000), 207-209, 135-138.

[7] The Holy Qur'ān, 3:64.

[8] The Holy Qur'ān, 49:13.

[9] The Holy Qur'ān, 9:80.

[10] Muḥammad Hamidullah, *The Life and Work of the Founder of Islam* (Luton: Apex Books Concern, 1975), 46.

[11] Al- Bukhārī, *Ṣaḥīḥ al-Bukhārī*, ḥadīth no., 89.

[12] Ibn Hisham, *As-Sirah an-Nabawiyyah*, vol. 2., 224; Muḥammad Hamidullah, *İslam Peygamberi*, vol. 2, translated by Salih Tug (Istanbul: Irfan Yayinlari, 2004), 1086.

[13] Kariminia, *Peaceful Coexistence in Islam and International Relations*, 293.

[14] Hamidullah, *Sokunat beinalmelli dolate eslami*, 315.

[15] Muḥammad Husayn Haykal, *The Life of Muḥammad*, translated by Islma'il Rāji al Fāruqi (n.p.: New Cresent Publishing House, 2008), 178-179.

[16] Quoted in Annemarie Schimmel, *Mystical Dimensions of Islam*, (North Carolina: University of North Carolina Press, 1975), 227.

Dialogue as Pedagogy:
Learning Together with the Other

Rudolf C. Heredia

Terms of Discourse

Dialogue is readily described as communicative exchange. However, it is more comprehensive than the 'communicative rationality' of Habermas, which he defines as: "oriented to achieving, sustaining and reviewing consensus – and indeed a consensus that rests on the inter-subjective recognition of criticisable validity claims."[1]

The nature of dialogic communication focuses less on rational meaning than on hermeneutical meaningfulness. Moreover, to be credible, dialogue must be sensitive to the differences of local situations, and to be effective it must consider their commonalities as well differences and thus develop an overall architecture for a more universally sustainable dialogue.

The Hermeneutics of Dialogue

For Panikkar 'dialogue' is a most fundamental condition of our existence. It is our way of being. He says, "Dialogue is, fundamentally, opening myself to another so that he might speak and reveal my myth.... Dialogue is a way of knowing myself and of disentangling my own point of view from other viewpoints and from me."[2]

'Myth,' Panikkar understands as a pre-rational, not an irrational but rather a trans-rational, comprehension, "the horizon of intelligibility"[3] that can only be expressed in symbol and metaphor. Once it is rationally articulated, myth is demythicised and then develops into an 'ideology,' which in this context Panikkar describes as: "the more or less coherent ensemble of ideas that make up critical awareness."[4]

Gadamer explains how "to be in conversation, however, means to be beyond oneself as if to another." For, as he insisted in 1960 all genuine dialogue must be premised on an authentic hermeneutic: "to recognize oneself (or one's own) in the other and find a home abroad – this is the basic movement of spirit whose being consists in this return to itself from otherness."[5] But we would emphasize a further implication of such dialogical hermeneutics: "the challenge to recognize otherness or the alien in oneself (or one's own)."[6]

'Difference,' then, as Gadamer insists "stands at the beginning of a conversation, not it its end,"[7] (awaiting the moment of coherence, of fulfilment, of a 'fusion of horizon' that will complete the hermeneutic circle and set it off again for us – "we who are a conversation."[8] For, we are constructed and deconstructed in dialogue with ourselves and others. Indeed, "the conversation that we are is one that never ends."[9] For dialogue and conversation are intrinsic to the human condition, the very language of our existence, the essential hermeneutic of all our experience. For "dialectics is the optimism of reason. Dialogue is the optimism of the heart."[10] Thus we can speak of a 'dialectical dialogue' which would pertain to the encounter of ideologies, while a 'dialogical dialogue' would be more pertinent to the meeting of myths.

We must dare beyond the constraints of dialectical reason, which no doubt has its uses – and limitations. In dialogue the 'self' and the 'other' are both discovered and enriched, the cultural 'other' and especially the 'counter-cultural other', within my own culture and across cultures too. For as we unveil our 'self' in the 'other', and the 'other' in our 'self', we will find that our deepest identity and bonding transcends all differences in an immanent I-thou communion. It this that makes a dialogue pedagogic: learning together with and from each other.

However, a dialogue within is an imperative for a dialogue without. An intrapersonal dialogue is the pre-condition for an interpersonal one: openness within the self so that one is open to other and not locked in a 'walled-in consciousness.' So too is an intra-community dialogue an imperative for an intercommunity one. It is precisely such openness that overcomes our prejudgments, our prejudices, the unconscious ideologies and mind-sets, which eventually can only bring a 'clash of civilizations.' If dialogue is to be pedagogic then there must be a 'fusion of horizons', each side learning from the other, and meeting on common ground to journey together to higher ground.

Human beings are meant to be interrelated and interactive, not isolated and alone. Yet, there is always the danger of celebrating our own 'difference' in isolation and seclusion from others, and not in dialogue with them. We fund examples if such 'withdrawal' among fundamentalists/radicals of various persuasions: religious communes, utopian communities …This "shades over into the celebration of indifference, non-engagement and indecision."[11] Such an inwardly turned dialogue eventually becomes a monologue, whether of individuals or groups. This inbreeding can only lead to a genetic decline of the group's cultural and intellectual DNA. This further negates creative pluralism, undermines respectful tolerance and destroys any real possibility of a dialogue across differences with the other.

The Asian Scenario

The socio-political trajectories of Asian societies though their various stages of development from agro-rural to urban industrial societies are spread across a wide spectrum of developmental models and political ideologies. Consequently there are wide variations in the levels of poverty and deprivation, both in intensity and scope, across societies and within each as well. Consequently, there are multiple modernity unevenly spread: whereas some regions are highly advanced other locales are left behind in an earlier historical age. Most Asian live in several different centuries simultaneously, even within their national boundaries.

Yet there are commonalities in the "family resemblance"[12] of those Asian cultures and religions which are premised on an understanding of a cosmos beyond or rather outside historical time. These developed locally and spread geographically beyond, many to other distant Asian civilizations. But they were largely within the continent, at least till 20th century. Abrahamic cultures and religions also have a common 'family resemblance' which is premised on divine revelations within human history. These are at times perceived as 'foreign' to Asia. But this is really a perception colored by the colonial experience and domination of the West. They are very much Asian, or rather West Asian from where they spread over to other parts of the continent and beyond as well.

All this makes for an intriguing Asian mosaic with positive possibilities for complementarities and exchange, but also real dangers of misunderstanding and conflict. Hence when the Federation of Asian Bishops (FABC) calls for a threefold dialogue, with the poor, with cultures, with religions, the purpose must be defined in terms of it a liberating, enriching, transformational promise. Such a dialogue must be both inclusively Asian and open to the world, universally global, and concretely local.

The Church in Asia must outgrow its colonial past to evolve into an authentic Asian Church, contributing to and learning from the Church universal in a pedagogic dialogue. In developing a contextual theology for this evolution Peter Hai list

> five of its major characteristics, which complement and enrich each other: (1) a synthetic contextual character, (2) a similarity between the FABC's theological methodology and that of Latin American liberation theologies, (3) a faith seeking dialogue, (4) an approach that encourages theological pluralism and aims to achieve harmony, and (5) a development that constitutes a paradigm shift in theology.[13]

In its Sixth Plenary in 1995 in Manila, the FABC recognized the specificities of the Asian churches and called for "a movement toward the triple dialogue with other faiths, with the poor and with cultures." The context for this triple dialogue must necessarily address the Asian situation characterized by three inescapable conditions: economic poverty, cultural diversity and popular religiosity.[14] For in Asia voluntary poverty still has a religious value represented as detachment from earthy goods and desires; popular religiosity runs too deep among our peoples to be easily dismissed and it expresses religious values that must not be discounted, rather it needs to be carefully and empathetically discerned for the genuine faith in which it is embedded; our cultural and religious diversity is an inescapable reality not just to be accepted but to be celebrated in authentic Asian religious traditions.

Most recently two events have opened new horizons of possibilities for renewal and reform for both the Catholic Church and the Society of Jesus: the election of Pope Francis on 13th March 2013, who has brought a tsunami of change in the Church: and the convocation of the 36th General Congregation for 2nd Oct 2016 and the expectation of a new General. Both events have significant relevance for the Church and the Jesuits in Asia. This is the ecclesial context for our pedagogic dialogue in Asia.

The Church in Asia is a very small minority in a very large and enormously complex, and increasingly problematic social situation. It has still not shaken off its colonial past and though Christians are a tiny per cent in the population they are still a significant presence there. We must learn in dialogue with the other: the poor, the *anawim* of the Bible, those culturally and religiously different. As Pope Francis said in his address to the conclave before his election: the Church cannot be a 'self-referential', 'worldly Church' it must be a "Church which evangelizes and comes out of herself , the *Dei Verbum religiose audiens et fidente proclamans*," hears and proclaims the word of God. In his speech to the pre-conclave general congregation of cardinals, he left us a compelling image of Jesus of this Church-for-the-world, "in which Jesus knocks from within so that we will let him come out."[15]

This makes the call and challenge of a triple dialogue in the Asian Church in distinctive and critical for the Church Universal as well and so is pedagogic for both. But it needs to be energized by the Spirit continuously: *eccelesia semper renovanda, ecclesia semper reformanda*, or in Luther's expression *eccelesia semper purificanda.*

Dialogue as Liberation: Learning from the Poor

The Contemporary Crisis

In Asia the transition from tradition to modernity, rural to urban, agriculture to industrialization has been uneven and inequitable. It has failed to deliver on its promise of a better world for all. The development model pursued has left an unconscionably large and increasing desperate poor population trapped in their deprivation in South Asia. Even those countries that have achieved rapid levels of growth have mounting social and political tensions that could put the gains at serious risk, as in China. And where economic affluence has arrived there is now is now a crippling stagnation, like Japan. Others are stymied by multiple conflicts and gross inequalities, e.g., India. Rather than tinkering with the present system, we need another more sustainable model of development that is just and egalitarian, participative and solidary, not a top-down neo-liberal globalization.

The capital intensive model whether led by the state or private enterprise has resulted in endemic inequalities and polarization across multiple dimensions. Authoritarian leaders come to power by fair means or foul and precipitate a majoritarianism that marginalizes minorities. Not surprisingly those in the lowest strata of society, the most vulnerable and disfranchised people become scapegoats as collective discontents simmers and boils over, and the discontents of modernity are visited on refugees, migrants, minorities, … the weak and vulnerable. Consumerist individualism breaks down social solidarity into an atomized mass society where mass leaders find a gullible following. Defensive communitarianism divides society into impervious and hostile compartments.

The economic inequalities of class in an earlier century precipitated a working class struggle that in places called for a class war. After two devastating world wars this was largely defused by the welfare state. But half a century later, in spite of a remarkable decrease in absolute levels of poverty the world over and Asia, even in developing countries, relative poverty, that is the differences between the rich and the poor, has jumped to unsustainable levels worldwide, even in poor countries. The evidence for this can be seen in the recent populist, majoritarian mass politics, in rich and poor countries alike that is compounded by nationalism and migration, and internal displacement. And as always it is the poor and minorities that are the worst off.

In a capitalist society where gross inequalities are ingrained over generations, class antagonisms can build up beyond class struggle into class war. The welfare state has helped to mitigate this, but a neoliberal capitalism is dismantling it and once again institutionalising a global free market with disastrous consequences for the vulnerable poor. Asia is seeing the worst of this. Thomas Piketty's monumental work on Capitalism in the Twenty-first Century (2014) challenges the conventional wisdom of neoliberal economists. He demonstrates how over centuries the system reproduces itself and increase as it embeds inequality. This is "the fundamental force for divergence"[16]: meaning that return on capital is generally higher than economic growth. In such a system class becomes caste, as status is inherited with capital rather than achieved through merit. But he is positive about remedial interventions in the system: "There are nevertheless ways in which democracy can gain control over capitalism and ensure that the general interest takes precedence over private interest while preserving economic openness and avoiding protectionist and nationalist reactions."[17]

Pope Francis has been severely indicting the profit driven, free-market system as inhuman and contrary to the Gospel values. His first encyclical *Evangellii Gaudium*, on the Joy of the Gospel articulated a critique of the present economic systems. It is premised on the basics Catholic social teaching, and his second, *Laudato Si* (praise be) an even more emphatic rejection of it in the context of the ecological crisis consequent on climate change and consequent environmental degradation.

Thus the inequities of class and caste, precipitate hostilities of ethnicity, and religion negate the life-chances of the weaker sections of our peoples; the violence of religious fundamentalism that traumatizes dissenting individuals and minority groups; political extremism hijacks human rights; the individualist consumerism of a market driven economy and money power displaces human concerns; invidious competition has been institutionalized to discount group cooperation; overt success and public recognition for individuals are valued far more than the silent sacrifice and unacknowledged contribution of persons;... these are just some of the characteristics of our social situation against which we must build counter-communities of solidarity for justice.

Solidarity for Justice
In this problematic context the individual pursuit of happiness and success displaces the common good and threatens to sunder our societies. To address this we need another developmental model for liberating the poor. Solidarity must stand against alienation. But this will require a counter-culture communitarianism, not on a self-centred individualism of the 'me generation', but on an 'other' centred social ethic of persons-for-others; a culture that does not place person and community in contradiction, but is premised on a complementarity of persons-in-community and a community-of-persons. It cannot be a community in which we pursue an illusory 'progress' for the privileged few, while we leave the disinherited masses behind. All this is even further exacerbated by the contemporary neo-liberal globalization.

We cannot be content to be ruled by the manipulative and elitist politics so current in societies today and the in egalitarian economic models they pursue. Rather we must strive for a more sustainable and equitable economy, a more transparent and participative polity. Together we need get beyond the individualist consumerism that is corroding our cultures across the continent and exorcise the aggressive religious fundamentalisms and the violent conflicts it generates and exploits. We need a participative down-up developmental process coordinated by top-down facilitation.

In other words, we must build a counter-cultural community that will seek 'another development' and an 'alternative politics' for a multicultural, a pluri-religious society, both on the national as well as the international scene. We must believe, as the World Social Forum keeps affirming: "Another World is Possible!" where economic status is not skewed, cultural identities are inclusive and religious traditions are harmonious. But to take such a counter-culture seriously, we need to articulate a value frame of reference in which we function and evaluate ourselves critically against the vision and inspiration of a counter-cultural community of solidarity, where the personal good of each is the common good of all. This is the only way to decolonize ourselves from the neoliberal capitalism encircling global village.

The contrast-community of Christian faith has much to offer here not just in terms of the vision of the kingdom: a reign of peace and justice, reconciliation and harmony, of beauty and truth. It can also point to a road map to get there: through renunciation and self-denial, with faith and hope, love and joy. This is what the Christian vision must be animated by: the experiences of its mystics and prophets, and articulate this in a contextualized theology of liberation for all, but preferentially for the poor, the last and the least.

Such a vision must has been so evocatively articulated in Dec. 4 of the 32nd General Congregation of the Society of Jesus (1974-75), "Our Mission Today" as the "the service of faith and the promotion of Justice": "If we have the humility and the courage to walk with the poor, we will learn from what they have to teach us what we can do to help them. ...to help themselves: to take charge of their personal and collective destiny."[18]

In practical terms this will demand a pedagogic dialogue with the poor in action-reflection praxis, a bottom-up process that reaches out to and embraces the whole of society in this movement.

What sets the context for his preferential option for the poor and the promotion of justice is not clerical bureaucratic administration but the Christian charism of love. Pope Francis is foregrounding once again a vision and mission for our world that was earlier articulated emphatically at the Latin American Bishops conferences at Medellin in 1968, Puebla in 1979,

Santo Domingo in 1992. It was affirmed for the universal Church in World Synod of Bishops in 1971 on "Justice in the World": "Action on behalf of justice and participation in the transformation of the world fully appear to us as a constitutive dimension of the preaching of the Gospel, or, in other words, of the Church's mission for the redemption of the human race and its liberation from every oppressive situation."[19]

And again the *Evangelii Nuntiandi* in 1975 reaffirms this in Nos. 25- 39, and rhetorically asks: "how in fact can one proclaim the new commandment without promoting in justice and in peace the true, authentic advancement of man [*sic*]?"[20]

This is a vision that still awaits a more comprehensive and convincing expression in the mission of the Church today, to be a truly prophetic Church in a world of "conspicuous consumption"[21] and desperate poverty; of power as the instrument of the privileged few and not at the service of the powerless multitudes; of the pursuit of self-referential individual goals not the common good of all. On 16th March, speaking to the media soon after his election, referring again to his choice of patron, Pope Francis left us a compelling vision for our mission: "Oh, how I wish for a Church that is poor and for the poor."

A pedagogic dialogue with the poor must be premised on an option for the poor that embrace both, faith and justice; a faith that does justice and a justice premised on Biblical faith. Our faith in God includes our love of God, but this is authenticated by our love of neighbour, especially the least and the last among them. Our promotion of justice is for all, but it is authenticated by our option for the poor. Biblical faith is not just intellectual consent, fides qui, but a total surrender to God, *fides qua*. This is the faith of the *anawim* of God. Moreover, Biblical justice necessarily includes forgiveness and reconciliation, which lead to peace and harmony. This is the justice of the prophets of God.

The poor have much to teach us about faith because in their life-situation, so vulnerable and always precarious, they have only their God as their one faithful protector. They experience endemic injustices at the bottom of society so their longing for a liberating justice is existential and genuine. Their very presence in our society challenges our lives with the question: Am I my brother's keeper? It confronts us with the affirmation of Jesus: as long as you did this to the least of my brothers you did it to me. It challenges all to learn from the poor even as we try "to help them help themselves." And dialogue is surely the best pedagogy for this. The poor are both, the most prepared to hear the word of God and the best able to witness to it.

Dialogue as Enrichment: Learning from the Cultural Other

Clash of Civilizations or Dialogue of Cultures

There is no denying the historical violence precipitated by collective differences of varying degrees and multiple kinds: political economic, religio-cultural. Today such collective violence is escalating everywhere. But there have also been exemplary creative synergy between different peoples, both across and within national borders. For social traditions do change even to the point of evolving into very new and rather different ones. Human identities based on them follow suit, or else there will inevitably be different degrees of dissonance and disorientation, as happens in times of rapid and radical social change when cultural traditions do not follow suit, or even resist the changes. Once we realize that cultures are socially constructed and so can be deconstructed, and we accept that religious affiliation to be a matter of freedom of conscience that can be informed and responsible, then the common concerns that bind the human community together can be brought back to centre stage in our shared lives to reverse the spiralling violence, to heal old wounds, to create a new future.

However, we cannot avoid the grim reality of divisions that mark our societies. For if common human concerns bring us together, different social interests set us apart. We cannot of course wish this away, nor can we impose uniformity or enforce a consensus on them and stay democratic and free. Too often the way of settling such differences was by confrontation and controversy, wherein each party tries not only to prove its own position, but at the same time to demolish the one of the other. This age of controversy settled nothing and neither did the religious wars it precipitated. For particularly with matters of personal and collective identity and dignity, human beings cannot be forced, or imposed on beyond a point indefinitely. Globalization has not made us more tolerant of each other, but rather the opposite seems to happen in our global village.

Yet there remains the temptation to fall back on inhuman and 'final solutions'! Ethnic cleansing and genocide await us at the end of this road. To escape such a scenario, a dialogue of cultures and religions is imperative, and for this we must overcome our prejudgments as the necessary precondition to find common ground from which to move to higher ground together. This further demands an acceptance and tolerance of 'the other' without which no dialogue is possible, only debate at best and violence at worst. Globalization has brought us closer, but it has not helped to make us more accepting of each other. Rather the opposite seems to have happened in the global village.

Celebrating Diversity

Yet diverse social groups coming together in some kind of a more inclusive social order, like a common polity, a common market, shared language and history, can construct an overarching civilizational order over time. Under such an umbrella diverse cultures and sub-cultures can survive and thrive as different "designs for living"[22] and "total ways of life."[23] In our world today plurality is an inescapable given, whether political economic or socio-religious or ethnic-linguistic or otherwise. For the complexity an imploding globalization in our modern world cannot be contained in any single worldview,[24] nor can a dominant one be imposed without destroying its freedom and openness.

In Asia, plurality is so deeply and intricately woven into the very fabric, the whoop and waft of our society that any attempt to homogenize it can only be suicidal. But ways of coping with it range from indifference and non-engagement, all the way to affirmation and celebration. Given the intricacies of our social interdependence, the first approach can only end with a nihilistic relativism if it does not collapse in annihilating chaos. The second must open into ever deeper levels of tolerance and broader dimensions of engagement.

As an ideological response 'pluralism' addresses this plurality with democratic equality and freedom. However, some common basis is necessary for social integration, involving some basic, even if minimal, orientation towards cooperation rather than conflict, lest the common meeting ground becomes the occasion for misunderstanding and hostility. This common basis can be shared histories and values, overlapping identities and interests.

We are now coming to value diversity as something potentially enriching and even uniting at a higher level of union. Such an enriching 'communion' or common union must inspire us not just to a 'unity in diversity', that accepts and respects differences, but rather to a 'diversity in unity', that appreciates and celebrates difference.[25]

The danger is that a majoritarian uniformity marginalizes minorities and creates an alienating hostility and even violent conflict between groups and communities. If these identities are exclusive, singular and solidary, rather than inclusive, multiple and fluid, then a re-socialization process will be needed lest fault lines get harden and mutual hostilities embedded. Such a situation must be anticipated and defused with a dialogue of cultures to create a climate of social tolerance and reciprocal acceptance. This is a precondition for a safe and stable, multicultural society.

Sadly our social tradition of tolerance seems to be increasingly displaced from public life. If the present crisis of intolerance is to be reversed, these need to be revived and extended. We must distinguish levels and dimensions in our understanding of tolerance, lest the ideal of tolerance we aspire to and the limits to intolerance that we set become both impractical and naive.

Ideal of Tolerance
However, tolerance is more than a matter of conflict resolution and emancipation. A constructive and creative response to pluralism cannot mean mere endurance of, and resignation to differences. It must include something more positive: the active acceptance of, and even the celebration of plurality. It must be as multifaceted the pluralism as the broad spectrum of social pluralities addresses: from political ideologies to economic systems, intellectual worldviews to ethical values, religious beliefs to cultural patterns, ethnic divisions to geographic regions.

As a response to pluralism we can distinguish progressive levels in our understanding, all deriving from a deepening realization of the reality, truth, *satya*, underlying our human situation; a reality that is radically pluralist and ultimately uniting, a truth that is essentially non-violent. These are not exclusive but rather overlapping dimensions and interpenetrating levels that form a continuous progression. This is the common ground we must seek for dialogue.

With Panikkar, we can distinguish several levels of tolerance[26]: first, tolerance as a practical necessity: bearing with a lesser evil for the sake of a greater good. But such political pragmatism does not cut deep enough to sustain itself under the stress and strain of rapid social change. A second, further understanding of tolerance is based on the realization of the essential limitations in any human grasp of truth or expression of reality: it must always be partial, it can never be complete. Such tolerance is but "the homage the finite mind pays to the inexhaustibility of the Infinite."[27] Such an intellectual awareness makes us accepting of what we do not understand and respectful of what we disagree with.

Beyond such acceptance and respect, however, we can still think of tolerance as a more positive and active moral imperative based on the ethics of doing good to others, of loving even our enemies. This is the third level of ethical or religious tolerance based on moral responsibility for the other and is often religiously inspired. But even in such an understanding of tolerance the 'different other' as the object of one's responsibility even love remains 'other'. Such 'objectivisation' of the other can only be transcended in a forth level of tolerance of what can only be called a spiritual or "mystical experience of tolerance,"[28] where "one being exists in another and expresses the radical interdependence of all that exists,"[29] where the other is the completion, the enrichment, the extension of oneself; where the other is no longer in definitional opposition to one's self, but where old selves become one new 'self', at one with the Self, *tat tvam asi*; where 'I' and 'thou' merge into the 'One I-Thou'!

There is a continuous spectrum across these various levels of tolerance. However the level of we live by is set by the way the 'self' perceives by the 'other': From perceiving the other as practical obstacle, to positive complement, to moral obligation, to mystical-spiritual fulfilment, our perception of the other is always complex and so the levels of tolerance will overlap.

Moreover, using the terms as explained earlier, 'myth' and 'ideology' are two dimensions of tolerance; consensual ideologies underpin the pragmatic and intellectual tolerance; while religious and spiritual tolerance is premised on shared myths.

Limits of Tolerance

Any understanding that does not consider how limits must be set to tolerance would be unviable and naive. If we are to cope with intolerance, we must set the social context within which tolerance functions at any of the levels or in either of the dimensions mentioned earlier. If tolerance is to be a viable social option in a plural society, it must not be high-jacked by a chauvinistic intolerance. For a cynical intolerance can easily and unfairly outmanoeuvre a trusting tolerance. Hence the limits of tolerance must be set within a regime of ethical values and norms, human rights and sensitivities.

However, to be sustainable our tolerance must go beyond legal norms and human rights. It must be founded on positive values and given in terms of: justice, truth, humanity, compassion, love ... It must be spelt out in behavioural norms that reflect these values: non-violence and respect for life, social solidarity and economic equality, political freedom and ethical truthfulness, in gender relations in terms of equality and fairness. Our tolerance must express sensitivity to the 'other' in multiple ways in the diverse arenas of inter-personal and social encounter.

But if tolerance must include tolerating the intolerable, how do we set responsible limits to intolerance without abandoning our own tolerance and becoming intolerant ourselves? This brings us to the necessity of dialogue as the *sine qua non* of tolerance and vice versa. For no dialogue is possible without a common and mutually agreed-upon level of tolerance, which must be reached in dialogue! Often dialogue collapses precisely because levels of tolerance are so different that people talk past, rather than to each other.

A regressive reaction seeking a haven in this heartless world by privileging and romantising earlier traditional societies and isolating ourselves in that cocoon is an inadequate and defensive response to the multicultural challenges we face today. Yet cultural nationalists do promote such surreal and unviable social and religious traditions so out of sync with our contemporary world. A cultural dialogue requires that we be open and rooted as well. Gandhi's aspiration can provide us with our best starting point here: "I do not want my house to be walled on all sides and my windows to be stuffed. I want the cultures of all the lands to be blown about my house as freely as possible. But I refuse to be blown off my feet by any of them."[30]

We are beginning to realize that uniformity is not the only or the most creative response to difference. Nor is mere co-existence a viable answer in an ever shrinking world. We need a dialogue of culture as a prelude to a dialogue of religions. Only then can we experience a *metanoia* in ourselves that will free us from the *paranoia* we have of each other.

Dialogue as Transformation: Learning from the Religious Other

Culture and Religion

Pascal wisely counselled: the heart has reasons that reason knows not off.[31] Indeed, a genuine dialogue pertains less to the dialectical mind than to the compassionate heart. We are still coming to terms with the implications of religious freedom and cultural rights for different groups within a single society. Much of the contemporary collective violence must be read in this context. Both culture and religion are symbol systems that bring meaning and motivation to individual and social life. But of the two, religion is the more fraught with a huge potential for explosive conflict because it is far more charged with emotion and passion than cultural ones.

Clifford Geertz's *Interpretation of Cultures* (1973) distinguishes the two. For him religion is a distinct domain within culture. Thus a culture "denotes a historically transmitted pattern or meanings embodied in symbols, a system of inherited conceptions expressed in symbolic forms by means of which men communicate, perpetuate, and develop their knowledge about and attitudes toward life."[32]

Whereas a religion is: "(1) a system of symbols which acts to (2) establish powerful, pervasive and long-lasting moods and motivations in men by (3) formulating conceptions of a general order of existence and (4) clothing these conceptions with such an aura of factuality that (5) the moods and motivations seems uniquely realistic."[33]

This explains why politics premised on the one or the other will then be qualitatively different and why religious identities are the more intractable of the two, especially in traditional religious societies. Moreover, when the two identities overlap and even merge and communities constructed on such identities are the more impervious and solidary.

Reason and Passion

Cultural and religious symbol systems are shared in society and across groups and communities. As such they necessarily exist in the public domain. They cannot be isolated in a private one, for the public and private domains are in constant and interpenetrative interaction. As collective identities they find their most appropriate, though not exclusive space in civil society. When collective interest are polarized along the fault lines of sectarian identities, they precipitate an 'identity politics', more subject to passion which displace by an 'interests politics' more amenable to reason. For interest politics is premised on ideological and/or economic differences among peoples and mobilize people along class divides. A rational politics of compromise will help to defuse this. Identity politics polarizes cultural and religious differences easily fall into a zero-sum game.

Precisely because religious identities are so emotional charged they are so readily co-opted to this politics of passion. And the more passionate, the more unreasonable and uncompromising this becomes. Far more than addressing the real interests and genuine concerns of people, this advantages group leaders, especially the extremists who claim to be better representatives of their peoples, whether there is any substance to their exaggerated claims or not. Such negative identity politics readily spills over into violent conflict. Communal riots and civil wars are so often based on such retrograde politics.

Science and Religion

A dichotomy between science and religion results in a dialectic rather than a dialogue between the two. Thinking in such binary opposites is more typical of Western than Eastern thought, where faith and reason are complementary, not opposed ways of seeking the truth. Both must be included in a more comprehensive understanding that opens to a genuine dialogue, not just between science premised on reason and religion premised on faith, but between religions as well. After all, more than just truth as knowledge, it is truth as reality, *satya* that cannot be contradictory.

After a corrosive rationalism rubbished religion, critical reason has turned in on itself and now undermines our confidence in the older rationalist optimism. Religious revivalisms and fundamentalisms are spreading like inkblots across countries and continents. To address such issues we need to understand the limits of positivist science based on the experimental method, and the horizons of religious faith based on an experiential quest. Each must be able to interrogate the other's truth in a constructive dialogue rather than in an antagonistic debate. However, faith must respect the legitimate domain and methods of reason, which in turn must be sensitive to the belief convictions and value commitments of faith. We must steer us of both a fideism that rejects reason in the domain of faith, and a rationalism which displaces faith with reason.

Beyond the incremental progress with experimentation, science proceeds with a 'paradigm shift'[34] that is an intuitive leap of imagination to a new model of interpreting data to resolve old contradictions and open new perspectives. This is not based on experimental logic, though it is post factum authenticated by it. The popular use of scientific technology is without much understanding of the theories and techniques that underpins it. It is pragmatically accepted because it works. This is an uncritical use of science quite alien to the scientific mind. Such uncritical pragmatism eventually instrumentalizes and dehumanizes science and leads to its misuse, as most obviously in modern warfare.

Religions are founded on the experience of charismatic persons whose teachings are institutionalized and experiences are ritualized into a tradition. This is meant to give later believers access to the original experiences and teachings. But these must be critiqued, interpreted and discerned to contextualize them in changing life-situations. A religious tradition must be renewed thus. This makes for a reasonable faith, not blind one. Unfortunately, much of popular religiosity gets distanced from such faith and mixed with superstition and magic. People seek assurance and certainty in their insecure and fluid world. Faith experiences no *Cost of Discipleship*.[35] It easily blinds itself to dogmatism and fundamentalism which eventually consolidate into religious extremism, even fanaticism. When politicized into a religious ideology, this can precipitates horrific violence, especially when religion is put on the defensive, as with a belligerent secularism or rationalism.

Ashis Nandy distinguishes between 'religion as ideology' and 'religion as faith.' All ideologies can help to interpret a social situation, and they can be as dysfunction ally aggressive: whether as religious fundamentalism or cultural nationalism, liberal capitalism or socialist Marxism. We need liberating and open ideologies, not closed and exploitative ones. Religious faiths too and can be oppressive or liberating, extremist or moderate. We need to recover "religious tolerance from everyday Hinduism, Islam, Buddhism, and/or Sikhism, rather than wish that ordinary Hindus, Muslims, Buddhists and Sikhs will learn tolerance from the various fashionable secular theories of statecraft." Tolerance in both domains to is needed to make dialogue viable.

Faith and Reason

The dichotomies between scientific reason and religious faith are but an extension of the dialectic between faith and reason. An interreligious dialogue cannot be premised on the one or the other because it must be underpinned by both. To facilitate such a dialogue the relationship between faith and reason must be clarified. Panikkar rightly insists on "Faith as a Constitutive Human Dimension"[36] and the content of faith must fulfil not negate the human, i.e., belief must humanize believers, not dehumanize them or demonize others. Tolerance then becomes the sign of 'good faith.'

Here in a few sutras is an epigrammatic summary our query: what does being 'reasonable' mean to faith, and again what does being 'faithful' to reason require?[37]

> Faith and reason are complementary not contradictory ways of seeking the truth;
>
> What we believe depends on whom we trust;
>
> A rational methodology transgressing its inherent limitations can never yield 'rightly reasoned' knowledge;
>
> Where we position ourselves influences how we reason;
>
> Whether or not we believe depends on our self-understanding;
>
> If to believe is human, then what we believe must make us more human, not less;
>
> Faith that is 'blind' is never truly humanizing; faith that is not humanizing is to that extent 'bad faith';
>
> Only a self-reflexive, experiential methodology is meaningful to the discourse of faith; a rationalist-empirical one is alien to it;
>
> Act of faith is constitutively human it necessarily has a common religious basis across varying cultures and traditions;
>
> An inclusive humanism must embrace both 'meaningful faith', as well as 'sensitized reason';
>
> The dialogue between faith and reason must be pursued in the context of tolerance and dialogue or it will degenerate into a hostile debate across an unbridgeable divide.

Indeed, both faith and reason are imperative to bring a healing wholeness to our bruised, broken world.

Domains in Dialogue

Dialogue is surely more than a verbal exchange. It is implies a reciprocity between the 'self' and the 'other' that can take place in various types of encounter and exchange between persons and groups. Hence a complex and more nuanced understanding of dialogue require a specification of various kinds of involvement of the 'self' with the 'other'. As with tolerance, so too with dialogue, we must distinguish various domains and dimensions of this involvement with one another, for dialogue is surely more than a verbal exchange.

Recently Christians have been urged by the Church to engage in a fourfold dialogue:[38]

> "*The dialogue of life*': where people strive to live in an open and neighbourly spirit, sharing their joys and sorrows, their human problems and preoccupations."

> "*The dialogue of action*': in which we which we 'collaborate for the integral development and liberation of people."

> "'The dialogue of religious experience': where persons, rooted in their own religious traditions, share their spiritual riches, for instance with regard to prayer and contemplation, faith and ways of searching for God or the Absolute."

> "'The dialogue of theological exchange': where specialists seek to deepen their understanding of their respective religious heritages, and to appreciate each other's spiritual values."

In our perspective, the dialogue of life is at the level of sharing and encounter of the myths we live by and, which then are deepened in the dialogue of religious experiences. This can be an even deeper level of not just mythic communication but mystical experience. The dialogue of action requires some level of ideological and political consensus, which can then be intensified and sharpened in a theological exchange. Thus life and experience are at the level of 'myth' and mysticism, action and theology at that of 'ideology' and politics, respectively.

In each of these areas of exchange, corresponding to the levels of tolerance delineated above, one can distinguish degrees of dialogue premised on differing understandings of the self and the other and the encounter between the two. Thus at the pragmatic level of tolerance the other is perceived as the limitation of the self. Here dialogue becomes a practical way of overcoming differences, rather than by confrontation that could result either in the assimilation or in elimination of the other. At the intellectual level, where the other is seen as complementary to the self, dialogue seeks to overcome the limitations of the self with help of the other, rather than instrumentalise the other in the pursuit of self. At the ethical level the self-accepts moral responsibility for the other. In this dialogue the self will reach out to the other to establish relationships of equity and equality. At the spiritual level, the other is perceived beyond a limitation or a complement or an obligation, as the fulfilment of the self. Here dialogue would call for a celebration of one another.

Raimundo Panikkar rightly insists that "dialogue is not a bare methodology but an essential part of the religious act par excellence."[39]

In 1995 the 34th General Congregation of the Society of Jesus in Decree 5 gave a particularly relevant mandate for dialogue to the Jesuits: "to be religious today is to be inter-religious in the sense that a positive relationship with believers of other faiths is a requirement in a world of religious pluralism." As Joshua Heschel insists, "No Religion is an Island"[40] the imperative for dialogue can now be summed up in a few pertinent sutras:

> To be a person is to be inter-personal;
> To be cultured is to be inter-cultural;
> To develop is to participate and exchange;
> To be religious is to be inter-religious;

Psychologists have convinced us of the first; sociologists are trying to teach us the second; political economists are promoting the third; theologians are coming to realize the fourth.

Dialogue as Disarmament for Peace

Metanoia for Peace

For all the progress we might congratulate ourselves on, the last century has been perhaps the most violent century in human history. It still continues into the present. Asia has not been exempted from this. Violence is still the final arbitrator to conflicts and divisions that increasing riddles our societies and our world. A catalogue the violence of these last years, genocides, atrocities, riots, terrorism, murders, rapes, ... are merely the external evidence of the constant social tension between countries, regions, communities, groups, individuals, ... that never to go away but too easily escalate out of control.

Non-violence seems to be an idea whose time has passed. We must reverse the spiral of violence that engulfs us like a cyclonic tidal wave, and reflect together on what peace and harmony today might mean for us. For, while the quest for power remains one of our most insidious human temptations, the longing for peace is part of our deepest human yearnings.

A sound and stable peace must be founded on such complementarity, not on domination. It must be 'the fruit of justice.' A just social order necessarily implies freedom if it is to be compatible with human dignity. Moreover, if the dialectical tension between justice and order is effectively and constructively resolved, then we would have a third element in our understanding of peace that is harmony. This is a treasured Asian value. Each of these three elements, justice, freedom and harmony, can be described, but we still need to put them together in a collective 'myth of peace,'[41] pursued both individually and collectively.

Vision and Mission

But for this dream to even begin to become a reality, we must divest ourselves of a great deal of, the presumptions and pre-options we have been, and still are being socialized into. We must not allow our history to control our destiny; we must come to terms with our collective memories and allow our wounded psyche to heal. More importantly for the dialogue among ourselves, and even within our 'self', this myth of peace must first be rooted in our hearts and minds, our cultures and religions. This is a most appropriate agenda in Pope Francis's year of mercy.

Tragically modern human with the loss of innocence in a disenchanted world, has no longer any abiding myths. Today more than ever we need such bonding myths to sustain our world. Now myths are collective, never individual projects, and the 'myth of peace' is one in which we can all share. Certainly it is one whose time has now come in our tired and torn, broken and, bruised world. But as yet we have no such common myths. Even the symbols and images we use for peace are quite inadequate or needlessly divisive. The tragedy of modern humanity seems to be that it has too few creative and inspiring myths to live by and too many competing ideologies to die for. And so in desperation we revive and cling to images and symbols that draw on the darkest recesses of our destructive potential.

If the myth of peace is to redeem us from such a future, it must become the common ground for our dialogues. This is the peace that is reflected in popular greetings, *pax*, shalom, salaam, shanti ... that needs to found for us a brave new world. At this profound level of myth, peace can be an end in itself, as in fact is so universally expressed by various salvation myths in other religious traditions and utopian ideologies.

A Triple Dialogue

Against the background of the historical trajectory of violence in religious traditions, and the alarming escalation of religious and other kinds of terror today, a comprehensive tolerance becomes the *sine qua non* condition for a multi-dimensional dialogue across political economic and religio-cultural and religious divides. As our globalizing world implodes further, even continents cannot isolate themselves, nor can countries and communities immunize themselves from the escalating violence.

In the bewilderingly plurality of societies in our contemporary world, and some Asian societies, especially those in the middle East and South Asia, are more so than most, violent conflict often reaches an impasse. With the rapid social change and the insecurities it brings, with technologies of mass communication and mass mobilization, of social media and individual connectivity, in which competing groups and conflicting interests implode, this impasse becomes a point of no return and no advance. National and local communities dig themselves into a kind of trench warfare. In such a war of attrition the one alternative seem to be to withdraw into isolation, if that were possible at all; in a globalizing world this would be dangerous and even unviable. The other is to mobilize for total war and mass destruction; this would be an inhuman price to pay even for the unlucky survivors.

To anticipate such a painful dilemma the viability of radical alternatives needs to be explored. We can surely find alternatives to make another world possible, where sustainable and regenerative technologies, participative and inclusive social systems, for free and equal citizens and communities are not beyond our reach even though not yet within our grasp. If can disarm ourselves from the prejudgments and prejudices, the fears and hostilities wherein we seek security, we could make a just society a more viable reality, where the personal good of each is subsumed into the common good for all.

However, for this we need to distance ourselves from, and critically examine our vested interests and unconscious ideologies, our exclusive identities and intolerant fundamentalisms, hidden fears and inarticulate apprehensions, to put the old negativities on hold and be open to the new possibilities to set a creative agenda for peace and harmony. This implies a kind of disarmament from all negativities that vitiates this. It will demand a daring, courageous leap of faith, but if not us then who, if not now, then when!

A Pedagogic Dialogue

For a pedagogic dialogue with the poor we must first detach ourselves from our embedded vested interests and political ideologies, when these provide the strong armour against change for a better, more humane world, a more just and fraternal society. Only when we put off this armour will we find the humility and the courage, the faith and commitment to walk with and learn from, and also with the poor to find our personal and collective destinies together. This is the liberation a pedagogic dialogue with the poor teaches us.

In a multicultural society, and Asian societies are more so than most, cultural conflict often becomes endemic. When cultural identities cease to be flexible and fluid but become solidary and exclusive, each cultural community digs itself into a kind of cultural trench warfare and once again a continuing war of attrition undermines our cultures. To defuse this we must cease absolutizing our cultures as an ultimate good. Rather we need a 'cultural disarmament,'[42] stepping back from our cultural entrenchments, bracketing away cultural negative identities and stereotypes, holding them in abeyance to facilitate a dialogue of cultures and come back to them less exclusive and more understanding, more open to, and appreciative of the cultural other whom we can celebrate our diversity as a mutual enrichment. This involves seeking common ground in our shared cultural values and loyalties from which to move together to higher ground of a more enriched and creative culture. A pedagogic dialogue with cultures teaches us to find a deeper understanding and appreciation of the cultural other in myself and my cultural self in the other.

Similarly in a society when a religious tradition is politicized it can explode into violence. Precisely because of its emotional charge of religious identities, such politicized religious violence becomes embedded and exorcising this demon may require a sustained effort over generations. We need to incisively critique our fundamentalist extremes and inflexible dogmatisms of all hues in our religious traditions, and bracket our differences to open ourselves to finding common ground in our religious beliefs and commitments to move together to the higher ground of a transformed religious tradition, with a renewed spirituality and mysticism. A pedagogic dialogue with religions can teach us to deepen our understanding of other religious traditions and our own as well.

A political economic, religio-cultural disarmament will demand a radical change of heart, a social *metanoia* from a history of violence to a commitment to non-violence, from the pursuit of power to the quest for peace, from a pragmatic to a deeper level of tolerance, from a self-righteous monologue with ourselves to a truly open and equal dialogue.

The threefold dialogue, with the poor, with cultures, with religions that the Federation of Asian Bishops' Conference (FABC) calls for must be premised on the Gospel myth of the kingdom of peace and justice, of equality and fellowship, of freedom and love is not a blue print but a vision, a prophetic critique of our present and a call to build a future with faith and hope together, already now but not fully yet.

Endnotes

[1] Jürgen Habermas, *Theory of Communicative Action*, vol. 2, translated by Thomas A. McCarthy (Boston: Beacon Press, 1984), 17.

[2] R. Panikkar, *Myth, Faith and Hermeneutics: Cross-cultural Studies* (Bangalore: Asian Trading Corp., 1983), 242.

[3] Panikkar, *Myth, Faith and Hermeneutics: Cross-cultural Studies*, 101.

[4] Panikkar, *Myth, Faith and Hermeneutics: Cross-cultural Studies*, 21.

[5] Hans-Georg Gadamer, *Truth and Method* (New York: Seabury Press, 1975), 15.

[6] Fred R. Dallmayr, "Hermeneutics and Deconstruction: Gadamer and Derrida in Dialogue," in *Dialogue and Deconstruction: The Gadamer and Derrida in Dialogue Encounter*, edited by Diane P. Michelfelder and Richard E. Palmer (New York: State University of New York Press, 1989), 92.

[7] Hans-Georg Gadamer, "Destruktion and Deconstruction," in *Dialogue and Deconstruction: The Gadamer and Derrida in Dialogue Encounter*, edited by Diane P. Michelfelder and Richard E. Palmer (New York: State University of New York Press, 1989), 113.

[8] Gadamer, "Destruktion and Deconstruction," in *Dialogue and Deconstruction: The Gadamer and Derrida in Dialogue Encounter*, 110.

[9] Gadamer, "Destruktion and Deconstruction," in *Dialogue and Deconstruction: The Gadamer and Derrida in Dialogue Encounter*, 95.

[10] Panikkar, *Myth, Faith and Hermeneutics: Cross-cultural Studies*, 243.

[11] Gadamer, "Destruktion and Deconstruction," in *Dialogue and Deconstruction: The Gadamer and Derrida in Dialogue Encounter*, 90.

[12] Ludwig Wittgenstein, *Culture and Value* (London: Blackwell, 1958), 14.

[13] Peter N.V. Hai, "Fides Quaerens Dialogum: Theological Methodologies of the Federation of Asian Bishops' Conferences," *Australian e-journal* 8/1 (2006).

[14] Aloysius Pieris, *An Asian Theology of Liberation* (London: T & T Clark International, 1988).

[15] "Bergoglio's Intervention: A diagnosis of the problems in the Church," http://en.radiovaticana .va/storico/2013/03/27/bergoglios_intervention_a_diagnosis_%20of_the_problems_in_the_church/en1-677269 (September 3, 2018).

[16] Thomas Piketty, *Capital in the Twenty-First Century* (Massachusetts: Harvard University Press, 2014), 25.

[17] Piketty, *Capital in the Twenty-First Century*, 1.

[18] 32nd General Conference of the Society of Jesus (1974-1975), no., 50.

[19] 32nd General Conference of the Society of Jesus (1974-1975), no. 6.

[20] 32nd General Conference of the Society of Jesus (1974-1975), no. 31.

[21] Thorstein Veblen, *The Theory of the Leisure Class* (New York: Macmillan, 1989), 64.

[22] Clyde Kluckhohn and W. H. Kelly, "The Concept of Culture," in *The Science of Man in the World Crisis*, edited by Ralph Linton (New York: Columbia University Press, 1945), 78-105.

[23] Ralph Linton, *The Cultural Background of Personality* (New York: Appleton-Century-Crofts, 1945), 30.

[24] Karl Rahner, *Theological Investigations*, vol. vi (London: Payton, Longman and Todd, 1969), 26.

[25] Rajni Kothari, "Integration and Exclusion in Indian Politics," *Economic and Political Weekly* 23/43 (October 22, 1988), 20.

[26] R. Panikkar, *Myth, Faith and Hermeneutics: Cross-cultural Studies* (Bangalore: Asian Trading Corp., 1983), 20-36.

[27] S. Radhakrishnan, *Eastern Religions and Western Thought* (Oxford: Oxford University Press, 1927), 317.

[28] Panikkar, *Myth, Faith and Hermeneutics: Cross-cultural Studies*, 23.

[29] Panikkar, *Myth, Faith and Hermeneutics: Cross-cultural Studies*, 23.

[30] *Young India*, June 1921: 170.

[31] Blaise Pascal, *Pensees* (New York: F.P. Dutton, 1958), 222.

[32] Clifford Geertz, *The Interpretation of Cultures* (New York: Fontana, 1973), 8.

[33] Geertz, *The Interpretation of Cultures*, 90.

[34] Thomas Kuhn, *The Structure of Scientific Revolutions* (Chicago: University of Chicago, 1970).

[35] Dietrich Bonhoeffer, *Cost of Discipleship* (New York: Macmillian, 1970).

[36] Panikkar, *Myth, Faith and Hermeneutics: Cross-cultural Studies*, 187-229.

[37] Cf. Rudolf C. Heredia, "Gandhi and the Myth of Peace," in *New Quest* 136 (July-August 1999): 231-239.

[38] "Dialogue and proclamation," Pontifical Council for Inter-Religious Dialogue, Vatican City, 1991, no. 42.

[39] Raimundo Panikkar, *The Intra-religious Dialogue* (New York: Paulist Press, 1978), 10.

[40] Harold Kasimow and Byron L. Sherwin, eds., *No Religion is an Island: Abraham Joshua Heschel and interreligious dialogue* (Maryknoll: Orbis Books, 1991), 3-22.

[41] Heredia, "Gandhi and the Myth of Peace," in *New Quest*, 231-239.

[42] Raimon Panikkar, *Cultural Disarmament: The Way to Peace*, translated by Robert R. Barr (Louisville: Westminster John Know Press, 1995).

Mercy and Compassion: The Womb of Interfaith Dialogue

Francis Gonsalves

Introduction

We live in a violent and wounded world. Through TV, Internet and the print media, we are daily made aware of terrifying forms of violence unleashed upon peoples, worldwide. What is most distressing is that much of this violence is ironically perpetrated and perpetuated 'in God's name', so to say, with fanatics of all religions murdering and maiming as if they were fulfilling God's will for humankind. While those who resort to violence and bloodshed can hardly be called 'religious', it is also alarming that not many of those who are 'religious' in one way or the other courageously critique those who masquerade as custodians of religion while actually indulging in diabolic activities. Therefore, those who desire to tap the treasures of religious traditions are faced with a dual task: (a) of taking a prophetic stand to denounce the irreligion of fanatics; and, (b) of discerning commonalities among religions that will help us to strengthen interfaith ties so as to build a better world. With the latter task in mind, this paper seeks to explore the concepts of mercy and compassion, which seem to be the heritage of all religions, presenting possibilities for fruitful interfaith dialogue and action. But, first, a brief note on the perspective from which this paper is written and the reason why this theme is chosen at this particular point of time.

The Perspective: 'Year of Mercy' as Inspirational for Interfaith Initiatives

I write this paper as a Catholic theologian seeking to dialogue with other religious traditions. Though I have been interested and involved in interfaith dialogue at various levels since many years, this year has evoked added interest to reflect upon the theme of 'mercy' at the behest of Pope Francis, who has declared this year—spanning December 8, 2015 to November 20, 2016—as a 'Jubilee Year of Mercy.' Pope Francis writes:

> There is an aspect of mercy that goes beyond the confines of the Church. It relates us [Christians] to Judaism and Islam, both of which consider mercy to be one of God's most important attributes. Israel was the first to receive this revelation which continues in history as the source of an inexhaustible richness meant to be shared with all mankind [*sic*]. As we have seen, the pages of the Old Testament are steeped in mercy, because they narrate the works that the Lord performed in favor of his people at the most trying moments of their history. Among the privileged names that Islam attributes to the Creator are 'Merciful and Kind.' This invocation is often on the lips of faithful Muslims who feel themselves accompanied and sustained by mercy in their daily weakness. They too believe that no one can place a limit on divine mercy because its doors are always open.[1]

The so-called 'Jubilee Years' announced by popes over the recent past are special times proposed to Catholics to reflect upon and respond to certain spiritual and religious needs and themes. Thus, Pope Francis earlier announced a Year of Faith, Year of Consecrated Life, Year of Family, etc. The current 'Year of Mercy' comes with his call, as follows:

> I trust that this year celebrating the mercy of God will *foster an encounter with these religions and with other noble religious traditions*; may it open us to even *more fervent dialogue so that we might know and understand one another better; may it eliminate every form of closed-mindedness and disrespect, and drive out every form of violence and discrimination.*[2]

Pope Francis's invitation to "more fervent dialogue" with a view to foster deeper understanding among religions and to eliminate close-mindedness, disrespect, violence and discrimination is not only addressed to Christians but to believers in all religions, and to those who explicitly endorse no religion whatsoever. Hence, this paper proposes mercy and compassion as twin themes in what might be called a 'womb for interfaith dialogue', hopefully begetting, as it were, more fecund responses and avenues for effective dialogue and prophetic action.

This paper is divided into three parts. Part one begins with a clarification of the terms mercy and compassion *vis-à-vis* other similar terms and then reflects on their significance in the so-called 'Abrahamic religions': Judaism, Christianity and Islam. Part two explores the understanding of compassion and its derivatives in the so-called 'Cosmic religions': Hinduism, Buddhism,

Jainism, Confucianism and Taoism. Part three views whether these terms could be meaningful to those who claim to be atheists and agnostics.

Part I: Mercy as Womb-Like Love in the Abrahamic Religions

In our daily conversations we use many words, which are seemingly synonymous with mercy: pity, sympathy, empathy and compassion. Though these words may be loosely used in our everyday exchanges, there are shades of meaning which distinguish one word from another. Let us see the differences that distinguish one from the others.

Pity, Sympathy, Empathy in Relation to Mercy and Compassion

Pity is a feeling of sorrow towards someone who suffers. We see beggars or handicapped persons by the roadside and feel sad for them. We may throw a coin to them and probably thank God that we are not beggars or handicapped. One who pities others may even do a little bit to alleviate their suffering. However, pity could evoke feelings of superiority and could make one feel like a patron and benefactor of those who are pitied. In the long run, pity is not constructive and neither engenders conversion and change in the one who pities nor in those pitied.

'Sympathy' and 'empathy' are stronger in meaning and evoke greater care, concern and commitment. Sympathy is a feeling '*with*' someone who is badly off in one way or another. For example, when the mother of a friend dies, we will probably go to her/his house and offer our 'sympathies'. We do feel '*with*' her/him since we have been in similar situations and know how painful it is to lose a loved one. Sympathy normally leads to action that can be helpful for the other. For instance, in the concrete case of the death of a friend's mother, we might promise to send her/him food until such time that s/he is able to come to grips with the loss and resume normal life, once again. Finally, empathy is a feeling '*into*' or getting '*into*' the skin of one who suffers. Empathy leads to action that enriches both parties, since both are deeply touched and affected. Empathetic actions are never concerned about benefit for the self, but are always selfless and other-oriented.

While pity, sympathy and empathy are used in our daily conversations, they are not much used in the moral, spiritual and scriptural spheres, where we often use 'mercy' and 'compassion.' Notably, these two words are frequently used synonymously though one can draw distinctions between them. Mercy has moral and legal content. One can plead for mercy from a judge or file a 'mercy petition.' Mercy is forgiveness of wrong—the 'being good' to someone who does not really deserve it. It is seen in parents' attitude towards wayward children or in God's attitude towards sinners. By contrast, compassion is a deep 'gut level' feeling for others who suffer or are deprived of something. For example, we may feel great compassion for the severely malnourished infants of Africa or the child laborers of Asia, but are not 'merciful' to them since these children have not offended us in any way. Conversely, a judge might be merciful to a criminal and revoke a death sentence without feeling truly compassionate towards him.

The Roots of Mercy and Compassion in Judaism and Christianity

Moving beyond the common nuances of mercy and compassion, and delving into their biblical roots, we become aware of many significant facts. First, although difficulties arise when we translate biblical terms from their original Hebrew and Greek into English, we can surmise that 'mercy' occurs approximately 150 times in the Bible, while 'compassion' appears some 50 times.[3] Second, the theological formula that appears about a dozen times in the Bible describing God as: "merciful and gracious, slow to anger, and abounding in steadfast love and faithfulness"[4] seems to summarize who God *is*: Mercy! Third, the Hebrew *ḥesed* is often translated as 'mercy' but it is also translated as 'loving-kindness' and 'goodness'. Thus, there is a close connection between mercy and love, with love being the final fulfillment of mercy. Fourth, the invisible God's love and mercy is incarnate or 'made fleshly visible' in Jesus' life, teachings and actions. Fifth, the Greek *splagchnizomai*—literally, to be moved in one's bowels or intestines—is characteristic of Jesus, who either provides for the poor or forgives sinners. In all the above, mercy and compassion are seen as heart-felt, gut-level emotions that always fructify in action favoring the poor and the sinner.

While a 'father image' or 'male terminology' for God is largely adopted for prayer life and religious discourses in Judaism and Christianity, the Hebrew word for 'mercy', i.e., *raḥamim* is etymologically related to the word *reḥem*, meaning, 'womb'. In Hebrew religious consciousness, then, "the meaning of mercy is rooted in and clarified by the root *reḥem*—womb. Thus, a whole range of merciful affectivity associated with *raḥamim* is, as it were, tightly associated with what might be called 'womb-like' love."[5] In using images, symbols, similes and metaphors for God, we must be aware that our God-talk is, always and everywhere, *anthropomorphic* (literally, 'man formed').

Down through the ages patriarchal systems and structures have drawn up discourses, painted pictures and suggested symbols of God deeply dyed in male/patriarchal color and contours. Today, many Christian theologians feel that these should be complemented with biblical imagery of God as mother, nurturer, feeder, nurse, midwife, etc.,[6] so as to get a rounded image of God who is beyond gender.[7]

Reflecting upon mercy as a form of 'womb-like love' can give us deeper insights into the nature of mercy; for, in biblical imagery, the womb is not merely a bodily organ or a receptacle for reproduction but evokes myriad meanings: symbolic, metaphorical, analogical and transcendental.[8] Indeed, at a most primordial level, God is the sole author of life whose Womb, figuratively speaking, brought forth the world. Then, womb is the place of the origin of life which God can "open" (as in the case of Rachel in the Book of Genesis 30:22) or "close" (as in the case of Hannah in 1 Samuel 1:5) or reach, so as to delicately "knit together" forms of life (Psalm 139:13). The womb is also a place of sacrificial love oriented towards nurturing the weak and vulnerable and a place of relationship where human life is sown through spousal love that will eventually flower in loving God (vertical) and all of creation (horizontal). Finally, the womb is a place of welcome, which militates against the 'culture of death' that Christianity strongly opposes.

Pope Francis's Teaching: Mercy as Visceral Love

In the current 'Year of Mercy', with his document entitled *Misericordiae Vultus*,[9] Pope Francis puts the spotlight on *'faces of mercy'*—uppermost among which are the merciful faces of Jesus and his mother, Mary [Miriam] who, conjointly, give visibility and voice to the face of God, the "Father of mercies" (1 Corinthians 1:3). In a simple and direct way the Pope begins with an assertion: "Jesus Christ is the *face of the Father's mercy*. These words might well sum up the mystery of the Christian faith."[10] This summation is quite central to Christian revelation condensable in the statement: God *is* Love-Mercy-Compassion. However, lest we get entrapped or enraptured by illusory images of some Platonic, merciful God dwelling 'up there' in the highest heavens, Pope Francis brings God down-to-earth, so to say, by asserting:

> The mercy of God is not an abstract idea, but a concrete reality with which
> he [God] *reveals his love as of that of a father or a mother*, moved to the very
> depths out of love for their child. It is hardly an exaggeration to say that this

is a '*visceral*' love. It gushes forth from the depths naturally, full of tenderness and compassion, indulgence and mercy.[11]

Indeed, every truly merciful and deeply compassionate act must overflow from a maternal-paternal movement of the heart, from a womb-like love, from a churning of the intestines, a gut-level, visceral feeling for those who suffer or have sinned. This was Jesus' feeling when he mercifully forgave sinners and compassionately catered to the poor and the 'least'. Without such a God-like visceral love, all manifestations of mercy are but mirages or dewdrops, at best, and patronizing poison, at worst.

Allah, Most Merciful: The Name of God in Islam

Similar to Judaism and Christianity, Islam teaches that Allah is The Merciful One. In prayer and meditation, among the 99 names of Allah that are commonly invoked, are the names *Al-Rahman* and *Al-Rahim*. Both these names are derived from the root '*rhm*', referring to a host of meanings, including, as we noted earlier, the word for the womb. '*Rhm*' suggests tenderness, kindness, gentleness, forgiveness, mercifulness and benevolence. Since the name *Al-Rahman* does not only mean 'The Merciful One' but also 'The Source of All Mercy', no person can ever be named *Al-Rahman*. At most one can be named *Abd Al-Rahman* or 'servant of The Merciful'. Significantly, Allah gives Prophet Mohammed the name *Al-Rahim* in the Qur'ān describing him as "full of kindness (*ra'uf*) and mercy (*rahim*)."[12] What is predicated of Mohammed is also said of other prophets like Nuḥ, Ibrāhim, Musā, Zakariā and Isā.

Of Allah's all-inclusive mercy, the Qur'ān explicates: "He encompasses everything in mercy (*rahma*)." Consequently, since Allah is Creator, Allah also demands that all people embrace as many creatures as possible with the bonds of mercy. Indeed, from the Qur'ān and Hadiths of the Prophet it is clear that dealing with others compassionately is indispensable for salvation. This enjoins on the believer four tasks: (a) to live in gratitude [*shukr*] for Allah's mercy, (b) to ask for more of Allah's mercy [*du'ā*], (c) to beg forgiveness for one's forgetfulness and cruelty [*istigfār/tawba*], and (d) to live intensely in mutual compassion [*tarahhum*].

Judaic-Christian-Islamic interreligious dialogue can be greatly fostered if the believers of these three major Abrahamic religions mine the treasury of their scriptures for common motifs and beliefs. Fifty years ago, Vatican Council II of the Catholic Church declared:

This sacred Council remembers the spiritual ties which link the people of the New Covenant to the stock of Abraham. The Church of Christ acknowledges that in God's plan of salvation the beginning of her faith and election is to be found in the patriarchs, Moses and the prophets. ... The Church cannot forget that she received the revelation of the Old Testament by way of that people with whom *God in his inexpressible mercy* established the ancient covenant.[13]

Of Islam the Vatican Council II's document entitled 'Nostra Aetate' no.3 specifically states: "The Church has a high regard for Muslims. They worship God, who is one, living and subsistent, *merciful and almighty*, the Creator of heaven and earth, who has also spoken to men [*sic*]." One can see that God's 'mercy' and 'merciful' attributes are common to these three Abrahamic religious traditions. These commonalities of belief are translatable into concrete common actions for the ennoblement of society, at large.[14]

Part II: Cords of Compassion in the Cosmic Creeds

With a strong focus on the Divine Being as revealed by their scriptures and prophets, the so-called Abrahamic or Prophetic religions derive their vision and mission of mercy from the very nature of Yahweh-God-Allah who *is* Love-Mercy-Compassion. From this foundation, since Yahweh-God-Allah created human beings, the divine attributes like love, mercy and compassion become God's gifts to humankind. In contrast, rather than endorsing compassion as an attribute of God, the Asiatic—particularly Indic religions like Hinduism, Buddhism, Jainism—focus on shared '*being*' or '*inter-being*'. The Life of all living beings demands deep respect and nurturing. These religions preach that compassion must flow from the basic premise of reciprocity, that is, the realization that as much as one wants to avoid pain and live in peace and prosperity, everyone and everything else yearns for the same, too.

Dayā as the Hindu Dharma to Divide and to Share

In Sanskrit, the words *karunā* and *dayā* are synonyms for mercy or compassion. The *Brhaspati Smrti* text of classical Hinduism of perhaps the 6th century teaches: "Complete love belongs to one who always delights in behaving towards all beings as equal to the self, for their good and for their welfare."[15] Other Hindu texts like the *Raghuvamsa* (2.11) and the *Hitopadesa* (1.60) remind us that authentic *dayā* is not dependent on the virtues of the being to which it is addressed; for, "Good people are compassionate even of beings that have no value."[16] This is reminiscent of Jesus' teaching to love even one's enemies and not just one's family and friends. While one might translate *dayā*—as in the injunction: "*Dayā karo!* Be merciful!"—to only refer to some sentiment, the word actually implies the deep desire welling up in the heart to remove the hardships of others, even if it implies great effort and sacrifice. Its semantic field is therefore not that of emotion or sentiment, but of active desire to help others. In Rig Vedic use, the verb '*day dayate*' would imply to divide, to distribute, to allot, to share and to partake of. Therefore, it means actively getting involved and sharing in the pain and suffering of others.

Today, Mata Amritanadamayi from Kerala—known as the 'Hugging Amma'—can be given as an example of love and compassion. At the 2nd Parliament of World Religions held in Chicago in 1993 she said:

> We have forgotten the love, compassion and mutual understanding taught by religion. The basic cause underlying all the problems that exist in the present day world is the lack of love and compassion. Love and compassion, alone, will wipe out the darkness, bringing light and purity to the world.... To show compassion towards suffering humanity is our obligation to God. Our spiritual quest should begin with selfless service to the world.

Karunā as the Cornerstone of Buddhism

In his book 'The Heart of Compassion', His Holiness the Dalai Lama writes: "It can be asserted rightly that loving-kindness and compassion are the two cornerstones on which the whole edifice of Buddhism stands." Compassion for others is one of the central teachings of Mahayana Buddhism wherein one sacrifices oneself in order to attain salvation for the sake of other beings.[17] Nonetheless, the self is also important since all of existence is regarded as interdependent and unless one has exercised self-restraint and developed self-awareness, one can never expect to reach out in compassion to others. The Buddha preached that one must never neglect one's own welfare (*attha*), which one must use by analogy to understand what the other's welfare consists in. Later, one must progress from the limited love of one's family and friends to the larger love of all creatures and of all of creation. Buddhism thus preaches that compassion (*anukampa*) is a universal ideal without boundary or limitation.

Buddhism does not merely teach compassion as a value to be attained, but advocates firsthand, direct experiences: "Contemplative reflection on the suffering of living beings is not enough; we must help diminish suffering through compassionate involvement... The lotus flower grows most beautifully when planted deep in the mud."[18] However, such involvement must not be equated with aimless social activism; but is born out of a liberated state of mindfulness that is the fruit of spiritual disciplines like the practice of *vipassanā*,[19] and *upāya*.[20] It is clear then that the Buddhist tenet of *karunā* involves active response to suffering and pain of other creatures.

Jainism's All-Embracing *Jiva Dayā*

Jainism propagates compassion and care for every living being, even microscopic insects. The Jain *jīva dayā* tenet stresses compassion towards everyone and everything. Closely connected to the practice of *dayā* is *ahimsā* (non-violence). All being (*sat*) is divided into nonliving (*ajīva*) and living (*jīva*) forms. While we might regard rocks, lakes and trees to be nonliving (*ajīva*), according to Jainism all these have the life force of *jīva*.[21] Ancient Jain texts explain that it is the intention to harm, the absence of compassion, which makes an action violent. Without violent thoughts there can be no violent actions. When violence enters one's thoughts, the Jain is exhorted to remember Lord Mahāvīr's words: "You are that which you intend to hit, injure, insult, torment, persecute, torture, enslave or kill." When one enters the other's skin, so to say, one will desist from harming the other(s). Furthermore, one will positively strive to cultivate an attitude of amity (*maitri*) towards all forms of life.

Without going into details, we see that religions of the Far East like Confucianism and Taoism too speak of compassion in various ways. For instance, Confucius' social philosophy largely revolves around the concept of *ren*, meaning, 'compassion' or 'loving others.' Cultivating or practicing *ren* involves deprecating oneself. Those who have cultivated *ren* are "simple in manner and slow of speech." For Confucius, such concern for others is demonstrated through the practice of forms of the Golden Rule: "What you do not wish for yourself, do not do to others." In similar vein, Tao Teh Ching asserts: "The sage has no interest of his own, but takes the interests of the people as his own. He is kind to the kind; he is also kind to the unkind: for Virtue is kind. He is faithful to the faithful; he is also faithful to the unfaithful: for Virtue is faithful."

Part III: Mercy and Compassion beyond Religious Confines

In the foregoing analyses, we have seen how mercy and compassion are understood in the Abrahamic/Prophetic and Cosmic/Mystic religious traditions, whose teachings have not remained theoretical, but have animated the lives of renowned world leaders. The Indic focus on respect for life and compassion towards all living beings inspired Mahatma Gandhi to translate the ideals of *dayā* and *karunā* into political praxis by evolving strategies of nonviolence (*ahimsā*). Moreover, *ahimsā* inspired the likes of Martin Luther King, Jr., and Nelson Mandela, who adopted similar strategies in their own contexts. The principle of *ahimsā* is based on the basic premise that the life of all creatures—especially human beings—is sacred and cannot be destroyed by violence. Nonetheless, in the struggle for justice and truth (*satyagraha*), one must be ready to suffer and bear pain oneself. This is where the need of self-sacrifice arises.

Self-sacrifice—which, in the extreme, entails even giving one's life for the welfare of others—is at the heart of all discourses on mercy and compassion. The rationale behind this thinking is simple: If I deeply desire the other's welfare, I will shed my ego, inconvenience myself, and reach out compassionately to help others. This is simply 'self-emptying' or what in Christian theological terms is *kenosis*. Jesus summarized the kernel of *kenosis* by saying: "No one has greater love than this, to lay down one's life for one's friends" (Gospel of John 15:13). *Kenosis* is the attitude of emptying oneself to embrace the other and promote life. It roughly parallels the *shūnyatā* of Buddhism, as well as Hinduism's ideals of *tyaga* (sacrifice), *vairagya* (renunciation) and *karunā*. Likewise, agnostic philosopher Gianni Vattimo speaks of 'weak ontology' of divine kenosis that is needed to respond to suffering humanity amidst the evils of secularization.[22] Ironically, this 'weak ontology' is strength; for, it takes great faith and fortitude to give one's life for another. Such a disposition is not only found among those who are 'religious', but among all those who dare to stand in solidarity with those who suffer.

Today, we concretely experience what has been termed the 'globalization of indifference.'[23] Huge sections of society are excluded, exploited and doomed to die slow deaths due to unjust, inhuman practices, on the one hand, and widespread apathy and indifference, on the other. In the face of this cancerous development, there is need to foster a 'globalization of compassionate solidarity'[24] that will feel the suffering of crucified humanity at the visceral, gut-level, and reach out with commitment to alleviate suffering and pain. Such solidarity will only be possible if we understand the root causes of the maladies that plague the poorest of poor. This creates the indispensable need for interfaith dialogue which engenders a process of 'knowing together' whereby: "We compassionately understand each other, our points of view, including those of the ones we confront and in the process our points of view become circles of view capable of more generous embrace."[25] History shows that socio-religious movements have responded effectively to global indifference in diverse contexts.

Conclusion: The Need for More 'Faces' of Mercy and Compassion

We have seen that all religions teach that mercy and compassion are spiritual values of the highest order. However, it often happens that religious ideals do not find adequate expression in the lives of believers. Thus, we urgently need 'faces of mercy and compassion'—i.e., religious men and women to serve as models of the power of mercy and compassion. Christianity has produced a Saint Mother Teresa and Islam can be proud of Nobel laureate Malala Yousafzai who prophetically espouses the cause of poor women and illiterate girls. The Dalai Lama tirelessly proclaims the need of compassion for world peace and Hindus like Baba Amte have shown what compassion truly is by caring for lepers. These 'faces' give abstract values like mercy and compassion a form and figure.

The power of compassion is unleashed only if one 'feels' the suffering of the other as if it were one's own suffering. This first gut-level feeling is a form of knowledge—accessible to all—that begets action. When one feels/ knows the others' pain and suffering, one acts to alleviate that pain and suffering. Whether one takes action as a result of religious motivation or mere humanism is unimportant. What is crucial, however, is that through merciful, compassionate actions we shall be able to tell those who suffer that we are *with them*. Wouldn't our concerted efforts to raise up those overburdened with suffering ensure the birth of a new world order?

Endnotes

[1] Pope Francis, *Misericordiae Vultus* (Vatican City: Libreria Editrice Vaticana, 2015), no., 23. This document was issued to inaugurate the 'Year of Mercy'. Copy of the text is available on the web-site https://w2.vatican.va/content/francesco/en/ apost_letters/documents/papafrancesco_bolla_20150411_misericordiae-vultus.html.

[2] Francis, *Misericordiae Vultus* (Vatican City: Libreria Editrice Vaticana, 2015), no., 23. Italics added.

[3] Leland Ryken, James C. Wilhoit and Tremper Longman III, eds., *Dictionary of Biblical Imagery* (Illinois and Leicester: Inter Varsity Press, 1998), 547-548.

[4] Exodus 34:6. Psalms 86:15; 103:8, etc.

[5] J. Sheila Galligan, "Mercy's Mystery: Womb-Like Love," in *Spiritual Life* 56/1 (Spring 2010), 49-55, examines four specific ways in which merciful love can be appreciated as a form of 'womb-like' love.

[6] God is referred to as 'father' in the First Testament about 22 times in images, similes and metaphors (see Deuteronomy 32:6; 2 Samuel 7:12-15; Isaiah 64:6-8; Psalm 89:26-29, etc.). God is also compared to a mother, nurse, feeder, midwife, etc. (Deuteronomy 32:18; Isaiah 49:15; 66:13; Hosea 11:4; Psalm 22:9).

[7] See the article 'God's motherly embrace,' written in the context of International Women's Day, 2016, which can be accessed on the web-link http://www.asianage. com/columnists/god-s-motherly-embrace-839.

[8] Ryken, et al., eds., *Dictionary of Biblical Imagery*, 962.

[9] *Misericordiae Vultus*, Latin, literally means 'Faces of Mercy.'

[10] *Misericordiae Vultus*, no.1.

[11] *Misericordiae Vultus*, no. 6; italics added.

[12] See Holy Qur'ān 9:128.

[13] See Vatican Council II's "Declaration on the Relation of the Church to Non-Christian Religions," *Nostra Aetate*, no.4.

[14] See, for instance, Maurice Borrmans, "A Light in the Inter-Religious Christian-Islam Dialogue: The Virtue of Compassion," in *Dolentium Hominum* 46/1 (2001), 61-65, for a personal, experiential account of how a hospital in Ain Sefra, Algeria, became "a holy temple of a merciful compassion in which Christians and Muslims [could] say many things under the gaze of God."

[15] For further details, see George Gispert-Sauch, ed., *"Dayā,"* in *Gems from India* (Delhi, ISPCK/VIEWS, 2006), 149-151. The original Sanskrit reads as: *"Ātmavat sarvabhuteru yad hitaya sivāya ca/vartate satatam hrsto krtsnā hy esā dayā smrtā."*

[16] Gispert-Sauch, ed., *"Dayā,"* in *Gems from India*, 151. The original Sanskrit reads as: *"Nirgunesv api sattvesu dayām kurvanti sādhavah."*

[17] Geshe Kelsang Gyatso, *Ocean of Nectar: Wisdom and Compassion in Mahayana Buddhism* (Delhi, Motilal Banarsidass Publishers Pvt. Ltd., 2000), 20-21, differentiates between the compassion of Hinayana and Mahayana Buddhism. Providing the analogy of a child who is drowning, he opines: "Hinayanists are like onlookers who want that the child be saved, but do not take that responsibility upon themselves. Mahayanists, on the other hand, are like the mother, for not only do they [*sic*] want all living beings to be free from suffering, they also take personal responsibility for protecting them."

[18] See Thich Nhat Hanh, *Interbeing: Fourteen Guidelines for Engaged Buddhism*, rev. & ed. F. Eppsteiner (Berkeley, California, Parallax Press, 1993), 18.

[19] Steve and Rosemary Weismann, *Meditation, Compassion & Lovingkindness: An Approach to Vipassana Practice* (Delhi: Sri Satguru Publications, 2000), 25-31,193-194, hold 'compassionate understanding' as the final fruit of *Vipassana*.

[20] John W. Schroeder, *Skillful Means: The Heart of Buddhist Compassion* (Delhi: Motilal Banarsidass Publishers Pvt., Ltd., 2000).

[21] See C.D. Sebastian, "Ahimsā and Compassion in Buddhism and Jainism," in *Jnanatirtha Journal of Sacred Scriptures* 3/1 (January-June 2009), 32-34.

[22] Gianni Vattimo, *Belief* translated by L. D'Isanto & D. Webb (Cambridge, Polity Press, 1999), 20-68, develops the idea of *kenosis* within a secularist context as an antidote against suffering in the world.

[23] See, Pope Francis's documents entitled '*Evangelii Gaudium*,' no.54, as well as *Laudato Si*', no.52.

[24] See Filo Hirota, "Globalization of Compassionate Solidarity: Challenges and Opportunities," in *East Asian Pastoral Review* 38/4 (2001), 351-365.

[25] See, Ananta Kumar Giri, "Knowing Together in Compassion and Confrontation: Social Movements, Gift of Knowledge and Challenge of Transformations," in *Jeevadhara* 39/229 (January 2009), 88-95.

Christian W. Troll's Engagement with Sir Sayyed Ahmed Khan

Victor Edwin, S.J.

Introduction

The noted Jesuit scholar Christian W. Troll engaged deeply with the writings of Sir Sayyid Ahmad Khan (henceforth Sir Sayyid) while studying the latter's intellectual life and work for his doctoral thesis. His work on Sir Sayyid Ahmed Khan is considered to be one of the standard works of the latter.

The first part of this article highlights the fresh approach of Sir Sayyid towards the Bible. Sir Sayyid affirmed that (1) since the Bible witnesses to the oneness of God, Muslims cannot afford to ignore it; and (2) studying the Bible in the light of the Qur'an could help Muslims to deepen their relations with Christian neighbors.

The second part of the essay describes how Troll responded to Sir Sayyid's thinking of reading one another's scriptures. It appears that Sir Sayyid's attitude towards the Bible shaped Troll's understanding with regard to the importance of Scriptures in dialogue between Muslims and Christians.

Sir Sayyid's Commentary on the Bible

Tabyīn al-Kalām is the fragmentary commentary of Sir Sayyid on the Bible.[1] He composed and published it in 1862 at the age of 42, and republished it in 1885. G. de Tassy refers to it as a testimony to Sir Sayyid's open-mindedness and broad vision and terms it as 'informative', 'interesting', and a 'synthesis of Eastern and Western learning and scholarship'.[2] Troll affirms that *Tabyīn al-Kalām* is an extraordinary text,[3] observing that it was "... not an aberration of his younger year literary adventurism."[4] It is worth mentioning here that *Tabyīn al-Kalām* comprises three parts: (1) Prolegomena to the Study of the Bible; (2) Translation of, and commentary on, Genesis 1-11; (3) Translation of, and commentary on, Matthew 1-5.[5]

Bible's Witness on *Tawḥīd*

Muslims cannot afford to reject the Bible since the Bible witnesses on *tawḥīd*[6] – the Oneness of God. Sir Sayyid emphasized that the Bible should be studied and commented upon by Muslims since the Bible witness to *tawḥīd*. This position is the key to his overall understanding of the Bible. This consideration is clearly radical in contrast to the general Muslim understanding.[7] One cannot miss this courageous approach of Sir Sayyid's approach towards the Bible in India. Troll makes note of this and writes:

> The question of the corruption of the Scriptures (*taḥrīf*) is an age-old issue among Muslims, Jews and Christians. It deliberately had been made the central point of the Controversy [in India] by Pfander and the subject of special treatment by Kairānawi in his *I'jāz-i 'Īsawī*. [However] Sir Sayyid claims that the errors and contradictions that doubtlessly are found in the present biblical Scriptures can be solved without the postulate of a deliberate, general textual corruption of the Biblical texts.[8]

Troll confirms that Sir Sayyid believed in the relevance of the gospel of Jesus. Troll writes: "... freed from the distortions and of an erroneous dogmatic interpretation and in the light of the Qur'ān's uniquely clear message of God's Unity, [Sir Sayyid believed that] the gospel of Jesus continues to be relevant."[9] It is important to observe that although Sir Sayyid would recognize corruption in the text and distortion of dogma, he would hold that since the Bible in its totality witness to *tawḥīd*, it should be studied and commented upon by Muslims. In short, the position of Sir Sayyid was that Muslims cannot afford to reject the Bible.[10]

One should not lose sight of the implications of Sir Sayyid's stand that the Bible witnesses to *tawḥīd*. In other words, Sir Sayyid may affirm that Muslims should recognize that Christians are monotheists. If this is so, it is important since the Trinitarian Monotheism of Christians is often misunderstood by Muslims to be tri-theism.

Bible and Muslims' Spiritual Life

Sir Sayyid drew from the Bible, the Qur'an and sound *aḥādīth* while interpreting biblical concepts like 'disciples', 'kingdom of God' and 'seeing God.' Troll affirms that for Sir Sayyid Jesus uncovers the inner truth and the essence of the teachings of the Bible. This point might be able to help Muslims be more attentive to the inner meanings of the teachings of the Qur'an. Thus, the Bible could help Muslims to grow in their spiritual life. Sir Sayyid suggested that a Muslim could deepen his/her faith in the light of the true moral teachings of the authentic pre- Qur'ānic scriptures. Troll stressed this significant element of the courageous endeavor of Sir Sayyid for the much needed promotion of interreligious scholarship in India and beyond.

Sir Sayyid makes two important assertions: Muslims cannot afford to reject the Bible since the Book witnesses to *tawḥīd* and that the Bible could help Muslims to grow in their spiritual life. Sir Sayyid's attitude towards the Bible appears to have an impact on Troll's own thinking on the use of Scriptures in relations between Christians and Muslims. Troll came to recognize that both Christians and Muslims need to read one another's scriptures if they want to deepen their understanding of each other and grow in mutual appreciation.[11]

Reading One Another's Scriptures: Critical Theological Questions

Troll is aware of the critical theological questions that could come up in reading one another's scriptures. For example, while using the Bible and the Qur'ān in religious conversation between Christians and Muslims, the question arises as to how we read each other's Scriptures cross-culturally and religiously, and what status we accord them.[12]

Troll lays down an important rule for profitable interaction between Christians and Muslims while reading together the Bible and the Qur'ān.[13] He writes that Christians and Muslims should "grasp the basic point that in the two faiths the Word of God addressed by God to the human race is understood in significantly different ways."[14] Christians and Muslims should not fail to grasp the profound differences in their convictions about the nature and message of their scriptures, otherwise conversations between them will not take off above the irrelevant criticism and confusion.[15] The revelation of the Qur'ān as the Word of God is understood by Muslims as "the final, unique and fully authentic manifestation of the Word of God, addressed to humankind through the ministry of Muhammad",[16] while for Christians the story of revelation comes to its fulfillment in Jesus of Nazareth, who Christians believe is the Word made flesh (John 1:14). In addition, Christians believe that public revelation ends with the death of the last Apostle.

It is important to note that within Catholic theology there are two different ways in which revelation is understood. Most Catholic theologians before K. Rahner recognized revelation as truths revealed by God. These revealed truths were gathered in a deposit of faith. These revealed truths, it was believed, should be acknowledged as true on the authority of God as mediated by the Church for one's salvation.

This could be called a static understanding of revelation. In this stream of thought, the revelations possessed by non-Christian religions were considered to be a preparation for the Christian gospel. In this scheme of things, there would be no place for the Qur'ānic revelation, as it came after Jesus Christ. In contrast to this school, K. Rahner argued that revelation is not static but dynamic. It is God's self-communication, to which human persons respond. Since revelation occurs within historical situations, there could be Jewish, Islamic, Indic revelations.[17]

For meaningful interreligious conversations between Muslims and Christians, Muslims should recognize that Christians believe that the Word did not become a book, but, rather, that it became incarnate in the person of Jesus, while Christians should recognize that Muslims believe that God's word is preserved in a book, the Holy Qur'ān.[18]

Muslims might ask: What about the Bible? Is it the Word of God? Muslims have the right to know about Christian thinking on this subject. Christians use the term 'Word of God' in a way different to that in which Muslims use it in reference to the Qur'ān. For Christians, the Word speaks in and through the words of men and women, the authors who composed the various books in the Bible.[19] The limitations of the writers' cultures, languages and customs are part and parcel of the Bible.

Also, Christians should recognize the spiritual significance of the Qur'ān in the lives of Muslims as the Book shapes the lives and spiritualties of more than a billion Muslims today. To enter the world of Muslims, Christians need to understand the status and agency of the Qur'ān and the way in which it is respected by Muslims.[20] Similarly, Muslims should recognize the place of the Bible in the lives of Christians for any meaningful interaction between them on the level of theology.

In the spirit of openness, Troll finds that there are Muslims and Christians who feel that it "is part of their vocation to get to know one another" by studying one another's scriptures. Among Muslims, many are "increasingly aware of the need to learn something from Christians themselves about their own understanding of the Bible" and "take the Bible seriously and get to know it properly", as is the case with Christians who learn about the Muslim understandings of the Qur'ān.[21]

'Scriptural Reasoning': Muslims and Christians Study of the Bible and the Qur'ān

Troll affirms that the "intense reading of paired passages" from the Qur'ān and the Bible as an important initiative.[22] The project, called 'Scriptural Reasoning', attracts educated Muslims and Christians to study the Bible and the Qur'ān together. M. Ipgrave finds that for any real progress in Christian-Muslim relations, Christian and Muslims should take both the Qur'an and the Bible and study seriously their contents and teachings.[23]

In 'Scriptural Reasoning', the onus is on the believer to explain his/her scripture in the light of one's faith as well as awareness of the presence of a believer who believes differently. Thus, the rules of exegesis are drawn in the light of one's faith with sensitivity towards the faith of the participant in religious conversation. Troll further clarifies:

> It is a non-negotiable basis for dialogue that each side should acknowledge that the Scripture on which the faith of the other community is founded forms the basis and the norm for the understanding and expression of that faith. This point [...] also implies the importance of Christians studying the Qur'ān and Muslims studying the Bible if the dialogue between them is to be meaningful.[24]

Although Sir Sayyid did not expand his thinking to the level of 'Scriptural Reasoning', it should be acknowledged that he walked an uncharted path, suggesting a theological place for the Bible in the spiritual blossoming of a Muslim. It would not be inappropriate to say that Sir Sayyid could be considered as one of the early pioneers for a project like 'Scriptural Reasoning.'

It can be affirmed here that Sir Sayyid's approach towards the Bible has a certain theological impact on Troll's thinking on Scriptures in dialogue between Christians and Muslims. While constantly displaying a sympathetic approach towards the Qur'ān, Troll maintains that a Muslim who reads the Bible should recognize unambiguously that the Bible, on which the faith of the Christian community is founded, forms the norm for the understanding and expression of Christian faith. Troll maintains openness towards Muslims and a witness to his faith together in a healthy dialogical tension. Discernment plays a vital role in this process.

Conclusion

If interreligious conversation is to be fruitful, both Christians and Muslims cannot afford to neglect one another's scripture. Some groups of Christians and Muslims do read both scriptures and draw spiritual nourishment for their lives. This spiritual *sādhana*, the reading of one another's scriptures, can help these Christians and Muslims to recognize the presence of the Spirit of God in one another's tradition. This will also eventually guide them to help each other to discern the presence of the Spirit of God in their lives as Christians and Muslims and facilitate them to grow in their commitment to the One God.

Endnotes

[1] Sir Sayyid wanted to deepen mutual knowledge and respect between Christians and Muslims. See, J.M.S. Baljon Jr., *The Reforms and Religious Ideas of Sir Sayyid Ahmad Khan* (Leiden: E.J. Brill, 1949), 77-84.

[2] M. Hasan, "Religions of the Edge: Perspectives on Faiths and the Faithful," in *A Moral Reckoning: Muslim Intellectuals in Nineteenth-Century Delhi* (Delhi: Oxford University Press, 2010), 102.

[3] C.W. Troll, "Sayyid Ahmed Khan (1817-98) Commentary on Mathew, Chapters 1-5, with special reference to his comments about the Beatitudes (Mt 5, 3-12)" (lecture, Aligarh Muslim University, Aligarh, March 22, 2013).

[4] C.W. Troll, "Some remarks on Sayyid Ahmad Khan's Commentary on Mathew 5" (paper presented at the Jesuits among Muslims Meeting, New Delhi, April 4, 2013).

[5] Troll, "Some remarks on Sayyid Ahmad Khan's Commentary on Mathew 5," (April 4, 2013).

[6] See, Syud Ahmud [Sayyid Ahmed] Khan, *Preliminary Discourse on the Mohamedan Commentary of the Holy Bible* (Ghazipur, 1862), 30, 39.

[7] Muslim scholars stress that Islam is a revealed religion and that previous revelations point to the coming of the Prophet Muhammad. They argue that all the Books that were revealed by God, including the Bible and the Qur'ān, contain essentially the same message. Muhammad came with the final message for humanity. The Qur'ān

confirms what had been said in the earlier revelations and corrects what has been misunderstood, misinterpreted, corrupted, changed and concealed. As a result, whatever conforms to the Qur'an is authentic and whatever does not, is unauthentic.

[8] Troll, "Some remarks on Sayyid Ahmad Khan's Commentary on Mathew 5," (April 4, 2013).

[9] CW Troll, "Modern Trends in Indian Islamic Thought – The Recent past" (unpublished papers, Sophia University, Tokyo, Japan).

[10] C.W. Troll, "Christian-Muslim Relations in India: A Critical Survey," *Islamochristiana* 5 (1979): 126.

[11] C.W. Troll, "Recent Studies in Nascent Islam," *Vidyajyoti* 44/5 (May 1980): 227.

[12] J. Basset, "Has Christian-Muslim Dialogue already begun?" *Muslim-Christian Perceptions of Dialogue Today* (Leuven: Peeters, 2000), 287.

[13] C. W. Troll, "Bible and Qur'an in Dialogue," *Bulletin Dei Verbum* 79/80, http://www.sankt-georgen.de/lese raum/troll37.pdf (December 10, 2010).

[14] C.W. Troll, *Dialogue and Difference: Clarity in Christian-Muslim Relations* (New York: Orbis Book, 2009), 132.

[15] M. Borrmans, *Guidelines for Dialogue between Christians and Muslims* (New York: Paulist Press, 1990), 104-105.

[16] Borrmans, *Guidelines for Dialogue between Christians and Muslims*, 104-105.

[17] K. Rahner, "Revelation," in *Sacramentum Mundi: An Encyclopaedia of Theology*, vol. 5, edited by K. Rahner, C. Ernest, Kevin Smyth (London: Burn & Oates, 1970), 358.

[18] See especially Chapter 2 (The Qur'an as Sign of God) in G. Dardess, *Do we Worship the same God: Comparing the Bible and the Qur'an* (Cincinnati, Ohio: St. Anthony Messenger Press, 2006), 27-39.

[19] C. Chapman. *The Bible through Muslim Eyes and a Christian Response* (Cambridge: Grove Books Limited, 2008), 5.

[20] N. Daniel, *Islam and the West: The Making of an Image* (Oxford: Oneworld [1960], 2000), 55-59.

[21] Troll, *Dialogue and Difference: Clarity in Christian-Muslim Relations*, 137.

[22] Troll, *Dialogue and Difference: Clarity in Christian-Muslim Relations*, 139.

[23] M. Ipgrave, ed., *Scriptures in Dialogue: Christians and Muslims Studying the Bible and the Qur'an Together* (London: Church House Publishing, 2004), 144-145.

[24] C.W. Troll, *Muslims Ask, Christians Answer*, translated by D. Marshall (Lahore: Multimedia affairs, 2012), 21.

HMI Publications

Islam
A Historical Survey (Indian Edition, 1979)
H.A.R. Gibb

Evangelism, Dialogue, Reconciliation: The Transformative Journey of the Henry Martyn Institute (1998)
Diane D' Souza

Approaches, Foundations, Issues and Models of Interfaith Relations (2001)
David Emmanuel Singh and Robert Edwin Schick

Jesus the Messiah in Muslim Thought (2002)
Olaf Schumann

From Converting the Pagan to Dialogue with Our Partners: HMI's Fifty Years Work of Evangelism and Interfaith Relations (2009)
Andreas D' Souza

The Jesus Verses of the Qur'ān (2011)
Karel Steenbrink

The Sufi Movement
East and West (2014)
Jan Slomp

Mysticism, Spirituality and Secularism
An In-depth Search for Meaning and Authenticity in a Pluralistic World (2015)
Varghese Manimala

My Father is a Farmer
Biblical Reflection on Sustainable Agriculture (2016)
Daniel Prem Kumar

Seeking Communion
A Collection of Conversations (2018)
Joseph Victor Edwin SJ

Letter to an Unknown Friend
Children Promote Peace between India and Pakistan (2018)
Joseph Kalathil SJ

Understanding Hinduism (2018)
Mahesh Badhe

www.ingramcontent.com/pod-product-compliance
Lightning Source LLC
Chambersburg PA
CBHW060411030726
47495CB00003B/526